Devotions With Wendi

5-Minute Moments to Build Your Faith in 365 Days

Wendi A. Irlbeck

DEDICATION

The devotional book you now hold in your hands started as a small seed that the Lord planted in my heart four years ago. I wrote each entry with you in mind, understanding the price Jesus paid for us and the redemption we share as God's children.

As you journey through these 365 devotionals, you will experience the same transformative grace that Jesus has poured into my life. He is the Firefighter who saved my life, and I want everyone to know about Him on the deepest level. Each page represents a step toward growing in our relationship with Christ, serving as a constant reminder that God's love is always within reach.

I am dedicating this book to a few of my close friends and family members. The first being my God-fearing grandmother, **Marijane Irlbeck**, who was like a mother to me. May she rest in power with the Lord. Grandma lived with mighty faith and she never wavered regardless of the storms life brought. She was kind, caring, and her hug felt like an embrace from Jesus Himself!

Her legacy of faith lives on and inspires me every day. She impacted many lives, especially mine.

"I am reminded of your sincere faith, which first lived in your grandmother . . . and, I am persuaded, now lives in you also."
— 2 Timothy 1:5

Acknowledgements

A special thank you to my dad, **Daryle**, who is truly one of a kind. He's always encouraged me to pursue my wild dreams and instilled in me a "work hard, never quit" mentality. Even when the odds were against me, he was the one telling me, "Keep going, Wendi. You'll get there—just don't quit."

Dad's voice brought light to my darkness before I found Christ, and I am forever grateful. My dad fought battles for our family that shaped me in ways I carry with me every day, helping me become a warrior for God's Kingdom. He also taught us to pray as children and reminded us that our guardian angels are always near. Turns out, dads are usually right. I love you, Dad.

I also want to thank **Aunt Arlene** and **Uncle Roger**, who supported me through tough times and encouraged my faith. To my friend **Dominique**, whom I met in Nashville—you sharpened me and gave me the courage to keep writing this book when I felt ill-equipped or "not Christian enough." Thank you for helping me grow in my faith. Finally, to my loyal client, **April**—your generosity made this book possible. Thank you for answering my prayer in obedience to God's provision.

And most importantly, thank you, **Jesus**. I love you with all my heart and soul. I live to honor and glorify you.

Preface

Writing these devotionals has been one of the most healing and transformative journeys of my life. For the first twenty-two years of my life, I didn't know our sweet Savior. I ran on ambition, self-reliance, and the lie that if God existed, He was too busy for people like me. But Jesus never stopped showing up. When people ask why I'm so passionate about my faith, my answer is simple: imagine being trapped in a burning building and a hero pulls you out. You'd never stop talking about your Rescuer.

This book began as private journals with the Lord during some of my darkest seasons. Through each entry, I found clarity in the chaos and beauty in the broken places. By sharing my journey, I was able to see God's powerful healing and the light only His presence can shine. My prayer is that as you read these pages, you'll experience our Heavenly Father's same healing touch and love.

For years, I lived as a high-achiever hiding deep pain. I walked through childhood adversity, wrestled with disordered eating, and endured the trauma of an abusive relationship. I also battled against perfectionism and performance anxiety as an athlete and aspiring dietitian. I knew how to strive, but I didn't know how to *rest* in grace. My wounds ran deep, but the healing hand of God reached deeper still.

This book was born from those very ashes. It is the fruit of surrender, not striving. These pages are honest—some downright raw and vulnerable but each one is offered with the hope that you'll encounter the mercy and kindness of a God who still works miracles out of messes.

Professionally, I'm a registered dietitian, certified sports nutritionist, entrepreneur, and speaker—but my true identity is being a daughter of Jesus Christ. I'm deeply passionate about merging health and fitness with faith, empowering others to take care of their spiritual, emotional and physical health. God really does want healing and wholeness for all of us.

My prayer is that these devotionals will meet you in your everyday moments and speak to the quiet corners of your heart. Always remember that God isn't just a Savior for someday—He's our Healer, Helper, and Hope of *right now*.

ABOUT ME

I grew up without my biological mother, which meant much of my childhood was shaped by the strong presence of my hardworking father, relatives and grandmother. My dad started a trucking company and worked relentlessly to build it up and provide for our family. Thanks to his dedication, we were blessed with everything we needed as children, including the opportunity to play sports, be well-fed, and attend college.

My dad's mom (my grandmother) stepped up and played a large role in my life, but as children, my siblings and I were often left to figure things out on our own. While it wasn't easy, those experiences molded me in ways I couldn't fully appreciate at the time. Looking back now, I can see how God was at work even in those moments, preparing me for a path I didn't yet know I would walk.

As a child, I spent my days fishing, hunting, playing sports, and doing what many would call "boy things." Those activities, while teaching me resilience and strength, also set me apart from other girls my age. I was often teased and bullied for not fitting in, and while that was difficult, it also taught me how to stand firm in the face of adversity.

One of the most challenging stages of my childhood was learning how to read. I attended a small rural elementary school and my teacher didn't teach me. My dad, despite the demands of operating and growing his trucking business, took on the responsibility of teaching me himself. He would sit in his living room chair while I kneeled beside him, learning from the trucking and agriculture books he held. Often, it was late at night, and the pressure mounted as we both grew tired and frustrated. It was a struggle we shared and a journey we undertook together.

I vividly remember those midnight sessions, piecing together sentences while my dad patiently and tirelessly worked with me. Though it was a painful period, those moments taught me resilience and perseverance. Slowly but surely, I learned to read—and today, I am a lover of the written word.

I realize how blessed I am to have had an earthly father who, despite his own challenges, did not quit on me. He was not a teacher, but God helped us. As painful as it was, my dad loved me and simply wanted his little girl to be able to read well. His dedication has fueled my deep empathy for children, especially those raised in single-parent households.

I know firsthand the hurdles divorced families face, so I'm passionate about supporting young people and helping them grow confidently during their most critical developmental stages. I'm also deeply committed to helping those who may have both parents in the household but still feel a disconnect or absence of love. Many of the young people I encounter express feelings of loneliness and isolation, and I strive to meet them where they are, offering guidance and showing them the love of Jesus Christ.

As I reflect on my life, I see how my struggles laid the foundation for something greater. The obstacles I faced as a child became the building blocks for my calling: writing this devotional and helping others through my sports and nutrition business. My life is a testament to how God works through hardships, transforming weaknesses into strengths for His purpose. What once felt like a struggle was God planting seeds that would one day bear fruit in ways I never imagined.

For many years, I felt empty, insecure, and broken as a young woman, which led me to fall victim to many shortcomings. But in God's mercy, He saved me. Ever since then, I have been seeking to become the woman I needed when I was younger. If I can help it, I never want anyone to experience the pain and struggles I did. If Jesus can rebuild a broken woman like me, He can do the same for you!

Now it's your turn to step into the story God is writing over your life. As we journey through these devotionals together, come with an open heart and an expectant spirit! Bring your journal, your prayers, your questions, and even your shattered pieces.

Each day is an invitation to meet with our Heavenly Father and encounter His absolute love for His children. The same Rescuer who found me in the fire is reaching for you, too. So let's begin this journey together, knowing that God will finish the beautiful work He has started in you.

Introduction

*"But first seek the Kingdom and His righteousness,
and all these things will be given to you as well."*
Matthew 6:33

If you would have told me years ago that I'd be writing a 365-day devotional, I probably would have laughed—or cried—depending on the season I was in. But here I am, inviting you into a journey that is both a devotional and a memoir of how the Lord worked in my life in ways I never expected.

This isn't just a collection of daily encouragements; it's a story of *transformation*—my story, but also *yours*. Because if there's one thing I've learned, it's that Jesus is always writing a bigger story than we can see.

I've walked through valleys of heartbreak, seasons of waiting, and moments where I questioned if I'd ever see breakthrough. I've wrestled with fear, doubt, and the deep wounds that life can bring. But through it all, I've also witnessed God's faithfulness, His mercy, and His miraculous hand guiding me forward.

As I wrote this devotional, I didn't follow a rigid formula or try to make each day fit into a neat pattern. Instead, I wrote with the Holy Spirit—allowing Him to lead, guide, and shape every word. That means each day follows a different flow, and that's by design. Some entries may challenge you, while others bring comfort. Some will lift your spirit, and others might cause you to reflect deeply.

As you walk through these pages, my prayer is that you see God's fingerprints all over your own life, just as I have seen Him in mine. It's my hope that you are reminded, day by day, that our Father is faithful, present, and working—even in the waiting.

No matter where you are right now—whether you're in a season of breaking or breakthrough—God is not done with your story. I pray this book brings you hope, healing, and the confidence to trust that the same God who carried me will carry you, too.

Let's take this journey together—one day, one prayer, and one miracle at a time.

With love,
Wendi

"At the right time, I, the Lord, will make it happen."
Isaiah 60:22

DAY 1

YOU ARE MADE IN GOD'S IMAGE

"God saw all that he had made, and it was very good."

Genesis 1:31

As a registered dietitian and certified sports nutritionist, I've had the privilege of helping individuals of all ages improve their health, wellness, and athletic performance through personalized nutrition coaching and education. True health and wellness isn't just about what we eat—it's also about *when, how much,* and *why*. Our eating habits are often deeply rooted in emotions, beliefs, and past experiences. Nutrition is more than a physical act; it's often a mirror reflecting how we view ourselves and the relationship we have with our bodies.

Recently, my heart broke during a conversation with a mom who was deeply worried about her daughter's relationship with food. She didn't want her daughter to suffer, and I couldn't help but think this is how God feels about us as His children. This mother desperately wanted to help but felt lost because her daughter couldn't see the dangerous path she was on.

I understood her pain—I've been there too. I used to obsess over every calorie, every meal, focusing on how it would make me "look" instead of how it would make me feel. This struggle is all too common in a world that values outward appearance over inner well-being, but God sees us through a completely different lens.

God made each of us unique and beautiful, crafting every detail—from our DNA to every strand of hair. He knew us before we were born. The devil tries to deceive us, filling us with shame and guilt over our imperfections. But in God's eyes, we are *"fearfully and wonderfully made"* (Psalm 139:14).

If we could learn to see ourselves through our Father's eyes and truly love the unique bodies He gave us, we would strip away the power that satan tries to hold over us. The enemy thrives on our insecurities, convincing us that we aren't enough—that we're flawed or unworthy. But those are lies designed to keep us trapped in shame. God didn't make a mistake when He created you. Every part of you, from your personality to your physical features, was crafted with intention.

Starting today, I want you to lift your head high with confidence, knowing that you are beloved by Jesus and deeply adored. Instead of letting thoughts of not being enough take root, choose to believe that in our Savior's eyes, you are already complete. There's nothing missing and nothing broken that He can't redeem. When God sees you, He says, *"You are my beloved child, perfectly created in My image, and I have a purpose and plan for your life beyond what you can imagine."*

Today's Verse:
"You are a chosen people, a royal priesthood, a holy nation, God's special possession, that you may declare the praises of him who called you out of darkness into his wonderful light."
—1 Peter 2:9

DAY 2

SURRENDERING THE STRUGGLE

"The Lord has done great things for us, and we are filled with joy."

Psalm 126:3

Have you ever shoved clutter into a drawer before guests arrived, just to keep up appearances? We do the same thing with our hearts—hiding the mess, tucking away the struggles, and presenting a polished version of ourselves to the world. But God sees beyond the surface. He knows what's behind closed doors, and He's not put off by the chaos. Instead, He's inviting you to bring it *all* to Him today. Why? Because when you stop hiding and lay everything before Jesus, He can bring order, healing, and purpose to your life. There's no shame in the mess—only an opportunity for His grace to transform it into something beautiful.

God isn't looking for flawless people; **He's looking for an open heart.** Until I released my need to appear perfect, I wasn't fully experiencing the depth of Jesus' love. Only through humbling experiences—like a broken engagement and the struggles I faced in becoming a dietitian—did I learn that God wanted my heart more than my accomplishments.

One of my toughest moments was failing the Commission on Dietetic Registration exam—the board exam for dietitians after completing 1,200 supervised practice hours and a master's degree. This is a very rigorous exam, with only a 60 percent pass rate the year I took it. This exam is the culmination of years of academic study, hands-on training, and clinical internships. It demands hundreds of hours of preparation in biochemistry, clinical nutrition, food service management, and more. Passing it is essential to becoming licensed, allowing one to practice professionally and make a difference in others' lives.

Like many, I had put pressure on myself to succeed on the first try. When I didn't, it felt devastating. But in hindsight, I can see how God used that time to teach me that my identity wasn't in a title or exam score, but in His love and purpose for me. Once I surrendered to God and stopped studying, I passed. I still remember that day so vividly, each moment carved into my memory as if it happened yesterday. In the quiet, sterile exam room in Ann Arbor, Michigan, I faced the final question. The clock ticked away, my heart hammering with each second. I knew that, in a few moments, one final screen would flash a verdict—pass or fail. I took a deep breath, fingers hovering over the submit button, and whispered a final, desperate prayer.

"Lord, if it's Your will for me to be a dietitian, let me see a pass on this screen. If not, I'll understand. I'll trust that You have another plan, something better, even if I can't see it right now. You've carried me through every moment of this two-hour test. Thank You for shielding my mind from fear and satan's whispers that I would fail. You've stayed by my side, holding my focus. I've given all I have—to this test and to You. Whatever happens, I know it's Your will."

With a steadying exhale, I clicked submit. For a moment, I couldn't breathe. Then, the screen lit up with a single word: **"Pass**." My hand flew to my mouth as I felt hot tears spring to my eyes. Relief, disbelief, and joy all poured through me at once! I was shaking, unable to contain the tidal wave of emotion. My shoulders sagged under the sudden release of tension, and I was overwhelmed with gratitude. I got up, still wiping away tears, and practically stumbled out of the exam room, needing air and needing space to process what had just happened.

Outside in the parking lot, the Michigan sky was bright and open above me. I couldn't hold it in any longer—I fell to my knees right there on the pavement, crying out my thanks to God! And then I was up again, laughing, dancing, just me and God in that parking lot, surrounded by nothing but gratitude and the thrill of this long-awaited moment!

After a few minutes, I pulled myself together enough to make a call to a very influential mentor from my undergrad and graduate studies. She picked up on the first ring, and I blurted out the news, still breathless with excitement. She laughed and said, "See, Wendi! I told you—you just needed to relax and trust. You always had the ability!"

But I knew it wasn't just me. "No," I told her, my voice thick with emotion. "It wasn't me at all. It was all God! I was so terrified I'd fail again, but He had other plans. I just had to let go and trust Him completely!"

That day wasn't just about passing an exam—it was a lesson in surrender, trust, and faith. It was about realizing that even in our smallest moments of fear, God is moving in ways beyond our understanding. He shapes our path in ways we have yet to see. All these years later, that memory still warms my heart. It's a reminder of the power of faith and the joy of stepping fully into God's plan.

Through my experience, I learned that failure doesn't define us but can build us. It taught me reliance on Jesus, reminding me that God's opinion is the only one that matters. The people who love me don't care how many times I took the test or what I scored; they value me for *who* I am, not what I've achieved. God sees us the same way—He doesn't measure our worth by our accomplishments but by our willingness to lean on Him. You are not defined by your career, performance, or any external validation. You are defined by God's love and grace.

Here's a tip that can spare you pain, tears, and frustration—don't root your identity in achievements, titles, or accolades. It's tempting, I know. We live in a world that glorifies success and rankings, but God's Kingdom values surrender and trust. When you place your worth in your job, test scores, or goals, it can quickly turn into idolatry—where these things become more important than God's love and purpose.

I learned this firsthand when I idolized my RD exam, believing my worth was tied to being the "most impactful dietitian." But that mindset was all about *me*. Today, my joy comes from glorifying Christ in my work. Whether or not I'm recognized as "elite" doesn't matter—what matters is that I reflect His love in everything I do.

Today's Challenge:

Today, take 10 minutes to reflect on one area in your life where you might be striving for perfection or forcing things to happen on your own. Write it down, and invite God into it, asking Him to guide you, renew your perspective, and help you release any unnecessary pressure. Then, finish with a short prayer of gratitude, thanking God for His love, His patience, and the freedom to be fully ourselves in His presence.

THE GIFT OF HIDDENNESS

"In their hearts humans plan their course, but the Lord establishes their steps."

Proverbs 16:9

Do you ever feel unseen, as if your work, your prayers, and your faithfulness go unnoticed by the world? Maybe you're in a season where God has hidden you away, and you don't understand why. You see others moving forward, stepping into new opportunities, and receiving recognition while you remain in the quiet place, tucked away in what feels like obscurity. But what if hiddenness is actually a *gift*?

Throughout Scripture, we see that before God raises someone up, He first hides them. Moses spent forty years tending sheep in the wilderness before leading Israel out of Egypt. David was anointed as king but spent years in caves, running from Saul. Even Jesus, the Son of God, spent thirty years in quiet preparation before stepping into His public ministry.

One of the clearest examples of hiddenness is Elijah. After boldly confronting King Ahab and declaring a drought (1 Kings 17:1), God did something unexpected—He told Elijah to go into hiding: *"Then the word of the Lord came to Elijah: 'Leave here, turn eastward and hide in the Kerith Ravine, east of the Jordan. You will drink from the brook, and I have directed the ravens to supply you with food there."* (1 Kings 17:2-4)

Elijah obeyed, and for a time, he was completely dependent on God's provision. The world may have forgotten him, but God had not. In that hidden place, Elijah learned trust, humility, and total reliance on the Lord. It wasn't punishment—it was *preparation*.

Maybe that's where you are now. Maybe God has drawn you into a season of stillness, where your impact feels small and your influence feels insignificant. But let me encourage you: God is doing something in the hidden places that cannot be accomplished in the spotlight. He is developing your character, deepening your dependence on Him, and preparing you for what's ahead.

The world glorifies visibility, but God treasures *intimacy*. If you are hidden, it's because God desires to be alone with you. It's because He is working on something deeper than what others can see. Jesus Himself often withdrew to quiet places to pray (Luke 5:16). If the Son of God needed moments of hiddenness, how much more do we?

So instead of resenting the season you're in, *embrace it*. Let God do His refining work. Trust that He sees you, even when no one else does. Hiddenness is not a delay—it's a divine invitation into deeper intimacy with Jesus.

Today's Verse:
"He has made everything beautiful in its time. He has also set eternity in the human heart; yet no one can fathom what God has done from beginning to end."
—Ecclesiastes 3:11

SEASONS DON'T LAST FOREVER

"Let us not become weary in doing good, for at the proper time we will reap a harvest if we do not give up."

Galatians 6:9

Perspective is a powerful thing. What you see as your worst day could be someone else's best day. Have you ever stopped to think about that? It's easy to get caught up in our own struggles, frustrations, or even disappointments. But God calls us to have an eternal perspective—to see beyond the present moment and recognize that every season has a purpose.

You may not be where you want to be today, but remember, seasons change. The good ones don't last forever, but neither do the hard ones. Genesis 8:22 reminds us, "As *long as the earth endures, seedtime and harvest, cold and heat, summer and winter, day and night will never cease."*

So it is with our lives. There are seasons of planting—where you're putting in hard work and seeing little reward—and there are seasons of harvest, where you see the fruit of your labor. Both seasons are necessary, and both are part of God's plan.

No matter what season you find yourself in today, know that God is with you. He hasn't forgotten you, and He is using this season to prepare you for what's to come. Often, the trials we face become the very tools God uses to shape us and to help others down the road. Your struggle today could be someone else's breakthrough tomorrow.

Encouragement for Today:

- **Be Grateful:** Even if today doesn't look like you expected, choose gratitude. God is doing something in this moment, even if you can't see it yet. Gratitude shifts your heart from focusing on what you lack to recognizing how God is providing for you.

- **Trust the Process:** Just like seasons change, your life will too. The hard season you're in won't last forever. God is working in the unseen to bring about a harvest in your life. Don't give up during the "seedtime," because the harvest is coming.

- **Remember—Your Story Has A Purpose:** The challenges you're facing today could be the very things that equip you to help someone else later. God uses our pain, our setbacks, and our trials to shape us and make us vessels of His love and wisdom for others.

Today's Verse:
"For our light and momentary troubles are achieving for us an eternal glory that far outweighs them all."
—2 Corinthians 4:17

TRUSTING GOD TO RESTORE THE IMPOSSIBLE

"Ask, and it will be given to you; seek, and you will find; knock, and the door will be opened to you. For everyone who asks receives; the one who seeks finds; and to the one who knocks, the door will be opened."

Matthew 7:7-8

O ne of the most beautiful things about prayer is how it invites God to move in the impossible. A man shared with me his heartache about a strained relationship with his daughter. Ten years had passed since she had left the family and even changed her last name. The distance felt permanent, yet something stirred in his heart that made him reach out. With humility, he wrote his daughter a letter, expressing his love and desire for reconciliation. He passed the letter through her mother, hoping but not knowing if it would ever reach her.

I remember journaling that night, praying for healing between them. I asked God to soften her heart, to bring peace, and to work a miracle. I wasn't expecting an answer so soon, but God's timing often surprises us. Just hours later, the man reached out with news that left me in awe—his daughter showed up at their family Christmas dinner! After a decade apart, she was there, present, and willing to reconnect. His words to me were simple but profound: *"Thanks for praying hard. It happened fast!"*

This moment was more than a family reunion; it was a testimony to the power of prayer and God's faithfulness. Like the story of the Prodigal Son in Luke 15, it reminds us that no relationship is too broken for Jesus to heal, and no heart is too distant for Him to reach. It took courage for this father to write the letter, and it took divine intervention for his daughter to take the first step back.

Sometimes, we hesitate to pray boldly, wondering if God will act. Yet, He promises in John 14:13-14: *"If you ask me anything in my name, I will do it."* This story is a testament to the fact that God not only hears but moves. When we trust Him with our deepest hurts and our boldest prayers, He works in ways we cannot predict.

If you're waiting for a breakthrough in your life, take heart. God moves swiftly when the time is right, and His plans are always perfect. Write the letter. Say the prayer. Open your heart. And trust that the same God who brought a daughter home after ten years can restore what's broken in your life too. Let this story inspire you to believe in the power of prayer and the beauty of His perfect timing.

Today's Verse:
*"The prayer of a righteous person has great power
as it is working."*
—James 5:16

PRAY BOLDLY

"Therefore I tell you, whatever you ask for in prayer, believe that you have received it, and it will be yours."

Mark 11:24

When was the last time you prayed with such conviction, **so fully believing that God would move, that it felt as though your whole heart was laid bare before Him?** Many of us pray, but often without the deep assurance that God hears and will act. We ask, but we hesitate to believe fully, or worse, we stop asking because we wonder if God is truly listening.

Maybe you're feeling forgotten. Maybe you've prayed for something so long that doubt has crept into your heart. It can be discouraging when we pray for something and it feels like there's no response. But here's a truth we sometimes forget: God listens to our prayers, and He desires to move on our behalf. He calls us to come before Him with boldness and faith. James 4:2-3 says, *"You do not have because you do not ask God. When you ask, you do not receive, because you ask with wrong motives."*

This scripture challenges us to check both our faith and our motives. Are we asking with a pure heart, trusting that God knows what's best for us? Or are we asking out of selfish desires, focusing only on what we want, not on what God desires for our lives? God is calling you to come before Him not only with requests but with a heart that aligns with His will.

Empowering Truths for Today:

- **God Wants You to Ask Boldly:** You are not bothering God when you come to Him with your requests. He desires for you to ask, to seek, and to knock with persistence. He is a loving Father who wants to give good gifts to His children (Matthew 7:7-11).

- **Pray with Faith and Expectation:** Mark 11:24 tells us that when we pray, we are to believe that we have received what we ask for. This kind of faith moves mountains. When you pray, do it with the belief that God is already working on your behalf.

- **Persevere in Prayer:** Don't give up because you haven't seen an immediate answer. God's timing is perfect, and He often works in ways we cannot see. Keep praying, keep seeking, and trust that He is moving behind the scenes for your good.

Today's Verse:
"Before they call I will answer; while they are still speaking I will hear."
—Isaiah 65:24

BENT BUT NOT BROKEN

"When Jesus saw her, he called her forward and said to her, 'Woman, you are set free from your infirmity.'"
Luke 13:12

Unresolved pain has a way of following us. The wounds of the past, if left unhealed, don't just stay in the past—they shape how we think, how we respond, and even how we see God. Trauma that isn't dealt with bleeds into every part of life, influencing relationships, decisions, and the ability to hope for the future. Maybe you've felt it too. Maybe you've asked God why He allowed certain things to happen. Maybe you wonder if healing is even possible.

I've been there.

For me, one of my deepest sources of pain was growing up without my mother. She and my father divorced when I was just a baby, and her absence felt like a silent wound—an ache I couldn't explain, a loss that followed me through every stage of life. It wasn't just missing her physical presence; it was the questions that had no answers. *Did she love me? Did she think about me?*

For years, I carried this pain like a burden. It was a heart wound I couldn't shake. But when I surrendered my life to Jesus, something unexpected happened—He met me *inside* the pain. He didn't ignore it, dismiss it, or tell me to get over it. Instead,

He showed me that He was there all along, even in the hardest moments. And as I walked with Christ, I began to see the purpose in my story.

What I once thought was my greatest weakness, God was turning into my greatest strength. Now I'm able to meet others who are experiencing the same kind of pain. I have a deep compassion for those who have lost a parent or lack stability.

Pain can either break us or shape us. The choice is ours.

The Bible tells the story of a woman who suffered for 18 years, bent over and unable to stand up straight (Luke 13:10-13). She was faithful—she still went to the synagogue—but her condition had weighed her down for nearly two decades. Then one day, Jesus saw her. He called her forward and said, "*Woman, you are set free from your infirmity.*" And in an instant, she straightened up.

How many of us are walking through life bent over by the weight of our past? How many of us believe we will never stand tall again?

Jesus is calling you forward.

The same Savior who saw that woman sees you now. He knows the pain you have carried. He knows how long you have suffered. And He is not content to leave you in that place.

Will you let Jesus heal you? Will you trust Him to lift the weight you were never meant to carry? Today marks the start of a new journey toward your future.

Today's Verse:

"*Even to your old age and gray hairs I am he, I am he who will sustain you. I have made you and I will carry you; I will sustain you and I will rescue you.*"

—Isaiah 46:4

LOVE GOD. LOVE OTHERS.

*"Therefore encourage one another and build each oth-
er up, just as in fact you are doing."*

1 Thessalonians 5:11

As we journey through life, it's easy to get wrapped up **in our own struggles and only see challenges.** But some-times, God places obstacles in front of us so that we have to rely on Him for help. He may also put people in our path who need an encouraging word, a listening ear, or a prayer spoken over them. In these moments, we have the opportunity to show the love of Christ and to be His hands and feet.

I want to share a personal story that touched my heart and reminded me of the power of prayer and encouragement. While out for a hike, I crossed paths with a man named Alan. He looked troubled, so I asked him how I could pray for him. It turned out that Alan was going through one of the most painful seasons of his life—he was recently divorced, and his adult children hadn't spoken to him in three years because of it. I could see the weight of his heartache, and in that moment, I simply offered my prayers and encouragement.

Later, Alan emailed me after seeing my business logo on my jacket. He thanked me for the prayers and words of hope I spoke over him, sharing how much it had uplifted him. I told him to keep in touch and to let me know when God answers our prayers for his relationship with his children. This encounter left me reflecting on how one small act of kindness, and one moment of prayer, can plant a seed of hope and even spark a relationship with Christ.

Every interaction we have with someone is an opportunity God has orchestrated. Sometimes, we don't know the battles people are facing, but God does. When we take a moment to speak life, offer prayer, or lend an ear, we are participating in God's redemptive work. Alan's story is a reminder that we don't need to have all the answers—just a willing heart to be present and to share God's love.

Think about it—how many times have we walked past someone who looked like they were carrying a burden? What if we paused, even for a moment, to ask how we could pray for them or encourage them? You never know how your words could be the spark that ignites faith in their life.

Today's Verse:
"By this everyone will know that you are my disciples, if you love one another."
—John 13:35

GOD'S APPROVAL IS ALL THAT MATTERS

"Whatever you do, work at it with all your heart,
as working for the Lord, not for human masters..."
Colossians 3:23

Do you ever feel weighed down by the need for approval?
Maybe it's the desire to be noticed by your boss, validated by your family, or praised by your peers. It's a heavy burden, isn't it? We crave recognition because we want to feel valued, but too often, this addiction to approval traps us. It convinces us that our worth is tied to what others think of us rather than what God says about us.

I used to take pride in my accomplishments, striving for accolades and the approval of my family. I vividly remember family members doubting whether I could start a business, write a book, or succeed in sports nutrition as a private-practice dietitian. It wasn't that they wanted me to fail; they simply wanted me to have a stable career and financial security. Those are valid concerns in modern culture.

However, in the Kingdom of God, the Lord does business differently than the world's systems. While the world seeks comfort and personal gain, God stretches us, teaching us to focus on people over profits and to trust Him for provision. Jesus teaches us a new way of living.

When I let go of my pride and stopped seeking others' validation, everything changed. Instead of chasing approval, I placed my faith in God, trusting that if it was His will, my work would flourish. **That peace has been immeasurable, shifting my desire from wanting my family to believe in me to wanting them to believe in Jesus.**

The Bible is filled with examples of business-minded individuals who glorified God through their work. Paul supported himself as a tentmaker while spreading the gospel, and Lydia, a successful businesswoman, became one of the first converts in Philippi. Their stories remind us that ministry and entrepreneurship can go hand in hand when aligned with God's purpose.

We all want to feel seen, appreciated, and validated by those around us, especially by our loved ones. But there's an incredible freedom in releasing that need for approval. When we surrender our pride and place our faith and trust in God's plan, we align ourselves with His greater purpose for our lives. It's not about *us*—it's about our *Savior*. When you let go of the need for recognition, you make room for God to work in ways far greater than you could ever imagine. He's the very best CEO.

Today's Verse:

"Serve wholeheartedly, as if you were serving the Lord, not people, because you know that the Lord will reward each one for whatever good they do..."
—Ephesians 6:7-8

DAY 10

IT'S YOUR GOLDEN HOUR!

"Those who look to Him are radiant; their faces are never covered with shame."

Psalm 34:5

Have you ever met someone who just **radiates joy?** There's something about them that draws you in—it's more than just a happy personality; it's the light of God shining *through* them. That's the **Holy Glow**, and the best part? It's not reserved for a select few—it's available to you, too! The Bible gives us the perfect recipe for a radiant life that shines from the inside out. So grab your spiritual apron, because we're about to mix up something divine to recharge your spiritual life!

Step 1: Start with the Light of God's Presence: Moses knew all about the Holy Glow. After spending time in God's presence on Mount Sinai, his face literally shone with God's glory (Exod. 34:29). That glow didn't come from Moses' effort; it came from being close to God. The first ingredient in your Holy Glow is time with Jesus. Spend moments in prayer, worship, and reading His Word, and let His light fill your heart. Jesus said, *"I am the light of the world. Whoever follows me will never walk in darkness, but will have the light of life"* (John 8:12).

Step 2: Add Generous Servings of Joy and Gratitude: Nothing dims your shine faster than grumbling and negativity. Instead, stir in joy and gratitude. Philippians 4:4 says, *"Rejoice in the Lord always. I will say it again: Rejoice!"* And in 1 Thessalonians 5:18, we're told, *"Give thanks in all circumstances; for this is God's will for you in Christ Jesus."* Joy isn't about pretending life is perfect; it's about choosing to focus on God's goodness, even in the mess. Gratitude turns your heart toward God and keeps your glow alive.

Step 3: Sprinkle in Kindness and Love: Your glow isn't just for you—it's meant to bless others! Jesus said, *"Let your light shine before others, that they may see your good deeds and glorify your Father in heaven"* (Matt. 5:16). Acts of kindness, encouragement, and love are like glitter for your soul—they make you shine even brighter. Whether it's offering a helping hand or sharing a smile, your glow grows when you reflect God's love to others.

Step 4: Finish with a Shield of Peace: Finally, protect your glow with peace. The world loves to throw stress, worry, and fear our way, but God's peace keeps our shine intact. Philippians 4:7 promises, *"The peace of God, which transcends all understanding, will guard your hearts and your minds in Christ Jesus."* Breathe, pray, and trust God with the things you can't control. A peaceful heart is a glowing heart. So there it is—your Holy Glow recipe! Mix these ingredients daily, and you'll shine like never before!

Today's Verse:
"You are altogether beautiful, my darling; there is no flaw in you." —Song of Solomon 4:7

DAY 11

DIVINE APPOINTMENTS AWAIT

"The Lord will watch over your coming and going both now and forevermore."

Psalm 121:8

There's something transformative about traveling. It's more than just visiting new places; it's an opportunity for God to work in ways we might never experience in the familiarity of home. Travel expands our vision, allowing us to see the needs of others and reminding us that God's work extends far beyond the boundaries of our everyday surroundings. When we step out in faith, even in small ways, we open ourselves to divine appointments that can bless both us and those we encounter.

On a recent trip to California, I felt the Lord nudging me to take the elevator at my hotel—something I don't usually do since I prefer the stairs. As I obeyed, I met a mom whose daughter was part of a softball team. Our conversation quickly turned to nutrition, which is my passion and calling. She pulled out her phone to show me a nutritionist she admired on social media and asked, "Is this you?" It was me! We laughed, and I realized this was no coincidence—it was a God-ordained moment.

The next morning, I had the privilege of talking to the team about nutrition and even praying with them before their game. Later, the girls knocked on my door, telling me how much they admired me. I quickly reminded them to idolize Jesus, not me. Moments like this remind me that the work God does through us isn't about elevating our own platform—it's about pointing people to Him.

Travel also gives us the chance to encounter people we might never otherwise meet. That same weekend, I met a famous children's author, someone who inspired me in ways I didn't expect. God often uses these moments to stretch us, teach us, and remind us of His bigger picture. We are not called to keep our light hidden; we are called to shine it wherever He sends us, even if that's an unexpected hotel elevator.

As you move through your own travels, whether near or far, I encourage you to look for opportunities to expand your vision and share God's love. Every encounter is a chance to reflect Christ's light and meet the needs of others. Trust that God has divine appointments waiting for you and be willing to step into them. Who knows? You may meet someone who inspires you—or someone who needs to see Jesus in you.

Always remember that we are God's hands and feet on the earth. Scripture says, "*Now you are the body of Christ, and each one of you is a part of it*" (1 Cor. 12:27). Every interaction is an opportunity to serve others and reflect the love of Christ.

Today's Challenge:
Intentionally look for one opportunity to serve someone and reflect God's love. This could be a kind word, a small act of service, a prayer, or simply listening to someone who needs encouragement. Ask the Lord to open your eyes to the needs around you and trust Him to guide your actions.

DAY 12

OVERWHELMED, BUT NOT OVERCOME

"In the world you have trouble, but cheer up! I have overcome the world."

John 16:33

Life can feel overwhelming sometimes, can't it? The world is loud with headlines of violence, wars, and hardship. It's easy to feel like the weight of it all is too much to bear, especially if your personal struggles seem to echo that same chaos. Maybe you're thinking, *"You don't know what I've been through."* And you're right—I don't. I can't possibly understand the depth of your pain, the weight of your grief, or the relentless challenges you face. But here's what I do know: **God understands it all.**

I've walked through my own seasons of heartache and uncertainty. For the past four years, I've been on a journey of singleness that brought with it personal hardships and moments of unworthiness. Yet, in the middle of that pain, God showed me how to turn it into something meaningful. I started a business from nothing and, through His grace, paid off over $80,000 in student loan debt!

At first, I thought financial freedom would change everything—that once the debt was gone, life would magically feel lighter. But here's the truth I discovered: freedom doesn't come from achieving milestones or checking off goals. True freedom comes from trusting God with your life and leaning into His purpose for you.

Let me ask you this: Where are you looking for peace? Are you waiting for your circumstances to change before you start living again? I've been there, waiting for something external to fix what's broken inside. But the deeper healing I needed couldn't come from paying off debt, building a business, or reaching a goal. It came from turning to Jesus and letting Him hold the pieces of my life.

I know how hard it can be. Maybe you're grieving, overwhelmed, or just exhausted from the fight. But let me encourage you—don't give up. Lift your eyes to Jesus. He sees you. He knows the burdens you're carrying, and He's not distant from your pain. Take a moment to reflect on where God has been faithful in your life, even in the smallest ways. If nothing comes to mind, that's okay—turn to His Word for hope. In Luke 12:22-23, Jesus says, *"Therefore I tell you, do not worry about your life, what you will eat; what you will wear. For life is more than food, and the body more than clothes."*

Friend, you're not alone. God is always working behind the scenes, even when it feels like nothing is happening. His love for you is constant, and His plans for you are good. Trust that He is holding you through the hard times, and know that Jesus hasn't brought you this far to leave you.

Today's Verse:
"Come to me, all you who are weary and burdened, and I will give you rest."
—Matthew 11:28

CHILDLIKE FAITH, FEARLESS TRUST

"Truly I tell you, unless you change and become like little children, you will never enter the kingdom of heaven."

Matthew 18:3

God has the power to do anything at any given moment. If He wants to transform your life in an instant—*He can.* This truth is something we need to hold on to, especially when we feel overwhelmed or doubtful. Every single one of us is a work in progress, and no matter how old we are, God is still shaping us. We are *all* under construction, and God is far from finished with the masterpiece He's creating in you.

One of the key things God asks of us is to have a childlike faith. Think about how a child trusts completely, without hesitation or fear. Jesus reminds us in Matthew 18:3, *"Truly I tell you, unless you change and become like little children, you will never enter the kingdom of heaven."* Children don't overthink or worry about whether they're good enough or whether they know enough—*they simply believe.* That's the kind of faith God calls us to have, trusting Him completely with our daily lives, our futures, and even our uncertainties.

But let's be honest—doubt has a way of creeping in, doesn't it? We all experience moments of hesitation where we feel unqualified or too inexperienced to follow through with what God has placed in our hearts. Maybe there's something God is prompting you to do right now—like take a new job, have an important conversation, or perhaps speak life into the heart of someone who needs encouragement. Whatever it is, fear and doubt can make you hesitate. But here's the good news: God never calls us to do something without giving us the tools to accomplish it. If He is asking you to step out in faith, you can trust that He *will* provide everything you need. You don't have to have all the answers or even be completely ready in your own strength. God will equip you for the task—He *always* does.

Reflection: Take a moment and ask yourself, *What is God prompting me to do? Is there something you've been putting off because of fear or uncertainty?* Maybe it's time to take that step of faith, trusting that God's got you, just like He always has. The Lord Jesus can speak to us in all sorts of ways. He doesn't mind when we ask Him for confirmation before taking a risk. In fact, He *rejoices* when we come to the Father like small children, eager to get His thoughts and plans about our important decisions.

Remember, the more we seek our Heavenly Father, the more we find His direction for our lives and the lives of those around us. And that begins with taking *action*, even if it's a small step, toward what God is calling you to do.

Today's Verse:

"By faith Abraham obeyed when he was called to go out to the place which he would receive as an inheritance. And he went out, not knowing where he was going."

—Hebrews 11:8

WHEN GOD SENDS ENCOURAGEMENT

"The Lord is my shepherd, I lack nothing."

Psalm 23:1

Today, I decided to break from my usual routine and work in a different space. What I thought would be a simple change of scenery turned into a divine appointment that I couldn't have planned even if I tried. I met an incredible woman named Morgan, and from the moment we started talking, it was as if God had hand-picked her to speak truth into my life. Despite battling nerves about an upcoming speaking engagement, she took the time to share scripture with me and pray over me.

Morgan's encouragement was like a direct message from God. It reminded me that Jesus truly does see me. Morgan didn't just speak into my life; she also had a sticker on her laptop from Moody Publishers—a reminder to write my book! I couldn't help but feel that this was more than a coincidence. It was a moment where God's presence felt tangible, and He reminded me that He is always orchestrating things behind the scenes, even when we don't see it.

Sometimes, God speaks to us in these quiet, unexpected moments, through the people He places in our path. Today was one of those days for me. It came right after a season of hurt and hardship like harsh comments online that stung, business losses that weighed heavily, and personal struggles that have felt like one hit after another. Thankfully, God knows when we need a reminder of His goodness. He is such a thoughtful and loving Father.

Right before I met Morgan, I received a call from an athletic director in Murfreesboro, Tennessee, who follows me on social media. He told me not to let the negativity overshadow all the good I've done. He reminded me of the countless people I've helped—people who may never say it out loud but have been impacted by what I've shared through social media posts and through my career. Isn't it amazing how God knows just the right time to send us the encouragement we need?

Today, I also took a big step of faith. I turned down a CEO opportunity that could have improved my financial situation and given me a more flexible personal life—something I haven't experienced since starting my business. It wasn't an easy decision, but I trust that God has a plan for me. I know that He's calling me to remain faithful in that plan while also taking the time to rest.

Just like I had to trust God's direction in my decision, you may also be facing a choice that requires faith. Maybe it's a career move, a relationship, or simply the need to slow down and rest. Whatever it is, know that God is guiding you, even when the next step feels uncertain. Surrender your worries to Him, and trust that His plans for you are good. **You don't have to have it all figured out—just take the next step in faith.**

Today's Verse:
Jesus said to them, "Come with me by yourselves to a quiet place and get some rest."
—Mark 6:31

FAITH WITH FLAVOR

"Devote yourselves to prayer, being watchful and thankful. And pray for us, too, that God may open a door for our message, so that we may proclaim the mystery of Christ, for which I am in chains."

Colossians 4:2-4

Lately, my greatest fear has been wasting my time and energy on things that do not honor or glorify God. This realization has convicted me to be as bold as possible in sharing the gospel. I don't want to reach the end of my life and realize I spent more time chasing temporary things rather than investing in eternity. One thing I've come to understand is that I was not praying nearly as much as I should be. Talking about Jesus and sharing the gospel is one thing, but praying without ceasing is another.

Only through prayer can we stay vigilant against trials and recognize divine opportunities. The Apostle Paul instructed us to share the gospel with wisdom and joy, speaking in a way that reflects the truth and grace of Christ. If we are truly seeking to glorify God, our words and actions must be aligned with Him.

Jesus Himself declared, *"You are the salt of the earth...."* (Matthew 5:13). As believers, we are called to *be* salt—not just to sprinkle it here and there but to live in a way that preserves truth, enhances the message of Christ, and makes the gospel irresistible to those who hear it.

As a registered dietitian, I understand how important seasoning is. Salt brings out the best flavors in food. Without it, vegetables can be bland, and an unseasoned steak lacks depth. The same principle applies to sharing the gospel—if our words lack wisdom and grace, they won't resonate. If we sound judgmental, rigid, or disconnected from people's struggles, they won't be drawn in. But when the gospel is presented with love, understanding, and authenticity, people listen.

This is true when sharing Christ with others. Pay attention to the people you meet and where they are in their walk with God. If someone is, for example, a committed vegan, you wouldn't immediately try to convince them to abandon their lifestyle and switch to animal protein. That approach would push them away. Instead, you might ask, *How can I help you right now?* Maybe they're feeling fatigued, and you have the opportunity to encourage them, pray for them, and see if they are open to a new way of living.

Pray for open doors. Pray for God-prepared opportunities and divine appointments to share the gospel. And above all, be relatable! When food is well-seasoned, people finish their plates. Likewise, when the gospel is presented with grace and wisdom, people are more likely to truly hear it—and even accept Christ into their lives.

Today's Verse:

"Rejoice always, pray without ceasing, give thanks in all circumstances; for this is the will of God in Christ Jesus for you."
—1 Thessalonians 5:16-18

THE POWER OF LETTING GO

"Be still, and know that I am God."

Psalm 46:10

O ne of the most important and life-altering decisions you will ever make is putting your faith and trust in Jesus Christ. He offers hope that goes beyond our circumstances, peace that transcends understanding, and provision for every need. When we surrender to Him, we find the kind of love and care no human can match. He sees our hearts, knows our struggles, and has a perfect plan for each of us. But the journey of faith isn't passive. It calls us to take action—to lay down what hinders our relationship with Him and to pick up what strengthens it.

In Matthew 16:24, Jesus tells His disciples, *"If anyone would come after me, let him deny himself and take up his cross and follow me."* Jesus wasn't speaking of a casual commitment but of total surrender. The cross is a symbol of sacrifice and devotion, a reminder that following Jesus requires us to let go of the things that keep us from Him. What is it today that you need to lay down so you can follow Him more closely?

Think about the rich young ruler in Matthew 19:16-22. He asked Jesus what he needed to do to have eternal life. Jesus replied that he needed to sell his possessions, give to the poor, and follow Him. The young man walked away sad, unwilling to part with what he held so dear. Jesus was not asking him to give up everything to leave him empty, but rather to free his hands and heart for the abundance Jesus was offering.

What is holding you back from fully embracing the life Jesus has for you? Maybe, like the rich young ruler, it's material possessions or financial security. Or maybe it's a relationship, a fear, a burden of guilt or shame that you've carried for too long. Whatever it is, Jesus is calling you to release it, to lay it down at His feet so you can pick up the fullness of life He offers.

The apostle Paul understood this trade-off well. In Philippians 3:7-8, he writes, "*But whatever were gains to me I now consider loss for the sake of Christ. What is more, I consider everything a loss because of the surpassing worth of knowing Christ Jesus my Lord.*" Paul laid down his achievements, his status, and his past to follow Jesus. And what did he gain? *Everything.* Christ became his ultimate treasure.

Prayer:

Lord, I lay down all that is keeping me from following You wholeheartedly. Help me pick up the cross and trust You to lead me on this journey of faith. Strengthen my relationship with You and remind me that in You, I have everything I need.

Amen.

JUST START BUILDING

"For God has not given us a spirit of fear, but of power and of love and of a sound mind."

2 Timothy 1:7

If you're feeling stuck in the same routine, it's time to take a leap of faith! The Bible gives us countless examples of God calling people to step out of their comfort zones and trust Him completely. Abraham's journey is a powerful reminder of this. When God told Abraham (Abram) to leave his home and everything familiar, the Lord didn't give him the full plan. In Genesis 12:1, the Lord simply said, *"Go from your country, your people and your father's household to the land I will show you."*

Abraham trusted God and obeyed, stepping into the unknown, believing that God's promises would come to pass even though he didn't see them yet. **That same trust is what God asks of you today.** King Jesus says just follow Him in obedience and simple trust, even when the details are unclear.

We often hold ourselves back because of fear—fear of the unknown, fear of failure, or fear of what others might think. But as followers of Christ, we are not called to live with a spirit of fear; we are called to live by faith.

Ruth took a courageous step of faith after her husband's death. She could have stayed in Moab, surrounded by the familiar, but instead, she chose to follow her mother-in-law, Naomi. Ruth declared, "*Where you go, I will go, and where you stay, I will stay*" (Ruth 1:16). She walked away from everything she had ever known.

Ruth had no idea that her future husband, Boaz, was waiting on the other side of her obedience. Her decision to leave Moab not only led to her marriage with Boaz but also made her part of a lineage that included King David—and ultimately, Jesus!

And then, let's consider Noah. When God told him to build the ark, Noah didn't waste time trying to explain himself to those who mocked or doubted him. The Bible says Noah "*did everything just as God commanded him*" (Gen. 6:22) even though it had never rained! He trusted God's instructions completely, even when they seemed impossible. Abraham, Ruth, and Noah all teach us that *obedience to God is worth more than the approval of people.*

The world may not always understand or support the steps God is asking you to take, but trust that *Jesus* sees the bigger picture! *What has God called you to build in your life?* It might be moving to a new city, losing weight, taking on a new venture, entering a relationship, or even reaching a deeper level of faith. Whatever it is, keep moving forward, knowing that God is faithful to complete what He has started in you.

Today's Reminder:
Noah didn't stop to explain himself to every hater or doubter. He kept building his ark because God said so! Everyone thought Noah looked crazy—until it started to rain! You should do the same and let the rain do the talking!

FIND YOUR SECRET PLACE

"Jesus often withdrew to lonely places and prayed."
Luke 5:16

When you're feeling overwhelmed, confused, or lost, it's important to find a place of retreat to pray—just like **Jesus did.** He often withdrew to quiet, solitary places to connect with His Father.

For me, when I need quiet time to hear from God, I go out into the woods, surrounded by nature—vegetation, flowers, sunlight, and water. In the stillness, I can feel the Holy Spirit's presence more deeply. Maybe for you, your place of solitude is your backyard garden, inside your car, or a quiet room in your home.

The concept of a garden holds deep biblical significance. In Genesis 2, God chose a garden as the first home for Adam and Eve. The garden was a place of shelter, delight, and protection—a space of retreat where they could commune with God. It was in this sacred space that God Himself walked in the garden, seeking fellowship with His creation (Genesis 3:8). It's no coincidence that many of us feel a special closeness to the Lord when we're in nature, surrounded by the beauty He created.

Taking time to reconnect with God in a quiet, natural setting allows us to hear His voice more clearly. When I go into the woods and leave my phone behind, I can pour out my heart to God without distractions. It's in those moments that I feel His presence most powerfully. Scripture promises that when we seek the Lord, we will find Him (Jeremiah 29:13).

So, where is your "garden"—aka your place of solitude? It doesn't have to be a physical garden, but rather any space where you can retreat and focus on God. *How can you set a goal to spend time in that place daily, allowing God to refresh and speak to your spirit?* Whether it's in nature or another quiet place, make it a priority to meet Jesus there regularly. When we intentionally seek Him, He meets us with His peace, guidance, and love.

Going Deeper:

The "secret place" with Jesus is more than just a physical location—it's a *spiritual sanctuary* where we meet with God intimately and personally. In Matthew 6:6, Jesus says, *"But when you pray, go into your room, close the door and pray to your Father, who is unseen. Then your Father, who sees what is done in secret, will reward you."* This secret place is a space where you can be completely vulnerable before God, free from distractions or the pressures of life. In the secret place, you're reminded that you are seen, known, and loved by God.

It's where you pour out your heart in prayer, listen for His voice, and receive His guidance. We have to fight for this time because distractions will always come our way. However, it's through an intimate relationship with our Heavenly Father that the greatest breakthroughs often happen.

DAY 19

GOD'S PROMISES SHINE BRIGHT LIKE A RAINBOW!

> *"I set My rainbow in the cloud, and it shall be for the sign of the covenant between Me and the earth."*
> Genesis 9:14 (NKJV)

Have you ever stopped and really looked at a rainbow? Not just glanced at it, but truly taken it in? There's something breathtaking about those vibrant colors stretching across the sky. It's no accident—it's the handiwork of God, a masterpiece placed right in front of us to remind us of His faithfulness.

Let's go back to the first time a rainbow appeared. Imagine what Noah had just been through. Forty days and forty nights of relentless rain, followed by months of waiting as the waters slowly recded. He and his family had been through a storm like no other—literally. And then, after all the chaos and destruction, God painted a promise in the sky. A bow in the cloud, a covenant saying, "I *will never flood the earth again.*"

But here's the thing—God didn't just give Noah the rainbow as a one-time sign. He gave it to all of us, for all generations. Every time you see a rainbow, it's as if God is whispering, "I *keep my promises.*"

God's Beauty in Creation

Noah wasn't the only one to recognize God's power through nature. Solomon, the wisest man who ever lived, marveled at God's creation too. He wrote about the beauty of the trees, the birds, the oceans, and the changing seasons. In Ecclesiastes 3:11, he reminds us that God has "made everything beautiful in its time."

Solomon knew what we sometimes forget—creation reflects the Creator. The world around us isn't something to be worshiped, but it is something to be noticed. Nature reveals God's handiwork, His creativity, and His attention to detail. The new age movement may look to the earth as something divine in itself, but as God's people, we look *through* creation to see the One who made it.

Every sunrise, every flower, every rolling wave is a brushstroke of God's artistry. And the rainbow? *That's His signature.*

Reflection Questions:

What "rainbows" has God placed in your life recently as reminders of His promises? Has something in nature caught your attention and reminded you of the love of Jesus? When was the last time you truly paused to admire God's creation?

Consider writing these special moments in your Bible or starting a new notebook. Record every "rainbow" moment that comes your way this season. Over time, this list will become a powerful testimony of God's faithfulness and goodness in your life. Take a moment today to thank our precious Savior for the beauty He surrounds you with!

DAY 20

JESUS IS YOUR KINSMAN REDEEMER

"May the Lord repay you for what you have done. May you be richly rewarded by the Lord, the God of Israel, under whose wings you have come to take refuge."

Ruth 2:12

What's **weighing you down today?** Maybe it's worry, fear, regret—or the need to control everything around you. I get it. Hebrews 12:1 tells us: *"Let us strip off every weight and the sin that hinders our progress."*

For me, that weight has often been control. I've spent years gripping the reins of my life, convinced that if I just worked harder, planned better, and held on tighter, I could make everything turn out the way I wanted. I've used work as a way to escape, pouring myself into it so I wouldn't have to sit with the deeper aches of the past. But the truth is, control is exhausting. God has been asking me to let go—not just once, but every single day.

Letting go isn't passive. It doesn't mean sitting back and doing nothing. It means loosening my grip, surrendering my plans, and trusting that He's working even when I can't see the outcome. And when I struggle with that, I think about Ruth in the Bible.

Can you imagine what it must have felt like for her? She left everything she knew—her home, her people, her sense of security—to follow Naomi into an uncertain future. They arrived in Bethlehem with nothing. No husband to provide for them. No guaranteed way to survive. They were two women in a culture that offered little protection or opportunity.

Ruth had every reason to be anxious. She could have let fear paralyze her. Instead, she did the only thing she could—she took the next step. She went to the fields to glean, picking up leftover grain so she and Naomi could eat. She didn't have a grand plan, but she did what she could and trusted God with the rest. And then, in a way only God could orchestrate, He led her straight to the field of Boaz—the very man who would not only provide for her needs but also redeem her story.

Boaz was her kinsman redeemer, a man with both the ability and willingness to restore what had been lost. And in the same way, **Jesus is our Kinsman Redeemer**. He steps into our brokenness, our uncertainty, our desperation, and He makes a way. He takes the weight of our burdens and trades them for His peace. He restores what was stolen, mends what was shattered, and turns our ashes into beauty.

Truth be told, letting go is hard. Ruth didn't know how her story would unfold. She just *trusted*. And maybe, just maybe, that's what God is asking of us too. Because when we finally let go, we find that we were never meant to carry it all in the first place.

Today's Verse:

"Whoever tries to keep their life will lose it, and whoever loses their life will preserve it."
—Luke 17:33

RUN YOUR RACE WITH ENDURANCE

"Therefore, since we are surrounded by so great a cloud of witnesses, let us also lay aside every weight, and sin which clings so closely, and let us run with endurance the race that is set before us."

Hebrews 12:1

As you step into today, know that you are not running the race of life alone. God has placed you on a path with a divine purpose, and although it may feel overwhelming at times, you have been equipped with everything you need to succeed. Just like a runner, part of the preparation involves shedding unnecessary loads and hindrances that might slow you down or distract you from your ultimate goal. Runners also don't look back; they look ahead.

Similarly, God invites you to cast aside the burdens that have been weighing you down—whether it's fear, doubt, or distractions that keep you from resting in Him. By doing so, you make room for the Holy Spirit's peace and strength to carry you through. Running with endurance means learning to trust God in every season. Sometimes, the wind of the Holy Spirit brings acceleration and speed; other times, we must maintain consistency in our walk with Christ.

Paul warns us in Galatians 5:7-10 that the enemy works over-time to pull us away from God. "*You were running a good race. Who cut in on you to keep you from obeying the truth? That kind of persuasion does not come from the one who calls you.*" This verse reminds us to stay vigilant. Distractions and obstacles are often subtle—they may come in the form of doubt, temptation, or discouragement.

Other times, people and drama may try to interrupt our good race. But Paul's words encourage us to shake off anything not rooted in God's truth, for those things are not from Jesus. *Keep running*, knowing that God has called you to freedom!

Today, choose to run with endurance. Lay aside any weight holding you back, and fix your eyes on Jesus, the source of your strength. You are empowered to overcome, not because of your own efforts, but because the same Spirit that raised Christ from the dead lives in you.

Prayer:

Lord, I thank You for surrounding me with a cloud of witnesses and for the strength You give me to run with endurance. Help me to lay aside every burden, trusting You fully as I navigate this journey. Empower me today to keep my eyes fixed on You and to run with perseverance, knowing You are my ultimate victory. Keep me alert to anything that tries to cut in on my faith, and guide me with Your truth. Amen.

DAY 22

CONFESSION BRINGS FREEDOM

*"Whoever conceals their sins does not prosper, but
the one who confesses and renounces them finds
mercy."*

Proverbs 28:13

Have you ever decided to lie or conceal something you knew was wrong out of guilt or shame? We all have. It's a common struggle—to hide our mistakes, sins, and shortcomings because we fear what others might think of us. But the truth is, keeping these things hidden doesn't protect us. Instead, it traps us in guilt, shame, and pain, preventing us from experiencing the freedom that God offers.

Satan wants nothing more than for you to carry the weight of your guilt. He wants to convince you that your sin disqualifies you from God's love and that it's better to stay silent than to expose your mistakes. But that is a *lie*. God's grace and mercy are greater than any sin we could ever commit. And when we confess, God doesn't condemn us—He *redeems* us.

Look at King David. He was a man after God's own heart, but he made a grave mistake by committing adultery with Bathsheba and then tried to cover it up. David's decision to hide his sin led to negative emotional, physical, and spiritual consequences. He wrote in *Psalm 32:3-4*: *"When I kept silent, my bones wasted away through my groaning all day long. For day and night your hand was heavy on me; my strength was sapped as in the heat of summer."*

David's silence didn't protect him—*it drained him.* But when he finally confessed his sin, God forgave him and restored him. This is the power of confession. When we uncover our sins before God, He covers them with His grace. When we bring our struggles into the light, He heals us and sets us free.

Repenting and confessing your sins doesn't just bring relief—it brings joy and peace. James 5:16 tells us to *"confess your sins to each other and pray for each other so that you may be healed."* Healing begins when we stop hiding and start trusting God with our brokenness.

I've experienced this firsthand. For years, I struggled with perfectionism and the shame of being involved in an abusive relationship. I was living with guilt, afraid of what people would think if they knew the truth. But when I finally confessed my sins to God, He embraced me with His forgiveness. I no longer had to carry the weight of failure or fear that someone would find out about my past. The moment I laid it all at Jesus' feet, He not only forgave me, but He also began to transform my life, one day at a time. Today, my personal and professional life has never prospered more.

God can redeem every part of your story, no matter how broken it may seem. He can take your guilt, shame, and fear and turn them into a testimony of His goodness and grace. Don't ever give up!

Today's Verse:
"If we confess our sins, he is faithful and just to forgive us our sins and to cleanse us from all unrighteousness."
—1 John 1:9

WORSHIP BEYOND THE MUSIC

"God is spirit, and his worshipers must worship in the Spirit and in truth."

John 4:24

If you've ever heard the phrase *"worship in Spirit and truth"* **and wondered what it actually means, you're not alone.** Jesus spoke these words in John 4:23-24, saying, *"But the time is coming—indeed it's here now—when true worshipers will worship the Father in spirit and in truth. The Father is looking for those who will worship him that way. For God is Spirit, so those who worship him must worship in spirit and in truth."*

But how do we live this out beyond Sunday services and worship songs? Let's break it down in a way that makes sense for everyday life.

To worship in **Spirit** means to engage with God beyond just rituals or routine—it's about a real, living relationship with Him. It's not about just going through the motions; it's about surrendering your heart. The Holy Spirit, who dwells within every believer, helps us connect with God in a deeper way. He moves in our prayers, guides us in truth, and reminds us that we are never alone.

I remember when God first nudged me to step out in faith and move to Nashville. At first, fear crept in, but as I leaned into the

Holy Spirit's guidance, I felt a peace that could only come from Him. That's what it means to walk in the Spirit—letting Him lead, even when the way forward isn't clear.

Worshiping in **truth** is about coming before God with honesty and aligning our lives with His Word. It's easy to put on a front, to act like we have it all together—but God isn't looking for perfect people; He's looking for real ones. Jesus *is* the Truth. He wants us to bring Him our struggles, our doubts, and even our questions. The "truth" part also reminds us that our faith isn't built on emotions or trends but on the unchanging Word of God.

Worshiping in Spirit and truth isn't just about singing in church—it's about how we *live* every single day. It's seen in the way we trust God with our decisions, love people well, and stay faithful even when things don't make sense. Worship happens when we choose to forgive, when we pray with expectation, and when we stand firm in God's promises.

So today, start small. Ask the Holy Spirit to guide your heart. Open your Bible and take in His truth. Let worship be more than a moment—let it become the way you live. Because when you truly worship in Spirit and truth, you'll experience God in a way that transforms every part of your life.

Today's Verse:
"Teach me your way, Lord, that I may rely on your faithfulness; give me an undivided heart, that I may fear your name."
—Psalm 86:11

SHINE BRIGHT, STAND APART

"You are the light of the world. A town built on a hill cannot be hidden."

Matthew 5:14

There's something unique about you, isn't there? Maybe you've felt it in the way people respond to you, how you seem to stand out even when you try to blend in. You might think it's your quirks, your personality, or even something you don't quite understand. But let me remind you of this prophetic truth: when you walk into a room, the atmosphere shifts because you carry the light of Jesus Christ within you.

In today's world, it seems like everyone wants to attach a diagnosis to their uniqueness. Society often labels creativity, sensitivity, or unconventional thinking as "issues" to be managed rather than gifts to be celebrated. But what the world sees as strange or flawed, **God calls chosen**. Your uniqueness is not an accident—it's a distinguishing mark of the Creator's hand on your life. He made you different *on purpose* so that you can carry His light into places others cannot.

As a believer, you are not just anyone—you are a carrier of God's *presence*. The Holy Spirit dwells within you, and with Him comes power, peace, and light. What others may see as "different" or "unique" about you is often the mark of Christ's hand on your life. You were never meant to fit in with the world; you were designed to be set apart, a reflection of heaven on earth.

That thing about you that feels "weird" or "quirky"? It's not a flaw; it's part of your God-given uniqueness. Perhaps it's your creativity, the way you think outside the box, or the compassion that others might dismiss as overly sensitive. These are distinguishing marks that God has woven into your being to set you apart for His work. Like a fingerprint, your uniqueness is evidence that God created you with intention and purpose.

When you step into a room, you bring more than yourself—you bring the hope of Jesus Christ. The peace you carry silences chaos. The light in you exposes darkness. The love you embody reminds others of God's heart. Even if you don't say a word, your presence speaks volumes because it's not just you—it's Christ *in* you, the hope of glory (Colossians 1:27). You are God's beloved vessel, uniquely designed to bring His Kingdom wherever you go.

Challenge:

This week, take a moment to reflect on the traits or habits that make you feel different or even out of place. Rather than trying to hide them or change them, ask God to show you how these "oddities" are actually a reflection of His DNA within you. Consider how your uniqueness might be the very way He's designed you to fulfill a specific purpose. Embrace the fact that what might feel unusual is actually a powerful expression of God's handiwork in your life.

DAY 25

FORGIVENESS BRINGS FREEDOM

"Be kind and compassionate to one another, forgiving each other, just as in Christ God forgave you."
Ephesians 4:32

To truly experience the fullness of God's glory, we must be willing to surrender the burdens we carry—our sins, **our grudges, and the pain others have caused us.** Forgiveness is the key that unlocks peace in our hearts. When we reflect on the grace Christ has extended to us, it becomes clear that forgiving others is not just a command but an act of love that mirrors His heart. Jesus bore the weight of our sins and forgave us, offering grace we didn't deserve. How could we withhold that same grace from someone else? But let's be honest: forgiveness isn't always simple.

Forgiveness is messy and often painful, especially when someone we trust has deeply hurt us. I know this personally. I once loved someone deeply and gave so much of myself, only to experience verbal abuse and emotional damage in return. The hurt ran deep, and for a long time, I held onto that pain. It wasn't until years of healing, reflection, and God's guidance that I realized forgiveness was the only way forward—not for his sake, but for mine. Forgiveness didn't excuse the wrong, but it freed me from the weight of bitterness that was keeping me stuck.

We all make mistakes, and we are all in need of grace. Just as God forgives us, He calls us to forgive others. Holding onto resentment doesn't change the past; it only hardens our hearts and pulls us further from God's peace. Jesus said we are to love our enemies. We can't repay evil with evil.

Forgiveness isn't meant to be limited—*it's a continual process.* This doesn't mean forgetting the hurt or allowing someone back into your life if it's unsafe. Forgiveness is about releasing the burden of bitterness, trusting God's justice, and making room for His healing in your heart.

Forgiveness is not about the person who hurt you; it's about you and your relationship with God. When you forgive, you release the heavy weight you've been carrying and allow God to fill that space with His peace and restoration. Healthy boundaries are sometimes necessary, and letting go doesn't always mean reconciliation. It means trusting God to handle the situation and choosing not to let anger or pain control your heart.

Today's Challenge:

Is there someone you need to forgive? Are you holding onto bitterness that's keeping you from experiencing God's peace? Take a moment to release that person into God's hands. Pray for the strength to forgive and let go. Remember, healed people heal others, but hurt people continue to hurt those around them. Choose to be a vessel of healing, allowing God to restore not just your heart but the hearts of those you touch.

BOLD FAITH: TOUCHING THE HEM OF HIS GARMENT

"And a woman was there who had been subject to bleeding for twelve years, but no one could heal her."

Luke 8:43

God can do the impossible at any moment. He works miracles out of messes. There is no situation too difficult for Him to transform. But here's the key—do we have the kind of *faith* that believes in the impossible, even when things seem hopeless? The woman with the issue of blood, as described in the Gospels, offers us a powerful example of what true faith looks like.

For 12 long years, this woman suffered from a condition that left her isolated and drained. She had spent all her money on doctors, trying everything humanly possible to be healed. Nothing worked. But she wasn't ready to give up. She heard about Jesus, and despite the risks, she believed with all her heart that if she could just touch the hem of His garment, she would be healed.

Think about that for a moment. She believed that even the very edge of His *clothes* held enough power to change her life! And she was right! As soon as she got in close proximity with the Savior, the woman was instantly healed. Her faith stopped Jesus in His tracks.

Do you have that kind of faith? A great definition of faith is "simple trust." Are you willing to take bold steps, trusting that Jesus can change your circumstances, even in the smallest ways? I'll admit, sometimes I struggle with this. There are days when I believe wholeheartedly that Jesus is with me and capable of doing the impossible. But other days, doubt creeps in, and my faith wavers.

Maybe you've been there too. But here's the truth: God cares about each of us, no matter our past or present struggles. He is willing to stop for us just as He did for her. The question is, are we willing to risk it all—our doubts, our fears, our comfort zones—to touch the hem of His garment? What's truly beautiful about the woman with the issue of blood is that Jesus didn't just heal her—**He restored her identity in front of everyone!** In those times, bleeding marked a woman as unclean and sinful, but Jesus made a point to call her "Daughter," affirming that she had done nothing wrong. In that moment, Jesus felt power leave Him because of her great faith! And here's the amazing part—you carry that same resurrection power in your heart through the Holy Spirit!

Jesus wants your healing even more than you do because He sees the whole, restored version of you that's ready to make waves in the Kingdom and impact many lives! He's always ready to step in and bring restoration to your life. The question is, are you ready to receive the healing He's offering?

Today's Verse:
"Then he said to her, 'Daughter, your faith has healed you. Go in peace and be freed from your suffering.'"
—Mark 5:34

FEARLESS FAITH: SHARING JESUS WITHOUT HESITATION

"If anyone will not welcome you or listen to your words, leave that home or town and shake the dust off your feet."

Matthew 10:14

God calls us to be bold in sharing our faith and to seize every opportunity to testify about His goodness. We may not always know the impact of our words, but when we step out in faith, trusting God to guide us, He places us in the paths of people who need to hear from Him. He gives us the right words at the right time.

Yesterday, I had one of those moments at my local Y. I met a woman recording an influencer video, and we began a conversation. She mentioned how she talks about politics on her page, despite the backlash. I asked if she ever talks about the Lord, and she admitted that while she's a follower of Christ, she avoids discussing faith because it's "too controversial." I laughed and said, "What isn't controversial today? Politics isn't?" She agreed, and I encouraged her, telling her that God has big plans for her and that she can boldly share her faith, using her platform to inspire others.

Before we parted ways, I invited her to church, and she gladly accepted, telling me how much better she felt after our conversation. In that moment, I was reminded of the power of stepping out in faith and encouraging others. We never know what someone is battling, but a simple word of encouragement can make a world of difference.

Sometimes, we're hesitant to share our faith because of fear—fear of rejection, criticism, or controversy. But Jesus reminds us in Matthew 10:14 that not everyone will welcome our message. That's okay. We are called to speak up anyway. If someone rejects it, we "shake the dust off" and keep moving forward, knowing that God will use our words in ways we might never see.

When you're feeling down, consider how you can help someone else. There's something deeply healing about stepping out of our own pain to encourage another. In fact, giving from the heart often leads to healing. The next time you feel sad or discouraged, ask yourself: *How can I serve someone else today?* You'll find that helping others draws you closer to God's heart and lifts your spirit.

So, how can you be a fisher of men today? Look for opportunities to share your faith, encourage someone, or simply listen. God will use your words, even when you feel weak. And as you step out in faith, He will strengthen you for His purposes.

Today's Verse:
"For I am not ashamed of the gospel, because it is the power of God that brings salvation to everyone who believes: first to the Jew, then to the Gentile."
—Romans 1:16

YOU ARE SEEN: GOD HAS NOT FORGOTTEN YOU

"Are not two sparrows sold for a penny? Yet not one of them will fall to the ground outside your Father's care. And even the very hairs of your head are all numbered. So don't be afraid; you are worth more than many sparrows."

Matthew 10:29-31

Have you ever felt unseen? Like your prayers aren't heard, or the dreams you've been holding onto were quietly slipping away? If you've ever felt forgotten, take heart—God hasn't lost sight of you. *Not for a moment.*

Sometimes, the waiting seasons of life can feel unbearable. We look around and wonder why others seem to be moving forward while we feel stuck. But what if the waiting isn't about being overlooked but about being prepared? God sees the bigger picture. He knows exactly what you need and when you need it. His timing is not just good; it's perfect.

Think about the sparrows Jesus spoke of in Matthew 10. They were considered insignificant, worth only a penny, yet not one of them falls to the ground without God's care. If God is so attentive to a small sparrow, how much more is He invested in you, His beloved child? Every detail of your life matters to Him. He sees your tears, hears your prayers, and knows the desires of your heart.

In the moments when you feel forgotten, remember this: God is working behind the scenes in ways you can't yet see. The waiting is never wasted. He's building your character, strengthening your faith, and preparing you for something far greater than you can imagine. Just because you can't see the outcome doesn't mean He's not moving.

Today, rest in the truth that you are deeply known and loved by God. The same God who numbers the stars in the sky also numbers the hairs on your head. You are not forgotten. You are cherished. Trust Him to bring His plans for your life to fulfillment, in His time and His way.

Today's Verse:
"Consider it pure joy, my brothers and sisters, whenever you face trials of many kinds, because you know that the testing of your faith produces perseverance."
—James 1:2-3

TRUSTING GOD IN THE WHAT-IFS

"Commit to the Lord whatever you do, and He will establish your plans."

Proverbs 16:3

When I recently hired two new contract dietitians, **I felt a mix of hope and fear.** On one hand, I was confident in the growth of my business and excited about the help I was bringing on board. But on the other hand, I was worried. One of them had left her full-time, salaried job to join my company, which meant I felt responsible for ensuring she had enough hours to support her family. The other also hoped for stable, consistent work. The pressure weighed on me. While my business has been growing, I couldn't help but wonder, *What if they leave? What if we invest in training, only for them to walk away? What if we can't get enough clients?*

The "what ifs" seemed endless. I knew God was asking me to trust Him, but it hasn't been easy. Since then, we've had some wins but also faced challenges. To stay anchored in faith, I started doing a team huddle prayer before each meeting. I know the power of prayer, and I wanted my team to lean into that faith as well.

Was I nervous about what they'd think? Maybe a little. But I trusted that this act of faith would help us all forge ahead with God at the center. And as we prayed, we started seeing subtle signs of God's provision—new clients signing up, doors opening. It was as if God was whispering, "*I am here, and I've got this.*"

Running a business is tough. There are ups and downs you wouldn't believe unless you've experienced it. But God uses our challenges, worry, and frustration for His good when we channel it properly. I want to be a leader who keeps my eyes on Christ and leads with faith even in the workplace. Still, it's not always easy.

Where in your life can you step out in faith and trust God where it's hardest to trust? He knows your path, and He will redirect you if something isn't meant for you. Whatever you're facing today, remember that God's timing is always perfect. We need to release our timeline to experience the fullness of His plans.

No matter the challenges, trust that God is working behind the scenes, orchestrating everything for your good and His glory. Stay faithful, stay prayerful, and know that He is with you every step of the way.

Today's Verse:
"*Trust in the Lord with all your heart and lean not on your own understanding; in all your ways submit to Him, and He will make your paths straight.*"
—Proverbs 3:5-6

DAY 30

FAITH GROWS IN THE WAITING

"I waited patiently for the Lord; He turned to me and heard my cry."

Psalm 40:1

Take a moment right now to pause and take inventory **of your heart.** What are you carrying that's weighing you down? Is it fear, frustration, or pain from the past? Whatever it is, God is inviting you to release it into His hands. He already knows every detail—your thoughts, your struggles, and even the things you haven't been able to say out loud. Why not let it go and trust Him? When I've laid my burdens before Christ, I've found that God meets me with overwhelming love, grace, and mercy. All He asks is that we come to Him honestly. He'll handle the rest. When I asked God to show me what I needed to release, He revealed something unexpected.

For years, I had buried painful memories tied to Michigan, a place I used to call home. Someone I trusted deeply hurt me there, and I let that pain overshadow all the good memories. It felt like I couldn't love Michigan anymore. But holding onto the past kept me from embracing what God wanted to do in my life. I realized I couldn't step into the future while clinging to old wounds. That's true for all of us—when we hold onto hurt, we're not fully open to what's next.

Here's the truth: God can't show you what's ahead until you're ready to trust Him with what's behind you. He asks us to let go, to trust, and to wait on Him—not because He's withholding answers, but because faith grows in the waiting. When we surrender control, we open the door to deeper understanding, greater peace, and clarity about His plans for our lives. Faith isn't passive; it's an active choice to trust God, even when we don't understand.

Today, as I write this on a cold winter day, I'm reminded of God's constant presence, even in the darkest times. I've faced seasons of deep struggle, battling suicidal thoughts and the pressure to carry more than I could bear. It's exhausting, and I know many of you have felt the same weight. But here's what gives me peace: even in the hardest moments, God is with me. Writing these devotionals is my way of drawing near to Him, and my prayer is that these words touch even one person—maybe that person is *you*.

Beloved, please remember that you matter. Jesus died for you so that you could live in freedom, hope, and love. Whatever you're holding onto, release it today. Let God take your burdens and make room for His healing, His plans, and His peace. You are not alone. You are deeply loved, and your future is secure in His hands.

Today's Verse:
"In this world you will have trouble. But take heart! I have overcome the world."
—John 16:33

DAY 31

WHEN GOD FEELS SILENT: TRUSTING HIM IN THE WAITING

"He brought me out into a spacious place; He rescued me because He delighted in me."

Psalm 18:19

The last few weeks have been heavy. I've felt my own fears, self-doubt, and ambition cloud God's mission for my life. Maybe you're in a season like this too—where everything feels harder than it should, and hope feels just out of reach. You're trying. You're reading your Bible, showing up at church, praying, and leaning on your community, but it still feels like God is silent. You wonder if He's even there. I know these feelings all too well.

I hit a breaking point recently. I needed to get away, so I retreated to a quiet spot in the woods and poured my heart out to Jesus—raw and unfiltered. All the anger, pain, and frustration I'd been holding onto spilled out. In that moment, I realized something I'd been avoiding: I'd been pretending to be "okay" when I was anything but. It's easy to go through the motions and put on a brave face, even when you're struggling inside. But being vulnerable—even with Jesus—takes far more effort.

On the surface, I seemed to have it all together. I'd paid off my student loans, hired two new team members, and was physically healthy. But deep down, I was angry and confused about my life's direction. As I fell to my knees in prayer, God didn't respond with thunder or an immediate solution. Instead, He sent a simple yet profound reminder of His love when a vibrant red cardinal fluttered nearby. To me, cardinals are a symbol of God's presence, a gentle way of saying, "I see you. I'm here." Even in silence, the Holy Spirit is with us. I love when the Lord speaks through His creation.

As I walked back to my car that day, I remembered that God rarely shows us the full picture; rather, He promises to walk with us through every storm. Faith isn't about having all the answers; it's about trusting Him with the next step. When the enemy whispers lies that God doesn't care or has forgotten you, remember that those are just distractions. God is faithful, even when we don't feel it.

I'll be honest—my heart is still healing. I'm feeling burnt out, confused, and in desperate need of God's renewal. But I'm learning that Jesus is closest to us in these tender, vulnerable moments. If you're feeling lost or unseen right now, know this: you are not alone. God hears your cries, sees your pain, and is with you, even when the silence feels deafening. Lean into Him. Pour out your heart. And trust that He's already working in ways you can't yet see.

Today's Verse:
"Answer me when I call to you, my righteous God. Give me relief from my distress; have mercy on me and hear my prayer."
—Psalm 4:1

GOD IS STILL WORKING: HE SEES YOUR PAIN AND HEARS YOUR QUESTIONS

"The Lord is close to the brokenhearted and saves those who are crushed in spirit."

Psalm 34:18

Every so often, a celebrity or someone of status will say there's no God because of the injustice or suffering they've faced. My heart goes out to them because I've been there, too. I used to have a victim mentality, thinking, *"If God exists, why did He allow such terrible things to happen to me and my family?"* I've questioned His existence based on the pain I've experienced, just like so many others do.

I once thought, *"If God were real, He wouldn't let horrific things happen to innocent people, including me, my brother, sister, and dad."* I struggled with the challenges my grandmother faced, and I blamed God for every hardship. But here's what I've come to realize: the very people who say "God does not exist" are often the ones who need Him the most. And God is working on them, just as He worked on me, even when I wasn't open to seeing it.

Before I became a believer, I idolized my work ethic, my achievements, and even my grandmother. I believed that I controlled my destiny, that my success was in my own hands. But when things went wrong, I would turn around and blame the very God I claimed didn't exist. I know I'm not the only one who has felt this way.

Megan Rapinoe, a famous soccer player, made a statement after suffering an injury during a game: "*If there was a God, this is proof there isn't.*" My heart breaks for her, and for others who feel this way. When we face hardship, it's easy to doubt God's goodness. But the truth is, God doesn't abandon us in our pain.

Psalm 34:19 reminds us, "*The righteous person may have many troubles, but the Lord delivers him from them all.*" Even when we face difficulties, God is still working to rescue us and bring us into a place of peace and healing. We may not always see it right away, but His timing is perfect.

If you find yourself doubting God's presence because of the suffering you see or experience, remember this: the very fact that you're questioning means you're wrestling with the idea of God. And God can handle your questions, your anger, and your pain. He invites you to bring it all to Him, to be honest about what you feel, and to trust that He is working even when you can't see it.

Challenge: Pray for those who are hurting today and those who doubt God's goodness because of the pain they're facing. And take a moment to reflect: *Where in your life can you praise God, not just for the good, but for being with you in the hard times, too?*

Today's Verse:
"*Cast all your anxiety on Him because He cares for you.*"
—1 Peter 5:7

IT'S TIME TO GET UP

"Then Jesus said to him, 'Get up! Pick up your mat and walk.' At once the man was cured; he picked up his mat and walked."

John 5:8-9

Have you ever found yourself feeling hopeless or stuck in self-pity? Maybe you've thought, *I'm never going to get out of this mess* or *Nothing is ever going to change, so why bother?* I know I've been there. If you have too, John 5:1-15 is a powerful reminder that Jesus wants to help us in our time of need.

But here's the thing: Jesus needs us to acknowledge that self-pity is not the way forward. When we give in to hopelessness, we're telling God that we don't fully believe in His ability to make us well.

Take a moment and ask yourself: **Do I want to get well?** Do you want to get out of that toxic relationship or workplace? Do you want to get out of debt? Do you want to stop making the same mistakes? Do you want to break free from anger, unhealthy choices, or overwhelming stress?

If your answer is an unequivocal **YES**, then the time to change and ask for help is **NOW**!

I recently faced this exact struggle. Just a few days ago, I found myself angry and frustrated. One of my employees submitted her resignation, leaving me with the burden of finding a replacement, retraining someone new, and managing all the clients in the meantime. I felt overwhelmed, exhausted, and, honestly, I had a bit of a pity party. I thought, *How will I ever find balance in my life? Maybe I'm not meant to grow this business I started four years ago.*

In that moment, hopelessness tried to take over. But here's what I had to remember: God loves me, and I can surrender that hopelessness to Him. For years, working 6 a.m. to 8 p.m. every day wasn't an issue. But now, as I've entered my mid-thirties, I've begun to ask, *Is there more? What needs to change?*

Burnout is not the life God wants for us. He calls us to come to Him for help—to be ready to change, to sacrifice, to endure, and to take action when needed. When Jesus healed the man by the pool of Bethesda, He didn't just offer pity. He gave a command:"*Get up! Pick up your mat and walk.*" And the man did—**immediately**. He was cured, not because he felt sorry for himself, but because he responded to Jesus' call with obedience and faith.

So, what about you? **Are you ready to get well?**

If so, it's time to pick up your mat and walk. Trust that God has something better for you—but you have to be willing to leave behind what's holding you back.

Today's Verse:
*"Immediately the man was made well,
took up his bed, and walked."*
—John 5:9

SCRIPTURE BEFORE SCREENS

Jesus answered, 'It is written: Man shall not live on bread alone, but on every word that comes from the mouth of God.'

Matthew 4:4

When Jesus said these words, He wasn't just responding to satan's temptation in the wilderness—He was declaring a truth for all of us. Just as our physical bodies need food to survive, our souls need the nourishment of God's Word to truly thrive. Without it, we're spiritually malnourished, vulnerable to the lies of the enemy and the stress of the world. But when we make God's Word our daily bread, it becomes the strength, wisdom, and peace that sustain us through every circumstance.

In a world full of distractions, it's easy to let God's Word take a back seat to everything else on our to-do list. But imagine if we approached the Bible the way we approach meals—with intention, desire, and consistency. As I often share on social media, *"scripture before screens"* is a key part of my daily discipline. I don't check my email, phone, or computer until I've opened my Bible. I share this today because it can be truly transformative for those who want to walk deeper in faith.

Here are some practical steps to get spiritual nourishment:

1. **Start Your Day with the Word:** Begin each morning with prayer and worship, then read your Bible before turning on any electronic devices. Just 10-15 minutes of focused reading can set the tone for your day. Prioritizing Scripture over screens helps transform your mind and spirit.

2. **Write Key Verses Down:** Writing verses by hand helps you retain them and trains you to listen for the Holy Spirit's guidance. Keep a verse in your heart and mind throughout the day to remind you of God's presence and peace.

3. **Apply the Verse to Your Life:** Don't just read the Bible—*live* it. Ask God how to apply the Scripture to your circumstances, and share it with others to strengthen your faith and theirs.

Today's Verse:
"Your word is a lamp for my feet, a light on my path."
—Psalm 119:105

INTEGRITY OVER INCOME

"A sterling reputation is better than striking it rich;
a gracious spirit is better than money in the bank."
Proverbs 22:1 (MSG)

Sometimes, I'll take on a project for a significant pay cut, **not because it makes financial sense, but because the Holy Spirit nudges me to.** In moments like those, I have to trust that God has a bigger plan—one that isn't about my bottom line but about His Kingdom. Whether it's helping someone who's struggling or making a decision that prioritizes people over profit, I've learned that when I follow His lead, He always provides.

Maybe you're a student right now, trying to balance school and work, or you're in a job where cutting corners might seem like the easiest way forward. Let me encourage you—choosing to honor God, even when it costs you, is always worth it. Integrity isn't just about big, public decisions; it's about the quiet, unseen moments where you choose what's right over what's easy.

The world often tells us that success is measured by how much we have or how far we get, but God's definition of success is very different. It's about living with character, reflecting His heart, and trusting Him to take care of the rest. When we lead with integrity, we're not just honoring God—we're inspiring others to do the same.

There have been times in my business when doing what was right felt harder and slower, but looking back, I see how God's faithfulness always came through. He blesses the steps we take in obedience, even when we can't see the full picture yet. Whether you're working on a group project, clocking in at your job, or running your own business, know that every time you act with integrity, you're making an eternal impact.

So, to the student, the employee, or the entrepreneur: keep putting integrity first. When you let the Holy Spirit guide your decisions, you're not just building a reputation—you're building a life that honors God and reflects His love to the world.

Today's Verse:
"Better a little with righteousness than much gain with injustice."
—Proverbs 16:8

THE YOU THAT YOU'RE BECOMING

"Being confident of this, that He who began a good work in you will carry it on to completion until the day of Christ Jesus."

Philippians 1:6

"If you could only meet the person you are becoming!"** Those words stopped me in my tracks. A client, Arthur, spoke them to me during a routine check-in call, but they landed like a direct message from God Himself. I wrote them down immediately, letting them sink deep into my heart.

Later that evening, I flipped through an old journal and found an entry from March 18, 2021. As I read my own words from years ago, I realized just how much had changed—how much I had changed. I had been in Michigan, on the cusp of a major transition that would lead me to Nashville. I was also still nursing the emotional wounds of an abusive relationship. I had felt lost, uncertain, and honestly, a little broken.

Arthur had walked with me through that season. He knew my struggles and had always encouraged me to keep praying—for healing, for growth, and even for the person who had hurt me. At the time, those prayers felt impossible. But looking back now, I see how God was working in ways I couldn't yet perceive.

Think about your own life. Where were you a year ago? Six months ago? Even a few weeks ago? Maybe you were wrestling with heartbreak, navigating uncertainty, or stepping into something completely new. Maybe you're still in the thick of it, wondering if you're really growing or if God is even moving at all.

I get it. But let me remind you of something powerful: **God is always at work, even when you can't see it.**

Ephesians 2:10 tells us, *"For we are God's handiwork, created in Christ Jesus to do good works, which God prepared in advance for us to do."* You are not an accident. Your life is not random. Every trial, every victory, every moment in between—it's all shaping you for something greater than you can imagine.

The hardest part? Trusting Him in the process. When growth feels slow, when prayers seem unanswered, when nothing makes sense—that's where faith comes in. Because even when we don't see the transformation, *God does.* He knows exactly who you are becoming, and He's not finished with you yet.

So take a deep breath. Reflect on how far you've come. And if today still feels heavy, hold on—because the person you're becoming is someone extraordinary. Not because of your own strength, but because of the One who is shaping you.

You're in His hands. And that's the safest place to be.□

Today's Verse:
"For we live by faith, not by sight."
—2 Corinthians 5:7

WHERE IS YOUR TREASURE?

*"For where your treasure is,
there your heart will be also."*

Luke 12:34

A **few days ago, I had an unexpected moment in downtown Nashville that gave me a fresh perspective.** While at my nail salon, I ran into a celebrity author whose book I read four years ago when I was just starting my business in Michigan. Talking with her about life, business, and God's timing felt surreal. It was inspiring—but even more so because I remembered how much I used to idolize her when I first read her book.

Back then, I put her on a pedestal. I studied her journey, measured my own progress against hers, and admired her success as if it held the blueprint for my own. But in that moment, I realized how much I had grown—both personally and spiritually. I no longer idolized her. I respected her as another person on a journey, just like me. And more importantly, I recognized something God had been teaching me all along: when we elevate people, careers, or achievements above Him, we create idols. And idols distract us from fully glorifying God.

Today, idolatry looks different than it did in biblical times. We may not be bowing to golden statues, but how often do we bow to the influence of others? Social media has created a culture where influencers, content creators, and public figures shape our views on success, beauty, relationships—even faith. We compare our lives to curated highlight reels, longing for what we think we're missing. It happens so subtly—watching influencers promote a lifestyle we think we need, following their advice more than we follow God's wisdom, and craving their approval without realizing it.

But Jesus gives us a different call: **Seek first His kingdom** (Matthew 6:33). It's easy to spend hours scrolling, taking in opinions and trends, but how often do we truly meditate on Scripture? Many of us can name five social media influencers or athletes and recall their stats, yet struggle to remember five of Jesus' parables. That's not a condemnation—it's a reminder that the enemy loves to distract God's people. If we're not careful, we'll fill our minds with voices that pull us away from the one voice that truly matters.

This is a pivotal moment in your life, and Jesus has sent me with a word to gently bring you back into His loving arms. He's inviting you to refocus. Here's how to start: "*Set your minds on things above, not on earthly things*" (Colossians 3:2).

Challenge:

This week, the Lord is calling us to reignite our passion for Him. We are invited to silence the distractions around us and refocus our hearts. If possible, take a day or two this week to fast from social media and set time limits on your apps. Rather than scrolling first thing in the morning, open your Bible and start with God's Word. Let go of anything or anyone you've been elevating above Him, and place Jesus back at the center of your life.

THE HOLY SPIRIT WILL GUIDE YOU

"They obeyed the Lord's order...."

Numbers 9:23

Have you ever felt out of place in the very location where you believe God has called you to be? Or perhaps you sense that your time in a particular place is nearing its end, but you feel uncertain about what lies ahead. You pray earnestly, seek God's guidance, and strive to hear His voice, yet the silence feels overwhelming. You may feel stuck, lost, or even frustrated, wondering if you are truly where God wants you to be.

Over the past few months in Nashville, I have found myself in this same space—wrestling with these questions, seeking answers, and feeling unsure of my purpose, even while holding onto the belief that God brought me here for this season.

One morning, I went for a walk between client sessions, hoping to clear my mind. I wandered down a new road, praying as I went, and passed by Lipscomb Academy. With tears in my eyes, I walked onto the track and field. That's when I saw a sign that said, **"You belong here."** If that wasn't a message from God, I don't know what is! At that moment, I was reminded that God has me in Nashville for a reason. Now, He is moving me to a new territory in Dallas, Texas. This is a powerful reminder that God's timing is always perfect—He's never early and never late. If you leave a place too soon or stay beyond His will, God can and will redirect your steps. His timing is PERFECT.

Oftentimes, when making bold moves for the Kingdom of God, the Lord will absolutely confirm His directions in very unique ways. He wants to remind you that you're on the right path. I have seen this countless times in my own life. A friend I met in Franklin, Tennessee, a former NFL coach named Lee Stuckel, once told me, *"God brought you to Tennessee for a reason. Keep trusting."* Those words stuck with me during my years there, but even with that encouragement, I still struggled at times. Serving God can be hard, and trusting Him when you don't see the results right away can feel like walking a tightrope.

Knowing when to go or stay is one of the most challenging aspects of following God's will. It requires discernment, prayer, fasting, and a deep trust in His timing. Sometimes, God may ask you to stay in a place longer than you expect, stretching your faith and growing your patience. Other times, He may lead you to move on, even when it's uncomfortable or unexpected. The key is to stay sensitive to His leading and open to the Holy Spirit's guidance, even when it doesn't make sense in the moment. When you feel uncertain, seek confirmation through prayer, scripture, and the peace that only God can provide. Trust that the Father's timing is always perfect, and when it's time to go or stay, He will make it clear. He is a God of order, and He will always direct your path when you seek Him wholeheartedly.

Today's Verse:
"At the Lord's command the Israelites set out, and at His command they encamped."
—Numbers 9:18

DAY 39

PEOPLE OVER POSSESSIONS

"The earth is the Lord's, and everything in it, the world, and all who live in it."

Psalm 24:1

God is in control. He spoke the heavens and earth into existence, carefully designed every living thing, and entrusted us to be stewards of His creation. But in all of this, there's something we must never forget—people matter most to God. More than the earth, more than systems, more than efficiency, more than the pursuit of progress. His heart beats for people.

It's easy to get caught up in managing resources, making wise decisions about sustainability, or advancing technology. And while those things can be good, they should never take priority over the well-being of souls. Jesus didn't lay down His life for nature—He laid it down for you and me. The most precious thing to God isn't the beauty of the mountains or the vastness of the ocean; it's the heart of His children. And if that's where His heart is, then ours should be too.

In today's world, there's a growing push toward artificial intelligence, efficiency, and perfect systems. But if we're not careful, we risk losing what makes us uniquely created in God's image—our ability to love deeply, to feel compassion, and to connect in ways no machine ever could. Technology can enhance life, but it cannot replace the Holy Spirit. It cannot replicate the kindness of a friend, the warmth of an embrace, or the life-changing power of a heartfelt prayer.

So, where do we go from here?

Yes, be a good steward of what God has entrusted to you. Reduce waste, care for the earth, be responsible with your resources. But even more than that, be a steward of people. Prioritize relationships. Show up. Love well. Forgive freely. Let your words bring life and your actions reflect the heart of Christ. Because in the end, what will truly matter is not what we built, but who we loved.

Jesus Himself said in John 13:34-35, "*A new command I give you: Love one another. As I have loved you, so you must love one another. By this, everyone will know that you are my disciples, if you love one another.*"

This is how the world will recognize Jesus in us—not through our accomplishments, not through our efficiency, but through the way we love. So today, ask yourself: Where can I love better? Who needs my compassion? How can I reflect the heart of Christ in my everyday life?

Let's not miss the greatest calling of all—to love people the way Jesus first loved us.

Today's Verse:
"*Do not store up for yourselves treasures on earth, where moths and vermin destroy, and where thieves break in and steal. But store up for yourselves treasures in heaven, where moths and vermin do not destroy, and where thieves do not break in and steal.*" —Matthew 6:19-20

ARISE AND SHINE—YOUR LIGHT CANNOT BE DIMMED!

"I know what it is to be in need, and I know what it is to have plenty. I have learned the secret of being content in any and every situation."

Philippians 4:12

Comparison is the thief of joy. We've all heard it before, but it's a truth we need to remind ourselves of constantly. The Apostle Paul teaches us that true joy comes from contentment—not from looking at what others have or what they're doing, but from being at peace with what God has given us and where He has placed us.

Think about it: stars don't compare themselves to other stars. They don't look around the sky and sigh because one star shines a little brighter than the next. No, they simply shine. They shine because that's what God created them to do. It's in their nature to shine, and they don't waste time worrying about how bright another star might be. Stars shine where they are placed, and they fulfill their purpose just by being what they were made to be.

We, too, are created to shine, but the moment we start comparing our light to someone else's, we lose sight of our own calling. Comparison leads to distraction, discontentment, and discouragement. God never asked us to compare—He called each of us to reflect His light in our own unique way. If we can't be content with what we have now, more will never satisfy us. After all, having more doesn't translate to true joy.

Jesus said in Matthew 5:14-16, *"You are the light of the world. A town built on a hill cannot be hidden. Neither do people light a lamp and put it under a bowl. Instead they put it on its stand, and it gives light to everyone in the house. In the same way, let your light shine before others, so that they may see your good deeds and glorify your Father in heaven."*

So, ask yourself today: *Where in my life am I comparing myself to others?* Is it in my career, my relationships, my ministry, or my personal life? Wherever it is, release it to God. He didn't create you to be like anyone else. He created you to reflect His light in your unique way. Contentment is not about settling for less. It's about recognizing that God has given you everything you need to fulfill the purpose He has for you. You are enough because *Jesus* is enough. And as you walk in that truth, His light will shine through you in ways that bring glory to His name. THIS IS YOUR GOLDEN HOUR!

Today's Verse:
"When Moses came down from Mount Sinai....he was not aware that his face was radiant because he had spoken with the Lord. When Aaron and all the Israelites saw Moses, his face was radiant, and they were afraid to come near him."
—Exodus 34:29-30

YOU RADIATE THE HEART OF JESUS!

"Those who look to him are radiant; their faces are never covered with shame."

Psalm 34:5

Have you ever noticed that after spending time in prayer or reading your Bible, your spirit feels lighter, your heart calmer, and even in the midst of chaos, you can sense God's peace?** That's because time in God's presence changes us. Just as Moses' face radiated with God's glory after meeting with Him on Mount Sinai, spending time with Jesus has a transformative effect. Moses didn't even realize his face was shining, but everyone around him did!

In the same way, when you spend time with God—whether in prayer, worship, or reading the Bible—His light begins to shine through you. While it may not be as visibly obvious as it was with Moses, people around you can still notice the difference. They sense the peace, love, and patience you carry with you. That inner transformation equips you to respond with grace and wisdom, no matter the challenges you face.

Today, the Lord is emphasizing the importance of immersing ourselves in His Word. In a world full of "fast food faith," where quick fixes are often sought, we need the depth that comes from digging into Scripture. As Charles Spurgeon once said, "A *Bible that's falling apart usually belongs to someone who isn't.*" The more time you spend in God's Word, the more deeply rooted and grounded you become in His truth. It's through these moments of study and reflection that God reveals His wisdom and fortifies your faith, preparing you for the trials ahead.

I also want to remind you that God meets you where you are, even in your hardest moments. Sometimes, when life feels overwhelming, it can be difficult to open your Bible or focus on prayer. *And that's okay.* Simply sitting still before the Lord and resting in His presence is enough. **Sometimes, the only worship we can offer is through our tears, and God honors that.** He sees your heart and is with you in the silence, the tears, and each step of your journey. He is not distant—He is close, offering comfort and peace. He is shaping you to better reflect His light, even when you can't yet see it. As you move forward today, remember this promise from the Lord: "*The Lord is close to the brokenhearted and saves those who are crushed in spirit*" (Psalm 34:18). In every moment, especially in the tough ones, He is right there with you.

Today's Verse:
"*You keep track of all my sorrows. You have collected all my tears in your bottle. You have recorded each one in your book.*"
—Psalm 56:8

ANSWER THE CALL—GOD GOES BEFORE YOU!

"The LORD himself goes before you and will be with you; He will never leave you nor forsake you. Do not be afraid; do not be discouraged."

Deuteronomy 31:8

God often calls us to places we never expected, to roles we may feel unqualified for, and on journeys that stretch our faith in ways we couldn't have imagined. He does this not because He wants to see us struggle, but because Jesus has already equipped us for the very things He is asking us to step into. The challenge isn't whether we're *ready*—it's whether we're *willing* to trust Jesus fully.

I have a dear friend who is stepping into one of these God-sized journeys. She is leaving everything familiar to take on a new opportunity in another state. As much as I'll miss her, I am in awe of her faith. Her obedience in walking with the Lord, despite the uncertainties, is a beautiful reminder of how we are all called to follow our Lord boldly, wherever He leads.

The truth is, God often asks us to step out in faith before we feel fully prepared. Maybe it's taking on a new job, leading a group, or even leaving behind what's comfortable for something unknown. It's easy to feel inadequate, but what matters is that

God doesn't send us alone. His presence is our assurance. He goes before us, makes the path straight, and equips us for the journey.

Where in your own life today can you surrender your fears and worries? Where is God asking you to trust Him more deeply? It could be in your work, relationships, or a personal dream that seems too big to achieve. Whatever it is, know that God is faithful. He will provide exactly what you need to fulfill the calling He has placed on your life.

Like my friend, you too are called to take those steps, trusting that God's plans are greater than your fears. His grace is sufficient for every new challenge, and His presence is constant, even when the road is unfamiliar. The Lord Jesus says today, *"Answer the call to move forward when afraid. Be brave, for the Lord your God shall be with you wherever you go."*

Today's Verse:
"And my God will meet all your needs according to the riches of His glory in Christ Jesus."
—Philippians 4:19

STAND FIRM—THE KING IS COMING!

"Look, I am coming soon! Blessed is the one who keeps the words of the prophecy written in this scroll."

Revelation 22:7

Dear brothers and sisters in Christ: I know there are moments when the weight of this world feels like too much to bear. When you look around and see injustice, suffering, and evil seemingly gaining ground, it's easy to wonder if things will ever get better. It's easy to lose hope when the battle feels relentless. But hear this—*don't lose hope*. Jesus has not forgotten us. He will return, and when He does, He will bring perfect justice, end all suffering, and take us home to be with Him forever.

The enemy wants nothing more than to deceive you into thinking that evil is winning, that God has abandoned His people, and that there's no hope for the future. But the truth is, satan is a defeated foe. **The victory was won long ago on the cross.** Jesus has already conquered death, sin, and all the powers of darkness. The devil may roar like a lion, but he is a lion with no teeth—he cannot devour those who belong to Christ.

So, don't be deceived by what you see in the world today. Don't let the chaos and the noise drown out the truth of God's Word. God's promises are still true. He has not abandoned His throne, and He is not blind to the suffering you endure. Hang on tightly to the promises He has given us in scripture. His Word is your weapon in this spiritual warfare, and now more than ever, it's time to stand firm in faith.

The Bible reminds us that Jesus will come again, and He will make all things right. In Revelation, we're told of a day when there will be no more death, sorrow, crying, or pain (Rev. 21:4). That day is coming. But until then, we are called to fight—not with fists or anger, but on our knees in prayer. If you've been brought low, if life has beaten you down, get on your knees and pray until you find the strength to rise again.

God says in Isaiah 46:4, "*I have made you; and I will carry you. I will sustain you and I will rescue you.*" Let this be the truth that anchors your soul in these turbulent times. No matter what happens, God *will* sustain you. He *will* carry you. And He *will* rescue you in His perfect timing.

So, pray for your fellow brothers and sisters. Encourage one another to keep the faith. We are all in this together, and we will not be overcome. Hold on to hope, because our Savior is coming soon.

Today's Verse:
"*Let us hold unswervingly to the hope we profess, for He who promised is faithful.*"
—Hebrews 10:23

RUN WITH ENDURANCE—THE VICTORY IS ALREADY WON!

*"I can do all things through Christ
who strengthens me."*

Philippians 4:13

Have you ever seen an athlete accomplish something incredible? Maybe a runner pushes through exhaustion to finish a tough race, a basketball player makes the winning shot just in time, or a team fights back to win against all odds. Moments like these inspire us, but what we don't always see is the hard work, discipline, and mindset that got them there.

As believers, we're called to face our own trials and obstacles with the same determination. Whether it's navigating a difficult season, overcoming fear, or stepping into a calling that feels beyond our ability, we're not meant to rely on our strength alone. **Philippians 4:13 reminds us that we can do all things—not through sheer willpower,** *but through Christ,* **who infuses us with His strength.**

Think of it like training for a race. An athlete builds endurance through repetition, discipline, and trust in their coach's plan. In the same way, we build spiritual endurance by staying connected to Christ through prayer, immersing ourselves in His Word, and trusting His guidance. Studies have shown that people who read the Bible at least three or four times a week experience significant improvements in overcoming struggles! They report feeling less stressed, making better decisions, experiencing greater peace, and even feeling less lonely. His Word becomes the fuel that powers us through life's challenges, giving us clarity, strength, and the deep assurance that we are held in His hands.

When trials come, picture yourself as part of God's team. Just as a coach sees the potential in their players and calls out their best, God sees your strength even when you don't. And just as an athlete studies their playbook, we must be equipped with God's Word, standing firm against the enemy's schemes. The battle is real, but we are called to stand in victory, firmly planted in Christ. The Word of God is our greatest weapon!

And remember—the Holy Spirit is your Head Coach. He is right there beside you, equipping you, encouraging you, and reminding you that the victory is already won. So keep training. Keep pressing forward. Keep your eyes on Jesus, and trust that He has already secured the victory.

Challenge:
This week, commit to studying your Bible at least four times. As you read, look for a verse that resonates deeply with you—one that speaks to your heart or addresses a challenge you're facing. Write it down and declare it over your circumstances, remembering that there is power and life in the words we speak. Then, place the verse where you'll see it often: in your car, on your work desk, in your locker room, or on your bathroom mirror. Watch how God's Word renews your strength, encourages your spirit, and equips you to persevere.

THE WAITING IS NOT A DELAY—IT'S A DIVINE PREPARATION

"For I know the plans I have for you, declares the Lord, plans to prosper you and not to harm you, plans to give you hope and a future."
Jeremiah 29:11

Have you ever felt caught in the tension of waiting on God, wondering when His promises will unfold? You've prayed, poured out your heart, and sought His direction, yet the answers seem out of reach. The waiting feels heavy, and doubt starts to creep in. But what if this season isn't a pause in your story, but part of God's greater plan? A "not yet" from Him isn't a "no." It's a deliberate moment of preparation, where He's crafting something far beyond what you can see right now.

Waiting can feel like circling an airport, so close to landing yet held in the air for reasons you don't understand. Frustration sets in because you're ready for the next step, the breakthrough, the blessing. But the pilot—God—knows when it's safe to land. He sees the full picture and knows what's waiting on the ground. His timing protects you and prepares the way for the promise.

Trusting Him in the waiting isn't easy, but it's the key to experiencing His best.

Think of Moses.

His time of waiting in Midian wasn't a detour; *it was a season of preparation.* For 40 years, God trained him to eventually lead the Israelites out of Egypt (Exodus 3:1-10). Those years were essential for the leadership and wisdom he would need. In the same way, your waiting isn't wasted. God uses seasons of waiting to shape your character, prepare your heart, and align circumstances to fulfill His promises in ways you may not yet understand (Isaiah 55:8-9). His timing is always intentional and never random (Ecclesiastes 3:11).

So, what do we do while we wait? We let go of control and take daily steps of faith. Trust isn't passive—it's active. It looks like choosing to believe that God is good, even when life feels uncertain. It looks like leaning into His Word, listening for His voice, and letting go of fear. The waiting may feel long, but it's a sign that something beautiful is on the horizon. Stay faithful, stay grounded, and remember that the One who holds the stars also holds your story.

Today's Verse:
"But those who hope in the Lord will renew their strength. They will soar on wings like eagles; they will run and not grow weary, they will walk and not be faint."
—Isaiah 40:31

REMOVE THE CLUTTER

"Above all else, guard your heart, for everything you do flows from it."

Proverbs 4:23

It's time to clean house. No, not just your physical space, but your mental, emotional, and spiritual spaces too. We often let clutter build up in our lives—old habits, toxic relationships, unnecessary distractions—things that don't serve the life God wants for us. Today, God may be asking you to take inventory of what's in your life and to make room for what He's calling you to.

Start with a question: *What do you need to clean out?* Maybe it's your closet, your pantry, or your desk. But what about your contact list, your inbox, or the people you spend the most time with? Are they helping you move forward into the purpose God has for you, or are they pulling you back? Sometimes, the biggest changes we need to make aren't physical, but relational and spiritual.

The Bible is clear: "*Do not be deceived: 'Bad company ruins good morals.*" (1 Cor. 15:33). The people we surround ourselves with and the things we let influence our hearts and minds have a direct impact on the direction of our lives. You may have dreams, goals, and a deep desire to follow God's will for your life, but if you're still holding on to distractions and relationships that don't align with that vision, you'll struggle to move forward.

<u>This is a call to action.</u> Today, make the decision to remove what's weighing you down and pulling you away from God's purpose. Cleaning out your closet is a start, but what about the deeper areas? Who or what do you need to let go of to make space for growth, peace, and alignment with God's will?

God is calling you to show up as the person He's called you to be—right now. Don't wait until everything is perfectly in place or until you feel ready. You will never be ready and the perfect conditions do not exist. God's transformation begins when you take that first step. When you remove the clutter—both physically and spiritually—you make room for Him to move in powerful ways.

Take ownership of your life today. Remove distractions. *What can you clear out to get closer to the life God has designed for you?* It might mean making hard decisions about relationships or letting go of habits that aren't serving you. But trust that God's plans are for your good. He's calling you to walk in freedom and purpose, but first, you need to clear the path.

Today's Verse:
"Let us throw off everything that hinders and the sin that so easily entangles. And let us run with perseverance the race marked out for us."
—Hebrews 12:1

STAY LOW, WALK BOLDLY—GOD WILL LIFT YOU UP!

"Now Moses was a very humble man, more humble than anyone else on the face of the earth."

Numbers 12:3

Humility is rarely celebrated in today's culture. We live in a time when self-promotion is normalized, and success is often measured by influence, status, and applause. The world teaches us that the loudest voices get heard, the most confident people get ahead, and the ones who fight for their recognition receive the greatest rewards. But God's ways are different. He raises up those who bow low, and He exalts those who surrender completely to Him.

Moses was a man who had every reason to walk in pride. God chose him to perform miracles, to stand before Pharaoh, and to lead an entire nation out of captivity. Yet, Scripture tells us that Moses was the most humble man on earth. His strength was not in his ability but in his dependence on God. He didn't seek recognition—he sought God's presence. He knew that without the Lord, he was nothing, and that posture of humility positioned him to walk in divine authority.

But in this age, humility is hard. It's tempting to want credit for what we've done, to be seen, acknowledged, and validated. Maybe you've been overlooked, feeling like the work you do goes unnoticed. Maybe you've obeyed God in secret, yet it seems others are receiving the rewards. Let me remind you—**Jesus sees what man overlooks.** God honors the heart that serves without seeking a stage, the hands that work without expecting applause, and the spirit that bows low so that He alone is glorified.

Jesus Himself demonstrated this kind of humility. He left Heaven's throne to walk among us, taking the form of a servant. And in the moment when He could have defended Himself before Pilate, He remained silent. He didn't need to prove His identity—He knew who He was in the Father's eyes. The Lord is calling you to that same humility, the kind that doesn't fight to be seen but trusts that *God* sees.

This is your moment to walk in a humility that unlocks Heaven's favor. If you will humble yourself, surrender your need for validation, and trust that God exalts people in His perfect timing, you will see His hand move in your life in ways you never expected.

Moses didn't chase greatness—God placed it upon him. He didn't seek his own name to be lifted high—God made his name known. What God is calling you to do is not about your recognition, but *His*. Stay low, stay obedient, and watch how He moves.

Today's Verse:
"Humble yourselves, therefore, under God's mighty hand, that He may lift you up in due time."
—1 Peter 5:6

LIVING IN THE POWER OF ZOE: THE ABUNDANT LIFE JESUS PROMISED

"Your beginnings will seem humble, so prosperous will your future be."

Job 8:16

Have you ever felt like you're just getting by—waking up, going through the motions, and wondering, Is this really all there is? Maybe you've been stuck in a cycle of struggle, waiting for something to shift, longing for a breakthrough that feels just out of reach. If that's you, hear this: **You were not created just to survive.**

Jesus didn't come so you could simply exist. He came so you could thrive. In John 10:10, He makes an extraordinary promise: "*I have come that they may have life, and have it to the full.*" But this "life" isn't just about getting through the day. The Greek word zoe used here means a divine, extraordinary, abundant life—one that flows directly from God Himself. And the best part? It's not just for eternity. It's for you, right here and now.

But let's be honest. Sometimes, life doesn't feel abundant. Maybe you're facing loss, uncertainty, or disappointment. Maybe you're asking, *God, where are You? Do You see me? Do You hear me?* If that's where you are today, let this truth settle in: Yes, He sees you. Yes, He hears you. And yes, He is working on your behalf.

Even in the silence, even in the struggle, He is moving.

You may feel like you're barely holding on, but God is holding onto you. He's not asking for perfect faith—just a mustard seed. That's all it takes for Him to move mountains. He specializes in turning tests into testimonies and messes into miracles.

So how do you step into this abundant life? You trust Him. You surrender your idea of what abundance *should* look like and embrace what God is doing—even if you can't see it yet. Because true abundance isn't about material things. It's peace in the storm. It's joy that defies circumstances. It's faith that anchors you when everything around you is shaking.

The waiting, the struggles, the unknowns—they are not wasted. God is using them to shape you, strengthen you, and prepare you for what's next. His promise of an abundant life isn't for *someday*—it's for today.

So right now, wherever you are, take a deep breath. Lean into His presence. Your story isn't over. Bring Him your mustard seed of faith, and watch as He breathes His *zoe* life into every dry and weary place.

You were not meant to simply exist. You were made for spiritual abundance. After all, your Heavenly Father is a King.

Today's Verse:
"Now to Him who is able to do immeasurably more than all we ask or imagine, according to His power that is at work within us."
—Ephesians 3:20

DAY 49

EMBRACE THE PROCESS

"Not one of all the Lord's good promises to Israel failed; every one was fulfilled."

Joshua 21:45

My organic chemistry professor used to say, *"The process in how you arrive at the answer is more important than the answer."* In my undergraduate studies, I didn't get it. I thought to myself, *Who cares how you arrive at the answer as long as it's correct?* But now, years later, and as a follower of Christ, I understand the profound truth behind that statement. The journey, the process, and the growth that happens during our faith walk is where the real gold is found.

Think about Joshua. Before leading the Israelites into the Promised Land, Joshua spent years serving as Moses' assistant, faithfully waiting in the background. His time in the wilderness wasn't wasted—it was a season of preparation. God used those years to build Joshua's courage, refine his leadership, and teach him to depend on the Lord for every victory. Even Jesus, the Son of God, spent years in silence before His public ministry. From His childhood to His baptism, much of His life remains unseen by us, but we know those "silent years" were essential for preparing Him to fulfill His mission. God was working in the hidden places, just as He does in our lives.

As believers, we must embrace the process, even when it's uncomfortable or confusing. God is not just interested in giving us the answers to our prayers—**He's interested in growing us into the likeness of Christ.** The trials, the waiting, the steps of obedience along the way—they're all part of His plan to bring out the "gold" in us. When we focus solely on the outcome, we miss the treasures He's placing along the path.

So, if you find yourself in a season of uncertainty or struggle, take heart. God is at work in the process, refining you and drawing you closer to Him. Trust that every step, every lesson, every moment of waiting is part of His good and perfect plan for your life. The journey may not always make sense, but in God's hands, it will always have purpose.

Today's Verse:
"Being confident of this, that he who began a good work in you will carry it on to completion until the day of Christ Jesus."
—Philippians 1:6

RELEASE THE NEED FOR PERFECTION

"My grace is sufficient for you, for my power is made perfect in weakness."

2 Corinthians 12:9

For years, I lived under the constant pressure of perfectionism. The world may have called it being "Type A," but in reality, it was exhausting—an endless cycle of chasing flawless performance and seeking approval at every turn. I took pride in being dependable, detail-oriented, and driven, yet beneath the surface, fear dictated my every move. Fear of failure. Fear of not being enough. Fear of disappointing others.

Then Jesus stepped in and showed me a better way. With His gentle, patient love, He revealed that He never asked me to strive for perfection. He wasn't measuring my worth by my accomplishments—He had already declared me worthy. I didn't have to earn His love; I simply had to receive it.

Perfectionism is often rooted in fear—fear of rejection, fear of falling short, fear of losing control. But the more I trusted Jesus, the more I saw the truth: my identity wasn't found in what I could achieve, but in what He had already accomplished on the cross. Long before I ever tried to prove myself, He had already called me loved, chosen, and enough.

Letting go of perfectionism hasn't been an instant transformation. It's a daily choice. If you've been carrying the burden of perfectionism, I encourage you to bring it to Jesus. He's not asking for flawless performance—He's inviting you into His rest.

Steps to Overcome Perfectionism

- **Recognize Your Triggers** – Pay attention to when and where you feel the pressure to be perfect. Is it in your work, relationships, or social media presence? Awareness is the first step toward breaking free.

- **Exchange Perfection for Grace** – When you catch yourself striving for perfection, pause and pray. Ask God to help you rest in His grace rather than your own effort. *"My grace is sufficient for you, for my power is made perfect in weakness"* (2 Corinthians 12:9).

- **Embrace 'Good Enough'** – Challenge yourself to finish something without over-editing, overthinking, or seeking constant approval. Whether it's a project, conversation, or decision, remember this: **obedience in faith is far greater than perfection in fear.**

Today's Verse:
"Fear of man will prove to be a snare, but whoever trusts in the Lord is kept safe."
—Proverbs 29:25

TRUST THE UNKNOWN, EMBRACE THE UNSEEN

"Now faith is confidence in what we hope for and assurance about what we do not see."

Hebrews 11:1

We often ask God to do something new in our lives—new opportunities, new blessings, new direction. Yet, how often do we hold onto the same old patterns, clinging to what's comfortable?

It's natural to want to stay in our comfort zones. They feel safe, predictable, and familiar. But the truth is, God doesn't work in stagnant places. He calls us to step out, to trust Him, and to move beyond the borders of what we know.

When God is ready to take you to a new level, it will often require you to leave behind what feels secure. The unknown can feel terrifying, but it's in that space where God does His greatest work. Think about it—every great moment in the Bible happened when someone stepped out in faith. Abraham left his homeland. Moses faced Pharaoh. Peter walked on water. Each of them had to step into the unknown, trusting that God's plan was better than their comfort zones.

Right now, God may be calling you to take a similar step of faith. It could be a career change, a move, a relationship shift, or a personal challenge. Whatever it is, He's asking you to trust Him—to rely on His strength instead of your own.

When you do, you open yourself up to a reality that's 100% reliant on Christ—a reality filled with joy, growth, and blessings far greater than what your comfort zone could ever provide.

Take a moment today to ask yourself: *How can I trust God in this very moment? Where is He calling me to step out in faith?*

Pray over Proverbs 3:5-6 this week, and let it guide your heart as you lean into His promises. Remember, it's in the unknown that God reveals His greatest plans. He is with you every step of the way.

Today's Verse:
"Trust in the Lord with all your heart, and do not lean on your own understanding. In all your ways acknowledge him, and he will make straight your paths."
—Proverbs 3:5-6

A FATHER'S LEGACY

"Start children off on the way they should go, and even when they are old they will not turn from it."
Proverbs 22:6

Growing up, my dad was my hero. As a single father raising my siblings and me, he stepped into a role that required incredible strength, sacrifice, and endurance. My mother was never present in our lives, but my dad filled that void as best as he could. My grandmother also stepped up and was like a mother to me.

I grew up fishing, hunting, and doing all the "boy things" that set me apart from other girls. I was bullied and teased for not fitting the mold, but looking back now, I see the blessings in those experiences. My dad taught me to embrace being different, reminding me that the challenges we faced—things other kids with two parents didn't experience—would ultimately make me stronger.

One memory that always stands out is when my dad ran his trucking business from our home. Later, he moved the company to an old, retired property, where the business still resides today. He had us kids working with him, using tools to pick rocks out of the semi tires. He'd say, *"If you don't get all those rocks from the tire tread, the semi won't go."*

At the time, I thought I was really helping him keep that truck running. In reality, it wasn't about the rocks—it was about teaching us responsibility, hard work, and the importance of doing our part, no matter how small.

Now, as an adult, I reflect on how hard it must have been for my dad—working constantly, struggling to get us to our sports and activities, all while trying to give us the best childhood possible. He sacrificed so much for us, and though we didn't understand it as children, I see it clearly now.

If you're a single parent reading this, know that your children may not fully grasp the battles you fight every day, but I promise you this: **God sees your effort, and He will use your pain for a greater purpose.** One day, your kids will look back and appreciate the sacrifices you made. They'll remember the lessons of grit, love, and perseverance you modeled for them.

What I once thought were hardships, I now see as treasures. My dad's wisdom, especially his saying, "*Always leave people and places better than when you found them,*" is now ingrained in me. It's more than advice—it's a calling.

So, if you're feeling weary, wondering if your sacrifices matter, hold onto this truth: God is with you. He sees you. And one day, you and your children will bond over the hardships that shaped you all.

Today's Verse:
"As a father has compassion on his children, so the Lord has compassion on those who fear him."
—Psalm 103:13

WHEN JUSTICE FEELS DELAYED, TRUST GOD'S TIMING

"For the Lord loves justice; He will not forsake His saints. They are preserved forever, but the offspring of the wicked shall be cut off."

Psalm 37:28

Persecution comes in many forms. Recently, I received hate messages and inappropriate texts on my work phone. It was painful, violating, and felt like an attack on my very being. Social media, a place where I often shared health, nutrition, and motivational posts, became a source of hurt. That experience made me realize how much stock I placed in my work and my online presence—more than I had been placing in Jesus.

In moments like these, when the battle between good and evil feels overwhelming, it's easy to question everything. I know God is real, but I also feel the struggle between faith and reality.

In 2020, I left an abusive relationship, praying fervently for justice. But justice didn't come right away. God's timing is different from ours, and sometimes it feels as though He's not responding when we need Him to. But God always moves. He may not serve justice immediately, but He will, in His perfect time.

David was a man after God's own heart, yet he wasn't immune to moments of intense anger and frustration. In Psalm 109,

David openly asked God to bring judgment upon those who had wronged him. His prayer was raw and honest:

"Appoint someone evil to oppose my enemy; let an accuser stand at his right hand. When he is tried, let him be found guilty, and may his prayers condemn him." —Psalm 109:6-7

David's emotions were real, but ultimately, he left justice in God's hands. This teaches us that while we can bring our frustrations to God, we must trust **His way of handling things, not our own.**

God reminds us that vengeance belongs to Him. We are called to resist the urge to repay evil with evil, even when our emotions scream otherwise.

If you've been wronged and you're waiting for justice, hold on. God sees it all, and He will handle it. Rest in His timing, not your own.

Today's Verse:
"Do not repay anyone evil for evil. Be careful to do what is right in the eyes of everyone."
—Romans 12:17

HELP IS ON THE WAY

"May the God of hope fill you with all joy and peace as you trust in Him, so that you may overflow with hope by the power of the Holy Spirit."

Romans 15:13

Dear Friend,

You are about to be blessed beyond measure in this season of your life. The Lord wants you to know that He sees you. Every tear you have shed, every prayer you have whispered, and every act of love and service you have poured out—none of it has gone unnoticed. Heaven has recorded every moment, and your faithfulness is about to yield a harvest greater than you can imagine.

Help is on the way. There are angels at your side, fighting on your behalf. Even though you may not see them, they are there—guiding your steps, opening doors, and moving mountains that seem impossible to overcome. You are not alone in this journey. God is with you, actively working all things together for your good.

I hear the Lord saying, **"I am proud of you."** Yes, *proud.* Your Heavenly Father has seen how you have persevered, even in moments of weakness. He has watched as you have chosen love when it would have been easier to walk away. He knows the weight you have carried, and yet, you have continued to trust in Him.

Jesus reminds us in John 16:33, "*In this world you will have trouble; but take heart! I have overcome the world.*" Troubles may come, but victory is already yours in Christ. You do not need to fear the chaos or uncertainties because God has already gone before you.

Here is what the Lord wants you to hold onto today:

- **Your prayers have power.** Even when it feels like nothing is changing, God is moving in ways you cannot yet see.

- **Your smile carries the light of Heaven.** Use it to transform the atmosphere around you.

- **God's promises are unshakable.** The world may change, but His love and faithfulness will never waver.

Beloved, take heart. Your breakthrough is closer than you think. Keep showing up. Keep trusting. Keep smiling. **God is with you, and your story is far from over.**

Today's Verse:
"*The Lord appeared to us in the past, saying:*
'*I have loved you with an everlasting love;*
I have drawn you with unfailing kindness.'"
—Jeremiah 31:3

DAY 55

MIRACLE ON THE HIGHWAY

"For He will command His angels concerning you to guard you in all your ways."

Psalm 91:11

A couple of years ago, I had the privilege of hearing an incredible testimony from a client named *Anna. Her story is one of God's miraculous intervention, and with her permission, I am sharing it with you today. During our coaching call, she recounted an event that reminded me just how present God is, even in life's most terrifying moments.

Anna and her children were driving in their suburban when the unthinkable happened. The vehicle flipped multiple times, rolling violently on a busy highway. Moments before the accident, her daughter, Charli, had unbuckled her seatbelt. When the vehicle rolled, she was ejected from the car and landed in the middle of the freeway. Anna, overwhelmed with fear, expected the worst.

But then, something incredible happened. The traffic on that busy highway came to a complete stop. Not a single car moved forward. Anna knew this was no coincidence—God's angels were watching over her daughter, protecting her from imminent danger. While some major injuries occurred, God's intervention was undeniable. Their specialist declared them "walking miracles."

Anna's two other children and their friends, who were in the car, walked away without a scratch. What should have been a day of devastation became a day of deliverance. Against all odds, every one of them survived.

As Anna shared her story, I had a profound realization. Though I was supposed to be the coach in that moment, I became the student. Her testimony breathed life into my spirit—exactly what I needed after enduring my own personal losses. It was a powerful reminder of the importance of sharing our stories. Testimonies of God's goodness fuel our faith and reassure us that we are never alone.

Perhaps you've been where I am—questioning God in the midst of pain, wondering why bad things happen to good people. I've wrestled with these thoughts, especially after hearing of tragedies involving children and innocent families. *Where is God in these moments? Why does He allow these things to happen?*

These are tough questions, and as humans, we may not have all the answers. But one thing is certain—satan thrives on doubt. He wants us to question God's presence and goodness in times of tragedy. However, as Christians, we must press in closer to God and lean on one another for support. The Bible reminds us: *"And we know that in all things God works for the good of those who love him, who have been called according to his purpose"* (Romans 8:28). Even when life feels overwhelming, we can trust that God is always working, even in ways we cannot see. Sometimes, all we have is faith the size of a mustard seed—but that's enough.

Today's Verse:
"The Lord is good, a refuge in times of trouble. He cares for those who trust in Him."
—Nahum 1:7

TRAINING FOR ETERNITY

"For physical training is of some value, but godliness has value for all things, holding promise for both the present life and the life to come."
1 Timothy 4:8

I magine an athlete preparing for a race. Every day, they commit to rigorous training, focusing on strengthening their body through proper nutrition, hydration, rest, and exercise. Their goal isn't just to start the race—it's to finish strong, with endurance and perseverance.

But physical strength alone isn't enough. Any seasoned athlete will tell you that the mind plays an equally important role. A well-trained body without a disciplined, focused mind is like a car with no steering—it may have power, but it lacks direction.

The Apostle Paul often compared the Christian life to a race. He wrote, "*Do you not know that in a race all the runners run, but only one gets the prize? Run in such a way as to get the prize*" (1 Corinthians 9:24). Paul understood that just as an athlete must discipline their body for competition, we must train our hearts and minds for our walk with Christ. The difference? While earthly athletes compete for a perishable crown, we are striving for an eternal one with Jesus (1 Corinthians 9:25).

To run this race well, we must develop spiritual discipline. Just as athletes train daily, our spiritual growth requires consistent practice. This includes spending time in God's Word, committing to prayer, and choosing faith over fear. Strength doesn't come overnight—it's built through perseverance, one step at a time.

However, discipline doesn't mean running ourselves into exhaustion. One of the most overlooked yet essential parts of training is **rest**. Athletes understand that without proper recovery, their muscles will break down instead of grow. The same principle applies to our spiritual lives. God never intended for us to run on empty. He calls us to trust Him enough to rest, knowing that He is still working even when we pause.

Jesus modeled this beautifully. Throughout His ministry, He often withdrew to pray and rest, demonstrating that time with the Father wasn't optional—it was necessary (Luke 5:16). If Jesus, the Son of God, made time to rest in His Father's presence, how much more should we?

If you're feeling weary today, remember: You are in a race, but you are not running alone. God is with you, strengthening and sustaining you. Stay faithful, keep moving forward, and trust that He will carry you to the finish line.

Just like an athlete in training, keep praying, keep pressing on, and let God take care of the rest.

Today's Verse:
"I will instruct you and teach you in the way you should go; I will counsel you with my loving eye on you."
—Psalm 32:8

WHEN BUSYNESS BECOMES A BURDEN

"He gives strength to the weary and increases the power of the weak."

Isaiah 40:29

There's a popular saying: **"If satan can't make you bad, he'll make you busy."**

This quote couldn't be more true, and I've seen it firsthand. The spirit of busyness is plaguing God's people, and we must be aware of the enemy's devices. If satan can't trip you up with obvious sin, he'll pile on distractions and endless tasks until you're so fatigued that your faith feels distant and your energy is depleted.

I learned this the hard way after months of being "too busy" for God, too busy for community, and too busy for true rest. It wasn't until I found myself isolated and burned out that I realized the enemy had been using my busyness to weaken my walk with Christ.

As Christians, we often confuse rest with laziness. However, true rest—resting in the Lord—is essential for our faith journey. Rest doesn't merely mean relaxing; it involves prioritizing what truly matters.

I spent so much time being "busy" with my business and responsibilities, thinking it was all for the right reasons. But instead of drawing me closer to God, it pushed me into a place where I started to resent the very blessings I had prayed for. My success, my responsibilities, and my life became burdens because I was trying to carry them in my own strength.

In my fatigue, I started to blame God. I felt like He had left me to handle it all alone. But the truth is, I had left *Him*. My sin wasn't just in being overly busy—it was in forgetting to surrender.

So, I ask you today: *What do you need to surrender to God? What busyness, worry, or responsibility have you been holding onto that's drained your energy and faith?*

Jesus can and will restore and renew you, but today, take a step of *surrender*. Stop trying to carry everything on your own. Right now, pause, take a deep breath, and pray. Lay your burdens at God's feet, trust Him with your responsibilities, and allow Him to refresh and strengthen your soul. His burden is light, and He longs to fill you with His mighty strength. Let God carry what you were never meant to bear.

Today's Verse:
"Be still, and know that I am God."
—Psalm 46:10

DAY 58

THE MINISTRY OF SINGLENESS

"She is clothed with strength and dignity; she can laugh at the days to come."

Proverbs 31:25

S ingleness is often viewed through the lens of what's missing—no spouse, no children, no family structure to lean on. But what if we saw our single years not as a season of absence, but of abundant opportunity? I like to call it the *ministry of singleness*. Many people in the Bible accomplished great things while unmarried, including Jesus Himself.

The Gospels show that both single and married women followed Jesus and played a vital role in His ministry. Some, like Mary Magdalene and Susanna, are believed to have been single, while others, like Joanna, were married (Luke 8:1-3). Their devotion to Christ was not defined by marital status but by their willingness to serve.

If you are unmarried, this season is a unique opportunity to serve God and others without the constraints of family responsibilities. It's a time to dedicate your gifts, time, and energy fully to God's plan. Whether through ministry, volunteering, or simply being available to help those in need, singleness allows for freedom in serving the Lord in ways that may not be possible in other seasons of life.

For me, as a single woman without children, there are moments when I wonder what I might be missing out on. Sometimes, I ask the Lord to speed up the process of fulfilling my desire for a family. But in His quiet whisper, I am reminded that He is my Kinsman Redeemer, my Protector, and the One who knows the perfect timing for everything. God has not forgotten me, and He has not forgotten you.

Singleness is not a delay in God's plan—it is part of it. Just as God called Jesus, John the Baptist, Elijah, Jeremiah, Paul, Anna the prophetess, and many of His followers to impactful ministries while they were unmarried, He is calling you to fulfill His purposes in this season.

To those who are married, I encourage you to recognize and honor the value of your single brothers and sisters in Christ. Be a voice of encouragement, affirming that God has a unique and purposeful calling for their lives. Rather than dwelling on what they may seem to lack, celebrate how they are using their gifts to serve others and build God's Kingdom. Your support, prayers, and genuine affirmation can be a source of strength during moments when they may feel overlooked or undervalued. By walking alongside them in community, you reflect the beauty of God's intentional design for every stage of life and His diverse family.

Today's Verse:
"An unmarried man is concerned about the Lord's affairs—how he can please the Lord."
—1 Corinthians 7:32

FROM BROKENNESS TO BREAKTHROUGH

"He heals the brokenhearted and binds up their wounds."

Psalm 147:3

Four years ago, I looked strong and healthy on the outside, **but inside, I was fighting a battle against my own sins while carrying the emotional weight of someone else's.** Over time, the cracks began to show—my physical health deteriorated, and my internal struggles bled into every part of my life. Despite my discipline in workouts and healthy eating habits, I wasn't consuming enough calories to sustain myself. I started shrinking—physically, emotionally, and spiritually.

My life was consumed by stress and pain as I endured the emotional abuse of a narcissistic relationship. The constant gaslighting, shaming, isolation, and manipulation left me feeling trapped and broken. Eventually, I could barely eat; my stomach was in knots daily, and heartache overshadowed everything. It felt as if I was living someone else's life, slowly becoming a shell of who I once was. I walked on eggshells, bracing for the next blow—unsure when or where it would come.

The home I shared with my fiancé became a nightmare that haunted me for years after I left. But by the grace of God, I finally broke free. I packed whatever I could fit into my vehicle and never looked back.

Today, I stand strong—physically, emotionally, and spiritually. My body now reflects the healing work God has done within me. The weight I've gained isn't just about numbers on a scale—it's a symbol of renewed strength, restored health, and the vitality that comes from God's grace and restoration.

Here's what I've learned: We serve a Lord who is both a Redeemer and Restorer. Jesus healed me—not just from the abuse, but from the false narratives that tried to define me. He reminded me of my worth—not in my physical appearance, my business, or my relationships, but in *Him* alone. My life is now a testimony of God's ability to transform the darkest seasons into stories of grace and redemption.

I know firsthand that life isn't always easy or fair. My journey has been filled with struggles, but through it all, God was present—ready to turn my mess into a miracle. As you continue reading these devotionals, I want to remind you: God's power is limitless. No matter what you're facing—whether it's sin, stress, or the weight of someone else's choices—you are not alone. These devotionals are here to remind you that God walks with you every step of the way, offering strength, guidance, and healing.

Today's Verse:
"When you lie down, you will not be afraid; when you lie down, your sleep will be sweet."
—Proverbs 3:24

DAY 60

ESCAPING THE TRAP OF ABUSE

"Be alert and of sober mind. Your enemy the devil prowls around like a roaring lion looking for someone to devour."

1 Peter 5:8

I **want to take a moment to be completely raw and honest with you.** I'm sharing my story not to dwell on the past, but because there is power in truth. Shame tells us to hide, to bury our experiences, to pretend they never happened. *But truth?* It sets us free—and sets others free as well. God is truth, and He works through our transparency to bring light into dark places.

Have you ever asked yourself, *Why am I here? How did I get to this point?* I have. In fact, I asked myself those very questions with a pistol pointed at my head.

In 2019, my life hit rock bottom. I was living with a man I despised, yet I kept going back. The truth is, I didn't even like him anymore. I loved the person I *thought* I fell in love with. But when his charming mask came off, I was left with someone who made me feel unworthy every single day. His behavior was a rollercoaster. One moment, he was kind. The next, his words were weapons, tearing me down until I questioned my own value. I was trapped—not just physically, but emotionally and spiritually.

Even after I escaped, the trauma followed me. But in the midst of my pain, I found God like never before. His presence became my refuge, my strength, my reason for hope. I know now that if I hadn't walked through that storm, I wouldn't be the woman I am today. If you need the courage to leave a toxic relationship, **let this be your sign.** You are not meant to live in chains—physically, emotionally, or spiritually. God created you for freedom, love, and a life that reflects His goodness. Leaving may feel impossible, but the moment you take that first step, God will meet you with His strength and provision.

Here's what happens when you finally leave:

You will feel fear—maybe even guilt—but you will also feel the weight begin to lift. As you move forward, you'll start to see God's hand in ways you never imagined. He will provide what you need: people who support you, resources to rebuild, and the courage to keep going.

It won't be easy, but freedom rarely is. Yet with each step, you'll grow stronger, more confident, and closer to the person God created you to be.

Healing is a journey, but it's one worth taking. God will not leave you to walk it alone. Your story is far from over.

Today's Verse:
"He will cover you with his feathers,
and under his wings you will find refuge;
his faithfulness will be your shield and rampart."
—Psalm 91:4

DAY 61

GOD SEES WHAT OTHERS OVERLOOK

But the Lord said to Samuel, 'Do not consider his appearance or his height, for I have rejected him. The Lord does not look at the things people look at. People look at the outward appearance, but the Lord looks at the heart.'

1 Samuel 16:7

Have you ever felt invisible or unseen? Maybe you've worked so hard to look the part—to appear strong, confident, or capable—while inside, you've been crumbling. I've certainly been there.

The world often judges us by appearance, accomplishments, or status. It can feel exhausting to keep up with those expectations, can't it? But here's the good news: God doesn't judge you by the world's standards. He isn't impressed by how polished you look or how well you're holding it all together. **God looks at your heart.**

But what does that really mean? When God looks at your heart, He sees the *real* you—the person beneath the surface, beyond the titles and achievements. He sees your motives, your desires, your struggles, and your faith. He knows when you're weary, when you're longing for more, and when you're doing your best even when it feels like you're falling short. Unlike the world, which sees only what's visible, God sees what's eternal.

When God sent the prophet Samuel to anoint the next king of Israel, Samuel assumed the choice would be based on outward qualities—strength, stature, or charisma. But God had a different perspective. He told Samuel, *"People look at the outward appearance, but the Lord looks at the heart"* (1 Samuel 16:7). While David's older brothers looked like kings, God chose David—a shepherd boy, overlooked by others—because his heart was fully surrendered to Him.

And that's what God sees in you, too. He sees beyond your struggles, beyond your scars, beyond the masks you may wear to hide your pain. He sees the person He lovingly created, the person He calls His own. He sees your potential, your unique gifts, and your desire to honor Him—even if you don't feel like you're enough.

Here's the truth: **You don't have to perform for God.** You don't have to meet a worldly standard to be loved by Him. He values who you are, not what you've done or how you appear. Jesus looks deep into your heart and sees the beauty He placed there.

Today's Prayer:

Lord, thank You for seeing me for who I truly am. Thank You for looking beyond the outward appearance and seeing my heart. Help me to live authentically before You, trusting that I don't need to impress the world to be loved by You. Teach me to value what You value and to find my identity in Your unchanging love. In Jesus' name, Amen.

KEEP PLANTING AND WATERING

"I planted the seed, Apollos watered it, but God has been making it grow."

1 Corinthians 3:6

I was on my way back to Nashville after delivering a presentation to a school in Boaz, Alabama—a town named after Ruth's husband in the Bible. His story is one of kindness and redemption, and it seemed fitting that this trip would bring a meaningful reminder of how God's hand moves in unexpected places. I hadn't been familiar with the area before, but I quickly discovered that Boaz is home to an incredible school filled with dedicated teachers, talented athletes, and students eager to learn. I was grateful for the opportunity to share about proper nutrition, hoping to leave them with something valuable.

After wrapping up my presentation, I started the four-hour drive back. I was making good time when I realized I needed to pull over for a quick restroom break. Oddly enough, I ended up stopping at a rival school's sports complex, thinking I could quickly use the restroom by the football field and get back on the road.

As I walked back to my car, I felt a nudge—why not step inside and thank them for letting me use their facility? It was a small thing, but acknowledging kindness never hurts. When I stepped inside, the coach greeted me with a surprised look.

"Whoa, you're Wendi from Twitter! I follow you!" he said. I was caught off guard. Here I was, in a small Alabama town, being recognized by someone I had never met. But he didn't stop there. "Let me show you something," he said, motioning for me to follow.

Down the hall in the weight room, several of my nutrition graphics were pinned to the wall—posters I had designed with fueling strategies and hydration tips. But the best part? Each one included scripture. So every time the student-athletes looked for guidance, they were also reminded of God's truth and how He sees them.

I stood there, humbled. It wasn't about me. This was about *Jesus.*

On this particular day, I was reminded of the quiet impact we can have, even when we don't realize it. The words we share, the kindness we extend, the faithfulness we walk in—it all matters.

You may never know how God is using your obedience, but that doesn't mean He isn't working. You may be planting seeds you won't see grow until years later, or perhaps you'll never witness their growth at all. But just because we can't see the fruit doesn't mean we should stop sowing.

So keep planting. Keep trusting. Keep walking in obedience. The work God is doing through you matters, even when you can't see it yet.

Today's Verse:
"Sow your seed in the morning, and at evening let your hands not be idle, for you do not know which will succeed, whether this or that, or whether both will do equally well."
—Ecclesiastes 11:6

TRUE WELLNESS STARTS FROM THE INSIDE OUT

"For physical training is of some value, but godliness has value for all things, holding promise for both the present life and the life to come."

1 Timothy 4:8

When it comes to health and wellness, much of the focus is placed on outward appearances—our weight, fitness levels, or how we look in the mirror. While these external markers have their place, true wellness begins within. It's about the condition of our heart, mind, and soul. Without addressing these internal aspects, no amount of external effort can bring lasting health.

God calls each of us to steward our bodies well, honoring Him with the resources and abilities He has given us. If you're unsure where to begin, start small. Dedicate just ten minutes a day to both physical and spiritual wellness. Take a walk while reflecting on a Bible verse, stretch as you pray, or simply sit in stillness before the Lord. Small steps of faithfulness can lead to lasting transformation.

Consistency is key to lasting change. If you have physical limitations or disabilities, remember that wellness looks different for everyone. Instead of focusing on what you cannot do, embrace what you can—whether it's gentle movement, deep breathing, or quiet reflection. What matters most is using this time to reconnect with God, honoring Him through the care of your body and soul.

Honoring our bodies also means honoring Jesus in our choices, particularly in how we approach purity and relationships. In today's culture, sexual immorality is often normalized—even celebrated. However, Scripture reminds us that our bodies are temples of the Holy Spirit. We were bought at a price. Just as we discipline ourselves physically, we are also called to exercise self-control in matters of purity.

Caring for your body honors God's creation, and nurturing your spirit prepares you for eternal impact. True wellness is about balance—strengthening both your body and your faith. Whether it's taking a walk, soaking in a warm bath, preparing a nourishing meal, or sitting in quiet reflection, every step toward wellness becomes an act of worship.

Take a moment today to reflect on how you can honor God with your body, mind, and spirit. Even the smallest step—whether in movement, prayer, or stillness—can draw you closer to Him and His purpose for your life. Choosing to walk in purity and self-control is not about restriction but about freedom—freedom to live in alignment with God's best for you.

Today's Verse:
"Do you not know that your bodies are temples of the Holy Spirit, who is in you, whom you have received from God? You are not your own; you were bought at a price. Therefore honor God with your bodies."
—1 Corinthians 6:19-20

WRITING YOUR WAY TO HEALING

"My heart is stirred by a noble theme as I recite my verses for the king; my tongue is the pen of a skillful writer."

Psalm 45:1

Journaling is not just a trendy self-help practice or a therapeutic outlet—it is a spiritual discipline that has the power to transform your mind and deepen your relationship with God. When you put pen to paper, you are creating sacred space to pour out your heart before the Lord, surrendering your worries, your fears, and even your unspoken struggles. What once felt chaotic and overwhelming begins to take shape, bringing clarity where there was once confusion.

Writing down your thoughts becomes even more vital in seasons of hardship. Science backs this up—studies show that expressive writing can help reduce anxiety, depression, and even the effects of trauma. But when we take this practice one step further and invite God into our journaling—through written prayers, reflections on Scripture, and reminders of His faithfulness—our notebooks become places of spiritual warfare and healing. Here, Jesus meets us in the deep places, speaking peace into our pain and renewal into our weary souls.

Throughout the Bible, God calls His people to **remember**. From the psalms of David to the written records of God's mighty acts, Scripture is filled with examples of believers documenting their struggles, their victories, and their encounters with the Lord. Journaling is our way of following in their footsteps, leaving behind a testimony of **God's faithfulness**—one we can return to in moments of doubt, discouragement, or waiting. What a gift to have tangible evidence that God has always been at work in our lives!

As you pour out your heart before Him, trust that Jesus is present in every stroke of your pen. Even in the ordinary practice of writing, He is whispering words of hope, reminding you that He is making all things new.

Action Step: Get a new notebook and label it "Victory Journal." Start to record every answered prayer, every breakthrough, and every moment of joy, no matter how small. Also jot down small moments that bring you a really big smile. When storms come, this will be your reminder that God is always faithful.

Today's Verse:

"I will remember the deeds of the Lord; yes, I will remember your miracles of long ago. I will consider all your works and meditate on all your mighty deeds."
—Psalm 77:11-12

DAY 65

DO YOU WANT TO GET WELL?

Jesus said to him, "Get up! Pick up your mat and walk."

John 5:8

For thirty-eight years, the man by the pool of Bethesda had been stuck in the same place, waiting for healing. He had grown used to his condition, resigned to his limitations. Then Jesus showed up, and in just one sentence, everything changed: *"Get up! Pick up your mat and walk."*

At first glance, this command may seem straightforward, but Jesus wasn't just telling him to stand—He was calling him to step into a new reality. The man had to respond in faith before he saw the miracle. He had to do something he hadn't done in nearly four decades.

How often do we find ourselves in a similar place? Maybe we've been stuck in a cycle of discouragement, fear, or complacency, waiting for the *perfect* conditions to change before we take action. Maybe we've convinced ourselves that breakthrough is only possible if someone else helps us, or if circumstances align just right. But Jesus doesn't wait for conditions to be ideal—He simply speaks, and His word is enough.

Pick Up Your Mat

Jesus specifically told the man to pick up his mat. Why? Because that mat represented his old life—the place of waiting, suffering, and limitation. Jesus wasn't just healing his legs; He was removing his identity as *the man who couldn't move*. By picking up his mat, he was making a declaration: *I'm not going back there.* What is the "mat" in your life? Maybe it's a mindset of doubt, a habit of procrastination, or an identity shaped by past failures. Jesus calls us not only to rise in faith but also to leave behind what once defined us.

Walk Forward in Faith

Jesus didn't just tell the man to get up and stand still—He told him to walk. Healing wasn't just about restoration; it was about movement. Faith isn't passive; it requires action. Sometimes we wait for God to do everything, but often, He calls us to take the first step. Maybe God is speaking to you today: "Rise. *Take up your mat. Walk.*" It's time to move forward. It's time to stop rehearsing past disappointments and start stepping into the future He has for you. *Will you trust His voice, even if it feels unfamiliar? Will you pick up your mat and leave behind what once held you back?* Today is the day to walk boldly into your future.

Today's Verse:
"Jesus went through all the towns and villages, teaching in their synagogues, proclaiming the good news of the kingdom, and healing every disease and sickness."
—Matthew 9:35

BLESSED ARE THE PEACEMAKERS

"If it is possible, as far as it depends on you, live at peace with everyone"

Romans 12:18

One morning, I was sitting in my local Starbucks in Nashville. Everything was going smoothly—coffee in hand, Bible open—until a guy inside started getting really upset. He was angry about losing money and being double-charged. His frustration grew louder by the second. I glanced up, wondering if things were about to escalate into a full-blown fight. Still, I kept my focus on the Bible, trying to stay absorbed while the tension in the room thickened.

Then, something strange happened.

A guy rode up on a motorcycle, parking it right out front. He had long brown hair, a beard, and work boots—the kind of rugged look that made me do a double take. As he walked inside, an odd thought popped into my head: *Does Jesus drive a motorcycle?* I know it sounds silly (go ahead and laugh), but the thought made me chuckle. Shrugging it off, I went back to my reading, not giving it much more thought.

The motorcycle guy got his coffee and went to sit outside. At one point, he looked straight at me through the window.

I can't fully explain it, but a chill ran through me. There was something about his presence—something peaceful, something steady. When the Holy Spirit radiates through someone, people notice—even in a coffee shop.

And that's when things got even more interesting.

The angry man, the one who had been making a scene earlier, suddenly walked outside and sat down next to the motorcycle guy. Just like that. No more yelling, no more frustration—just two strangers sitting together, talking like old friends. I sat there, stunned. One encounter with a faith-filled person, and the entire atmosphere changed. A sense of calm filled the space where chaos had been just moments before.

That moment reminded me of something profound: the peace of Christ can show up anywhere. Our King can use anyone to bring harmony into the midst of turmoil. It doesn't always look like a dramatic miracle. Sometimes, it's as simple as a conversation between two strangers or the quiet presence of someone who carries the gentleness of the Holy Spirit.

The next time you find yourself in a tense situation, remember—God might be working behind the scenes in ways you'd never expect. He calls us to be **peacemakers**, not just peacekeepers—not just avoiding conflict, but actively bringing reconciliation and unity. And in doing so, we reflect His heart to a world in desperate need of His healing touch.

Today's Verse:
"Blessed are the peacemakers,
for they shall be called children of God."
—Matthew 5:9

WHEN YOU FEEL FORGOTTEN, GOD IS NEAR

"We were under great pressure, far beyond our ability to endure, so that we despaired of life itself."

2 Corinthians 1:8

Have you ever felt so broken, forgotten, and overwhelmed **by pain that you went numb?** If that's where you are today, you're not alone. I've been there too—trapped in a cycle of depressive thoughts, wrestling with pride, and wondering if God even noticed my struggle. I'd love to say I powered through with sheer will, but sometimes willpower just isn't enough.

My wake-up call came when even getting out of bed on weekends felt impossible. The vibrant, motivated person I used to be seemed like a distant memory. I was drained—so much so that the thought of helping one more person or facing one more problem felt unbearable. I had worked tirelessly to build my business, coach others, and pour into my calling, yet in the quiet moments, I kept asking God the same desperate question: *"Why aren't you helping me?"*

It's easy to believe God has forgotten us when life feels unfair or overwhelming. I found myself slipping into the same victim mentality I always tell others to avoid—and I felt ashamed of it. But as I cried out to Him, He gently revealed what I couldn't see:

my selfishness, my tendency to place my work above Him, and my fixation on worldly goals. He reminded me that my identity isn't found in my achievements but in Him *alone*. I am His beloved child, and so are you. No matter how lost or broken you feel, your worth in His eyes has never changed.

God wasn't punishing me for feeling weak; He was inviting me to trust Him in a deeper way. I had been so focused on *doing*—achieving goals, fixing problems, making things happen—that I forgot how to simply *be* in His presence. When I cried out, expecting a quick fix, all I heard was a soft whisper: "*Wait.*"

Waiting isn't easy. For someone who thrives on action, it felt like the opposite of progress. But God was teaching me an essential truth: sometimes, we need to stop striving and start trusting. Healing comes when we surrender our burdens and rest at His feet.

One verse that carried me through this season was *Isaiah 60:22*: "*When the time is right, I, the Lord, will make it happen.*" If you're battling depressive thoughts or just trying to stay afloat, take heart—God sees you. He hears every cry and is working in ways you can't yet see. Our King is with you in this battle.

Today's Verse:
"*God is our refuge and strength,*
an ever-present help in trouble."
—Psalm 46:1

WHEN GOD SAYS IT'S TIME TO MOVE

The Lord our God said to us at Horeb, 'You have stayed long enough at this mountain. Break camp and advance into the hill country...'

Deuteronomy 1:6-7

When someone asked me, "*Wendi, why did you pick up and move to Nashville?*" my answer was simple: "*Jesus brought me here.*" Did I know anyone in the city? Not a single person. But that didn't stop me.

I've moved over 40 times throughout my life, often led by career opportunities, aspirations, and, most importantly, faith. Meeting new people and building fresh connections has always been part of my journey. Starting over doesn't scare me because I've learned that when I show up with my shovel in hand, God will guide me to where I need to dig. He has never failed me yet.

Now, the glory cloud is moving again, and the Holy Spirit is leading me to Dallas, Texas! I don't have all the details, but I am confident that God has a new mission waiting for me there. It humbles me to think that He has called me to move through so many different states, shaping me for His purposes. As I close this chapter in Nashville, I reflect on the impact I've had—helping others through their challenges, offering encouragement, and simply being a kind presence in coffee shops and conversations. I leave with a heart full of gratitude for the community God placed around me.

This journey of faith reminds me of *Hebrews* 11:1: "*Now faith is the assurance of things hoped for, the conviction of things not seen.*" Faith doesn't always come with clear instructions or guarantees. Often, it calls us into the unknown, requiring us to trust that God is leading us even when we can't see the outcome. Abraham left his homeland without knowing exactly where he was going, yet he walked in obedience. We are called to do the same—to walk by faith, not by sight.

When the Holy Spirit stirs your heart to move, take a risk, or embrace a new season, remember: **it's not about having all the answers.** It's about being willing to show up, bring your *shovel*, and let God direct where you dig. He may call you to new places, new jobs, or even new relationships. But wherever He leads, He will equip you with the courage and grace you need to succeed.

So, if you find yourself standing at the edge of uncertainty, wondering if you should take that next step—**go.** You don't have to see the whole picture to begin. Just trust, move forward in faith, and watch as God turns your obedience into a beautiful testimony of His faithfulness.

Today's Verse:
"*I will instruct you and teach you in the way you should go; I will counsel you with my loving eye on you.*"
—Psalm 32:8

SERVING AN AUDIENCE OF ONE

"Am I now trying to win the approval of human beings, or of God? Or am I trying to please people? If I were still trying to please people, I would not be a servant of Christ."

Galatians 1:10

Let's be real—people-pleasing is exhausting. We chase approval, measure our worth by others' opinions, and feel the sting when our efforts go unnoticed. We want to be liked, to fit in, to be celebrated. But in Galatians 1:10, Paul delivers a truth bomb: If our focus is on pleasing people, we're missing the bigger picture.

Here's the good news: You were never meant to live for the applause of the crowd. Your life is for an audience of One.

Think about it. Jesus didn't live for popularity. He wasn't worried about impressing the religious elite or curating the perfect image. He walked in truth, spoke with boldness, and fulfilled His purpose—regardless of who approved. And here's the kicker: Not everyone liked Him for it. Some misunderstood Him. Some rejected Him. But He never let that stop Him from walking in obedience to the Father.

So, what about you? Are you living for *likes* or for the Lord? Are you adjusting your words, actions, and decisions to fit what people expect, or are you standing firm in what God has called you to do?

The pressure to please people will always be there. But when you shift your focus from *Who notices me?* to *Am I walking in obedience?*—everything changes.

Living for God's approval brings peace. It frees you from the exhausting cycle of trying to measure up. It anchors your identity in something unshakable. People's opinions will change, but God's love for you never will.

So, take the pressure off. You don't have to impress, perform, or strive to be enough. You already are—because He says so. Walk confidently in your calling. Show up boldly in the gifts He's given you. Stop waiting for permission from people who weren't meant to approve your destiny in the first place.

You are loved. You are chosen. And you are fully approved by the One who matters most.

Today's Verse:

"However, I consider my life worth nothing to me; my only aim is to finish the race and complete the task the Lord Jesus has given me—the task of testifying to the good news of God's grace."

—Acts 20:24

LIVING THE DASH WELL

"Teach us to number our days, that we may gain a heart of wisdom."

Psalm 90:12

Hugging my grandma was like embracing a force of nature. She wasn't just my grandmother—she was a source of strength, wisdom, and unwavering love. Raised by a single father, I had the blessing of being nurtured by his mother. She didn't just help raise me; she shaped me.

One memory stands out from before I became a believer. A Christian boy I was dating broke up with me because I wasn't a follower of Jesus. I was devastated. As I cried, my grandma hugged me and said, *"Put your problems on God because He is up all night anyway."* I didn't fully grasp her words then, but I felt something in her embrace—a comfort that surpassed human understanding.

That night, like many before, I couldn't sleep. But over time, my grandma's words took root. As my faith grew, I started to trust that God truly is up all night, holding every burden in His hands. I began to sleep better—not because my problems disappeared, but because I learned to lay them at the feet of the One who never stops watching over me.

That Christian boy later wanted to get back together, but by then, my walk with Jesus had deepened. God had used that painful moment to draw me closer to Him in ways I hadn't expected. My grandma's wisdom—her gentle push toward faith—was part of the beautiful tapestry God was weaving in my life.

Grandma's life taught me something profound: God places us in roles to nurture, protect, and shape others. She never preached a sermon, but she ministered through every hug, every word of comfort, and every reminder to lean on God.

Life is short. The dash between our birth and death holds immense significance. Yet, we often chase distractions, worrying about the future and striving for things with no eternal value. But my grandma's life showed me that it's not the number of our days that matters—it's how we live them.

What will you do with the dash between your birth and death? Will you chase success, or will you invest in people, leaving behind a legacy that echoes into eternity?

The Lord is saying to our hearts today: *"Live the dash, and live it well. Do not waste your days on things that bear no fruit. Seek Me first, and everything else will fall into place."*

Today's Verse:
"A good name is better than fine perfume, and the day of death better than the day of birth. It is better to go to a house of mourning than to go to a house of feasting, for death is the destiny of everyone; the living should take this to heart."
—Ecclesiastes 7:1-2

DROP THE WEIGHT

"I will proclaim the name of the LORD. Oh, praise the greatness of our God!"

Deuteronomy 32:3

We all carry things that weigh us down—memories of past mistakes, disappointments, relationships that didn't turn out the way we hoped, or dreams that seem out of reach. Sometimes, we hold on because we think letting go means losing control. Other times, we cling to the past because we're afraid of what's ahead. But God calls us to release what no longer serves us so that we can step into the future He has prepared.

One of the most powerful scriptures on this is found in Isaiah 43:18-19: *"Forget the former things; do not dwell on the past. See, I am doing a new thing! Now it springs up; do you not perceive it? I am making a way in the wilderness and streams in the wasteland."*

God is constantly at work, renewing, restoring, and setting things in motion for our good. Yet, if we keep looking back, we risk missing what He's doing right in front of us. Holding on to what is behind us can keep us from stepping into the new opportunities, relationships, and blessings He has in store.

Think of it like carrying a heavy backpack on a long journey. The more weight you carry, the harder it is to move forward. Maybe it's time to take some things out of that backpack—old regrets, fears, and disappointments—and leave them with Jesus. He never intended for you to carry them alone.

Jesus says in Matthew 11:28-30, "*Come to me, all you who are weary and burdened, and I will give you rest. Take my yoke upon you and learn from me, for I am gentle and humble in heart, and you will find rest for your souls. For my yoke is easy and my burden is light.*"

What a beautiful exchange! When we lay down our burdens at His feet, He gives us peace in return. When we release control, He leads us with wisdom. When we surrender our past, He opens the door to a new beginning.

So, what is God asking you to let go of today? Maybe it's an old habit, a toxic mindset, or even your own timeline of how things should unfold. Trust that He knows what's best. He sees the full picture when we can only see a piece of the puzzle. Your future isn't found in the past; it's found in the hands of the One who holds time itself.

Prayer:

Lord, I give You my past, my present, and my future. Help me to trust You completely, to release what is weighing me down, and to embrace the new things You are doing in my life. I believe You are making a way, even when I cannot see it. Amen.

A NEW BEGINNING

"He is faithful to complete the work
He has started in you..."

Philippians 1:6

Are you ready for change? It doesn't have to be overwhelming or complicated—just start today with one thing. One prayer a day, one walk a day, one strength training session, one date, one phone call, one veggie a day. These small, intentional steps can transform your life.

God doesn't need you to be perfect, but He does want you to be healthy and whole—spiritually, mentally, and physically. When we take these steps, we invite the Holy Spirit into the ordinary moments of our lives, allowing Him to work in us in extraordinary ways.

Consider the story of Daniel in the Bible. When faced with the temptation of indulging in the king's rich food and wine, Daniel chose a simple, disciplined diet of vegetables and water (Daniel 1:12-15). This small act of obedience, rooted in a desire to honor God, resulted in great blessings.

Daniel and his companions were found to be healthier, stronger, and wiser than those who had indulged. God honored their small, intentional choice. In the same way, when we choose one small step in our health, spiritual life, or mindset, God sees our obedience and blesses our efforts. The Lord is not asking you for perfection or to become vegan; He's asking for your heart and obedience.

I believe the Lord Jesus is calling us in this season to take bold steps toward *true* healing—healing that encompasses every part of who we are. It's not enough to simply seek healing in our spirit while neglecting our physical health, or to focus on our bodies without tending to our souls. Jesus is asking us to bring our whole selves—mind, body, and spirit—into alignment with His will, making way for the King to reign in every area of our lives. This kind of healing requires us to be intentional and faithful.

The Apostle Paul reminds us of this approach in 1 Thessalonians 5:23, where he writes, "*May God Himself, the God of peace, sanctify you through and through. May your whole spirit, soul, and body be kept blameless at the coming of our Lord Jesus Christ.*" Paul shows us that our spiritual life cannot be separated from our physical and emotional well-being. God desires to sanctify every part of us and to bring healing to the wounds in our soul, strength to our bodies, and peace to our spirits.

Today's Verse:
"You are not your own; you were bought at a price. Therefore honor God with your bodies."
—1 Corinthians 6:20

SOMETIMES THINGS TAKE TIME

"Do not forget to show hospitality to strangers, for by so doing some people have shown hospitality to angels without knowing it."

Hebrews 13:2

I **met Dave on the sidewalk in Green Hills, Tennessee, after a meeting I had just finished.** Feeling overwhelmed and unsure of what God wanted for my life, I decided to take a walk and pray. The night before, I had hardly slept, and you know how the enemy always attacks when we are *hungry, angry, lonely, or tired*—the HALT acronym I often share with clients. Maybe you can relate.

As I was walking, a man came out of a local business with a bag and nearly bumped into me. I quickly turned and said, "Oh, excuse me." He smiled and replied, "Beautiful day!" I agreed, "Yes, the weather is wonderful." That's when he began to tell me his story.

Dave had been homeless for 16 months. Yet, despite all he had endured, his words weren't filled with bitterness or despair—they were filled with praise. Over and over, he kept saying, "*God is good.*"

I nodded, my eyes welling with tears. *Yes, God is good.* But as he shared his story, I realized just how deeply he believed it.

Life on the streets had been brutal. He had been robbed, losing everything he had left. Survival was a daily battle. And yet, he clung to faith. He refused to give up.

Then, on Christmas Eve, everything changed. As he stood on a street corner downtown, Dave's former boss happened to pass by. It was a moment of divine timing—one that ultimately helped him get off the streets.

Dave looked me in the eyes, his voice steady with conviction. "*You just can't quit,*" he said. "*Sometimes things take time.*"

His words weren't just advice; they were lived-out truth. It was a reminder that even in our hardest seasons, God is still working. Even when the breakthrough seems delayed, Jesus hasn't forgotten us. And sometimes, the miracle is simply in **holding on.**

Jesus Himself experienced homelessness at times (Luke 2:7; 9:58), yet He never lacked what He needed to fulfill His mission. His life proves that God's provision is always on time, and His grace is always enough.

As you wait on God's promises, don't forget those who are in a season of waiting too—especially those without a home. Jesus had deep compassion for the poor and the outcast, reminding us that when we care for the least among us, we are serving Him (Matthew 25:35-40).

Today's Verse:
"For I was hungry and you gave me something to eat, I was thirsty and you gave me something to drink, I was a stranger and you invited me in, I needed clothes and you clothed me, I was sick and you looked after me, I was in prison and you came to visit me." —Matthew 25:35-36

GOD'S AMBASSADORS

"But you are a chosen people, a royal priesthood, a holy nation, God's special possession, that you may declare the praises of him who called you out of darkness into his wonderful light."

1 Peter 2:9

Early one morning at 5:30 a.m., I sat in an Uber on my way to the airport after presenting at the International Society of Sports Nutrition Conference. As we drove through the quiet streets, I felt a nudge in my spirit to ask my driver if there was anything I could pray for him about.

Without hesitation, he opened up. "Well, actually yes, there is," he said. "My son has been dealing with depression and trauma. He lives in Boston, and I'm really worried about him. He survived a car wreck when he was 16, but his friends didn't. He's 33 now, and he's still struggling to understand why he's alive and they aren't."

My heart broke for this father and his son. I asked for his son's name and promised to pray for Gabe, believing that God has a purpose for his life. His father nodded and said, "We have to believe in something. If we don't believe, we have no peace." His words struck me deeply. They were a reminder of how fragile life is and how the burdens we carry often pale in comparison to what others are enduring. But even in brokenness, there is hope because we serve a God who heals, restores, and brings peace.

As I said goodbye to the Uber driver, I prayed that God would lift his heavy heart and bring healing to Gabe. Even in deep pain and confusion, God is working behind the scenes for our good and His glory.

As you reflect on this, consider the people around you—your Uber driver, a coworker, or a stranger in passing. We never know the burdens someone is carrying, but God does. He calls us to pray, to listen, and to be vessels of His love.

In your own life, no matter what you're facing, trust that God is at work. He's healing broken places, mending wounds, and using even the darkest moments for good. So keep praying, keep believing, and trust that even when you can't see it, God has a plan.

Today's Verse:
"We are ambassadors of the Anointed One who carry the message of Christ to the world, as though God were tenderly pleading with them directly through our lips..."
—2 Corinthians 5:20 (TPT)

LIVING OUT LOUD FOR JESUS

"When they saw the courage of Peter and John and realized that they were unschooled, ordinary men, they were astonished and took note that these men had been with Jesus."

Acts 4:13

The stage lights dimmed as I stepped away from the podium, my nutrition presentation at a major sports conference in Florida finally wrapped up. I exhaled, expecting the usual post-talk questions about performance strategies. But as the crowd thinned, a line began to form—not for advice, but for something else. They wanted to talk about Jesus.

In my presentations, I often share how Jesus is the source of my real strength and hope. Years ago, I might have hesitated. I might have worried about how people would react or whether I should keep my faith separate from my profession. But the truth is that I *can't*. My faith isn't just a part of my life; it *is* my life. Everything I am today is because of Jesus Christ.

Without Him, I honestly don't know where I would be. I might still be caught in the cycle of perfectionism, crushed under the weight of impossible expectations. I might still be lost in the darkness of depression and self-doubt. I might be even worse off. But I do know this—every time I was on the edge, God pulled me back. Every time I believed the enemy's lies, He whispered the truth. Every time I thought I had messed up too much, Jesus reminded me that He wasn't done with me.

If you have ever felt crushed, overwhelmed, or stuck in a place you never wanted to be, I want you to know that God is with you. He is not distant, and He is not waiting for you to clean yourself up or figure everything out. He is close—right here, right now—ready to lift you up.

That is why I cannot be silent about my faith. It is not because I have all the answers or because I have done anything special, but because I know what it is like to be saved by grace. I have experienced what it means to have my life completely transformed.

So, what about you? Maybe God has placed something on your heart—something you have been hesitant to share because you are worried about how people will react. But here is the truth: Your faith is not meant to be hidden. **Someone, somewhere, needs to hear your story.**

Be bold. Speak truth. Live unashamed. When you do, people will notice the sweet aroma of Jesus Christ bursting through your life! And that's what matters most.

Today's Verse:

"But in your hearts revere Christ as Lord. Always be prepared to give an answer to everyone who asks you to give the reason for the hope that you have. But do this with gentleness and respect." —1 Peter 3:15

YOU ARE SAFE

*"There you saw how the Lord your God carried you,
as a father carries his son, all the way you went until
you reached this place."*

Deuteronomy 1:31

I **want you to pause for a moment.** Take a deep breath. Think back to a time in your life when you felt completely exhausted—physically, emotionally, or spiritually. Maybe it was a season of loss, of heartbreak, of uncertainty. A time when you didn't think you could take one more step.

Maybe you're in that place right now.

Life has a way of wearing us down. There are moments when the journey feels too long, the road too steep, the burdens too heavy. We think we have to keep pushing forward in our own strength, but the truth is—we were never meant to walk alone.

God carries us.

In today's verse, God reminds His people that He has been with them all along. As they wandered through the wilderness—frustrated, afraid, and uncertain about the future—He never left their side. Like a loving father carrying a tired child, He sustained them, guided them, and protected them, even when they didn't see it.

The same is true for you.

I know there are days when it feels like you're trudging through the wilderness, wondering if you'll ever make it to the other side. Maybe you've prayed for direction but feel lost. Maybe you've fought battles that have left you weary. Maybe the weight of responsibility is pressing down so hard that you don't know how to keep going.

But listen—**your Father is carrying you.**

He's carried you through every sleepless night, every tear, every disappointment. He was there in every moment when you thought you couldn't take another step. One of the Holy Spirit's roles is Comforter. He has never left your side.

And He is here now.

You don't have to strive. You don't have to figure everything out on your own. You don't have to pretend you're strong when you feel weak. Your Father is not asking you to prove yourself. He's inviting you to rest in His arms.

Let Him carry you today.

Close your eyes and imagine a child being held by their father, head resting against his shoulder, completely at peace because they know they are safe. That's the kind of love God has for you. That's how He is carrying you right now.

Will you let Him?

Today's Verse:
"Even to your old age and gray hairs I am he, I am he who will sustain you. I have made you and I will carry you; I will sustain you and I will rescue you."
—Isaiah 46:4

THE HOLY SPIRIT MOVES THROUGH YOU

"Each of you should use whatever gift you have received to serve others, as faithful stewards of God's grace in its various forms."

1 Peter 4:10

L et's be real for a second—sometimes we overcomplicate serving God. We think we need a microphone, a massive social media following, or the ability to preach like Billy Graham to make an impact. But here's the truth: God has already given you exactly what you need to serve Him right where you are.

Think about it. What's something you love to do? Maybe you're the friend who always knows what to say when someone's struggling. Maybe you're the planner, the one who organizes game nights or makes sure everyone feels included. Maybe you're creative, turning ordinary moments into something meaningful. Whatever it is—that's a gift. And Peter is telling us in today's verse: *Use it!*

God isn't asking you to be someone you're not. He's not expecting you to suddenly become an extrovert if you'd rather have deep, one-on-one conversations. He's not requiring you to lead worship if your only musical talent is playing the triangle (no shame in that). He wants you to steward the gifts He's already placed inside you.

But here's the key—your gift isn't just for you. God gave it to you so you could bless others. Imagine if everyone held onto their gifts and never used them. No encouragers, no teachers, no helpers, no one to bring people together. The body of Christ would be incomplete! But when you lean into your God-given strengths and use them to serve, you become a channel of His grace in the world.

Maybe you're thinking, *Okay, but how do I know what my gift is?* Start by paying attention to what brings you joy when you do it for others. If you feel energized when you encourage someone, maybe your gift is encouragement. If you love making meals for people, maybe hospitality is your thing. If you're always offering wise advice, God may have given you the gift of wisdom. You don't have to force it—just follow where He's already leading you.

And here's the best part: You don't have to be perfect at it to use it. God doesn't expect you to have everything figured out before you start serving. He just wants you to be willing.

So, what's one way you can use your gift today? Maybe send a text to encourage a friend. Maybe volunteer, offer a helping hand, or simply *show up* for someone who needs you. Whatever it is, don't wait. The world needs what God has placed inside you.

Today's Verse:

"We have different gifts, according to the grace given to each of us. If your gift is prophesying, then prophesy in accordance with your faith; if it is serving, then serve; if it is teaching, then teach."—Romans 12:6

THE POWER OF FORGIVENESS

"And when you stand praying, if you hold anything against anyone, forgive them, so that your Father in heaven may forgive you your sins."

Mark 11:25

I t was 5:30 a.m. in the quiet hotel lobby when I met Todd—a man who, though he didn't realize it at first, was starving for God's truth. I had only planned to grab a cup of coffee, but God had something much bigger brewing that morning.

As I waited for my drink, Todd glanced at the book in my hand. "What are you reading?" he asked casually. I smiled. "The most important book of all—God's Word!" He hesitated for a second, shifting on his feet. "Oh, the Bible. Okay."

I could tell there was more behind that response, so I leaned in. "What's your favorite part of the Bible?" I asked. "Or what do you love most about Jesus?" He paused, as if he wanted to answer but didn't quite know how. I could see something was weighing on him, something he had been carrying for a long time.

Then, I felt the Holy Spirit nudge me. Ask him the real question. So I did. "Todd, if the Lord came back today, would you be ready?"

His entire demeanor changed. His eyes flickered with pain, and suddenly, the conversation shifted from small talk to something much deeper. He exhaled, as if releasing years of bottled-up emotion, and then he told me his story.

Todd had been married for 18 years. He and his wife had three children together, and for most of that time, he thought their life was solid. But then, out of nowhere, she betrayed him. She left him—for another woman. And when she walked away, she took everything—his home, his possessions, and what felt like his dignity.

He had been carrying the weight of that betrayal ever since.

I told him that resentment is one of the enemy's greatest weapons—because when we hold onto it, it holds onto us. Unforgiveness isn't just a burden; it's a thief. It steals our peace, our joy, and our readiness to stand before God with a pure heart.

"Todd, forgiveness isn't about whether your ex-wife deserves it. It's about whether you deserve peace. And you do."

I let the words sink in before asking him again, "If Jesus came back today, would you be ready?"

Tears welled up in his eyes. He was quiet for a long moment, then finally looked up at me. "I wish I had met you years ago."

I smiled. "God is never late, Todd. He's always on time."

That early morning encounter reminded me of something powerful: Forgiveness isn't just an act of obedience—it's an act of freedom. It's what releases us from the weight of the past and opens the door to healing and restoration.

God is ready to heal and restore all who come to Him. The only question is—will we let Him?

Today's Verse:
"Be kind to one another, tenderhearted, forgiving one another, as God in Christ forgave you."
—Ephesians 4:32

KEEP YOUR FORK—THE BEST IS YET TO COME!

"You prepare a table before me in the presence of my enemies. You anoint my head with oil; my cup overflows."

Psalm 23:5

Have you ever been at a dinner party where someone clears your plate, and just as you're about to settle in for post-meal conversation, they lean in and say, "Keep your fork?" If you grew up in a home that served dessert, you know what that means—something good is coming! Not just something good, but something sweet. Something rich. Something worth the wait.

That phrase, "Keep your fork," is a little nudge of anticipation. It tells you the best is yet to come.

God is saying the same thing to you today.

Maybe you've been in a long season of waiting, feeling like your plate has been taken away. Maybe you've experienced loss, heartbreak, or the weariness that comes from giving your all and still not seeing the breakthrough. But hear this: God is not finished. The feast isn't over. There is more ahead for you, **and it's going to be good.**

Psalm 23 reminds us that God prepares a table for us—even in the presence of our enemies. That means He is setting things up for you, even while circumstances seem against you. Your cup isn't just full—*it's overflowing!*

Now, let's talk about the **"fork moments"** in life. These are the times when God whispers to your spirit, *"Hold on. Keep believing. Stay expectant."* Even when it looks like nothing is happening, God is working behind the scenes.

Think about Joseph. He was thrown into a pit, sold as a slave, falsely accused, and locked in prison. But God wasn't done. Joseph's story didn't end in the pit—it led to the palace. His "fork moment" came when Pharaoh called him up, gave him a new robe, and placed him in charge of Egypt.

Or consider Sarah, who laughed at the thought of having a child in her old age. But laughter turned to joy when Isaac was born. God's promise was fulfilled, and it was sweeter than she could have imagined.

And what about you?

Whatever you've been walking through, know this: If God is telling you to keep your fork, it's because something greater is ahead. **Not just crumbs, not just leftovers, but the best part of the meal!**

So today, shake off discouragement. Hold onto hope. Keep trusting, keep praising, and keep your fork close—because your story isn't over. The best is yet to come!

Prayer:

Father, thank You for being a God of abundance. Even when I can't see what You're doing, I trust that You are preparing something amazing for me. Strengthen my faith, renew my hope, and help me to stay expectant. I know that my story doesn't end here. The best is yet to come! In Jesus' name, Amen.

DAY 80

THE STORY OF PHOEBE

"I commend to you our sister Phoebe...."
Romans 16:1

Phoebe isn't exactly a household name in the Bible. She doesn't get the same attention as Paul, Peter, or Mary Magdalene. But tucked away in Paul's letter to the Romans is a powerful glimpse of a woman who broke the mold of what ministry looked like in her time—and still speaks to those of us who feel like we don't "fit" into traditional roles today.

Paul introduces Phoebe with two key descriptions: she was a **deacon** of the church in Cenchreae, and she was a **benefactor** to many, including Paul himself. The Greek word used for deacon means *servant* or *minister*, and it's the same word Paul uses to describe himself in other letters. This tells us something important—Phoebe was not just a helper in the background; she was a *leader*. In a time when women were often overlooked, she was entrusted with responsibility in the early church.

More than that, Paul entrusted her with the delivery of his letter to the Romans. Scholars widely believe that Phoebe personally carried the letter from Corinth, where Paul wrote it, to Rome—a journey of roughly 700 miles across land and sea. This was no small task. Travel in the ancient world was dangerous, requiring physical endurance, resourcefulness, and courage.

It's likely that Phoebe boarded a ship across the Adriatic or Aegean Sea, navigated Roman roads, and endured weeks—possibly months—of travel to reach her destination.

But her role didn't end when she arrived. Letters in the ancient world weren't just handed off like today's mail. The person delivering them was often responsible for reading them aloud, explaining their meaning, and answering any questions. That means **Phoebe wasn't just a messenger—she was a teacher and interpreter of Paul's words to the Roman church**. She wasn't just carrying a scroll; she was carrying one of the most theologically rich letters in the New Testament!

Why does this matter? Because Phoebe's story is proof that God doesn't put people into ministry boxes. She wasn't an apostle or a prophet, yet she was essential to the spread of the Gospel. She wasn't famous, yet her faithfulness carried Paul's message to one of the most influential churches of the time. In the same way, we all carry the message of Jesus into the world!

Phoebe's life reminds us that **ministry isn't about titles—it's about faithfulness.** It's about saying yes when God asks you to carry something, even when you don't fully understand the weight of it yet. *What has God placed in your hands?* What message, gift, or role has He entrusted to you? It may not look like what you expected, but if Phoebe's story tells us anything, it's this: **when you walk in obedience, you might just be carrying something far more important than you realize.**

Prayer:
Lord, thank You for the example of Phoebe and her faithful service to Your Kingdom. Give me the courage to step into my calling, knowing that even small acts of faithfulness can make an eternal impact. Amen.

DAY 81

THE GOD WHO SEES YOU

"You are the God who sees me."

Genesis 16:13

Have you ever felt invisible? Cast aside, mistreated, or forgotten? Maybe someone you trusted betrayed you. Maybe life has forced you into a situation you never asked for, and now you're left wondering if anyone—even God—sees the pain you're in. Hagar knew exactly how that felt.

Hagar was an Egyptian servant who found herself in a situation she never chose. Sarah, Abraham's wife, was unable to have children, so she gave Hagar to Abraham, hoping to have a child through her. When Hagar became pregnant, the household tension grew. Sarah mistreated her so harshly that Hagar ran away into the wilderness—alone, rejected, and carrying the burden of choices that were never her own.

And that's when God found her.

Hagar sat by a spring of water in the desert with no plan, no future, and no one to care for her. But God saw her, called her by name, and acknowledged her pain. Overwhelmed by His presence, she gave Him a name—**El Roi**, **"the God who sees me."**

Maybe you feel like no one truly sees the hurt you carry. Maybe you've been mistreated or left to pick up the pieces of someone else's decisions. But just like Hagar, you are not forgotten.

Jesus sees you.

He sees the betrayal you endured. He sees the tears you cry when no one is watching. He sees the struggle, the unfairness, and the pain you never asked for. And God is not absent in your suffering—He is working all things for your good. Jesus understands mistreatment. He was rejected, falsely accused, and abandoned by the very people He came to save. But He never let the actions of others define Him—only the love of the Father.

And that same love covers you.

So today, instead of believing the lies that say you're forgotten, believe the truth—you are **seen, loved, and fiercely valued** by God.

- The same God who found Hagar in the wilderness sees you now.

- The same Jesus who endured betrayal understands your pain.

- The same Holy Spirit who strengthens you is walking with you every step of the way.

He is El Roi. The God who sees you.

Today's Verse:
"The Lord will fight for you; you need only to be still."
—Exodus 14:14

NO SUCH THING AS LUCK—ONLY GOD'S TIMING

"And we know that in all things God works for the good of those who love him, who have been called according to his purpose."

Romans 8:28

Every Sunday morning, I call my dad to check in before heading to church. During one of these calls, he shared his frustration about some issues with his planter. He hadn't been able to plant beans or corn *on his timeline*, and rain had further delayed the process. Anyone who knows farming understands that timing is everything, and these delays were a source of stress for him.

However, when I called him another morning, the story had changed. Despite planting later than planned, my dad shared that other farmers in the area were now replanting due to crop failure. In contrast, his fields were thriving. I told him, *"God clearly wanted to save you the stress, cost, and time of having to replant."*

My dad chuckled. *"Just dumb luck,"* he said.

That's when I had to step in. *"Luck is a scam, Dad. You know this. It doesn't exist. What you saw as a setback was actually a setup by the Lord. No luck here—that was the Lord paving the way for you."*

In that moment, I realized how easy it is to mistake God's hand for something as fleeting as chance.

How often do we label God's divine timing as "luck" or coincidence? It's easy to get frustrated when things don't go according to our plans. We want everything to happen on our timeline—whether it's planting crops, starting a new job, or seeing the results of a long-standing prayer. But what we see as **delays or setbacks are often God's way of protecting us**, setting us up for something better down the road.

What seemed like a delay in planting was actually God's perfect timing at work, sparing him the extra labor and costs that others now have to face. **It wasn't luck—it was God's provision, His plan unfolding in a way we couldn't foresee.**

We all have moments when life doesn't go the way we hoped. Maybe you've experienced a delay in a personal goal, a setback in your career, or a disappointment in your relationships. It's easy to get discouraged when things don't go as planned.

But as we learn from my dad's story, **God is always working behind the scenes**. What feels like a roadblock might just be His way of **preparing the path ahead.**

Today's Verse:
"Prepare your work outside; get everything ready for yourself in the field, and after that build your house."
—Proverbs 24:27

MUSTARD SEED FAITH

"Truly I tell you, if you have faith as small as a mustard seed, you can say to this mountain, 'Move from here to there,' and it will move."

Matthew 17:20

This afternoon, I had an unexpected encounter with my apartment complex's mailman, Rocky. I saw him filling the mailboxes and didn't want to be in his way, so I took another lap around the building. When I returned, he was finishing up. I grabbed my mail, thanked him, and wished him well, hoping he'd stay dry since it had been raining all day.

As I turned to leave, I felt the Holy Spirit nudge me. I hesitated but couldn't shake the feeling. Finally, I turned back and asked, "Is there anything in your life right now that you might need prayer for?"

At first, Rocky politely declined. "No, ma'am, I'm good." His response was kind but guarded. I felt God prompting me to ask again. "Are you sure? Maybe a family member or a friend?" He hesitated but shook his head. Still, something inside me wouldn't let it go. "Are you really sure?"

That's when Rocky looked at me, smiled, and finally opened up. "Well, actually, I have type 1 diabetes, and it's been tough. I take insulin three times a day. It sucks."

I paused, grateful he trusted me. "Rocky, I'm sorry you're going through that. I'll be praying for you. And as it happens, I'm a registered dietitian." He seemed surprised, and we continued talking. As we did, I felt the Spirit prompting me to share my faith.

"I love the Lord, and He loves you. Prayer has always been powerful in my life. I used to be a nonbeliever. Are you a believer, Rocky?"

He smiled but looked unsure. "I believe in something. Not sure what. I hated how religion made people feel superior."

I nodded. "I hear you. I spent most of my life not believing in Jesus either. But I've learned that while religion can be broken, Jesus is not. He is the way, the truth, and the life. People will let you down, but God won't. He saved my life, and I trust Him completely."

Rocky listened, thoughtful but open. "I can see it on your face—you really believe this. Thanks for sharing and praying for me."

As I walked away, gratitude filled me. The conversation hadn't gone as I expected, but God was in it. As I climbed the hill back to my apartment, a bright red cardinal flew by—a little reminder that the Spirit moves when we trust Him.

We often overcomplicate the Gospel, but it is simple. **Love God. Love others. Share Jesus.** Plant the seed, and let Jesus take care of the rest.

Today's Verse:

"The harvest is plentiful but the workers are few. Ask the Lord of the harvest, therefore, to send out workers into his harvest field." —Matthew 9:37-38

THE POWER OF QUIET FAITHFULNESS

"But when you pray, go into your room, close the door and pray to your Father, who is unseen. Then your Father, who sees what is done in secret, will reward you."

Matthew 6:6

In a world that constantly pushes us to be louder, bolder, and more visible, there's something deeply countercultural about *quiet faithfulness.* Success today is often measured by attention—how many likes we get, how many people know our name. But Jesus invites us into a different way of living—a life that finds meaning in what is done in secret.

When we think about faith, we often picture grand gestures—mission trips, preaching to crowds, or starting ministries that change lives. And while those things are beautiful and important, there's also incredible power in the small, hidden acts of faith that no one sees.

The daily choices to love, forgive, and serve—even when no one is watching—are often the most transformative.

Some of the most profound work God does in and through us happens in the quiet moments. When we choose to pray in stillness, open the Word in solitude, and love others without expecting recognition, that's where God shapes our hearts the most.

Jesus himself modeled this kind of life. He often retreated to quiet places to be with the Father—away from the crowds, away from the applause.

The world may not celebrate quiet faithfulness, but *God* does. He sees every whispered prayer, every unnoticed act of kindness, and every moment of obedience when it would be easier to walk away. He doesn't measure success the way we do—God looks at the heart.

There's a quiet strength that comes from being faithful in the little things. When we make a habit of meeting God in the secret place, we build a foundation of trust, peace, and intimacy that sustains us through life's challenges.

We may not see the fruit of those quiet moments right away, but God is working—often in ways we don't even realize.

Getting into the secret place with Jesus takes intentionality. But once you commit to showing up, that's where all the beauty happens.

Our Heavenly Father loves one-on-one time with His children. All you have to do is show up.

So, set your alarm! You have a date with God in the morning.

Today's Verse:
"Very early in the morning, while it was still dark, Jesus got up, left the house and went off to a solitary place, where he prayed."
—Mark 1:35

THE LEGACY OF FAITH

*"A good name is better than precious ointment, and
the day of death than the day of birth."*

Ecclesiastes 7:1

Death is one of life's greatest mysteries, and no matter how much we try to prepare for it, the experience can leave us feeling deeply unsettled.** When someone who once seemed so strong and full of life becomes frail and childlike in their final moments, it is a surreal reminder of how temporary this life truly is. I learned this in a profound way when I sat by my grandmother's side as she took her final breath. Grandma had been like a mother to me, the backbone of our family—always steady and strong. Watching her become vulnerable in those final days was both heartbreaking and humbling.

I was called home from college to say my goodbyes, and for that, I will always be grateful. Many people never get the chance to say farewell, and I recognize how precious those moments were. Yet, even with the opportunity, the experience was overwhelming.

As I sat by her side, watching my family give her medicine, we locked eyes. A single tear rolled down her face, and I could feel the weight of her love and something deeper being communicated. She refused the medication, and I softly pleaded, *"Grandma, please."* Her gaze spoke words her mouth no longer could. It was as though she was saying, *"Wendi, I love you. Grow in your faith and encourage others in this family."*

At the time, I did not fully understand what she was imparting. The moment felt heavy, surreal—almost as if time itself had paused. It was only later that I realized the depth of her message. In that tear, in that unspoken connection, my grandmother passed on a legacy of faith. The weight of her years of prayer, sacrifice, and devotion to God had been entrusted to me in her final moments.

We do not talk about death enough, but perhaps we should. In our culture, it is often seen as something to avoid or ignore, yet it is a part of life's natural rhythm. Sitting with my grandmother in her final moments was painful, but it was also a profound privilege. It reminded me that while we grieve the loss of those we love, for believers, death is a passage into something far greater.

At the beginning of this book, I dedicated it to my grandmother. She never got to see it come to fruition, but her influence is woven into every page. Her love shaped who I am and gave me the foundation I needed to walk in God's purpose. The seeds of faith she planted in me have grown into something beautiful, and I carry her legacy with me every day.

Death is not the final chapter for those who know Christ. It is the beginning of an eternal story, one where all tears are wiped away, and the faith of those who came before us continues to bear fruit for generations to come.

Today's Verse:
"I thank my God in all my remembrance of you."
—Philippians 1:3

BE A MARY IN A MARTHA WORLD

"Martha, Martha, you are worried and upset about many things, but few things are needed—or indeed only one."

Luke 10:41

I **just love talking about Jesus!** Whether it's over coffee, at the grocery store, or even mid-workout at the gym, I'm always on the lookout for someone to chat with about the goodness of God. By nature, I'm upbeat, personable, and always ready to connect—it's just how I'm wired!

But here's the thing—sometimes God just wants *me* to Himself. He's like, 'Hey, can we have this time together?' And yet, there I am in the sauna, suddenly deep in conversation with a new friend about their life. *Ever been there?*

I think a lot of us can relate! We *want* to be like Mary, sitting at the feet of Jesus, soaking in every word. But more often than not, we find ourselves in full-on Martha mode—buzzing around, filling every moment with activity and conversation. And while God loves our passion for people, He also longs for those quiet, intimate moments with us.

In Luke 10:38–42, Jesus visits Mary and Martha's home. Martha is busy preparing the meal, while Mary sits at His feet, *listening.*

Frustrated, Martha asks Jesus to make Mary help, but He gently tells her that Mary has chosen the better part—the one thing that truly matters.

What a powerful lesson! Martha wasn't doing anything *wrong*—she was serving Jesus! But she was so caught up in *doing* for Him that she missed the joy of simply *being* with Him. Meanwhile, Mary chose the *one thing* that mattered most: sitting in His presence.

If we're honest, many of us have Martha tendencies. We're busy, always moving, always pouring out for others. We pack our schedules, chase productivity, and—even in ministry—sometimes prioritize *working for God* over *walking with Him*. But Jesus reminds us that the *best* thing we can do isn't found in a to-do list—it's found in sitting at His feet. Now, does this mean we should stop serving or talking to others? Absolutely not! God calls us to love people, to build relationships, and to share His Word. But if we're always talking, always moving, always *doing*—when do we stop to *listen*? When do we sit still long enough to hear the whispers of the Holy Spirit?

So, maybe today, God is inviting us to *pause*. To take a deep breath. To put down our phones, step away from distractions, and just sit with Him. Because while Jesus delights in our passion for sharing Him with others, He also delights in *us*. Let's be intentional about finding those Mary moments—even if it means pausing mid-rep at the gym to hear what He's whispering to our hearts. Because when we prioritize time in God's presence, everything else flows from there.

Today's Verse:
"Mary has chosen what is better, and it will not be taken away from her."—Matthew 10:42

CHASING THE SON, NOT THE SUN

"Dear friends, I urge you, as foreigners and exiles, to abstain from sinful desires, which wage war against your soul."

1 Peter 2:11

Sometimes, I get caught up in the hustle of life. I love what I do, and I'm passionate about the work Jesus has given me. But if I'm being honest, there are moments when I realize I've been chasing after the sun—pursuing worldly achievements, goals, and tasks—and I start to feel drained. That's when I know it's time to step back and remember a hard truth: God could return at any moment, and all the things I'm running after won't matter. This life is temporary.

I struggle with the sin of working more than I pray or worship. I often believe I need to do everything, that my effort is what makes things happen. But God doesn't need us to do it all—He needs us to trust Him. That's always been hard for me, as I'm sure it is for many others who feel driven to accomplish. Yet, when God returns, our earthly achievements won't matter. Everything we've built will fade, and we will step into eternity—our true home.

The apostle Peter reminds us in 1 Peter 2:11 that we are foreigners and exiles in this world. We are not meant to feel at home here. This life, with all its toil and striving, is temporary. Our true home is in Heaven, where all striving will cease, and we will be with God forever. Peter urges us not to get caught up in worldly desires that pull us away from God's purpose.

It's easy to forget this truth when the world demands our attention and tempts us with things that seem urgent. We chase success, comfort, and recognition, losing sight of our eternal purpose. But Peter's reminder calls us back to a higher perspective—one that anchors us in God's promises rather than fleeting concerns. When we live with eternity in mind, our priorities shift. We start to seek God's will above our own, finding peace in His presence rather than in our accomplishments.

Challenge for the Week:

Take time to pause and reflect: *Where are your time and energy going? Are you chasing after the sun, or seeking the Son?* This week, commit to spending as much time in prayer, worship, or meditating on God's Word as you do working toward your goals. Start small—set aside 15 minutes each day to focus on eternity rather than the temporary. Ask God to show you what truly matters and help you rest in His promises. Let this be the week you step off the hamster wheel of busyness and into the peace that only God can give.

Today's Verse:
"But our citizenship is in heaven. And we eagerly await a Savior from there, the Lord Jesus Christ."
—Philippians 3:20

THE 3 A.M. WAKE-UP CALL

"Shortly before dawn Jesus went out to them, walking on the lake."

Matthew 14:25

Have you ever found yourself waking up in the middle of the night for no apparent reason? You glance at the clock, roll over, and try to go back to sleep, but something feels different. Maybe your heart is restless, your mind won't quiet down, or there's a stirring in your spirit that you can't shake.

What if God is waking you up on purpose?

Throughout Scripture, God often spoke to people during the night. Samuel was just a boy when he heard a voice calling his name in the darkness. At first, he thought it was Eli, but after the third time, Eli realized it was the Lord. He told Samuel, "If He calls you, say, 'Speak, Lord, for Your servant is listening'" (1 Samuel 3:9-10). In that quiet moment, Samuel received a message from God that would shape his future.

Jacob also had a life-changing encounter at night. He wrestled with God until daybreak, refusing to let go until he received a blessing. By morning, he was no longer just Jacob—he was Israel, a man transformed (Genesis 32:24-28).

Paul and Silas were in prison at midnight, praying and singing hymns to God when suddenly, an earthquake shook the ground, opening the prison doors and breaking their chains (Acts 16:25-26). Even Jesus sought solitude at night, rising early before dawn to pray (Mark 1:35).

So, why does God move in the quiet hours? Because that's when we're still enough to hear Him. The distractions of the day fade away, and our hearts are more open. If God wakes you up at 3 a.m., it may not be random—it may be an invitation.

Instead of rolling over, ask Him what He wants to show you. Open your Bible. Pray. Pay attention to the time—He may even be directing you to a specific verse. If you wake up at 3:16, think of John 3:16: "*For God so loved the world that He gave His one and only Son, that whoever believes in Him shall not perish but have eternal life.*" If you see 4:13, consider Philippians 4:13: "*I can do all this through Him who gives me strength.*"

God is always speaking, but are we *listening*?

The next time you find yourself awake in the stillness of the night, don't ignore it. It might not be a coincidence. It might not be stress or a random wake-up call. It might be God. *Will you answer?*

Today's Verse:

"*I wait for the Lord more than watchmen wait for the morning, more than watchmen wait for the morning.*"

—Psalm 130:6

BOLD FAITH IN A FEARFUL WORLD

"But blessed is the one who trusts in the Lord, whose confidence is in him."

Jeremiah 17:7

Trusting God fully is one of the greatest gifts you can give yourself. It means surrendering your plans, fears, and uncertainties, believing that His plan is far greater than anything you could imagine. Even when life feels unclear, God sees the whole picture. He knows exactly where He is leading you, and He is preparing your heart for something greater.

As you read this, know this truth: God loves you deeply. His purpose for your life isn't small or insignificant. He wants to fill you with peace, strength, and boldness so that you can shine His light in a world that desperately needs it. And one of the most powerful ways to do that is by sharing your faith.

But let's be honest—talking about Jesus is not always easy. Fear of judgment, rejection, or not having the "right" words can hold us back. We hesitate, wondering if we'll say the wrong thing or if the conversation will be awkward. But here's what you need to know: no one who has ever stepped out in faith to share Jesus has regretted it.

God isn't asking you to have all the answers. He's simply asking you to be available. When you step forward in obedience, He takes care of the rest. The Holy Spirit moves in ways we can't always see, working in the hearts of those around us. What seems like a small conversation to you could be a life-changing moment for someone else.

Yes, it might feel uncomfortable. You might wonder how people will respond. But God does not call us to play it safe—He calls us to trust Him. And when you do, He will give you the words, the courage, and the open doors you need.

So if God puts it on your heart to share the gospel with someone, don't hesitate. Take the step. Speak His name. Pray with boldness. Even if your voice shakes, even if you stumble over your words, God is moving through you.

Every time you share Jesus, you are aligning with His purpose. You are glorifying His name. And most importantly, you are saying yes to being part of His greater plan.

Will you step out in faith today?

Today's Verse:
"In the same way, let your light shine before others, that they may see your good deeds and glorify your Father in heaven"
—Matthew 5:16

WHEN THE BROOK DRIES UP

"Then the word of the Lord came to him: 'Leave here, turn eastward and hide in the Kerith Ravine, east of the Jordan. You will drink from the brook, and I have directed the ravens to supply you with food there.' But some time later the brook dried up because there had been no rain in the land."

1 Kings 17:2-7

Elijah was a prophet who followed God's instructions. During a severe drought, God led him to a hidden brook where he could drink water, and He even sent ravens to bring him food. It was a miraculous provision! But after a while, the brook dried up. The water that once refreshed him was gone.

Maybe you've been in a place like that. Life seemed to be going well, and you felt like you were exactly where God wanted you. Then, things changed. A job that once provided stability is gone. A relationship that felt secure has ended. A dream you worked hard for is no longer within reach. And you're left wondering, *God, what happened? Why did this dry up?*

It's easy to feel confused when something you relied on disappears. But here's the truth: **when something dries up, it doesn't mean God has abandoned you—it means He is redirecting you.**

Elijah's story didn't end at the dried-up brook. God spoke to him again, telling him to go to a town called Zarephath, where a widow would provide for him (1 Kings 17:8-9). That might not have made sense to Elijah at first—how could a poor widow help him? But when he obeyed, he found that God had already prepared the next provision for him. Not only did Elijah receive what he needed, but he was also able to help the widow and her son, blessing them with a miracle of their own.

If something in your life has dried up, **don't panic—pause and listen.** Could it be that God is guiding you somewhere new? Instead of clinging to what used to be, ask, *Lord, where are You leading me next?* Sometimes, we hold on too tightly to a season that was never meant to last forever. But when God closes one door, it's because He has another already prepared.

If your "brook" has dried up, take heart. **God is still your provider.** He is still leading you. What looks like an ending is actually the beginning of something greater. Trust Him, even when the next step isn't clear yet.

Today's Verse:
"See, I am doing a new thing! Now it springs up; do you not perceive it? I am making a way in the wilderness and streams in the wasteland."
—Isaiah 43:19

YOU DON'T BELONG HERE

"They are not of the world, even as I am not of it."
John 17:16

Ever feel like you just don't fit in? Like you're speaking a different language while everyone else is tuned into the world's frequency? That's because, as a follower of Jesus, you don't belong here—and that's actually a great thing.

Jesus made it clear in John 17 that His followers aren't like everyone else. We may live in this world, but we aren't defined by it. That means we don't have to chase what everyone else is chasing, stress over what the world stresses over, or conform just to make life easier. You, my friend, are set apart for something greater.

So What Does That Actually Look Like?

Think about it: Jesus didn't pray for you to be taken out of this world, but He did pray for you to be protected while you're here. Why? Because He knows you'll face challenges, pressures, and temptations that make you question your identity. The world will try to squeeze you into its mold, but God's calling you to break out of it.

How to Live Like You Belong Somewhere Else

1. Own Your Identity

You weren't made to blend in. God designed you to stand out! Romans 12:2 says, "*Do not conform to the pattern of this world, but be transformed by the renewing of your mind.*" That means you're not here to copy trends, seek approval, or follow the crowd. You're here to reflect Jesus. Let your thoughts, actions, and even the way you love others point back to Him.

2. See Life Through a Kingdom Filter

The world measures success by money, status, and influence. But Jesus flips that upside down. His Kingdom values faith over fame, humility over hype, and love over likes. When you hit a rough patch, don't ask, *Why is this happening?* Instead, ask, *What is God doing through this?* A Kingdom mindset lets you see trials as training grounds, not roadblocks.

3. Represent Heaven Everywhere You Go

You are not just here to get through life. You are here on a mission. Every place you step into — your job, your classroom, the grocery store, even online — is a chance to reflect Heaven. It is not about being perfect. It is about letting your words, your attitude, and even your kindness leave people wondering, "*What is different about them?*" Here is the secret: it is Jesus, alive and beating inside you, shaping everything you do.

Today's Verse:
"*But seek first his kingdom and his righteousness, and all these things will be given to you as well.*"
—Matthew 6:33

A TEST OF GENEROSITY

*"Listen, my beloved brothers, has not God chosen
those who are poor in the world to be rich in faith and
heirs of the kingdom, which he has promised to those
who love him?"*

James 2:5

It happened in a Publix parking lot in South Nashville. A woman approached me, her eyes filled with desperation. "I need money to feed my kids," she said softly. I felt a nudge in my spirit. This moment wasn't just about her—it was also about what God was asking *me* to do.

"How many kids do you have? What are their names?" I asked gently. She hesitated. No answer. A small ache settled in my heart. *Was she being truthful?* Doubt tried to creep in, but then another thought interrupted: *What if this is Jesus?* (Matthew 25:35–40). A battle stirred within me. One voice whispered, *Be cautious. Protect what's yours.* The other reminded me, *Be generous. Trust Me.*

I had responsibilities—bills, student loans, dreams of owning a home. And yet, here I was, standing before a woman in designer clothing, my own simple gym clothes and messy ponytail feeling like a stark contrast. Then, another gentle prompting. *Everything you have belongs to Me. This isn't about her—it's about you. Will you trust Me?* A twenty-dollar bill sat in my wallet—the only cash I had. *She doesn't look like she's struggling,* I thought. But the Holy Spirit nudged again, soft but firm.

I handed her the money. She looked me in the eyes, thanked me, and walked away. As I loaded my groceries, I noticed her get into a Lexus. A *nice* one. My heart tightened. *Had I just been fooled?* Frustration stirred, but before it could take root, a different prayer slipped from my lips: *"Lord, bless that woman. And help me not to judge."*

I know what some might say: *You were scammed.* Maybe. But that wasn't the point. The real test wasn't about *her*—it was about *my obedience.* Would I give when God prompted me, even when it didn't make sense? Would I trust Him to take care of me? Romans 8:32 reminds us: *"He who did not spare His own Son but gave Him up for us all, how will He not also with Him graciously give us all things?"* Generosity isn't about being reckless—it's about faith. It's about knowing that our security doesn't come from what's in our wallets, but from a God who never runs out of provision.

If I had clung to that twenty dollars, I might have felt safer for a moment. But I also would have walked away with something heavier—disobedience. What if this moment wasn't about the woman at all? What if God was using it to refine *me*? **At the end of the day, our job is to trust, obey, and let God take care of the rest.**

Today's Verse:
"Each of you should give what you have decided in your heart to give, not reluctantly or under compulsion, for God loves a cheerful giver."
—2 Corinthians 9:7

THE SHEPHERD'S CARE

"The Lord is my shepherd, I lack nothing."

Psalm 23:1

Psalm 23 is one of the most well-known and comforting passages in the Bible, but its depth is often overlooked. This opening verse alone carries a powerful truth: God is our Shepherd, and because of that, we lack nothing. *But what does that really mean?*

The Shepherd and His Sheep

In ancient Israel, shepherds weren't just caretakers—they were protectors, providers, and guides. Sheep are completely dependent on their shepherd for survival. They don't know how to find food on their own, they wander into danger, and they are prone to fear. Sound familiar? We, too, are completely dependent on God, though we often act like we can manage on our own. When David declares, *"The Lord is my shepherd,"* he is making a profound statement of **trust and surrender.** He isn't just saying God takes care of him; he is acknowledging that his life is **fully in God's hands.**

A Deeper Look at "I Lack Nothing"

The Hebrew phrase for "I *lack nothing*" means **to be completely satisfied, to have no deficiency, to be whole.** This doesn't mean we will never experience need or hardship, but it does mean that in God's presence, we already have everything we need. The world constantly tells us that we need *more*—more money, more success, more approval, more security. But David is reminding us that true satisfaction comes from the Shepherd, not from circumstances. When we live under His care, we are never truly lacking, because He provides everything we need—physically, spiritually, and emotionally.

How Do We Live Like We Lack Nothing?

1. **Trust the Shepherd's Provision** – If God is our Shepherd, then He already knows our needs before we ask. Instead of striving, we are called to **rest in His care**.

2. **Let Go of Fear** – Sheep are easily frightened, but when they see their shepherd, they calm down. **Are you carrying fears today?** God is saying: *"Trust me. You are not alone. I will take care of you."*

3. **Find Contentment in Christ** – True satisfaction isn't found in *things*, but in **God's presence.** When we focus on what we don't have, we feel like we are lacking. But when we focus on Jesus, we realize **we already have enough.**

Today's Verse:
"He makes me lie down in green pastures, he leads me beside quiet waters."—Psalm 23:2

DAY 94

WHEN FEAR TRIES TO TAKE OVER

"When I am afraid, I put my trust in you."

Psalm 56:3

F ear is a natural response to life's challenges, but God's Word reminds us that we don't have to live in fear. Whether it's the fear of war, financial stress, uncertainty in relationships, or health concerns, God promises to be with us in every situation. Psalm 56:3 reminds us that when fear rises, we must shift our focus—not onto the problem, but onto the One who holds all things in His hands.

Jesus is our anchor in every storm. Your marriage, career, finances, purpose, future, and health are under His constant care. No matter how uncertain things feel, the Lord has already gone before you, preparing the way. He is always with you, even in the darkest valleys. The key is not to let fear take hold but to trust that God is in control, working all things for your good.

When fear threatens to overwhelm us, it's easy to lose sight of God and fixate on the storm. But the truth is, we are never alone. God has given us His Word to guide us, His love to sustain us, His Spirit to empower us, and His people to support us. Our job is to keep our eyes on Him, even when the waves of fear try to pull us under.

Take a moment today and ask yourself: *What am I worried about right now?* Is it your future, a relationship, finances, or your health? Write it down and surrender it to Jesus. Whatever it is, He is inviting you to release it into His hands. Allow His truth to replace the lies that fear whispers. God is faithful, and He will carry you through this season—just as He has done before.

When fear rises, the Bible gives us practical steps to find peace in God's presence:

- **Reflect on His promises.** *"Do not fear, for I am with you"* (Isaiah 41:10).

- **Pray and release your worries to Him.** *"Do not be anxious about anything, but in every situation, by prayer and petition, with thanksgiving, present your requests to God. And the peace of God... will guard your hearts and your minds in Christ Jesus"* (Philippians 4:6-7).

- **Practice gratitude.** Giving thanks shifts our focus from fear to God's faithfulness.

- **Be still and trust.** *"Be still, and know that I am God"* (Psalm 46:10).

God is bigger than whatever you're facing. Let go of fear, hold onto faith, and trust that He is leading you through this moment with His love, strength, and unfailing presence.

Today's Verse:
"I sought the Lord, and he answered me; he delivered me from all my fears." —Psalm 34:4

WHEN THE BURDEN FEELS HEAVY, TRUST GOD

"Yet the LORD longs to be gracious to you; therefore He will rise up to show you compassion. For the LORD is a God of justice. Blessed are all who wait for Him!"

Isaiah 30:18

One morning, **I found myself staring at an unexpected $1,300 bill I couldn't cover.** My heart sank. It felt like everything I had worked for was slipping away. Exhausted and emotional, I knew this was the kind of moment when satan attacks the hardest. After four years of sacrifice, I couldn't help but wonder—*Was it all for nothing? How would I ever get ahead?*

I didn't blame God. I knew He was the reason I had come this far. But at that moment, I hit my limit. Falling to my knees, tears streaming down my face, I cried out for direction. *Take this burden, Lord, or give me the strength to keep going.* So, I surrendered—again.

In that raw moment, I asked God to search my heart, remove anything misaligned with His will, and give me courage for whatever came next. I repented, prayed for peace, and reminded myself that my struggle was temporary. His plan, His purpose, and His timing were far greater than the obstacles in my way.

As I wept in my closet, I asked God to walk with me through the storm. Even though nothing had changed yet, peace settled over me. I stepped outside for a walk, and that's when I saw it—a bright red cardinal zipping through the trees. It was a reminder that God sees me, He hears me, and He will provide.

Years have passed since that day. Our business is thriving, my $80,000 in student loans is paid off, and I now have a few incredible dietitians on staff. God answered my prayers in ways I never imagined. He has been faithful every step of the way. The journey isn't over, but I trust Him completely.

If you're feeling tired, frustrated, and ready to give up, remember—God hears your prayers. He sees your sacrifice. When you surrender everything to Him, He meets you in your brokenness and gives you the strength to keep going. He may not change everything overnight, but He will always provide what you need for the next step. Trust Him, and take it one step at a time.

Today's Verse:
"And my God will meet all your needs according to the riches of his glory in Christ Jesus."
—Philippians 4:19

WHEN TROUBLE COMES, HOPE IS BORN

"We also boast of our troubles, because we know that trouble produces endurance, endurance brings God's approval, and his approval creates hope. This hope does not disappoint us, for God has poured out his love into our hearts by means of the Holy Spirit, who is God's gift to us."

Romans 5:3-5 (GNT)

I **know you're tired.** Maybe life has felt like a constant uphill battle, and you're wondering when things will finally get easier. The weight of your struggles—whether financial, emotional, physical, or spiritual—has been pressing down on you, making it hard to breathe, hard to move forward, hard to believe things will change.

But hear me today: **Jesus is using this season for something greater.**

Romans 5:3-5 reminds us that trouble isn't pointless—it's a process. It produces **endurance**—the strength to keep going when you feel like quitting. Endurance leads to **God's approval**, meaning He is refining you, shaping your faith, and preparing you for what's ahead. And His approval creates **hope**—real, *unshakable* hope that will never disappoint you.

Maybe you're struggling to see the purpose in your pain. But what if this hardship is growing something in you that nothing else could? What if the struggle that feels unbearable today is the very thing that will make you unshakable tomorrow?

Jesus isn't asking you to enjoy the pain, but He is asking you to trust that He is working *through* it. God has already poured His love into your heart through the Holy Spirit. You are not alone. He is with you, strengthening you, preparing you, leading you into a hope that will never fail.

So take a deep breath. Keep going. This season won't last forever, but what God is building in you *will*.

Today's Verse:
"The LORD himself goes before you and will be with you; he will never leave you nor forsake you.
Do not be afraid; do not be discouraged."
—Deuteronomy 31:8

JESUS SEES YOU IN THE STORM

"He saw the disciples straining at the oars, because the wind was against them. Shortly before dawn he went out to them, walking on the lake."

Mark 6:48

Have you ever been caught in a storm—overwhelmed, anxious, and desperate to hear God, but your mind is racing too fast to focus? I've been there more times than I can count. I want to hear God's voice, but when life feels chaotic, my thoughts spiral, doubt creeps in, and before I know it, I'm trying to handle everything on my own.

If you've ever felt that way, you're not alone. The disciples experienced the same thing. After Jesus miraculously fed the five thousand, He told them to get into a boat and cross to the other side. They obeyed—but even in their obedience, they still faced a storm. As they rowed, the wind and waves battered them, and they were struggling against the storm (Mark 6:45-48).

Jesus saw them. Even though they couldn't see Him in that moment, He saw their struggle.

Isn't that how life feels sometimes? You do exactly what God asks, yet the storm still comes. The waves crash, the wind howls, and it feels like you're rowing against everything life throws at you. But here's the beautiful truth: Jesus never takes His eyes off you. Just as He saw the disciples fighting against the wind, He sees you now. And in the middle of their storm, He came to them—walking on the water, stepping into their chaos. With a word, He calmed the storm and brought them safely to shore.

Following Jesus doesn't mean we won't face storms. Obedience doesn't guarantee smooth sailing—but it does guarantee His presence. He sees you straining, and He is not distant. He is near, walking toward you even when you can't see Him, ready to step into your storm at just the right time.

If you're facing a storm today, take heart—Jesus sees you. He knows every detail of your struggle, every whispered prayer, and every longing in your heart to hear His voice. Even when the waves feel relentless and your thoughts won't slow down, God is with you. Right now, in the middle of your chaos, He is reaching out, ready to calm the storm and fill your soul with His peace. You are not alone—the Holy Spirit is closer than you think, holding you steady, reminding you that His love never fails.

Today's Verse:
"He got up, rebuked the wind, and said to the waves, 'Quiet! Be still!' Then the wind died down and it was completely calm."
—Mark 4:39

GOD SPEAKS IN A WHISPER

"And after the fire came a gentle whisper."
1 Kings 19:11

Imagine stepping into Elijah's shoes for a moment. He was told to stand on the mountain because the Lord was about to pass by. What an incredible, awe-inspiring moment! You would expect something powerful, right? Maybe God would appear in the roar of the wind, the rumble of an earthquake, or the blaze of a fire. But Elijah learned something profound that day—God wasn't in the dramatic, earth-shaking events. After all the chaos had subsided, God spoke in a gentle *whisper*.

How often are we like Elijah, expecting God to show up in big, obvious ways? We look for Him in miraculous signs, powerful emotions, or loud declarations. But what if, like Elijah, we've been searching in all the wrong places? What if God is speaking—not in the noise, but in the stillness? Whispering is one of His favorite ways to communicate.

We live in a world that never stops—our schedules are packed, our phones buzz non-stop, and our minds race from one thing to the next. It's easy to get swept up in the whirlwind, forgetting to pause long enough to hear God's voice. But here's the truth: a whisper can't be heard from a distance. You have to be close. To hear God's whisper, you need to slow down, draw near to Jesus, and be still.

So how do we become better listeners? By making space for stillness. Every day, we need to set aside time to be with God—reading His Word, praying, and seeking Him. But beyond that, we need moments of silence—sitting in His presence, allowing Him to speak without distractions or demands.

Think of a parent rocking their newborn in the stillness of the night. In those quiet moments, there are no words—just a deep, unspoken bond of love and security. The baby feels safe, and the parent's heart overflows with love. This is how God longs to draw near to us. It's in the silent moments of surrender that we build intimacy with Him, experiencing His love and peace in ways that words could never express.

God's voice isn't always found in the wind, the earthquake, or the fire. The most profound revelations often come as a gentle whisper. And you don't want to miss it.

As you go about your day, remember this: God is near. He is always speaking, always waiting for you to draw close. Slow down. Be still. Listen. In the stillness, you will hear the whisper of His love.

Today's Verse:
"He wakens me morning by morning, wakens my ear to listen like one being instructed."
—Isaiah 50:4

DAY 99

GOD IS A REDEEMER

"You intended to harm me, but God intended it for good to accomplish what is now being done, the saving of many lives."

Genesis 50:20

Have you ever looked back at a painful season in your life and wondered, *Why did I have to go through that?* Maybe someone betrayed you, hurt you deeply, or left scars that still affect you today. It's hard to see purpose in the pain when we're in the middle of it. But Genesis 50:20 reminds us that God is always working behind the scenes, turning what was meant for harm into something good.

Joseph knew what it meant to suffer. Betrayed by his own brothers, sold into slavery, falsely accused, and thrown into prison, he had every reason to feel abandoned and bitter. But instead of being defined by what happened to him, Joseph clung to the truth that God was still in control. Years later, when he stood before his brothers—now a powerful leader in Egypt—he didn't seek revenge. Instead, he recognized God's greater plan. What they meant to harm him, God had used to position him for a purpose far bigger than himself.

Maybe you've been through something that felt like it would break you. The betrayal, the heartbreak, the loss, the unfair circumstances—they weren't part of your plan. But they never caught God by surprise. Just like with Joseph, the Lord is using every piece of your story for something greater.

Here's what you need to know: The enemy may have tried to take you out, but he didn't win. That setback was actually a setup for something far greater. God is using what you've been through to strengthen you, to shape you, and to prepare you for what's ahead. Even the most painful moments in your life are being woven into a testimony that will impact others in ways you can't yet see.

God never wastes your pain. *He redeems it.*

You are not forgotten. You are not a victim. You are a child of God, and He is working all things together for your good (Romans 8:28). The very thing that was meant to harm you will be the thing God uses to elevate you, to bless you, and to bring glory to His name.

So, hold your head high. Jesus is turning your story into something beautiful. Keep trusting, keep believing, and know that even in the struggle, He is working behind the scenes. God loves you so very much!

Today's Verse:
"The Lord is good to those who wait for him,
to the soul who seeks him."
—Lamentations 3:25

THE STRENGTH YOU DIDN'T SEE COMING

"Do not grieve, for the joy of the LORD is your strength."

Nehemiah 8:10

Ever felt like life is crumbling around you, and you're just barely holding it together? Maybe you're juggling work, family, finances—trying to stay strong in your faith—but deep down, you're running on empty. If that's where you are, here's some truth to hold onto: **God is rebuilding you.**

Let's rewind to Nehemiah's time. God's people had been through devastation. Their city had been destroyed. They had been exiled, scattered, and worn down by years of hardship. But when they finally returned and rebuilt the walls of Jerusalem in just 52 days, it wasn't just a construction project—it was a picture of God restoring His people.

And yet, when they heard the Book of the Law read aloud, instead of throwing a party, they *wept*. Not just a quiet tear, but full-on, deep, heart-wrenching sobs! They realized how far they had drifted from God, and the weight of it hit them hard.

But Nehemiah flipped the script.

"Do not grieve, for the joy of the Lord is your strength" (Nehemiah 8:10). Wait... joy? Now?

Yes. Because this wasn't a time for shame—it was a time for *grace*. God wasn't holding their failures over them. He wasn't focused on their brokenness. He was celebrating their return, their rebuilding, and their restoration. *And He's doing the same for you.* You don't have to hold it all together. You don't have to be strong on your own. God is rebuilding the broken places in your life.

How to Step Into God's Joy Today

- **Shift your focus:** Instead of dwelling on what's missing or broken, start looking at what's being rebuilt. God is with you. He's for you. He's working things out, even when you can't see it.

- **Celebrate the progress:** The Israelites had just rebuilt the walls of their city. That was huge. Take a moment to recognize the progress in your own life—you're not where you used to be.

- **Choose worship over worry:** Joy doesn't come from perfect circumstances. It comes from knowing God is still God. So put on some worship music. Dance. Sing. Laugh. Let His joy fill you again.

Today's Verse:
*"David, wearing a linen ephod,
danced before the Lord with all his might."*
—2 Samuel 6:14

ANSWER THE CALL TO COMPASSION

"Do not withhold good from those to whom it is due, when it is in your power to act."

Proverbs 3:27

Have you ever been in a situation where helping someone felt like a burden? Maybe you were busy, tired, or it was simply inconvenient. In those moments, it can be tempting to look the other way. But what if the help you give could change someone's eternity?

Our time on earth is limited, and God places us here for a purpose: to serve others and glorify Him through our actions. We are called to love our neighbors, even when it's hard, and to be the light in dark places. Sometimes, offering help may seem like a small gesture, but in God's Kingdom, it can have eternal significance.

A Story of Compassion: In the Gospel of Luke, we see the parable of the Good Samaritan (Luke 10:25-37). A man is beaten and left for dead on the side of the road. Two people pass by without offering help. Finally, a Samaritan—someone who would typically be despised by the Jews—stops to help. Not only does he bind up the man's wounds, but he also takes him to an inn and pays for his care.

The Samaritan didn't allow inconvenience to stop him from showing compassion. His help wasn't just a one-time act; he committed to making sure the man was fully cared for. Jesus uses this story to highlight the importance of loving others, even when it costs us something.

We don't know the impact our actions might have. Like the Good Samaritan, you may be the only person who stops to help someone in need. And that moment of kindness could open their heart to God's love and ultimately lead them to salvation.

Choosing to Help: It's easy to justify not helping, especially when life is hectic or we're overwhelmed with our own struggles. But think about what it would mean to look back on your life and regret not helping someone when you had the chance. You might be the only person who crosses their path at just the right moment. And what if, one day, in heaven, that person comes up to you and says, *"You helped me when no one else did. Because of you, I came to know Christ!"* Imagine the joy of hearing God say, *"Well done, good and faithful servant"* (Matthew 25:23).

Reflection: Today, consider the people around you. Is there someone in your life who needs help, even if it's inconvenient for you? Pray and ask God for the strength and willingness to help, knowing that He sees and rewards every act of kindness done in His name.

Today's Verse:

"Which of these three do you think proved to be a neighbor to the man who fell into the hands of robbers?"

"The one who showed mercy to him," he said. Then Jesus told him, *"Go and do the same."*
—Luke 10:36-37

THE SECRET TO TRUE CONTENTMENT

"I have learned to be content whatever the circumstances."

Philippians 4:11

Discontentment—it's that nagging feeling in your heart that whispers, **"What you have isn't enough."** It's the longing for something more, the restless ache that tells you your life is somehow lacking. Maybe it's the desire for a relationship, a different career, a bigger house, or a family of your own. Discontentment makes you believe that if you could just attain that one thing, everything would be perfect.

I know the feeling well. I'm blessed with health, success, and a thriving relationship with God. Yet, I sometimes find myself longing for what others have—the marriage, the children, the home filled with family. A few years ago, as I have shared in previous devotions, I left a toxic, emotionally abusive relationship. It wasn't easy, and I wouldn't wish what I went through on my worst enemy, but it was a necessary part of my life that I've learned and grown from. By God's grace, I'm alive, healthy, and spiritually thriving. Still, there are moments when I miss the idea of what I gave up and the dreams I had for a future that wasn't part of God's plan.

What is Discontentment? Discontentment is the heart's cry for what it believes is missing. It's when we start focusing on what we don't have, instead of appreciating what God has already given us. It's an internal tug-of-war between where you are and where you wish to be. It leads to envy, comparison, and a sense of dissatisfaction that robs us of peace.

The thing is, discontentment often blinds us to the beauty of the present. It makes us feel like we're behind, like our lives aren't measuring up to some invisible standard set by others. But God doesn't want us to live in a constant state of wishing for more. He calls us to rest in His perfect provision, trusting that He knows exactly what we need and when we need it.

Escaping the Trap of Envy: James 3:16 warns us that where there is envy, *"there you find disorder and every evil practice."* Envy and discontentment go hand in hand, drawing us into a place of comparison and dissatisfaction. But when we bring our desires to God and surrender them to His will, we open ourselves up to true contentment—the kind that isn't dependent on external circumstances.

Take a moment to ask yourself: what is it that's causing discontentment in your life? Is it something you can hand over to God? Surrendering doesn't mean giving up on your dreams; it means trusting that God's timing and methods are far better than our own.

Today's Verse:

"But godliness with contentment is great gain. For we brought nothing into the world, and we can take nothing out of it."
—1 Timothy 6:6-7

GOD'S DESIGN FOR RELATIONSHIPS

Then the LORD God caused the man to fall into a deep sleep. And while he was sleeping, he took out one of the man's ribs and closed up the wound. And the LORD God made the rib that he had taken from the man into a woman, and brought her to the man. And the man said, "This is now bone of my bones and flesh of my flesh!"

Genesis 2:21-23

I n a world where marriage rates are declining, divorce rates are rising, and gender roles are being distorted, it's easy to lose sight of how God originally designed men and women to live in harmony. We werc never meant to compete with one another but to complement and support each other, especially in marriage and relationships. When we keep God at the center of our relationships, we lay a solid foundation that can withstand the storms of life and the temptations of sin.

I was reminded of this powerful truth when I met a couple who had been married for 70 years. We struck up a conversation while I was traveling for a speaking event, and their story left me in awe. They shared how they always put God first, and because of that, they were able to weather the inevitable challenges that came their way. They spoke about teamwork, unity, and mutual respect, and their love for one another was a living testament to the power of a God-centered relationship. It was inspiring to witness the beauty of a relationship built to last.

As a single woman, their words deeply encouraged me. They reminded me that the key to any relationship—whether it be a friendship, dating relationship, or marriage—is putting God first. When we build on that unbreakable foundation, the relationship is strengthened and empowered to endure whatever life brings. The storms will come, but when God is our anchor, the relationship becomes unshakable.

I want to encourage you today: whether you're single, dating, or married, make sure God is the foundation of your relationships. Invite Him into your heart and ask Him to guide you in your interactions with others. Remember, we aren't meant to go it alone or to fight for control. When we align ourselves with God's design and purpose, we can experience the peace and unity that He intended for us all along.

Today's Verse:
"Though one may be overpowered, two can defend themselves.
A cord of three strands is not quickly broken."
—Ecclesiastes 4:12

BUILDING ON THE RIGHT FOUNDATION

"For every house is built by someone, but God is the builder of everything."
—Hebrews 3:4

I **recently went on a date with a man named Bob, and from the start, we had a great connection.** He was funny, kind, and it felt like God had brought us together. As we got to know each other, Bob shared that while he didn't read the Bible or attend church, he was curious about faith. I saw this as an opportunity to encourage him and began praying for him, hoping he would grow in his relationship with God. I shared how prayer had shaped my life and spoke about the Bible as the foundation for spiritual growth.

As time went on, though, I began to feel unsettled. It wasn't that Bob was a bad person—far from it—but something about our connection felt spiritually off. He would say things like, "Take credit for all the hard work you've done." While that might sound empowering, I knew in my heart that everything I have is because of God's grace. Hard work matters, but at the end of the day, it is God who opens doors and provides. This experience led me to reflect on my priorities and my walk with Christ. Faith isn't just something I practice—it's the core of who I am. And when we build our lives, especially our relationships, they need to be rooted in that foundation.

That means honoring God's design for relationships, including waiting until marriage for intimacy. It means seeking Him first in all things, rather than relying solely on human wisdom. It means surrounding ourselves with people who strengthen our faith and encourage us spiritually.

In the end, I realized that while I cared for Bob and wanted to see him grow in faith, he wasn't at a place where he was ready to surrender his heart fully to God. That's something no one can force—it has to be a personal decision. There will be times when we meet people who are searching, and we can pray for them, encourage them, and plant seeds of faith. But at the same time, we need to be mindful of our own walk with God and ensure that our closest relationships draw us closer to Him, not further away.

As 2 Corinthians 6:14 reminds us, "*Do not be yoked together with unbelievers.*" This isn't about judging others—it's about choosing to align our lives with those who share our deepest values and commitment to God. Choosing a spouse is one of the most significant decisions we will ever make, second only to putting our faith in Jesus Christ. If you ever find yourself in a similar situation, I encourage you to pray and seek God's wisdom. He is faithful to lead you toward relationships that strengthen your faith and bring Him glory.

Today's Verse:
"*Do not be misled: 'Bad company corrupts good character.'*"
—1 Corinthians 15:33

PRAISE IS YOUR POWER

"I will bless the Lord at all times; his praise shall continually be in my mouth."

Psalm 34:18

When you're in pain, *praise God.*

When you're happy, *praise God.*

When you're sad, *praise God.*

When you win, *praise God.*

When you lose, *praise God.*

When you're broke, *praise God.*

When you're financially stable, *praise God.*

When you achieve success, *praise God.*

No matter what, **PRAISE GOD.**

Dear Friend: Praise changes things. It lifts our eyes above the temporal and reminds us of the eternal. When we praise God, even in the valley, it strengthens our spirit and realigns our hearts with His promises.

Praise is a declaration of trust, saying, *"Jesus, I know You are bigger than this situation."* Whether you're at your highest or lowest, praise becomes a weapon that defeats fear, discouragement, and doubt.

It's hard to praise the Lord when we are suffering or in pain, but that's often the moment when breakthrough happens. Do not give up! No matter where you find yourself today, make praise your response, because Jesus is always worthy.

Today's Verse:
"Let everything that has breath praise the Lord.
Praise the Lord."
—Psalm 150:6

GOD RESTORES

"At that time I will gather you; at that time I will bring you home. I will give you honor and praise among all the peoples of the earth when I restore your fortunes before your very eyes," says the Lord.
Zephaniah 3:20

There are seasons in life where we feel scattered, broken, or forgotten—times when it seems like our lives are falling apart and nothing is going as planned. In those moments, it's easy to wonder if God is still working, if He still has a purpose for us, and if restoration is even possible.

But God's promise in Zephaniah 3:20 speaks directly to those feelings of uncertainty. This verse is a beautiful reminder of God's heart for His people: He promises to gather us, to bring us home, and to restore what was lost. God assures us that, in His timing, He will not only restore our fortunes but also give us honor and praise among the nations.

Maybe you're in a season where it feels like you've lost something important—maybe a relationship, an opportunity, or even a sense of purpose. God's word in Zephaniah reminds us that He is a God of restoration. He is gathering the pieces of your life, and He's working behind the scenes to bring you into a place of blessing and honor. His promise is not just to restore what was lost, but to do it **before your very eyes**—in a way that will leave no doubt that His hand was at work.

The key is to trust God's timing. I know it's hard when you're longing for quick fixes and immediate answers, but let me encourage you—God's timing is perfect, and when He moves, it will be in ways beyond anything you could imagine. He won't just restore what's broken; He'll create something even more beautiful and purposeful from it.

As you wait for His promise of restoration, hold tight to this truth: **God is faithful.** He has not forgotten you, and when the time is right, His plans for you will unfold in ways that will leave you in awe. Stay strong, and trust that His perfect timing will bring the breakthrough you've been praying for.

Today's Verse:
"And the God of all grace, who called you to His eternal glory in Christ, after you have suffered a little while, will Himself restore you and make you strong, firm, and steadfast."
—1 Peter 5:10

EMBRACING YOUR NEW SEASON

"See, I am doing a new thing! Now it springs up;
do you not perceive it? I am making a way in the
wilderness and streams in the wasteland."

Isaiah 43:19

There's something special about new beginnings. There's a sense of excitement, hope, and anticipation for what's to come. Whether it's starting a new job, moving to a new place, or stepping into a new season of life, new beginnings carry the promise of fresh opportunities and untapped potential.

God is always at work in our lives, bringing forth new things, even in places that once seemed barren or hopeless.

Today, I believe the Lord is speaking a word of newness over His people. He is calling us to let go of the past—the disappointments, the failures, and even the successes—and to embrace the new things He is doing. Isaiah 43:19 reminds us that God is making a way in the wilderness and streams in the wasteland. Where there once was dryness and confusion, God is bringing clarity and refreshing. He's not just doing the same old thing; He's creating something entirely new in your life.

It's easy to let fear or uncertainty creep in when facing the unknown, but remember that God has already gone before you.

In Jeremiah 29:11, He promises, "*For I know the plans I have for you*," declares the Lord, "*plans to prosper you and not to harm you, plans to give you hope and a future.*"

God's plans are full of hope, purpose, and goodness, even if we don't see the full picture yet. The excitement of new beginnings comes not from knowing every detail but from trusting Jesus who holds our future in His hands.

As you embark on this new chapter in your life, invite God into every step. Ask Him to guide your decisions, open the right doors, and align your heart with His will. The joy of a new beginning is knowing that God is in control and that His plans for you are good.

Today's Verse:
"*He who was seated on the throne said, 'I am making every-thing new!' Then He said, 'Write this down, for these words are trustworthy and true.'*"
—Revelation 21:5

HEAVEN'S ENCOURAGEMENT

"Look at the birds of the air; they do not sow or reap or store away in barns, and yet your heavenly Father feeds them. Are you not much more valuable than they?"

Matthew 6:26

This morning, I went for a run, and let's just say—it was a struggle. My legs felt heavy, my breath was short, and as I approached a steep hill, I seriously considered throwing in the towel and power-walking my way to the top. But right as I was about to slow down, a bright red cardinal swooped across my path, like a little messenger straight from heaven.

In that moment, something shifted. My exhaustion didn't magically disappear, but a fresh burst of energy kicked in. My legs felt lighter, my stride picked up, and before I knew it, I was pushing forward with new determination. I couldn't help but whisper, "Thanks, God!"

That cardinal was more than just a bird—it was a reminder that God sees me, that He's with me, and that I don't have to run this race (literally or figuratively) on my own. I've shared before how cardinals have always been a special God-wink in my life, little reassurances from the Holy Spirit that say, "*I'm here. Keep going.*"

Before my run, I had prayed—nothing fancy, just a simple, "Lord, help me today." And I truly believe that prayer opened my heart to receive His strength in that moment. God isn't just in the big, life-changing moments; He's in the small, everyday ones too.

Jesus often spoke through nature—He pointed to the birds as reminders of God's care, just as Solomon did in Ecclesiastes. God is always speaking. The real question is, *are we listening? Do we take the time to look up from our phones and notice Him?*

So, here's your reminder today: God is near. He's cheering you on. He's sending you signs—even in the smallest, most unexpected ways. Keep your eyes open, and don't be afraid to pick up the pace.

Today's Verse:
"I know every bird in the mountains,
and the insects in the fields are mine."
—Psalm 50:11

LOVE WITHOUT CONDITIONS

"Whoever oppresses a poor man insults his Maker,
but he who is generous to the needy honors him."

Proverbs 14:31

L ast night, I was heading into Panera to meet a friend for dinner when a man suddenly approached me out of the dark and asked, "Got any change?" I paused for a moment and asked him what he needed the money for. He replied, "To get something to eat." Without a second thought, I asked for his name and invited him to join me for dinner. His name was Ian, and he agreed.

As we walked inside, the bright lights revealed his bruised and battered face. Ian shared that he had recently been beaten up and robbed, and had just been released from the hospital. I wasn't afraid; instead, my heart ached for him. He thanked me multiple times, smiling the entire time. It felt good to help, but I made sure to let Ian know that he should thank God, not me. The money wasn't mine—it was the Lord's, and I was simply grateful for the chance to provide him with a hot meal.

Reflecting on this moment, I realized how much my heart has changed since becoming a follower of Christ. In the past, I would have been quick to judge the homeless, making comments like, "Why don't they just get a job?" The reality is, we never know what brought a person to where they are, so we can offer them compassion.

God has opened my eyes to the fact that I have no idea what these people have gone through. Ian had been beaten and robbed, and he didn't turn down my offer of food. Not every homeless person is seeking money for drugs—many are genuinely hungry and hurting. You won't know their story unless you take the time to help them without judgment, just as Jesus helps us without hesitation or conditions.

Even when we make poor choices or find ourselves in messy situations, God doesn't turn His back on us. He doesn't say, "I told you so, now deal with this on your own." Instead, He shows up in our lives with love, grace, and provision, asking for nothing in return. That's the example we should follow as believers—offering unconditional love and help, not judgment.

I hope that if I were hungry and in need, someone would stop to help me, just as I helped Ian. That's what it means to live by the golden rule: treating others the way we want to be treated. I pray that Ian feels God's presence in his life, that he knows how deeply loved he is by his Heavenly Father.

When I look at Ian, I don't see someone homeless or broken—I see a fellow sibling in Christ.

Reflection: Who in your life might need help, love, and kindness today? Sometimes, it's as simple as listening, offering a kind word, or lending a hand. Like Jesus, let's love and help others without hesitation.

Today's Verse:
"Give to the one who asks you, and do not turn away from the one who wants to borrow from you."
—Matthew 5:42

I LOVE YOU, JESUS!

"I love you, Lord, my strength."

Psalm 18:1

David's life was marked by battles, betrayals, and seasons of deep distress.** He knew what it meant to run for his life, to be rejected, and to wait on God in the wilderness. Yet, in Psalm 18, after years of hardship, he opens with a declaration of love:**"I love You, Lord, my strength."**

This is the only time in all of Scripture that this particular phrase for love is used in addressing God. It carries a deep emotional intensity, almost like a longing embrace. David wasn't simply acknowledging God's goodness—he was clinging to Him, expressing a love that had been forged in the fire of suffering.

A LOVE SHAPED IN THE STRUGGLE

Psalm 18 was written after God had delivered David from the hands of Saul and all his enemies (2 Samuel 22). This wasn't a casual psalm—it was a **song of survival**.

David had been hunted by Saul, betrayed by those he trusted, and forced to live in caves while the very people he had once served turned against him. At times, his future looked hopeless. Yet, in all of it, he discovered something profound:

God was his rock. His fortress. His deliverer. His strength.

David didn't just love God because his life was spared. He loved Him because, even in the darkest places, God had never left him. When people turned their backs, God remained. When fear crept in, God gave him courage.

By the time he wrote this psalm, David's love for God had matured beyond surface-level gratitude. It was the love of a man who had wrestled, waited, and won—not by his own strength, but by the faithfulness of God. David wasn't just saying, "I love You, Lord."

He was saying:

- **"I hold onto You with all I am."**

- **"You are my lifeline."**

- **"I love You in a way that comes from dependence. I would not be here without You."**◻

Today's Verse:
Jesus replied: 'Love the Lord your God with all your heart and with all your soul and with all your mind.'
—Matthew 22:37

GOD IS WATCHING OVER HIS WORD

The word of the Lord came to me: "What do you see, Jeremiah?" "I see the branch of an almond tree," I replied.

Jeremiah 1:11

Let's talk about Jeremiah—a young man called by God at a time when his people were heading straight for disaster. Judah had turned away from the Lord, and God needed a prophet to warn them and call them back. But Jeremiah? He wasn't exactly jumping at the chance. He was young, insecure, and hesitant. Sound familiar? Maybe you've felt like God has put something on your heart, but you're not sure you're the right person for the job. Maybe you feel unqualified or unsure of what He's saying.

Then God does something interesting—He asks Jeremiah, *"What do you see?"* God wasn't just testing his eyesight; He was training him to recognize divine messages in the everyday. Jeremiah sees an almond branch. It's a simple image, but it carries a powerful message.

Here's the cool part: In Hebrew, the word for "**almond tree**" sounds almost identical to the word for "**watching**." So God was using this image to say, "*I am watching over My word to fulfill it.*" That's a promise. Just like the almond tree is the first to bloom in spring, God was saying, "*My plans are already in motion. What I have spoken will come to pass.*" Now let's bring it home—how does this relate to you?

God often speaks to us in ways that seem small at first:

- A **Bible verse** that keeps coming up in different places.

- A **story from Scripture** that sticks with you.

- A **dream** that lingers in your mind.

- A **word or phrase** that won't leave your heart.

- A **cardinal** that dances before your eyes.

When that happens, pay attention. God is asking, "*What do you see?*" because He wants to show you something deeper. Maybe you're waiting for a promise to come true, wondering if God still sees you. Maybe you're questioning if He's really moving in your life. Jeremiah's vision is a reminder: God is watching over His word, and it will happen in the right season.

So here's your challenge: Start writing things down. When you notice a repeated scripture, a dream, or a pattern, keep track of it. Pray over it. Reflect on it. Sometimes we don't recognize God's voice because we don't take time to listen. But when we do, our faith grows, and we start seeing His hand at work in ways we never expected.

Today's Verse:
"The Lord said to me, 'You have seen correctly, for I am watching to see that my word is fulfilled.'"
—Jeremiah 1:12

A SEAT AT THE TABLE

"The LORD is my light and my salvation; whom shall I fear? The LORD is the stronghold of my life; of whom shall I be afraid?"

Psalm 27:1

Recently I found myself sitting down with a representative from a women's entrepreneur group in Nashville. It was a surreal moment for me—a seat at the table with leaders ready to scale their businesses. After years of struggling and pushing through challenges, I was finally sitting in a profitable position to join this group. But as exciting as it was, I knew I had to be cautious. I didn't want to align myself with a "material-driven" mindset, where money becomes the ultimate goal. While money isn't inherently bad and can be used for good, I don't ever want to serve it. I want to serve God. As Jesus says in Matthew 6:24, *"You cannot serve both God and money."*

During the conversation, the rep asked me about my business. I smiled and told her, "I am Jesus Christ employed." She seemed surprised by my response, even smirking a little. I explained that I wouldn't be profitable without the Lord guiding and providing for me. About 30 minutes into our talk, I shared a brief version of how God saved my life one dark night in my apartment in Michigan in 2018—before I started my business in 2019. To my surprise, she was shocked by my story, and I could see her faith grow as she asked more questions. It was an unexpected opportunity to share my testimony, and I realized that God had orchestrated that moment for His glory.

Later that same day, two clients canceled their appointments, and I heard God say, "Now. Today is the time to share your testimony." So, I sat down, filmed my story, and on February 23rd, 2023, I shared the tragedy and triumph God had led me through. By March 3rd, the YouTube video was uploaded and sent out in my newsletter. The amazing part? I didn't feel any anxiety sharing my past, struggles, and redemption because I knew God was in control.

This was a difficult decision—a leap of faith—but it was possible because of Christ. I trusted that God was guiding me and that He would use my testimony for His purposes. In sharing it, I found peace. Jesus tells us in John 14:27, "*Peace I leave with you; my peace I give you. I do not give to you as the world gives. Do not let your hearts be troubled and do not be afraid.*"

What difficult decisions are you facing today that require great faith? Maybe it's a conversation you need to have, a step you need to take, or a decision you've been avoiding. Or, perhaps you have a testimony to share with more people. I want to encourage you—God can replace your anxiety with His peace when you surrender control to Him. After all, He is the Prince of Peace.

Today's Verse:
"*As the body without the spirit is dead, so faith without deeds is dead.*" —James 2:26

52 DAYS TO CHANGE EVERYTHING

"So the wall was completed....in fifty-two days."
Nehemiah 6:15

Did you know God can change your life in 52 days? In the book of Nehemiah, we see a powerful example of how much can change in a short period of time when we step into God's plan with faith and determination. Nehemiah was called by God to rebuild the broken walls of Jerusalem—a task that seemed impossible. The walls had been in ruins for decades, and the people were discouraged. Yet, with God's help and guidance, Nehemiah led the people to complete the entire wall in just 52 days.

What's significant about those 52 days isn't just the physical rebuilding of the wall, but the spiritual renewal and hope that came with it. Nehemiah's story reminds us that no matter what we are facing—whether we're athletes pushing through rigorous training, students overwhelmed with studies, professionals juggling work and life, or retirees wondering what's next—God can work miracles in our lives in a short amount of time. The key is our willingness to step out in faith, trust His timing, and keep our eyes on the goal He has set before us.

The Lord is saying to you today, "*I can restore, rebuild, and renew what feels broken in your life—often faster than you think. Don't be discouraged by the obstacles in front of you. I am with you, just as I was with Nehemiah. What seems impossible to man is possible with Me. I can bring change, healing, and breakthrough in your life in a short season. Trust My timing.*"

Before Nehemiah took on the monumental task of rebuilding the wall of Jerusalem, he didn't rush into action. Instead, Nehemiah spent time in prayer, fasting, and seeking the Lord's guidance. Nehemiah 1:4 tells us, "*When I heard these things, I sat down and wept. For some days I mourned and fasted and prayed before the God of heaven.*" His heart was broken over the state of God's people, but instead of immediately jumping into action, Nehemiah sought the Lord first.

As you consider embarking on your own 52-day challenge—whether it's a personal goal, a spiritual endeavor, or a project you feel called to pursue—take a lesson from Nehemiah. Don't rush into action without first sitting with the Lord. Pray, fast, and intercede for the guidance and wisdom you'll need. Spend time in God's presence, aligning your heart with His. The success of your journey depends on this foundation.

Today's Verse:
They were all trying to frighten us, thinking, 'Their hands will get too weak for the work, and it will not be completed.' But I prayed, 'Now strengthen my hands.'
—Nehemiah 6:9

FASTING FOR BREAKTHROUGH

"When you fast, do not look somber as the hypocrites do, for they disfigure their faces to show others they are fasting. Truly I tell you, they have received their reward in full."

Matthew 6:16

As a registered dietitian, I spend a lot of time teaching people how to fuel their bodies properly, emphasizing the importance of balanced nutrition. Food is a gift from God—something designed to nourish and sustain us. However, as a servant of Christ, I've also come to understand that there are moments when God calls us to lay aside physical nourishment so we can experience a deeper spiritual filling.

Fasting is not a diet, nor is it about restricting food for the sake of health or weight loss. It is a spiritual *discipline*—one that Jesus Himself modeled. Before beginning His ministry, He fasted for 40 days in the wilderness (Matthew 4:1-2).

Jesus didn't do this to punish His body but to draw closer to the Father and prepare for what was ahead. And when teaching His disciples, He didn't say *if* they fasted—but *when*—revealing that fasting was expected as part of a faithful life. In Matthew 6:16-18, Jesus gave clear instructions on how to fast in a way that honors God, showing us that this practice remains a vital pathway to intimacy with Him. Here are some key points to remember about fasting.

Fasting is Private and Personal

Jesus made it clear that fasting is not meant to be a performance. It is not about proving your holiness to others or making yourself suffer for God's approval. Instead, fasting is an intimate act of *worship*—a private time between you and the Lord. When we fast, we aren't just skipping meals; we are choosing to feast on His presence.

The world teaches us that hunger is something to avoid, that we must satisfy every craving. But fasting teaches us something different: our deepest hunger can only be satisfied in Christ.

Let the Lord Lead Your Fast

As a dietitian, I tell people to listen to their bodies. **As a believer, I tell people to listen to the Holy Spirit.** God will tell you how long to fast and what kind of fast to do. Some may fast for a day, others for longer. Some may do a full fast, while others may fast from distractions like social media. The key is obedience, not length.

Fasting is an invitation, not an obligation. It is not something we "have to" do, but something we "get to" do—a privilege to grow closer to God. And in our hunger, we are reminded that Jesus alone is the true Bread of Life, the only One who truly satisfies.

Today's Verse:
"So we fasted and petitioned our God about this,
and he answered our prayer."
—Ezra 8:23

SHINE WHERE YOU ARE

"You are the light of the world. A town built on a hill
cannot be hidden."

Matthew 5:14

O ne day, while working from the lobby of a local YMCA, **an employee turned to me and said, "Wendi, I hate this job. I just hand out towels and spray bottles, and I feel like I have no impact."** Her frustration was real, and I could sense her discouragement. Many often overlook the significance of our daily tasks, especially when they seem small or mundane. I gently reminded her that her job was incredibly important, both in the Kingdom of God and to the people around her. Her smile was the first thing people saw when they walked in, and for some, it could be the only positive interaction they'd experience that day.

In the Kingdom, no task is too small. When we do the "little things" with love and a positive attitude, we allow God to work through us in ways we can't always see.

After our conversation, she smiled brightly at the next few people who walked in, and one person responded, **"Wow, I needed that encouragement today."** It was a reminder of the power of choosing to be extraordinary in ordinary circumstances.

So, I ask you today—how can you shine the light of Jesus through your actions and thoughts in your current role, no matter how small it seems? Whether you're a teacher, single parent, an office worker, a coach, or stay at home parent doing many jobs. The Bible tells us in Colossians 3:23, **"Whatever you do, work at it with all your heart, as working for the Lord."** When you approach your tasks with this mindset, the ordinary becomes extraordinary, and God can use even the smallest acts to make a big impact. Jesus washed feet and so should we!

Today's Verse:
"Let your light shine before others, that they may see your good deeds and glorify your Father in heaven."
—Matthew 5:16

GOD'S PLANS ARE GREATER

"For I know the plans I have for you," declares the Lord, "plans to prosper you and not to harm you, plans to give you hope and a future."

Jeremiah 29:11

Jeremiah 29:11 was one of the first verses that truly impacted me in my walk with the Lord. Back in 2012, when I had just discovered my faith and began building my relationship with Christ, this verse became a source of hope and comfort as I navigated uncertainties and challenges. It reminded me that no matter what I faced—a failed exam, a broken relationship, or an unjust circumstance—God had a plan for my life. A plan that nothing and no one could alter. Even when I couldn't see the next step, I knew God was walking with me, and nothing could harm me to the point where I couldn't endure.

Have you ever found yourself reciting this verse? It's one of those promises from God that has the power to anchor us in the midst of life's storms. When the future feels uncertain, and our present circumstances seem overwhelming, we can hold onto the truth that God's plans are for our good. He promises us hope and a future, even when our situation seems hopeless. The same God who had a plan for His people during Jeremiah's time has a plan for you today. He sees your struggles, your fears, and your uncertainties, and He is actively working to bring good out of every situation.

It's easy to feel lost or anxious when we can't see what's coming next, but that's where faith steps in. God invites us to trust Him, not only in the good times but also in the hardest moments. Even when our plans fall apart, His remains steady. The storms in life are not meant to break us but to shape us. With God by our side, we can remain calm, knowing that He is in control. As we trust in His timing and surrender our own understanding, we open the door for Him to turn our mess into a miracle.

The Lord is saying to you today, *"I know the plans I have for you. Even when you can't see them, trust Me. Your struggles are not wasted, and I am working behind the scenes to bring about a future filled with hope."* Sometimes the very misery we experience becomes a ministry down the road, as God redeems our pain and uses it to help others. He turns our tests into testimonies, and what seems like a setback is often a setup for something greater.

Today's Challenge:
Take a moment to reflect on a time when things didn't go according to your plans, yet looking back, you can see how God was working through it. Write down one area of your life where you feel uncertain or discouraged right now. Then, pray over it, surrendering it to God and declaring Jeremiah 29:11 over your situation. **Choose to trust that God's plans are good, even when you can't see them yet.**

DIVINE REDIRECTION

"Commit to the Lord whatever you do, and He will establish your plans."

Proverbs 16:3

We've all sketched out dreams for our future, only to watch life unfold in unexpected ways. Maybe you mapped out your education, your career path, even the city you thought you'd call home. But when you look back now, you might find yourself smiling—or even laughing—at how different reality turned out. That's because, no matter how carefully we plan, it is God who ultimately establishes our steps.

I had grand plans of becoming a dietitian, working in corporate wellness, or with professional athletes at a prestigious hospital. Yet, none of those plans panned out—and I'm so grateful they didn't! Instead of the path I envisioned, I became a small business owner, moving countless times in just over 30 years of life. And you know what? It's been better than anything I could have imagined! Through the twists and turns, I've met amazing people, grown in my faith, and learned to rely on God in ways I never would have if I'd stayed on my original path. This journey has been far richer and more fulfilling than the plans I thought I wanted. Thank God for His divine redirection.

We often get stuck trying to figure out every detail of our lives, thinking we need to have it all mapped out. But here's the truth: God's plans are so much greater than our own. When we commit our ways to Him, He doesn't just follow along with our ideas—He establishes our steps, bringing us into alignment with His purpose. If you're feeling uncertain or confused about your next steps, remember that our God is not a God of confusion but a God of truth and light.

We may not always understand the *why* behind the changes in our plans, but we can trust that God's redirection is always for our good. His plans are perfect, filled with purpose, and designed to lead us to a life we couldn't even dream of on our own. So, if you find yourself questioning where to go or what to do, commit your plans to the Lord. Let go of trying to control every detail and allow Him to guide your steps. In time, you'll look back and see that His way was always better, filled with blessings, growth, and fulfillment beyond what you could have imagined.

Today's Verse:
"Many are the plans in a person's heart, but it is the Lord's purpose that prevails."
—Proverbs 19:21

CARRYING EACH OTHER'S BURDENS

"Carry each other's burdens, and in this way, you will fulfill the law of Christ."

Galatians 6:2

When I met David, he was staring blankly at apples in the produce aisle at my local Kroger. His wife of 49 years had recently passed away, and he was now navigating life alone. Even the simple task of grocery shopping felt overwhelming since it's something his wife had always done. God knew we both needed to cross paths that evening.

I had just finished a long day meeting with clients and was running on empty. In fact, I wore a ball cap and hood to send the signal that I wasn't interested in engaging with anyone—a rarity for me. But as I overheard David express his uncertainty about which apples to choose, something stirred in me. Despite my exhaustion, I turned my cart around and introduced myself.

"I'm Wendi, and I happen to be a registered dietitian and apple connoisseur," I said. "I can help you find the best apples and anything else you need." In our conversation, he shared that he had lost his wife. "I'm so sorry," I said. "I can't imagine that pain, but I know that God loves you, and she is in Heaven with the Lord."

We talked for about 20 minutes, and in that time, God reminded me of something powerful: we are called to carry each other's burdens. In that simple act of helping David, I realized God was empowering me with the energy and strength to be a light in his life, even when I felt I had nothing left to give. God gave me the words and the compassion to meet David where he was.

Sometimes we think we have to be at our best to help others, but God meets us in our weakness and fills us with His strength. He often places people in our lives for a reason—because He knows we can carry each other through the hard moments. This is how we live out the love of Christ.

Prayer:

Lord, thank You for the opportunities You give me to carry the burdens of others. Help me to see those around me who are hurting, and give me the strength and courage to reach out, even when I feel weary. May I be a vessel of Your love and compassion, fulfilling the law of Christ in every interaction.

Amen.

HONORING GOD WITH YOUR BODY

"You are not your own; you were bought at a price.
Therefore honor God with your bodies."
1 Corinthians 6:19-20

As a dietitian and certified sports nutritionist, I've spent years exploring how food and nutrition impact our bodies. Many assume my work is limited to crafting meal plans or encouraging high school athletes to eat their veggies, but it goes far deeper. It's about recognizing that our bodies are sacred creations of God made in His image to point others to Christ! Caring for our physical health is not just a practical necessity but a spiritual act of stewardship.

The Bible calls us to treat our bodies—and the bodies of others—with love, respect, and compassion. Just as we would tend to a physical church building, keeping it clean and in good repair for worship, we are called to nurture our bodies. This stewardship extends beyond vanity or appearances; it is an act of gratitude and reverence for the gift of life God has given us.

Just as we wouldn't defile a physical church with something damaging, we must be vigilant about what we allow into our bodies. Substance abuse, addiction, and harmful habits not only affect our physical health but also hinder our ability to live fully in the Spirit and hear God's voice clearly. You can't hear God's voice if you are sick, depressed, and unhealthy because of gluttony or listening to lies of the enemy.

God has used my work to touch lives in unexpected ways, reminding people of His love and the importance of honoring Him through their choices. What may have started as a simple conversation about nutrition has often turned into a moment of healing and hope on a much deeper level. When we commit our work to the Lord, He multiplies its impact—reaching hearts in ways we may never fully see or understand.

Remember: you can't pour into others if you're running on empty. Take care of yourself—mind, body, and spirit—so you can be a vessel of God's love to those around you.

Today's Verse:
"Dear friend, I pray that you may enjoy good health and that all may go well with you, even as your soul is getting along well."
—3 John 1:2

THE WELL THAT NEVER RUNS DRY

"Whoever drinks the water I give them will never thirst. Indeed, the water I give them will become in them a spring of water welling up to eternal life."
John 4:14

The story of the woman at the well in John 4 is one of redemption, grace, and purpose. When Jesus met her, she was burdened by her past, coming to the well in the heat of the day to avoid the shame and judgment of others. She had been married five times and was living with a man who wasn't her husband. Yet, in the midst of her brokenness, Jesus did not condemn her. Instead, He offered her living water—something far greater than the physical water she came to draw.

What's remarkable is that despite her past, Jesus saw her potential. He revealed Himself to her as the Messiah, making her one of the first people to know who He truly was. Her encounter with Jesus transformed her life, and she became an immediate witness to others, running back to her village to tell everyone about the Man who *"told me everything I ever did"* (John 4:29). Because of her testimony, many from her town believed in Jesus.

This story is a powerful reminder that no matter our past, God can use us for His purpose. The woman at the well could have been defined by her mistakes, her failed relationships, or her shame, but Jesus saw her differently. He saw her as someone worthy of love, redemption, and purpose. In the same way, God sees past our mistakes and shortcomings. Jesus invites us into His plan, offering grace and the chance to be a vessel of His love to others.

You may feel like your past disqualifies you from being used by God, but Jesus is not concerned with where you've been—He's focused on where He's taking you. The Lord doesn't waste anything; even the broken parts of your story can be used for His glory. When we come to Jesus, He fills us with living water, refreshing our souls and equipping us to fulfill His purpose for our lives.

Action Item: Find a quiet space and slowly read through John 4:1–42 today, picturing yourself walking toward the well. Imagine going in the heat of the day, weighed down by shame or burdens you've carried. As you step into the story, invite the Holy Spirit to uncover any places in your heart still thirsty for healing. Don't rush. Let Jesus meet with you and write down anything He places on your heart. Then, in the weeks to come, revisit what you wrote and look for signs of how He's been healing and leading you. Trust that even if you don't see it right away, living water is already flowing beneath the surface.

Today's Verse:
"Therefore, if anyone is in Christ, the new creation has come: The old has gone, the new is here!"
—2 Corinthians 5:17

THE BLESSING OF GIVING

"It is more blessed to give than to receive."

Acts 20:35

When Jesus teaches that it is more blessed to give than to receive, He invites us into a deeper joy rooted in reflecting God's heart. There is something uniquely fulfilling about giving—whether it's a material gift, your time, or simply your presence. When we give to someone in need or surprise a loved one with an act of kindness, the joy and gratitude we witness stir something profound within us: a sense of purpose and connection that far exceeds the fleeting happiness of receiving.

Think about a time when you gave selflessly to someone who truly needed it. Perhaps you offered food to a struggling neighbor, gave a thoughtful gift, or simply lent a listening ear to a friend in need. In those moments, you likely felt a deep sense of joy and fulfillment, knowing that your actions reflected God's love. This special kind of joy arises when we align ourselves with Jesus' example of sacrificial love.

Giving doesn't always involve money or material possessions. Often, the most meaningful gifts are our time, attention, and compassion. In a world that encourages us to focus on gaining, Jesus reminds us that true blessing comes when we give. When we give of ourselves, we mirror the heart of God, who gave us the ultimate gift of life and salvation through Jesus. In giving, we become more like Christ, embodying His love and grace.

GIVING CHALLENGE

1. Secret Encourager: Each day this week, ask God to put one person on your heart. Without telling them, pray for them and find a way to bless them anonymously—whether through a note, a small gift, or a kind act. Watch how God uses you behind the scenes.

2. Overflow Note to a Caregiver: The ministry of caregiving is one of the most beautiful and selfless callings, and yet it's often overlooked by the world. This week, take time to write a handwritten note to a caregiver who gives everything they have to care for someone else—a nurse, a hospice worker, a parent of a child with special needs, or a relative caring for a loved one. Tell them specifically how their daily sacrifices, quiet strength, and unseen love reflect the very heart of Jesus. Remind them that even when no one applauds, Heaven is standing and cheering them on. Your words could be the living water they need to keep going.

3. Bless a Child: Speak life into a child. Tell them something specific and encouraging about how God made them special. Even a simple word of love can plant seeds of confidence and faith that last a lifetime.

Today's Verse:
"*A generous person will prosper;
whoever refreshes others will be refreshed.*"
—Proverbs 11:25

THE BEGINNING OF WISDOM

"The fear of the Lord is the beginning of knowledge,
but fools despise wisdom and instruction."

Proverbs 1:7

L et's get straight to it—how often do you truly seek God's wisdom *first*? Not as an afterthought, not after everything else has failed, but first. The Bible makes it clear: wisdom doesn't begin with age, experience, or intellect. It doesn't come from the world's opinions, self-help strategies, or even personal success. Wisdom begins with one thing—**the fear of the Lord**.

But what does that mean?

The fear of the Lord isn't about terror or dread. It's not the kind of fear that makes you want to run and hide. It's a deep, holy reverence—an awe of who God is, an understanding that He alone holds all power, all knowledge, all truth. It's recognizing that **He is King, and we are not.** That's where wisdom begins—by knowing your place before Him.

Fools Reject What Could Save Them

The second part of this verse is a warning: *"Fools despise wisdom and instruction."* Ouch. No one wants to think of themselves as a fool. But every time we reject God's wisdom—every time we ignore His instruction, brush off correction, or do things our own way—we are walking in foolishness.

Think about it. How many times has God warned you through His Word, through a sermon, through the voice of a godly friend, and yet, you ignored it? Maybe you thought, **"I've got this. I know what I'm doing."** But then, later, you found yourself in a mess you could have avoided.

That's what happens when we reject the fear of the Lord. We end up relying on our own understanding, and that always leads to confusion, regret, and unnecessary pain.

A Different Kind of Fear

The enemy wants you to live in fear—but the wrong kind of fear. He wants you to fear failure, fear people's opinions, fear the unknown. **However, the only fear that brings life is the fear of the Lord.**

When you truly fear God, you don't have to fear anything else. When you revere Him above all, you stop making decisions based on fear of rejection, fear of lack, or fear of the future. Instead, you start making choices based on trust—trust in the One who sees everything you can't. That's real wisdom.

Today's Verse:
"If any of you lacks wisdom, you should ask God, who gives generously to all without finding fault, and it will be given to you"
—James 1:5

DAY 123

WHEN IT'S TIME TO MOVE ON

"I waited patiently for the LORD; he turned to me and heard my cry."

Psalm 40:1

Have you ever felt trapped, stuck, or confined with no way out? The good news is that God always provides a way, even when you can't see it and feel imprisoned. When I was in an emotionally abusive, controlling and toxic relationship, I felt hopeless. *I felt trapped, unsure of how to leave let alone keep living.* I felt ashamed to be stuck in something many warned me about including my own intuition and the Holy Spirit. I struggled to muster the strength to crawl out of the dark pit that almost took my life. But the Holy Spirit said, "Let's GO". I finally took hold of God's hand and He pulled me out of the darkness that almost became my demise.

Countless times I prayed for God to take my life because I couldn't see a way forward. I even prayed for God to change the man I was with or to change me, but He didn't. God was pruning me in ways I couldn't yet understand. He knew what I could handle, and when the time was right, He gave me the strength and spiritual armor I needed to escape. I didn't know it then, but God's delays were not His denials.

As I prayed and waited, God was working behind the scenes, preparing me for the day I would leave and never look back. That experience taught me something profound: when it's not God's time, you can't force it. **But when it is God's time, nothing can stop it.** I took action, created an escape plan, and trusted that no matter what evil came my way, God had me covered. When the time came, the Lord walked me out of that relationship, and we never looked back! God will clear the path and HE will cover you.

Jesus allows challenging circumstances to create crusaders for Christ. My life is living, walking, breathing proof of that. If God can take my mess and turn it into the miracle you are reading right now, think about what He can do with you and your life! Today is the first day of your future. Get moving.

Today's Verse:
*"The LORD is good to those who wait for him,
to the soul who seeks him."*
—Lamentations 3:25

FINDING JOY IN TRIALS

"And my God will meet all your needs according to the riches of his glory in Christ Jesus."
Philippians 4:19

Someone reading this is standing in the middle of transition. God is stirring your heart to do something unfamiliar. You may be wrestling with questions like, "Why now?" or "How will I make it?" But let me reassure you: you are not lost—you're being led.

As I sit here in my new home in Dallas, Texas, I sense peace in the atmosphere. It's the kind of peace that comes when you know you're exactly where God wants you to be. Just like you, I've faced seasons of uncertainty. When God called me to move to Nashville in October 2021, I didn't know a single person. He said, "Go." And I went. Jesus met me there. He provided. He surrounded me with the kind of community that only He could orchestrate.

Throughout the Bible, we see how God moves His people when He's ready to do something new *in* them and *through* them. Abraham left his home without knowing where he was going. The Israelites journeyed through the wilderness under a cloud by day and fire by night. Even Jesus moved from place to place, always led by the Spirit, always on assignment.

You are no different. The stirring you feel? It's not random. It's a holy summons.

You may not have all the answers, but you have *The Answer*—and God is faithful. If He's calling you to step out, He's also preparing provision, protection, and people ahead of you. You won't have to force your way in—Jesus will open the right doors. You won't have to strive to be seen—He already sees you. And you don't have to worry about how it will all come together—because He's already in your future, weaving the pieces together.

Today's Verse:
"The Lord will guide you always..."
—Isaiah 58:11

DAY 125

BUILDING WISELY

"The wise woman builds her house, but with her own hands the foolish one tears hers down."

Proverbs 14:1

Have you ever thought about the kind of "house" you're building? Not just the walls you live in, but your life—your relationships, your faith, your character, and the impact you leave on others. Every choice you make today is either strengthening or weakening that foundation. Proverbs 14:1 reminds us of this incredible truth: a wise person builds with care, but foolishness can tear it all down. The question is, which one will you be?

Here's the good news: God has given you everything you need to build wisely. You don't have to rely on your own strength or figure it all out alone. Wisdom starts when you invite Him into your daily life—when you pause and ask for His guidance before speaking, acting, or making decisions. Think about the relationships in your life: are you using your words to encourage and uplift, or are you unintentionally tearing down with criticism or impatience? Every word, every action, is a brick in the house you're building.

The truth is, we've all made mistakes and knocked down parts of our "house" along the way. Maybe you've let pride, fear, or frustration pull you off track. But here's the amazing thing about God: He's in the restoration business. He can rebuild anything we've torn down, no matter how broken it may seem. All He asks is that we surrender it to Him. So, if there's a mess in your life right now, don't lose heart. Bring it to God, and watch Him turn it into something beautiful.

Today, step out with intention. Speak life into your relationships. Choose kindness over frustration. Take time to pray and ask God to show you how to build with wisdom. You are creating something far greater than you realize—a life that reflects God's love and invites others to experience it too. Start building wisely, brick by brick, with Him leading the way. You've got this, and God's got you!

Today's Verse:
"By wisdom a house is built, and through understanding it is established; through knowledge its rooms are filled with rare and beautiful treasures."
—Proverbs 24:3–4

CHOOSING COMPASSION OVER JUDGMENT

> "Do not judge, or you too will be judged. For in the
> same way you judge others, you will be judged, and
> with the measure you use, it will be measured to
> you."
>
> Matthew 7:1-2

I used to say things I'm not proud of—harsh words like, "I can't believe how many homeless people sit on the sidewalk begging for money. They're perfectly capable of getting a job like the rest of us." In my early twenties, walking out of Minnesota sports venues like the Metrodome or Target Field, I'd feel frustration rise up. I had taken out student loans, worked hard to "become something," and here were people asking me for money. I judged them without a second thought.

At the time, I wasn't walking with God. My heart was hardened, and I didn't yet understand the weight of my words or the condition of my spirit. I thought I was better, more responsible, more worthy. But I see now—I had no idea what led those individuals to where they were. I didn't know their stories, their heartbreaks, their battles. I didn't understand that by judging them, I was inviting judgment upon myself (Matthew 7:1-2).

Life is unpredictable. None of us are immune to hardship. The Bible calls us to humility, not pride—to compassion, not condemnation.

A decade later, I find myself in a completely different posture. I now carry food and water in my car to give to the homeless in various communities. But this time, I don't just hand things out—I look them in the eye. I speak to them with honor. I pray for them. Why? Because God has softened my heart. He showed me that love changes things far more than judgment ever could.

If you've ever caught yourself thinking like I once did, I invite you to let God work on your heart, too. You don't need to carry shame—but you do need to allow the Holy Spirit to bring correction and renewal. We are called to *love*, not judge.

Today's Verse:

"For judgment is without mercy to one who has shown no mercy. Mercy triumphs over judgment."
—James 2:13

THE POWER OF YOUR WORDS

"Brothers and sisters, do not slander one another. Anyone who speaks against a brother or sister or judges them speaks against the law and judges it. When you judge the law, you are not keeping it, but sitting in judgment on it."

James 4:11

Words are powerful. They can breathe life and healing—or sow pain and destruction. With a single sentence, we can lift someone's spirit or crush their heart. That's why Scripture speaks so seriously about the weight our words carry.

When we speak with grace, we don't just change the tone of a conversation—we shift the entire atmosphere. Grace-filled words invite peace, love, and unity into the room. But on the flip side, slander doesn't just hurt feelings—it wounds identities. It's a form of character assassination, and it deeply grieves the heart of God.

Slander isn't just "venting" or being blunt. It's a distortion of truth that tears down instead of builds up. Even those who've wronged us—those who've made mistakes or hurt us—still belong to Jesus. When we speak against them, we're attacking someone He died to redeem.

Here's the hard truth: slander and manipulation are often rooted in the same spirit as witchcraft. They aim to control, divide, and wound. And the enemy loves to use them to break families apart, sabotage friendships, and create walls between people who are supposed to walk in love.

I've been there. I've let frustration guide my words. I've judged loved ones for their choices and made comments that weren't rooted in love but in pride or hurt. And every time, the Holy Spirit gently convicted me. Because we're not called to sit in the seat of judgment—we're called to sit at the table of grace.

Jesus didn't just preach love—He embodied it. Even when He corrected, it was to restore, not to ruin. And that's our standard too.

So let me ask you: is there someone in your life you've spoken harshly about? A family member, coworker, friend, or even a stranger whose choices rubbed you the wrong way?

The enemy is clever. He knows that if he can poison your words, he can poison your relationships—and rob you of the joy God wants you to live in.

But you can take it back. You can choose to speak life. You can repent, forgive, and begin again.

Today's Verse:

"Let no unwholesome word proceed from your mouth, but only such a word as is good for edification according to the need of the moment, so that it will give grace to those who hear."
—Ephesians 4:29

DAY 128

NEW LIFE IN DRY PLACES

"The wilderness and the dry land shall be glad; the desert shall rejoice and blossom like the crocus; it shall blossom abundantly and rejoice with joy and singing."

Isaiah 35:1-2

Today, I believe God is placing this word on my heart because many of us are going through seasons that feel dry and empty. Maybe you're facing a personal struggle, a relationship that feels broken, or a time when your faith feels distant. In these moments, God wants to remind you that He is the one who brings life to the dry places. He is speaking to the areas of your life that feel like deserts and promises that healing, renewal, and growth are coming. Isaiah 35 shows us that God can turn our most hopeless situations into places filled with joy and life.

The prophet Isaiah spoke about a time when barren land would be transformed into something beautiful and abundant. This wasn't just about physical land, but also about what God does in our hearts. The deserts of our lives—where we feel stuck, hopeless, or tired—can be renewed by God's power. When He steps into our situation, even the most difficult circumstances can be turned into places of joy, beauty, and new life.

Isaiah's vision is full of hope. He promises that God will not only restore His people but also transform everything around them. The barren land will blossom, and those who feel weak and weary will find new strength and joy. This points to the coming of Jesus, who would bring ultimate healing and restoration. When Jesus enters our lives, He heals the broken places and renews areas we thought were beyond repair.

Isaiah also talks about the **"highway of holiness"** (Isaiah 35:8), which represents the journey of faith we are on when we follow Jesus. It's a path of freedom and restoration where we can walk safely, guided by God. Even though we may face tough times, God promises to help us along the way. Miracles—both physical and spiritual—happen on this path: the blind will see, the deaf will hear, and the lame will leap for joy (Isaiah 35:5-6). This symbolizes the freedom and wholeness that Jesus brings into our lives.

As you reflect on Isaiah 35 today, ask yourself: *What areas of my life need God's healing and restoration?* Trust that God is working behind the scenes to bring new life, and even in the dry places, He is making all things new. It might not happen instantly, but God is faithful to restore and renew what feels lost or broken. Rejoice, knowing that new life is on the way!

Today's Verse:
"And the ransomed of the LORD shall return
and come to Zion with singing;
everlasting joy shall be upon their heads;
they shall obtain gladness and joy,
and sorrow and sighing shall flee away."
—Isaiah 35:10

GOD HEARS YOUR PRAYERS

*"Then you will call upon me and come and pray to
me, and I will hear you. You will seek me and find me,
when you seek me with all your heart."*

Jeremiah 29:12-13

You are on the verge of a big breakthrough! God sees you.
He sees the way you've been showing up in the face of difficulty, the way you've cared for others even when you struggled
to care for yourself. The Lord hears every prayer, even the ones
whispered in the stillness of the night, and He's telling you that
help is on the way.

The angels of heaven are standing beside you, ready to move at
the command of God. Though the world may seem chaotic and
uncertain, God's promises remain unshaken. His love for you is
unchanging, and His plans for you are still unfolding. You have
not been forgotten, and the prayers you've prayed are not lost.
The waiting season has not been in vain, and you're about to see
blessings beyond what you can imagine.

This is your reminder that when you seek King Jesus with all
your heart, you will find Him. God's presence is near, closer than
you think, and He is working in ways you cannot yet see. You
may feel like you're in the wilderness, but just as He promised in
Isaiah 43:19, He is making a way in the desert and streams in the

wasteland. The path is being cleared, the door is being opened, and what felt impossible is about to become your reality.

Let your heart be filled with hope. Even if everything around you seems unstable, God's plans for you are firm. He is your rock, your refuge, and your source of strength. The breakthrough is coming, and when it does, you will stand in awe of what the Lord has done. So keep seeking Him, keep trusting Him, and watch how He turns your faithfulness into a harvest of blessings. You are on the edge of something new, something powerful, and something good. Do not give up, for God is about to move mightily on your behalf.

Today's Verse:
"See, I am doing a new thing! Now it springs up; do you not perceive it? I am making a way in the wilderness and streams in the wasteland."
—Isaiah 43:19

DON'T GIVE UP—THE HARVEST IS COMING

"Let us not become weary in doing good, for at the proper time we will reap a harvest if we do not give up. Therefore, as we have opportunity, let us do good to all people, especially to those who belong to the family of believers."

Galatians 6:9-10

Galatians 6 reminds us that we will reap what we sow, as long as we don't give up. God sees the seeds you're planting, even if you can't see the harvest yet. When we put our faith in Jesus Christ and allow Him to fill us with His strength and grace, we will not grow weary or dry. And even when we do feel drained, we can trust that God will replenish what has been depleted. Our daily prayer should be: "Lord, *give me the strength and energy to pour into people, but please also pour into me first. Give me the ability to love people with Your heart."*

A few years ago, I had a conversation with a single mom through social media who was going through a rough time. It was a 20-minute chat, and I didn't think much of it after, but I tried to encourage her the best I could. Fast forward two years, and I received a handwritten note from her, thanking me for that conversation. She told me that it lifted her out of a low point and gave her hope. I had no idea at the time that those few minutes would have such a lasting impact, but God knew.

Doing good can feel thankless at times. **But don't stop doing good even when it feels like your efforts are going unnoticed.** God will refill your empty cup. He will bless you beyond measure for your faithfulness.

Galatians 6:9 promises, at the proper time, we *will* reap a harvest if we do not give up. You never know who you're impacting, and in God's perfect timing, the seeds you've sown will bear fruit. Trust that God sees you, and He will bless your efforts.

Today's Verse:

"Therefore, my dear brothers and sisters, stand firm. Let nothing move you. Always give yourselves fully to the work of the Lord, because you know that your labor in the Lord is not in vain." —1 Corinthians 15:58

BOAST IN YOUR WEAKNESS

"If I must boast, I will boast about the things that show I am weak. God knows that I am not lying. He is the God and Father of the Lord Jesus, and he is to be praised forever."

2 Corinthians 11:30-31

When you feel unprepared or uncertain, you're actually standing in the perfect position for God to show His strength. Scripture reminds us that if we're going to boast, let it be in our weakness—because that's where Christ's power rests most beautifully. It's often not in our polished moments, but in our *unfiltered, trembling yes* that Jesus reveals His glory.

All of us have been uniquely crafted with the fingerprints of our Creator. And when we begin to walk in our spiritual gifts from a place of submission, something powerful happens—we are strengthened, but even more importantly, others are lifted.

From a young age, I had the "gift of gab." I always had the ability to speak freely, to connect with strangers, and command a room. But over time, I came to realize—it wasn't just charisma. It was a spiritual gift given by Jesus to fulfill my Kingdom assignments in this world.

When I speak now, I often operate in the gifts of exhortation, evangelism, and leadership. But I've learned something crucial:

when I try to operate in my own strength, it can fall flat or feel prideful. When I yield to the Holy Spirit, He connects me with those who need His love.

In the early days of building my business, I felt the pressure to sell myself—to highlight my strengths, promote my work, and make sure people knew what I could do. But I've since learned to let go of the spotlight. Now, I ask Jesus to be the one who speaks through me. His presence does more than my promotion ever could.

The more I lift up Christ, the more peace I have. I no longer feel the urge to prove myself. When God is the one working through you, He becomes your credibility. The world says: show off your strengths. **Jesus says: boast in your weaknesses.** There's a radical freedom in that.

So let me ask you: *Where in your life can you allow God to show up and show off? Is it in your work? Your relationships? Your daily challenges?* Let Jesus do the heavy lifting. I encourage you to take time with the Lord to fully understand your spiritual gifts so you can harness what the Holy Spirit has already placed within you.

The world doesn't need a perfect performance—it needs the presence of God flowing through you. Some of the most anointed people I know aren't in the spotlight—they're interceding behind the scenes, raising Godly families, or quietly obeying God in places no one sees. We all have a purpose in God's beautiful Kingdom.

Today's Verse:

"But he said to me, 'My grace is sufficient for you, for my power is made perfect in weakness.' Therefore I will boast all the more gladly about my weaknesses, so that Christ's power may rest on me." —2 Corinthians 12:9

DAY 132

LIVING SET APART

"Make every effort to live in peace with everyone and to be holy; without holiness no one will see the Lord."

Hebrews 12:14

You can't live to please both the world and God. A true man or woman of God isn't worried about winning everyone's approval—they're set on pleasing Jesus. When you choose to follow the Lord, your desire shifts to doing God's will, no matter who might take issue with it.

Hebrews 12:14 reminds us that living a holy life is essential if we want to see the Lord. And yes, it can feel lonely; choosing God's way often means standing apart from worldly pressures and behaviors. But remember, while others might see you as different or even strange, God sees your bold choice to live set apart—and He is proud of you.

You'll know you're people-pleasing when your choices and actions are driven by the desire to keep others happy, even at the cost of your own convictions or what you know is right in God's eyes. If fear of disapproval, rejection, or criticism shapes your path more than God's truth, it's a sign your focus has shifted. On the other hand, when Jesus is your sole focus, your decisions align with His Word and purpose, and you find peace in knowing you're living to honor Him, even if others don't understand or agree.

Living this way is challenging because it requires standing firm in situations where it's easier to blend in. I see this often in my personal life and work as a dietitian.

When I was younger and less mature in my faith, I wanted to please everyone—whether it was by laughing along with mean jokes or going along with the crowd's behavior. I wasn't concerned with whether or not I was pleasing God.

As I grew in my walk with Jesus, I came to understand that pleasing Him is what truly matters. He showed me that we are not of this world—and because of that, we're often called to stand apart from the culture around us. That means choosing kindness when others are being cruel, resisting gossip even when it's spreading fast, and living in a way that reflects Jesus, even when it goes against the grain.

We can't live a Godly life by following people. We must follow Christ—even if it means feeling like outsiders.

Today's Verse:
"Dear friends, I urge you, as foreigners and exiles, to abstain from sinful desires, which wage war against your soul."
—1 Peter 2:11

A NEW HEART, A NEW SPIRIT

"I will give you a new heart and put a new spirit in you; I will remove from you your heart of stone and give you a heart of flesh."

Ezekiel 36:26

Do you ever feel like your heart has become heavy, hardened by the weight of life? Maybe you've been hurt by people you trusted, let down by circumstances, or simply worn out from trying to hold everything together.

Sometimes, without even realizing it, we begin to protect ourselves by closing off parts of our hearts—pushing away people, burying emotions, and even distancing ourselves from God. But here's the beautiful truth: God sees the places in your heart that no one else does, and He longs to bring healing and restoration.

In Ezekiel 36:26, God makes a powerful promise to His people. He promises to replace our hearts of stone with hearts of flesh—soft, alive, and responsive to Him. He's not asking us to fix ourselves or try harder to feel close to Jesus. He's asking us to come as we are, with our brokenness, pain, and even our doubts, and let Him do the transforming work. His desire is for your heart to beat in rhythm with His—to feel the fullness of His love, to experience His peace, and to overflow with joy and purpose.

But here's the key: we have to let our Father in. Sometimes that means facing the things we've avoided—old wounds, fears, or disappointments. It can feel vulnerable, even scary, to open ourselves up, but when we do, God meets us with gentleness. He begins to soften what's been hardened, to heal what's been wounded, and to breathe life into places that have grown dry. He doesn't just mend what's broken; He makes us new.

Today, ask God to give you a new heart. Invite Him into those places you've kept guarded. Trust Him to replace the weight of a hardened heart with the beauty of a heart fully alive in Him. No matter where you've been or how far you've wandered, His heart for you has never changed. You are loved, chosen, and worth restoring. Let Him give you the newness you've been longing for—it's His gift to you, and it will change everything.

Today's Verse:
"I will give them a heart to know me, that I am the Lord. They will be my people, and I will be their God, for they will return to me with all their heart."
—Jeremiah 24:7

WALKING IN THE SPIRIT

"You, however, are not in the realm of the flesh but are in the realm of the Spirit, if indeed the Spirit of God lives in you. And if anyone does not have the Spirit of Christ, they do not belong to Christ."

Romans 8:9

You are chosen. Handpicked by God Himself to do extraordinary things! You don't need to be famous, wealthy, or hold a prestigious title to serve God and impact the world. The Spirit of God lives in you, and because of that, you belong to Christ—marked with purpose. The world might tell you that greatness is measured by status, fame, possessions, finances, or achievement, but God measures things differently.

Beloved, you carry a divine assignment, even when it feels like you're just going through the motions. Whether you're at the grocery store, picking up your kids from school, or sitting at work, you are a vessel for God's love. You never know who you might encounter that is suffering in silence, weighed down by pain or struggle.

The Spirit of Christ lives in you, and that means everywhere you go, you carry the presence of Jesus. In this world, we have limitations—but we serve a God with unlimited resources, power, and authority! Today, be mindful of the opportunities around you to bring hope, peace, and love to those you meet.

You're marked for a greater purpose—and that is to advance the Kingdom. You are an ambassador for Christ, *and through you*, God is touching lives and changing hearts through small moments that lead to God-sized transformations!

Today's Verse:
"You did not choose me, but I chose you and appointed you so that you might go and bear fruit—fruit that will last."
—John 15:16

DAY 135

SEEK WISE COUNSEL

"Plans fail for lack of counsel, but with many advisers they succeed."

Proverbs 15:22

How many times have you tried to face a problem—or battle an addiction—on your own, thinking, *I've got this, I can fix it?* It's easy to fall into the trap of isolation. But the truth is, God never intended for you to fight your battles solo.

Scripture reminds us that *"plans fail for lack of counsel, but with many advisers they succeed"* (Proverbs 15:22). That's not just good advice—it's God's design. Community is a *gift* from Him. It offers wisdom when you're unsure, strength when you're weary, and encouragement when you're ready to give up.

I've seen firsthand how going it alone can delay healing and growth. Whether someone is battling emotional eating, struggling to stay consistent with their health goals, or navigating depression as a teenager, the turning point almost always comes when they reach out for help. The ones who try to tough it out in silence often end up facing even deeper discouragement, getting stuck in cycles that were never meant to be walked alone.

Even the strongest among us need a support system. I'll never forget the words my dad would often say to me:

"Wendi, if you need help, I'm here. Don't ever be ashamed or

embarrassed to ask. I love you. No matter what or how bad it gets, I'm here."

My dad wasn't perfect—and he'd be the first to admit that—but one thing he made clear was this: I didn't have to walk through hard things by myself.

Maybe you didn't have a father or a safe place to fall. But here's the good news: you *do* have a Father—your Heavenly Father—who is always present, always listening, and always ready to help. He sees you. He hears you. And He's not going anywhere.

Society may try to tell you that asking for help is a sign of weakness. But God says that *in your weakness, His strength is made perfect.* That strength is what will carry you forward.

If you're in a season where asking for help feels heavy—take heart. God is already moving. He's aligning the right people, the right support, and the right timing. Don't let shame or pride silence your cry for help. You're not failing—you're *trusting.* And trust always leads to freedom.

You are never alone. God is working on your behalf, even now.

Today's Verse:
"And I will ask the Father, and He will give you another advocate to help you and be with you forever—the Spirit of truth."
—John 14:16-17

TRUE BEAUTY COMES FROM WITHIN

"Your beauty should not come from outward adornment, such as elaborate hairstyles and the wearing of gold jewelry or fine clothes. Rather, it should be that of your inner self, the unfading beauty of a gentle and quiet spirit, which is of great worth in God's sight."

1 Peter 3:3-4

I've lived in both Nashville and Dallas, and if there's one thing those cities know how to do, it's show up and show out in style! The women there can dress! And honestly, I love fashion too. There's something joyful about getting dressed up, throwing on a cute outfit, doing my hair, and feeling confident in my own skin. God isn't against beauty—He's the one who created it!

But somewhere along the way, in a world full of filters, followers, and "who wore it best," we started letting the mirror define us more than the Master.

Here's the truth: your value isn't hanging in your closet. It's not wrapped up in your brand-name bag or how snatched your waist looks. It's not even in how "put together" you appear. Because God doesn't measure greatness the way the world does.

He's looking for something deeper.

He's drawn to the man or woman who radiates peace in a chaotic room. The one who loves when it's hard. The one who walks in humility, even when they have every reason to boast. That inner glow—the one the world can't sell or replicate—that's what pleases Him most.

You can rock your outfit *and* a heart that honors Him. There's no shame in loving fashion—but don't let fashion become your foundation. Don't let the pressure to "keep up" make you lose sight of who you are in Christ.

Because what God has placed in you? That's your real beauty. That's the light that sets you apart in rooms where everyone is trying to fit in.

So go ahead—put on the outfit. Just remember to clothe yourself in grace, humility, and a confidence that doesn't come from the world—it comes from the One who handcrafted you.

Heaven isn't looking for hype. Heaven is looking for those who know where their worth really comes from.

Today's Verse:
"The Lord does not look at the things people look at. People look at the outward appearance, but the Lord looks at the heart"
—1 Samuel 16:7

HONOR GOD WITH YOUR HEALTH

"Whether you eat or drink or whatever you do, do it all for the glory of God."

1 Corinthians 10:31

God cares deeply about every aspect of our lives—including how we care for our bodies. The Lord often provides strategy for how we manage our physical health, just as He gives us wisdom for spiritual matters. In His grace, God places people in our lives who can guide us on this journey of health and wellness, offering wisdom and encouragement to help us get started.

When we treat our bodies well, we honor the temple of the Holy Spirit (1 Corinthians 6:19). The first step is learning to fuel our bodies with the right foods in the right portions. When we know what to eat and how much, we no longer have to stress over tracking every meal. We can live in the freedom of balance and trust that God has equipped us with what we need.

Here's a practical strategy to help you optimize your health and athletic performance:

- **Breakfast:** 2-3 eggs + milk + sourdough avocado toast

- **Second Breakfast:** String cheese + jerky

- **Lunch:** Whole grain chicken sandwich + grapes + carrots + RXbar

- **Pre-Workout:** Greek yogurt + berries + honey + oats

- **Post-Workout:** Chocolate milk + banana + creatine blended up

- **Dinner:** Ground beef or steak, rice or sweet potato, roasted veggies, watermelon

- **PM Snack:** Cottage cheese + cherries + dark chocolate

This simple meal plan can be a great starting point for those looking to fuel their bodies with nourishing, wholesome foods. It's about consistency and eating to nourish your body instead of your emotions.

Today's Verse:
"My flesh and my heart may fail, but God is the strength of my heart and my portion forever"
—Psalm 73:26

GOD SEES YOUR FAITHFULNESS

"The Lord was with Joseph so that he prospered...."
Genesis 39:2

There's something so beautiful about knowing that our smallest, unseen efforts are never wasted in the eyes of God. Every little seed we plant in faith is being nurtured by the King who sees all things—even the things no one else notices.

But let's be honest: we live in an Amazon Prime world. We want quick results, fast answers, and overnight breakthroughs. Yet God doesn't operate on two-day shipping. His timing is perfect, and He's always working behind the scenes—often in ways we can't see.

Take Joseph, for example. Betrayed by his own brothers, sold into slavery, falsely accused, and thrown into prison—his life seemed full of one setback after another. But through every season of hardship, Joseph kept showing up. He worked with integrity, honored God, and remained faithful in the little things—whether it was managing a household or running a prison. And in God's perfect time, those small, faithful steps led to something *huge*. Joseph was promoted to a position of great authority in Egypt and used to save countless lives—including the very family that once betrayed him.

Joseph's story reminds us that God's timeline may not be immediate, but it's always intentional—and far greater than anything we could imagine.

The same is true for you.

When you're faithful with the little—whether it's in your family, your workplace, your friendships, or your personal growth—God sees it. You may not always see the fruit right away, but the harvest *will* come. Because in the Kingdom, there's always a set time for every season.

So be encouraged. God makes up the difference. He brings the increase. And when your breakthrough comes, it won't be a second too late.

Let the Holy Spirit be your strength in the waiting, and trust that God's plan for your life is not just good—it's *better* than anything you could've rushed into on your own.

Today's Verse:

"Joseph found favor in his eyes and became his attendant. Potiphar put him in charge of his household, and he entrusted to his care everything he owned"

—Genesis 39:4

LISTENING TO GOD'S WHISPERS

"And in the fourth watch of the night Jesus went unto them, walking on the sea."

Matthew 14:25

God is always speaking—but are we truly listening? Sometimes, we miss His voice because we've already made up our minds about what we *think* He said. Other times, we're so focused on our own plans that we can't hear His. We live in a loud world—and if we're not careful, the noise can drown out the very voice we need the most.

But God knows how to get our attention. In Scripture, we see a powerful pattern: God often moves and speaks during what's known as the *fourth watch of the night*—between 3 a.m. and 6 a.m. This was when Jesus walked on water toward the disciples in the middle of the storm (Matthew 14:25). It's a time when fear meets faith, and heaven intersects with earth. The fourth watch is when God reveals Himself in a way we can't ignore.

Recently, I experienced this for myself. I woke up two nights in a row at exactly 4:48 a.m. The first night, I dismissed it. But the second night, I knew—this wasn't random. God was calling me to be still and listen. I turned to Philippians 4:4–8, and the words spoke straight to the worries I had been carrying—decisions in my business, concern for loved ones, and the weight of not knowing what's next. Through His Word, God brought peace, clarity, and gentle redirection. It was a reminder that He sees me—and He speaks when I slow down enough to listen.

The Bible is called the *Living Word* for a reason. God still speaks through it today. But here's the challenge: we often run to His Word or to prayer only after we've tried everything else. We treat His voice as a last resort when it should be our first response.

Ask yourself:

Is God's voice the loudest in my life?

Am I waiting to hear what He wants me to do—or am I just hoping He agrees with my plan?

Don't miss the fourth watch. Don't miss the moment He's drawing you close.

Let His voice be the one that grounds you, guides you, and gives you peace—even before the sun comes up.

Today's Verse:

"And he saw them toiling in rowing; for the wind was contrary unto them: and about the **fourth watch** of the night he cometh unto them, walking upon the sea, and would have passed by them." —Mark 6:48

THE POWER OF INTEGRITY

"For God has not given us a spirit of fear, but of power and of love and of a sound mind."

2 Timothy 1:7

Fear loves to dress itself up as wisdom. It whispers, "Be cautious," when God says, "Step out." It says, "What if?" when the Holy Spirit says, "I go before you."

Fear is one of the most subtle yet aggressive tools the enemy uses to paralyze believers. That's why Paul reminded Timothy that fear isn't just a feeling—it's a *spirit*, and it doesn't come from God.

When you gave your life to Christ, you were filled with the Holy Spirit. And the Holy Spirit doesn't breed fear—He breathes boldness. The word Paul uses for "fear" here in the Greek language means *timidity, cowardice,* or *shrinking back.* That's not who you are in Christ!

You've been given a spirit of power, the same explosive power that raised Jesus from the dead (Romans 8:11). You've been filled with love—the kind that casts out fear (1 John 4:18). And you've been gifted a sound mind—meaning clarity, discipline, and stable thinking, even when the world around you is chaotic.

Sometimes fear feels like a blanket we've wrapped ourselves in for safety. But that blanket becomes a trap. God doesn't call us to live wrapped in what feels safe—He calls us to walk by faith. That doesn't mean we ignore danger or act recklessly. It means we recognize the voice of fear and reject it in the mighty name of Jesus Christ!

If you're facing a moment that feels too big, too scary, or too uncertain—remember this: that spirit of fear is not your inheritance. Speak back to it with truth. Declare what is yours: power to walk forward, love to remain steady, and a sound mind to discern what's true.

You don't have to wait for courage or motivation to act bravely. The power is already within you—His name is Jesus.

Today's Verse:

"Therefore, my dear brothers and sisters, stand firm. Let nothing move you. Always give yourselves fully to the work of the Lord, because you know that your labor in the Lord is not in vain." —1 Corinthians 15:58

CHOSEN AND CHERISHED

"I am my beloved's and my beloved is mine; he browses among the lilies."

Song of Songs 6:3

Let this truth settle in—God chose you. Not just the polished, put-together version of you, but every part. He sees your struggles, your wounds, and the silent battles you've fought. He knows the injustices you've endured and the pain you've carried alone. And still, He calls you His beloved. You are not overlooked or forgotten. His love for you is constant, pursuing you even in your darkest moments.

Maybe life has felt unfair. You've faced betrayal, rejection, or wrongs that were never made right. But hear this: God sees it all. Jesus is your defender, and He promises to bring justice. You don't have to carry this weight alone. Trust Him. He is working in ways you can't see, making things right in His perfect time.

I believe you're stepping into a season of restoration. The peace, joy, and hope the enemy tried to steal from you? God is giving it back. What has been delayed will not be denied. The trials you've endured weren't for nothing. They've shaped you, strengthened you, and prepared you to help someone else. One day, you'll cross paths with a person facing the same struggles you did, and because of what you've walked through, you'll be able to encourage them. That's how God works—He handpicks us to be a light for others.

I remember helping a woman years ago, coaching her through a tough season. I didn't expect anything in return. I just wanted to help. Recently, she reached out again, this time asking me to coach her family and speak at local events. That small act of obedience turned into a month's worth of income and new opportunities.

At the time, I had no idea how God would use that moment. I felt stretched thin, wondering if my efforts even mattered. But He reminded me—nothing is wasted in His Kingdom. Every quiet act of faithfulness, every unseen sacrifice, He sees it all.

So keep going. Keep giving from a pure place. The prayers you've prayed, the kindness you've shown, the love you've poured out—it's all recorded in Heaven. When your heart is in the right place, God will surprise you in ways you never expected.

Today's Verse:
"You are altogether beautiful, my darling;
there is no flaw in you."
—Song of Songs 4:7

YOU ARE BEAUTIFUL

"We do not dare to classify or compare ourselves with some who commend themselves. When they measure themselves by themselves and compare themselves with themselves, they are not wise."

2 Corinthians 10:12

The enemy comes to kill, steal, and destroy all things good—including our joy and identity. One day, I sat in the sauna, unaware that God had a purpose for me there. But it quickly became clear—perhaps I was there to speak truth into the lives of two young women absorbed in their phones, comparing themselves to others online.

As they scrolled through social media, admiring famous fitness influencers, I listened as they made comments like, "She's so beautiful and skinny," and "I wish I looked like her."

So I took a deep breath, and the Holy Spirit spoke through me: "Ladies, you are both absolutely beautiful—inside and out. Don't waste another moment comparing yourselves to those models you see online. God created you with purpose. You are real—unlike the edited images and filtered posts that flood social media. Jesus loves you just as you are, and I don't want you to ever feel less than or wish to look like someone else. Forget about the latest weight-loss fads or harmful diets. When you're ninety, you won't care about cellulite or what size jeans you wore. What will matter is that you were healthy, strong, and full of life—that your body carried you through a long, vibrant journey. Don't starve your body to be skinny; fuel it to be strong. We are all real people with real flaws, and what makes us beautiful is that we are created in the image of God. Your worth is not found in your body—but in Christ. If you want to be a model, be a model for Jesus. We are all ambassadors of Christ!"

Both girls looked at me with tears in their eyes. "Wow, thank you so much," one said. "I really needed to hear that." The other added, "Yes, me too!" As I finished speaking, another woman—who had quietly been listening—leaned over and thanked me for standing firm in truth. "We need to use our voices more to share the love of Jesus," she said. That same woman has since become one of my first friends here in Dallas, Texas. What started as a normal moment in a sauna became a divine appointment. God used a moment of obedience to not only minister to two young women battling comparison but to also connect me with someone I didn't even know I needed in this new season.

Don't you dare compare. The enemy loves to whisper lies in the quiet—especially when we're alone, scrolling, and subtly measuring our worth against others. But when we speak truth, the atmosphere shifts. The weight lifts. And freedom enters. That's what happened in that sauna. It wasn't just a conversation—it was spiritual warfare. And praise God, truth won.

Today's Verse:
"For we are God's masterpiece. He has created us anew in Christ Jesus, so we can do the good things he planned for us long ago." —Ephesians 2:10

DAY 143

FROM PAIN TO PURPOSE

"In peace I will lie down and sleep, for you alone, Lord, make me dwell in safety."

Psalm 4:8

Today, I write with confidence, no longer a victim of my past or ashamed of my mistakes, ready to share the moment I surrendered my life to Christ. Every trial and painful moment that satan meant to break me has become a tool in God's hands for my freedom and His glory. The enemy tried to keep my story hidden in shame, convincing me that silence was safest. But now, my pain has purpose, and my faith has grown in ways I never imagined. Jesus saved me—both literally and spiritually.

What was the turning point in the moment that nearly cost me my life? I was drowning in stress, feeling like a failure, and convinced I'd never become a registered dietitian—a life-long goal since I was a little girl. In my despair, I turned to stress eating and hit rock bottom, overwhelmed with sickness and fullness. In 2018, I used a spatula to make myself vomit. It got stuck, and each time I reached for it, it pressed further down my throat. I remember the final breaths I took, thinking I wouldn't see my family again, that I wouldn't see my nephew Westin, and that this would be how I'd be found and remembered.

At that moment, I cried out, "GOD, HELP ME." He reached in and pulled the spatula out, flinging it across the room—saving me before the enemy could take me. Praise God! I'm not proud of what happened, and looking back, I would have recommended outpatient treatment for anyone in my situation. But I was lost in darkness. Then, God intervened. Just as I was about to lose consciousness, He stepped in, pulling the spatula from my throat and tossing it across the room. I drove myself to the ER, too ashamed to have my family contacted. By God's grace, I walked out of the hospital without a single injury to my body. That's the kind of God we serve—amazing, merciful, and full of grace. Jesus gave me another chance to surrender and trust Him.

However, satan didn't stop coming for me. After I healed, I shared my story with my boyfriend at the time, who later tried to use it to blackmail me into staying in the abusive relationship I was desperately trying to leave. But over time, I realized my life was worth fighting for. I no longer struggle with bulimic tendencies or the need to be perfect. I am fully healed, thanks to God's grace.

Satan may try to trap you in darkness, but with Christ, you can break free and walk in the light. Your pain can be healed and become a testimony of hope—if God transformed my life, He can transform yours too!

Today's Verse:
"We are hard pressed on every side, but not crushed; perplexed, but not in despair; persecuted, but not abandoned; struck down, but not destroyed."
—2 Corinthians 4:8-9

THE FREEDOM OF CONFESSION

"If we confess our sins, he is faithful and just and will forgive us our sins and purify us from all unright-eousness."

1 John 1:9

When we try to hide our struggles, sins, or shame, it's like carrying a weight that grows heavier each day. Proverbs 28:13 reminds us, *"Whoever conceals their sins does not prosper, but the one who confesses and renounces them finds mercy."* This is a testament to the power of bringing our pain to God—laying it down with honesty and receiving His mercy in return.

Sharing my struggles openly has been a journey of redemption. It's freed me from the chains of shame, and now, I offer my story as a survival guide for anyone who feels trapped in silence. My healing didn't come overnight—it came through surrender. For years, I buried my pain, afraid of judgment, even from those closest to me. But when I finally allowed the light of Jesus to touch my hidden places, He revealed that He had been with me all along. Not just watching—but weeping with me, waiting for me, and ready to heal.

My story is not just about healing; it's about finding the courage to be seen and loved anyway. God took my journey through perfectionism, anxiety, and the pressure to succeed, and turned it into something He could use to uplift others. As I released my burdens, I discovered a deeper freedom that only His love could offer.

If you're carrying the heavy weight of shame—*let go.* Shame is not your identity. It's not your inheritance. It clings to our hearts, even after we've sought forgiveness, whispering lies that we're still unworthy. But here's the truth: shame is from the enemy. Conviction is from Jesus. Shame traps. Conviction sets free. Shame says you'll never change. Conviction says, "Come to Me, and I will make you new."

Today, I believe the Lord is saying:

"You don't have to carry this anymore. What you've hidden, I already see—and I'm not running away. Bring it to Me. I'm not ashamed of you. I'm ready to clothe you in righteousness, to give you beauty for ashes, and joy for your mourning. The enemy wanted to use this to bury you, but I will use it to build you. You are not too far gone. You are Mine."

Lay your shame at the altar—and don't pick it up again. He doesn't. Neither should you.

Today's Verse:
"There is therefore now no condemnation for those who are in Christ Jesus." —1 Peter 5:7

BREAKING THE GRASSHOPPER MINDSET

"But because my servant Caleb has a different spirit and follows me wholeheartedly, I will bring him into the land he went to, and his descendants will inherit it."

Numbers 14:24

Today I want to address the grasshopper mindset, because you are not called to be one. You're a faithful warrior in the Kingdom of God! In Numbers 13, the Israelites sent spies to explore the Promised Land. When they returned, most reported that the land was filled with giants, describing themselves as mere grasshoppers in comparison (Numbers 13:33). But Joshua and Caleb saw things differently. They were confident, not in themselves, **but in God's power to fulfill His promises**. They believed, even in the face of impossible odds, that God would make a way! This is what sets a faithful warrior apart from a grasshopper mindset. A person lives with a heart that trusts God's ability over the obstacles that seem insurmountable.

In this season, God may be calling you to step into unfamiliar territory and places that stretch your faith. You might face challenges that seem beyond your capacity. At that moment, it's important to reflect back on Joshua and Caleb. They *chose* to stare fear right smack in the face.

Remember, God doesn't call you to things He won't equip you for. When you walk in His will, He will give you the courage, strength, and wisdom you need for each step. The Holy Spirit wants you to remember that you're never alone. He is right beside you, forging a path where none seems to exist.

Many people shy away from God's call because they feel inadequate or overwhelmed. They may look at the task before them, the obstacles, and the opposition, and feel as if they don't have what it takes. But God is not looking for a flawless warrior; **He's looking for a willing one.** He's asking you to trust Him over your own limits, to believe that He's using every experience—good and bad—to shape you into who He created you to be. In this season, Jesus is not asking for perfection; *He's asking for faith.*

So stand tall, faithful warrior, knowing that God is working all things for good. Step into this season with a heart of faith, looking not at the giants before you, but at the God who is for you.

Oh, and the next time you see a grasshopper, go ahead and speak back to it! Remind yourself that you're not one to shrink back in fear. After all, you're a giant-slayer in God's Kingdom! Jesus has already claimed victory!

Today's Verse:
"Then Caleb silenced the people before Moses and said, 'We should go up and take possession of the land, for we can certainly do it." —Numbers 13:30

GOD'S SOVEREIGNTY IN ALL THINGS

"The Lord has made everything for its purpose, even the wicked for the day of trouble."

Proverbs 16:4

As we reflect on today's verse, it's natural to question how every person and circumstance fits into God's divine plan. We might wonder: How can even the wicked have a purpose in God's grand design? To understand this, we need to take a step back and view it through the lens of God's sovereignty and wisdom.

God, the Creator of all things, has designed everything in this world. Nothing exists outside of His plan. From the breathtaking beauty of creation to the challenging and perplexing situations, every part of the world has a place in God's purpose. Though we may not always understand or see the reason behind everything, we can trust that God's plan is certain. His wisdom, far beyond ours, ensures that every person and every event contributes to His larger story.

There have been times in my life when I've been hurt by others, when plans fell apart, or when I faced struggles that seemed impossible to overcome. But in hindsight, I can see how each of these moments was used by God to strengthen my faith, build resilience, and even open doors I never thought possible. What once seemed like setbacks or unnecessary hardships now makes sense in the light of God's bigger picture. God used those experiences to shape me, preparing me for new chapters and showing me that even difficulties have purpose when entrusted to Him.

Proverbs 16:4 reminds us to trust God with our lives and decisions, knowing He can bring good out of every situation—even when we don't fully understand it. Our role is to remain faithful, trusting that God's ways are higher than ours and His plans are always good. So, as we face the uncertainties of life, we can take comfort in knowing that our Heavenly Father is in control and has a purpose for every season.

Today's Verse:

"The Lord is my strength and my shield; my heart trusts in him, and he helps me. My heart leaps for joy, and with my song I praise him." —Psalm 28:7

THE TABLE OF LOVE

"It is better to eat vegetables with those who love you than to eat meat with those who hate you."
Proverbs 15:17

As a dietitian, I'll tell you that vegetables are essential—eating the rainbow is an easy way to stay healthy! A plate full of colorful, nutritious veggies can do wonders for your physical *and* spiritual health. But today's verse isn't just about food; it's about the value of the people around us. Proverbs 15:17 reminds us that the quality of our relationships matters more than the luxury of our circumstances. Would you prefer a simple meal with those who genuinely love and care for you, or a lavish feast with people who hold resentment or hidden motives? True nourishment comes from authentic love, not wealth or status.

God created us for fellowship, knowing that true joy comes from love and trust—not material things. Feasts and riches may provide temporary satisfaction, but relationships grounded in love and truth bring lasting fulfillment. We're called to prioritize relationships that reflect God's heart—marked by peace, respect, and kindness.

In our culture, we're often drawn to power and prestige, even if it means sacrificing authentic connections. But with time, we realize that being surrounded by those who lift us up and love us genuinely is far more valuable.

I have learned that true relationships are more precious than "feasting" with people who don't have my best interests at heart. I'd rather share a humble meal with loyal friends than a banquet with those who don't honor God's love.

Today, pray for God to help you focus on meaningful relationships. Ask Him to guide you toward people who reflect His love and away from environments where love and kindness are lacking. May we choose genuine connection over fleeting wealth or status.

Today's Verse:
"Better a little with the fear of the Lord than great wealth with turmoil." —Proverbs 15:16

PRAISE THROUGH EVERY SEASON

"And God is able to bless you abundantly, so that in all things at all times, having all that you need, you will abound in every good work."
2 Corinthians 9:8

Win or lose, praise God. In times of abundance or struggle, **PRAISE GOD!** Faith isn't just trusting God when things go well, but choosing to praise Him through the storms. True trust means lifting our praise regardless of circumstances, knowing that God is always good—even when life doesn't feel good.

Today's verse invites us to have a deeper faith rooted in God's unchanging character. His goodness isn't tied to our success or ease; He remains faithful, and His love never shifts with our situation. As 2 Corinthians 9:8 reminds us, God will bless us abundantly and provide for every good work.

In a world where it's easy to feel overlooked, remember that God knows your needs and promises to provide. Even in tough times, don't lose hope—God's faithfulness will come through in His perfect timing. Keep trusting His heart and stay rooted in His promises. You are never alone.

God WILL provide! Let today's praise be a declaration of faith. Even when life doesn't make sense, hold on and trust Him. He's with you, providing strength and preparing blessings aligned with His perfect plan. Keep praising, for He is working in ways you can't yet see. Stay faithful—God will fulfill His promises to you.

Win or lose, PRAISE GOD! **A true mark of a Christian is praising God no matter the circumstances.**

Today's Verse:
"The Lord is near to all who call on him, to all who call on him in truth." —Psalm 145:18

DIVINE APPOINTMENTS

"But I trust in you, Lord; I say, 'You are my God.' My times are in your hands."

Psalm 31:14-15

God has a powerful way of intervening in our lives—often when we least expect it, but when we need it the most. Whether it's a quiet nudge of encouragement or a door opening at the perfect moment, God is always at work. Trust this: He *can* and *will* fulfill every promise He makes in His Word! I experienced this firsthand on a busy Tuesday.

I had just finished a call with a web designer. Their services were exactly what our business needed to grow, but the costs were far beyond my small business budget. I prayed, asking God to provide the amount we needed for this next step. I didn't know how—but I trusted God would provide.

As I was leaving the coffee shop where my meeting had taken place, I bumped into my friend Andrew. He began sharing a story about how a generous donation had helped him open his coffee shop ministry. I told him about my need and asked for prayer. He smiled and said, "I have a friend who provides exactly what you need." Within minutes, I was sitting with that very friend—who happened to be at the same coffee shop—discussing our business needs.

Andrew's friend turned out to be the exact person I needed, with the skill set and integrity I had been praying for. It felt even better knowing I could support a fellow small business owner—a freelancer with kids—rather than a large firm. God had orchestrated every step of that day to bring me what I needed at just the right moment.

God's hand is often at work through the people He places in our lives. What feels like coincidence is often divine alignment.

Today's Verse:
"And God is able to bless you abundantly, so that in all things at all times, having all that you need, you will abound in every good work."—2 Corinthians 9:8

WISDOM AND WITTY INVENTIONS

"I, wisdom, dwell with prudence, and find out knowledge of witty inventions."

Proverbs 8:12

God's wisdom is rich and layered, and it often shows up in ways we don't expect. In Proverbs 8:12, wisdom says she finds knowledge of "witty inventions." What might this mean for us today? Witty inventions aren't just clever devices; they're *creative solutions, inspired ideas,* and *new ways of approaching the situations we face.* For each of us—whether we're a student athlete, a single parent, someone working hard in their career, or even a young adult figuring out their future—this verse speaks to the limitless potential of God-given wisdom in our lives.

For the Student Athlete: God's wisdom can help you see the game from new angles, giving you strategies and insights to elevate your performance. Pray for creative ideas and leadership that set you apart on the field.

For the Single Parent: Juggling it all can feel overwhelming, but God sees your sacrifices and wants to provide creative solutions. From organizing your day to creating moments of joy, He'll guide you with fresh ideas to lighten your load.

For the Career Professional: In a fast-paced career, God's wisdom offers innovative solutions and out-of-the-box thinking. Invite Him into your work and watch how He helps you approach challenges with fresh insights and excellence.

For the Young Adult Seeking Direction: As you navigate the uncertainty of your future, God's wisdom can open creative pathways, giving you insight into your passions and career choices with confidence and purpose.

God's wisdom is never outdated or irrelevant. It's alive, active, and ready to bring new ideas into every area of our lives.

So, today, ask the Holy Spirit for witty inventions. Let His wisdom lead you to creative breakthroughs, small or big, that inspire and uplift those around you. Remember, the Lord delights in sharing His wisdom, and He's ready to guide you with new ideas and insights perfectly suited for your journey. Embrace it, and watch as His wisdom brings fresh life to whatever you're facing.

Today's Verse:
"Call to me and I will answer you and tell you great and unsearchable things you do not know."
—Jeremiah 33:3

LETTING GO OF
PEOPLE-PLEASING

*"The fear of man lays a snare, but whoever trusts
in the Lord is safe."*

Proverbs 29:25

Life can feel exhausting when we focus too much on
pleasing people instead of pleasing Jesus. It's like being
stuck on a relentless rollercoaster of expectations—constantly striving to meet everyone's needs while losing sight of who
God uniquely created us to be.

But God promises *life to the full*—a life that is deeply satisfying and fulfilling because it's aligned with His love and purpose for us. This kind of fullness doesn't come from gaining
the approval of everyone around us. It's found in pleasing *Him*.

Here's an analogy I often share with my young athletes and
clients, especially when they struggle with feeling left out or
misunderstood for doing the right thing:

Even if you were the perfect double-scoop chocolate mint
Oreo chip ice cream cone, someone would still find a reason to
dislike it. One person might be lactose intolerant, another might
not like chocolate, and someone else may wish for a completely
different flavor. Trying to satisfy everyone's preferences leaves

us depleted and uncertain—robbing us of the true purpose God has designed for us.

Jesus didn't come so that we could live for the approval of others. He came to *free* us from that exhausting need and guide us into a life filled with peace, meaning, and lasting joy.

As Paul reminds us: "*Am I now trying to win the approval of human beings, or of God? Or am I trying to please people? If I were still trying to please people, I would not be a servant of Christ*" (Galatians 1:10).

When we shift our focus toward God's approval, our lives begin to reflect His purpose, peace, and love—not the ever-changing opinions of others.

So today, release the pressure to please. Lay it down at the feet of Jesus—and let Him remind you that His opinion is the only one that truly matters.

Today's Verse:
"*If you love me, keep my commands.*"
—John 14:15

FOLLOWING GODLY LEADERSHIP

"Remember your leaders, who spoke the word of God to you. Consider the outcome of their way of life and imitate their faith."

Hebrews 13:7

Great mentors, coaches, and leaders don't just tell us what to do—they *show* us. As followers of Christ, we're called to live a life modeled after Him. That means bearing the fruits of the Spirit: love, peace, kindness, integrity, selfless service, and an unshakable faith and love for Jesus.

A great leader doesn't simply hand out playbooks. They equip their team with the tools, systems, and mindset to handle adversity, overcome obstacles, and grow stronger. A mentor's role is to point us to where we can discover truth and wisdom for ourselves, building resilience and independence along the way.

This is exactly how the Holy Spirit works within us. He doesn't give us every answer immediately. Instead, He teaches us—guiding us through real-life experiences that shape our faith and develop our character. God uses mentors, pastors, teachers, and even friends to help mold us into who He's called us to be. If He gave us all the answers up front, we might miss the deeper lessons of faith, patience, and trust.

You don't need all the answers to take the next step. Just like a great coach meets you where you are and helps guide you to where you belong, God will meet you right where you are today.

The Holy Spirit is the ultimate Counselor and Encourager, guiding us with wisdom, comfort, and strength in every circumstance. He teaches us, prompts us, and gently nudges us in the right direction—especially when we feel weak or uncertain (John 14:26).

Is there a situation in your life where the Holy Spirit is teaching you to rely on Him more deeply? Let Him lead you. He is faithful to guide you every step of the way.

Today's Verse:
"But the Helper, the Holy Spirit, whom the Father will send in my name, he will teach you all things and bring to your remembrance all that I have said to you."
—John 14:26

WRESTLING WITH GOD

"So Jacob was left alone, and a man wrestled with him till daybreak."

Genesis 32:24

There's something powerful about wrestling. It demands strength, focus, and persistence. Wrestlers know the grit it takes to keep pushing forward—even when every muscle burns and every ounce of energy feels depleted. As a sports dietitian, I've had the privilege of working with many wrestling student-athletes—not just to help them meet weight goals but to fuel their bodies for peak performance. What I've learned over the years is that wrestling is just as much a *mental* battle as it is a physical one. Sometimes, your toughest opponent isn't the one across from you on the mat—it's your own mind.

The Bible gives us a striking image of this in the life of Jacob. One of the patriarchs of Israel, Jacob found himself at a turning point. Alone, uncertain, and preparing to face his estranged brother Esau, Jacob encountered God in the form of a man. The two wrestled throughout the night in one of Scripture's most unforgettable moments. Jacob could have let go—but he didn't. He clung to God, refusing to release his grip until he received a blessing. By morning, Jacob was forever changed—both physically and spiritually. He walked away with a limp and a new name: *Israel*, which means "he struggles with God."

That limp was a reminder of his encounter with the divine, proof that he had not only wrestled with God but had *persevered*. Jacob was no longer defined by his past mistakes. He had become a man of faith, chosen to lead God's people. His struggle wasn't wasted—it was transformational.

This story speaks volumes—not just to athletes on the mat, but to anyone walking through a season of difficulty. The truth is, life will bring moments when surrender feels easier than holding on. But God doesn't call us to surrender to the *struggle*—He calls us to engage, to wrestle, and to press in.

For parents, this story offers encouragement too. The strength it takes to support a child through the highs and lows of life can feel like its own kind of wrestling match. Wrestling isn't just about physical competition—it's a battle of will, a test of resilience, and a spiritual metaphor for persistence in faith. Just as you cheer on your child to stay focused and fight through fatigue, God is encouraging *you* to press on in your journey with Him.

If you're facing a challenge today—wrestling with a decision, a relationship, or even wrestling with God Himself—*don't let go*. Stay in the fight. God is not distant in your struggle; He's *in it* with you. And if you'll hold on, He'll use this season to shape, strengthen, and bless you in ways you never imagined.

Today's Verse:

Then the man said, 'Your name will no longer be Jacob, but Israel, because you have struggled with God and with humans and have overcome.'

—Genesis 32:28

TRUE GREATNESS IN CHRIST

"Repent, then, and turn to God, so that your sins may be wiped out, that times of refreshing may come from the Lord."

Acts 3:19

For most of my life, I lived by one rule: *work harder, be better, earn it.* I chased wins, accomplishments, approval. But even when I succeeded, I couldn't enjoy the moment. The voice in my head always whispered, *You could've done more.* Nothing was ever good enough. Deep down, I carried a quiet emptiness—a void that success couldn't fill. At the time, I didn't know what was missing. I only knew I felt like I was running a race with no finish line.

Then came the breakup. I was in college at UW-Stout in Menomonie, Wisconsin, dating a baseball player from a strong Christian family. One day, out of the blue, he and his mom decided I wasn't good enough—not church-going, not Christian, not raised in a "normal" home. I was stunned. But instead of getting angry, something in me stirred. *Why do they believe this so strongly? What do they know that I don't?* Curiosity drove me to a local Lutheran church. Ironically, the pastor there knew my ex's family. I started showing up every Wednesday at 6:30 a.m. for Bible study—not to win anyone back, but to explore this Jesus

I kept hearing about. I couldn't change where I came from, but I *could* be open.

One morning, we were learning about the Trinity when the pastor drew a simple image: an arrow pointing down. God came down to *us*. That flipped everything I thought I knew. I had spent my whole life trying to climb up, earn love, prove worth. But here was Jesus—coming down, arms wide, offering grace I didn't have to work for. I cried all the way home.

God wasn't asking me to earn anything. **Jesus had already paid for it.** My value wasn't in my grades, job titles, or people I helped. My identity wasn't in my family history or how others viewed me. My worth was found in the One who gave His life so I could have mine.

I laid down the weight of trying to be perfect. I surrendered the pain of judgment from people who looked at my "messy" story and labeled me unworthy. I let it all go. And in return, God gave me peace—and purpose. Years later, when I moved to Nashville, I visited a church in Smyrna. The pastor? The same one who taught that early morning Bible study. He smiled and said, "I still share your story. It's helped so many." **God is amazing like that.**

Maybe you know someone chasing greatness but still feeling empty. Maybe *you* feel that way. Don't underestimate what God can do with a curious heart and a surrendered life. You don't have to earn it. You just have to *receive* it.

Today's Verse:

Then Jesus said to his disciples, 'Whoever wants to be my disciple must deny themselves and take up their cross and follow me. For whoever wants to save their life will lose it, but whoever loses their life for me will find it.'
—Matthew 16:24-25

FAITH WITHOUT SIGHT

"Then Jesus told him, 'Because you have seen me, you have believed; blessed are those who have not seen and yet have believed.'"

John 20:29

True faith is believing without seeing. As someone who once questioned God, I understand the power of encountering Him in unexpected ways. I often explain my belief in Jesus like this: it's like feeling the wind. We can't *see* the wind—but we *can* see the trees moving as a result of it. In the same way, I've seen the movement of Jesus in my life. I am alive today because of Jesus Christ, as you've learned in previous days, and as seen throughout the countless testimonies in the Bible.

There's beauty in trusting—even when we don't have all the answers. This walk of faith is filled with reminders that God is present, and He desires that we share Him with those who do not yet know Him.

One day, I struck up a conversation with a fellow science enthusiast who was wearing a shirt that celebrated evidence-based thinking. His T-shirt read, "*Science does not care about your feelings.*" Honestly, I thought it was a cool shirt—I loved it because I'm an evidence-based dietitian myself. As we talked, he shared his skepticism about God, saying, "You can't prove Jesus is real."

My heart sank, but I felt the Holy Spirit nudging me to share my story, especially because I once thought like him. That moment reminded me that faith and science don't have to be enemies. God is not afraid of our questions—He meets us in them.

What made the encounter even more special was that Julia, a fellow believer, overheard us and felt inspired. She later came up to me and said, "Thank you for sharing your faith—it reminded me why I believe, too." Her words were a beautiful reminder that when we live out our faith openly, it doesn't just plant seeds in non-believers—it also strengthens and encourages other believers. When we speak about Jesus, God rejoices.

Here's the truth: *we're not responsible for changing hearts.* That's the Holy Spirit's role. But we *are* responsible for showing up, sharing the truth, and planting seeds.

So don't be afraid to speak about your faith—even in unexpected conversations. You never know who's listening or what God is preparing behind the scenes.

Plant the seed. Let God do the rest.

Today's Verse:
"Be on your guard; stand firm in the faith; be courageous; be strong. Do everything in love."
—1 Corinthians 16:13-14

THE SIXTY DOLLAR EFFECT

"*A generous person will prosper; whoever refreshes others will be refreshed.*"

Proverbs 11:25

Pastor Tom from Calvary Church in Grand Rapids once said something that stopped me in my tracks: "*True contentment doesn't come from what we accumulate. It comes from God.*" I didn't realize how much I needed to hear that until I found myself living it out.

That same Sunday afternoon, I went for a walk through downtown Grand Rapids. I had just been reflecting on Pastor Tom's message when I prayed a quiet, simple prayer: "*Lord, help me find some change so I can bless someone in need.*" I had passed by a homeless man earlier, and while I didn't have anything to give at the moment, I wanted to. It wasn't about the money—it was about trusting God to provide something small so I could be a blessing.

I searched the sidewalks as I walked. Nothing. Not even a penny.

But the next day? God showed up in a way I didn't expect. I found three crisp $20 bills—just sitting there. Sixty dollars. Not spare change. Not coins. *Bills.* And immediately I knew: this was from Him.

It felt like God whispering, *You asked for a little, but I'm capable of so much more.* It wasn't just provision—it was a reminder of His abundance, His kindness, and how He delights in showing up when we simply ask in faith.

But He didn't stop there. I felt a nudge in my spirit to match it. So I added $60 of my own, making it $120 total. With it, I bought bottled water, fruit, and passed them out to people on the streets of Grand Rapids.

That simple act of obedience turned into something bigger than me. I had just wanted to bless one person. But God used it to reach many.

And here's what I learned: when you open your heart to give—even a little—God often multiplies it. He expands what you thought was small and uses it to create impact.

Pastor Tom was right. Contentment isn't about how much you have—it's about learning to see what God is doing right now, right where you are. It's about walking with open hands and a soft heart, ready to say yes when the Holy Spirit nudges you.

So, here's my challenge for you: don't wait for the "perfect" time or a pile of money to be generous. Ask God to show you someone to bless today. Buy someone a coffee. Leave an encouraging note. Offer a prayer. Trust that God will take your simple yes and turn it into something more.

Because with Him, even the smallest seed can lead to a harvest.

Today's Verse:
"But godliness with contentment is great gain. For we brought nothing into the world, and we can take nothing out of it."
—1 Timothy 6:6-7

THE POWER OF PRAYER

"Then you will call on me and come and pray to me,
and I will listen to you. You will seek me and find me
when you seek me with all your heart."
Jeremiah 29:12-13

Prayer is one of the greatest gifts God has given us—an open invitation to experience His love, peace, and guidance. When we pray, we aren't just speaking into the air; we're opening our hearts to the One who knows us completely. In those quiet moments, God reveals truths we may not even recognize, bringing clarity to our fears and peace to our worries.

Romans 8:28 reminds us, *"In all things God works for the good of those who love Him, who have been called according to His purpose."* This promise reassures us that we are never alone in our struggles. God isn't surprised by our needs, nor is He distant from our pain. Prayer lifts the weight of our burdens and places them into His capable hands. Whatever is keeping you up at night—anxiety about the future, uncertainty in relationships, or financial stress—God is already working it out for your good.

Jesus Himself modeled the power of prayer. Before every major decision and during times of trial, He withdrew to spend time with the Father. When the disciples asked Him how to pray, He didn't respond with a list of rules or religious rituals. Instead, He gave them a simple, heartfelt prayer (Matthew 6:9–13), teaching that prayer is about trust, surrender, and relationship with God.

The size of our prayers reflects the size of our faith. When we pray boldly, we honor God's power to transform even the most impossible circumstances. When we release our worries into His hands, we are acknowledging that His wisdom far surpasses our own.

Today, bring everything—big or small—to God in prayer. Don't wait for the perfect words. Just come as you are. Let His peace guard your heart and His wisdom guide your steps.

Father God is not just listening—He's responding in love.

Matthew 6:9-13 (NIV):

This, then, is how you should pray:
'Our Father in heaven,
hallowed be your name,
your kingdom come,
your will be done,
on earth as it is in heaven.
Give us today our daily bread.
And forgive us our debts,
as we also have forgiven our debtors.
And lead us not into temptation,
but deliver us from the evil one.'

ROOTED IN GOD'S PRESENCE

"Look to the Lord and His strength; seek His face always."

1 Chronicles 16:11

People will come and go in your life—some will support you, others will stretch or even challenge you. But every encounter, every shift in relationship, can become a mirror that reflects how much you've grown.

Not long ago, I reconnected with a friend I hadn't spoken to in over two years. As we talked, I realized something had changed—*me*. I didn't feel the same pull for attention, validation, or control. I no longer needed to prove anything or perform to be accepted. Why? Because I've been learning to trust God more deeply. I've come to know that His approval is the only one that really matters.

Psalm 1:1–3 paints a picture of what it means to be truly grounded: a tree planted by streams of water, flourishing and unshaken through every season. That's what happens when we root ourselves in God's Word. When prayer and Scripture become our foundation, we're no longer ruled by perfectionism or the need to please others. The more we filter life through His truth, the more peace we find—no matter what's happening around us.

Here's a simple check-in: when doubt or anxiety rises, ask, "Is *this voice bringing me peace, love, hope, or encouragement?*" If the answer is no, it's likely not from God. The world is loud and crowded with opinions, expectations, and noise. But God's voice? It's still. It's steady. It leads you into rest, not chaos.

If you're wondering whether you're growing spiritually, don't look at your circumstances—look at your *response* to them. Are you turning to God in prayer? Are you anchoring yourself in His Word? True growth shows up in your ability to find peace in His presence, not in a perfect life.

Stay rooted today. Let His voice be your guide. Let His Word steady your heart.

And remember this: what God has for you can't be missed. He's not late. He hasn't forgotten. Every promise He's made, He intends to fulfill.

Your roots are growing deeper than you think.

Today's Verse:
"For no matter how many promises God has made, they are 'Yes' in Christ. And so through Him the 'Amen' is spoken by us to the glory of God."—2 Corinthians 1:20

UNTANGLING LIFE'S KNOTS

"He brought them out of darkness, the utter darkness, and broke away their chains."

Psalm 107:14

One night, I was reminded of how God works in the small, seemingly insignificant moments of our lives. While at a friend's house carving pumpkins and sitting by the fire, I listened as he shared his struggles—many of which I had once faced myself. As he spoke, I realized just how far God had brought me, using painful seasons to reveal His greater purpose.

Before heading out that evening, I wanted to wear my favorite necklace—a delicate piece with a bird charm, symbolizing my freedom after leaving a difficult relationship. But there was a problem: a stubborn knot near the clasp that I had never been able to untangle. Frustrated, I debated whether to wear it as it was. In a quiet moment, I whispered a simple prayer: *"Lord, could You help me with this knot?"* I tried again, but it wouldn't budge. So I chose to wear it anyway—knot and all—trusting that it was still beautiful and enough.

When I got home later that night, I placed it on the counter and went to bed. The next morning, after spending time in prayer, I picked up the necklace—and to my amazement, the knot was completely gone. Not a single twist remained.

That simple yet powerful moment reminded me of how God moves. We often come to Him tangled—ashamed of our messes, convinced we need to be "fixed" before we're worthy of His presence. But God never asks us to have it all together. He simply invites us to come—knots and all.

He doesn't need perfection. Jesus desires trust. And when we offer Him even our smallest frustrations or deepest wounds, He gently works through them in ways we can't.

That necklace, now untangled, became more than an accessory. It became a symbol of freedom, healing, and God's loving attention to the tiniest details of our lives. He is not only the God of grand miracles but also the God of intimate, personal moments that reassure us He is near.

If you're facing something in your life that feels impossible to untangle, bring it to God. You don't have to have it all figured out—just trust Him. Whether it's a broken relationship, a decision that weighs heavy, or a private struggle no one sees, He is able to restore, repair, and bring peace.

Let this be your reminder today: there is no knot too tangled, no mess too big, and no detail too small for God. Trust Him with everything—both big and small—and watch as He works His beautiful miracles in your life.

Today's Verse:
"This is the confidence we have in approaching God: that if we ask anything according to his will, he hears us. And if we know that he hears us—whatever we ask—we know that we have what we asked of him."
—1 John 5:14-15

TESTED AND REFINED

"But He knows the way that I take; when He has tested me, I will come forth as gold."

Job 23:10

Today, **God wants you to know that He sees you, even in your hardest trials.** You may be facing challenges that feel overwhelming or circumstances that have shaken your faith. But take heart: just as God was with Job through every part of his journey, He is with you, working even in the pain. Job's story shows us that while trials can feel isolating and confusing, they have the power to bring us closer to God, refine our faith, and reveal His faithfulness like nothing else.

In the Book of Job, we meet a man who was known for his faith and integrity, yet he faced unimaginable loss. Job lost his family, health, and wealth in a rapid series of events. Friends accused him of hidden sins, and he wrestled with questions about why God allowed such suffering. But through it all, Job held onto his faith, declaring, *"Though He slay me, yet will I hope in Him"* (Job 13:15). This powerful statement of faith is a reminder to us: our circumstances may change, but God's goodness and love do not.

There's a profound mystery in how God uses our trials to refine us. Job's trials revealed not only his resilience but also God's deep, unshakeable love for him. God restored Job's life, blessing him even more than before. *But the true miracle was the transformation within Job himself*—his understanding of God became more personal, his faith stronger, and his heart refined like gold.

This story reminds us that trials, though painful, are never wasted in God's hands. He is using every hardship to draw us closer, refine our character, and deepen our trust in Him.

If you find yourself in a season of testing, remember that God sees you and knows the way you take. He hears your prayers, even those whispered in moments of doubt or despair. Trust that the Holy Spirit is present, actively working behind the scenes. God is using this season to refine and strengthen you, just as He did with Job. What seems like loss or setback today may be the very thing that brings you closer to God and reveals His purpose in your life.

Today's Verse:
"After Job had prayed for his friends, the Lord restored his fortunes and gave him twice as much as he had before."
—Job 42:10

YOU ARE CALLED BY NAME

"Do not fear, for I have redeemed you; I have called you by name; you are Mine."

Isaiah 43:1

In my work, I'm blessed to meet people who embody resilience, hope, and faith in a world often marked by brokenness. While I call them clients, they are truly brothers and sisters in Christ—each with a unique story that strengthens my own faith. We are all called to serve one another, especially when we allow Jesus to reign in our hearts and actions, reminding us that our ultimate purpose transcends any career or duty.

Many of the people I work with experience not only physical transformation but also emotional and spiritual healing. Today, I want to share Ashley's story—one that deeply inspired me. She came seeking physical health, but God also used that journey to reconnect her heart to His. Ashley's testimony reminds us that God places people in our lives to shape and teach us in ways we least expect.

When Ashley first arrived, she felt lost—physically, emotionally, and spiritually. She had tried quick-fix diets in the past, but this time, she was searching for lasting change. She chose our team because of the compassion we showed her, which she later recognized as the love of Christ in action. Through our sessions,

I openly shared my faith in Jesus, and that space of vulnerability allowed Ashley to renew her relationship with God. Though she came from a different faith background, she found a deeper faith in Christ.

Ashley has become like family to me, and her favorite verse, Isaiah 43:1, continues to guide her: "*Do not fear, for I have redeemed you; I have called you by name; you are Mine.*" Her words echo in my heart: "*God knew what I needed and got me there. I'm so thankful for Him.*"

Ashley's story is a humbling reminder that every interaction holds the potential for God's grace. May we walk forward, reflecting Christ's love and helping others encounter His presence—one heart, one moment, one life at a time.

Today's Verse:
"*He lifted me out of the slimy pit, out of the mud and mire; he set my feet on a rock and gave me a firm place to stand. He put a new song in my mouth, a hymn of praise to our God. Many will see and fear the Lord and put their trust in him.*"
—Psalm 40:2-3

PROVISION IS COMING

"And my God will supply every need of yours according to his riches in glory in Christ Jesus."
Philippians 4:19

Dear Friend: there are moments when life feels weighed down by lack, when it seems as though the very ground beneath you is crumbling. It's easy to wonder if God truly sees your need and if He will come through. Yet, let this be a reminder that God, in His infinite wisdom and love, promises to provide. This provision doesn't come merely as a quick fix or a fleeting solution, but as a transformative, faith-building experience. God is intimately aware of each heartache and every prayer spoken in private. His provision is on its way and tailor-made for this season.

When life's blessings seem to dry up, and resources feel stretched thin, you may be tempted to slip into worry or even despair. The enemy wants you to believe that God is far off, but know this: **God's silence is not absence.** He is drawing you into a place of deeper reliance, asking you to press in, to seek His face, and to trust His timing. These are moments when faith is purified, a faith that is no longer based on visible blessings but on the deep assurance that God is who He says He is.

During this time, be vigilant against bitterness and frustration. It's easy to feel hurt or overlooked, especially when you're pouring into others and feeling emptied yourself. Yet, God reminds us to give without expectation and to trust that our reward is secure in Him. When you surrender your own needs to His hands, you open yourself up to a peace that can only come from God. Let Jesus refine your heart in this season, teaching you to rest in His sovereignty and grace.

God often allows these valleys to shape us, to deepen our faith and draw us closer to Him. Instead of withdrawing, use this time to lean in more than ever. Bring your frustrations to God openly, confessing every fear, every doubt, and every moment of weariness. In doing so, you are reminded of His unchanging nature. Our Heavenly Father has carried you before and will carry you again. Remember, hardship can be a holy invitation to encounter God's faithfulness in new and profound ways.

Allow today's difficulties to build tomorrow's testimony. What looks like lack now is often the soil for growth and at the right time, the seeds of uncertainty that you planted in the past will burst forth. Release your fears and embrace greater faith, knowing that the God who supplies for the sparrows has a specific plan to meet your every need. In His hands, even the barren places of your life are full of promise.

Today's Verse:

Then the Lord said to Moses, 'Behold, I am about to rain bread from heaven for you, and the people shall go out and gather a day's portion every day...'

—Exodus 16:4

LEAVING YOUR EGYPT BEHIND

"For my thoughts are not your thoughts, neither are your ways my ways," declares the Lord."

Isaiah 55:8

Today, God is calling you out of an "Egypt" season, a time marked by bondage to old patterns, mindsets, and limitations. In the story of Israel's exodus, Egypt represented more than just a place of physical captivity—it symbolized a way of thinking and living that was far from God's intended purpose. Similarly, God wants to lead you out of any place in your life where you've been confined, defined by past fears, or shaped by the standards of this world. He is inviting you to embrace a new mindset—one rooted in the Kingdom of God, where His higher ways and deeper truths set you free to walk in purpose and identity.

To leave your "Egypt" means shedding the familiar habits and thought patterns that have kept you bound. It's easy to conform to the culture around us, absorbing its values, desires, and priorities without realizing how they can distance us from God's heart. But God's Kingdom operates on a different standard. Where the world may glorify power, status, and self-sufficiency, the Kingdom honors humility, servanthood, and dependence on God. God is calling you to embrace this upside-down Kingdom and to trust that His ways, though they may seem countercultural, are life-giving.

The journey out of Egypt requires learning to see with spiritual eyes, trusting in what is unseen rather than the fleeting things of this world. In the wilderness, God taught Israel to depend on Him daily for provision, guidance, and protection. Similarly, He invites you to cultivate a mindset of daily surrender and trust, believing that He will provide for every need and lead you through every challenge. God's ways are not always easy to understand, but they are infinitely wise and crafted to grow you into the fullness of who you are meant to be.

In this season, God is inviting you to think bigger and to believe that there is more to life than what the world offers. The Kingdom of God is about eternal values—love, faith, hope, and purpose that transcends the temporary. By shifting your mindset from worldly goals to Kingdom principles, you begin to experience peace and joy that circumstances cannot shake. Trust that God's ways, though higher and often mysterious, are exactly what you need to walk in true freedom and purpose.

So, step forward in faith, knowing that God has called you out of your "Egypt" not to abandon you but to transform you. His plans are higher, His thoughts deeper, and His love for you unshakable. Lean into this new mindset and let the Spirit renew you, drawing you closer to the heart of the Father and empowering you to live according to His Kingdom's truth.

Today's Verse:
"Set your minds on things above, not on earthly things."
—Colossians 3:2

STANDING FIRM IN THE FACE OF COMPROMISE

"I will bless you greatly, and I will multiply your seed greatly like the stars of the heavens, and like the sand which is on the seashore."

Genesis 22:17-18

Stand firm in your commitment to God, even when it costs you.

I once faced rejection after delivering a sports nutrition presentation to a school because I refused to remove Scripture from my final slide. The verse—*"Iron sharpens iron"* from Proverbs 27:17—was deemed "offensive" to those who were not Christians. I was also told I couldn't openly share my faith or mention the name of Jesus.

It was a defining moment that revealed a choice every follower of Christ must eventually face: do we compromise our faith to fit in with the world, or do we stand firm in God's truth? I chose to hold the line. With gentleness and kindness, I reminded the woman that Jesus loved her—and that no one in the room would be preached at. They would simply be encouraged by a message that pointed to hope, truth, and practical nutrition.

It is our calling as Christians to share the gospel. If we don't, who will?

As someone who once lived without faith, I know firsthand the emptiness that comes from a life without Jesus. But God transformed me—personally and professionally. The road hasn't been easy. I've sacrificed, worked hard, and faced countless challenges to get to where I am today.

Jesus says in Matthew 10:32–33, "*Therefore everyone who acknowledges me before others, I will also acknowledge before my Father in Heaven. But whoever disowns me before others, I will disown before my Father in Heaven.*"

Christ makes me a better person, a better dietitian, and a better voice in the world. His wisdom guides my decisions, conversations, and every step I take. In every accomplishment, I see His hand at work. I wouldn't be alive today without Jesus—let alone a successful sports nutritionist. So He will always get the glory. I will never stay silent about my faith—and neither should you.

Today's Verse:
"*For I am not ashamed of the gospel, because it is the power of God that brings salvation to everyone who believes.*"
—Romans 1:16

THE COST OF COMPROMISE

"Do not be yoked together with unbelievers. For what do righteousness and wickedness have in common? Or what fellowship can light have with darkness?"

2 Corinthians 6:14

Bad company corrupts good character.

Sometimes it's easy to convince ourselves that compromising our faith in small ways isn't that serious—whether in a relationship, a job, or even in social circles. But the truth is, if "it" costs you your faith or causes you to water down the voice of the Holy Spirit, it costs too much. God desires that we remain close to Him, unyielding in our commitment. He calls us to be bold, even if that means walking away from things that lead us into sin or pressure us to hide our faith. It's a challenging call—but one that ultimately protects our relationship with Him.

Dating someone who knowingly leads us into sin or causes us to compromise our faith is a clear sign that this person isn't aligned with God's will for our lives. God has promised to provide the right person—someone who encourages us, helps us grow, and points us closer to Christ. Waiting on God is always worth it. We were never meant to walk this journey of faith alone—but He desires us to walk it in godly, Christ-centered community.

The world often rejects this way of living. When you set bound-aries or declare your commitment to follow Jesus, you may expe-rience judgment, rejection, or even loneliness. But Jesus reminds us, *"If the world hates you, remember it hated me first"* (John 15:18). The discomfort we feel is often an indication that we're walking in step with Him rather than with the world. Standing firm in our faith isn't about gaining approval from others—it's about prioritizing God's truth above all else, even when it costs us relationships or opportunities.

Ask yourself: Is anything causing you to stray from God's pres-ence or compromise your faith? If so, be bold and take action. As followers of Christ, we are called to a higher standard—to follow Jesus, not the ways of this world.

Today's Verse:
"You adulterous people, don't you know that friendship with the world means enmity against God? Therefore, anyone who chooses to be a friend of the world becomes an enemy of God."
—James 4:4

TRUSTING GOD THROUGH THE UNKNOWN

"Commit your work to the Lord, and your plans will be established"

Proverbs 16:3

I 'll never forget when I started my business in 2019. I had no money, a mountain of student loan debt, and I left my full-time job to pursue my dreams—despite criticism from family, friends, and even mentors. It was terrifying, but I knew I couldn't ignore what God had placed in my heart.

My dad encouraged me, saying, *"Wendi, you can do it. You always finish what you start, you don't quit, and with your drive and passion, you're going to change lives."* His words stuck with me. To be honest, my dad was the only one at the time who believed I could be successful. He's always supported me—no matter how big or crazy my dreams were. I trusted him, because he always tells the truth, even when it hurts.

I had no business coach, no step-by-step guide—I just trusted God, put people first, and focused on solving problems. I refused to spend another moment building someone else's dream while neglecting my own calling.

Those first years were tough—long days, countless sacrifices—but I kept showing up, serving, and trusting. And now, six years later, by the grace of God, we are thriving. I have a team of dietitians, paid off all my student loans, invested wisely, grown as a leader, given to charities, started a nonprofit, and even have my first book coming out. Looking back, I see how God's hand was in every step—guiding, providing, and refining.

But here's the truth: it wasn't just about working hard. It was about *trusting* God through the uncertainty. I lived below my means, sacrificed, and stayed faithful—but He opened the doors. And now, as I sense Him shifting my focus toward ministry, I trust that He will place me exactly where I belong, using my abilities for His glory.

If I have one regret, it's that I didn't start sooner. But even that reminds me—God's timing is always perfect. If you're standing at the edge of something scary, something God is calling you to do, I hope this encourages you to step out in faith. God works His best miracles when we are willing to trust Him and put in the work.

Thank You, Jesus!

Today's Verse:
"Do not despise these small beginnings,
for the Lord rejoices to see the work begin."
—Zechariah 4:10

CALLED TO LEAD, EVEN WHEN YOU FEEL UNQUALIFIED

"But Moses said, 'Pardon your servant, Lord. Please send someone else.'"

Exodus 4:13

Leadership doesn't always come with a title or position. It's not about waiting for the perfect moment or for someone else to act—it's about taking steps, big or small, to make a positive impact on those around us. True leaders recognize needs and respond to them, often in simple but impactful ways. Jesus showed us the kind of leadership that puts others first, serving humbly and with purpose. We don't need fame or wealth to make a difference; we just need willing hearts. Like Jesus, we can lead by choosing to love, serve, and help others right where we are.

The life of Moses is a powerful example of this type of leadership. Moses didn't feel qualified to lead. In fact, when God first called him to rescue the Israelites from slavery, Moses hesitated, saying, *"Who am I that I should go to Pharaoh and bring the Israelites out of Egypt?"* (Exodus 3:11). Moses doubted his ability and feared he didn't have the skills or influence to lead such a massive task. Yet, God saw something in Moses that he didn't see in himself—a heart willing to obey and serve. Despite his doubts,

Moses stepped into leadership, not through his own strength, but by relying on God.

Like Moses, we may not always feel like leaders. We might doubt our influence or feel we're not "important" enough to make a real difference. But leadership isn't about position or power; it's about *willingness*. God often calls us to lead by doing the small things, like picking up trash, helping a neighbor, or volunteering our time. It's these simple actions, when done with a heart for God and others, that make a lasting impact. Moses' leadership started with simple acts of obedience, each step preparing him to lead the Israelites to freedom.

So today, consider how you can lead where you are. It could be as simple as helping someone in need, being a positive example in your community, or offering your time to a worthy cause. Remember that God uses ordinary people to do extraordinary things when we're willing to step forward in faith.

You don't need to be perfect or have everything figured out; you just need to say "yes" to God and trust that He will equip you.

Just as He did with Moses, God will work through your willingness, making you a leader who blesses those around you and brings glory to Him.

Today's Verse:
"Now Moses was a very humble man, more humble than anyone else on the face of the earth."
—Numbers 12:3

LIVING BOLDLY FOR JESUS

"Greater love has no one than this: to lay down one's life for one's friends."

John 15:13

Matthew 5:16 reminds us, *"Let your light shine before others, so that they may see your good works and give glory to your Father who is in heaven."*

This verse isn't just encouragement—it's a call to live our faith openly and unashamedly. Think about how naturally we talk about a beloved family member. If someone told us our earthly father "wasn't real" or that we shouldn't speak about him, we'd find it absurd. And yet, in today's world, we're often pressured to downplay our faith in God—to stay quiet about the One who created us.

Our culture is moving toward a reality where God is sidelined. Society offers us a "seat at the table" only if we soften our faith, dilute the truth, or leave Jesus out of the conversation. But for those of us who know the love and sacrifice of Christ, we understand that the only table that truly matters is the one He has prepared for us.

As I write this, it is Easter—a time to reflect on the suffering Jesus endured for our sins. His sacrifice wasn't just an act of love—it was the ultimate display of selflessness. If we would be heartbroken to see our earthly father suffer for us, how much more should the weight of Jesus' suffering impact our hearts? He willingly bore the cross, not out of obligation, but out of boundless love—for each of us, even those who still reject Him.

Before I came to Christ, I respected believers, but I didn't understand the peace they carried. Now, having experienced God's love firsthand, I can say with certainty that nothing in this world—no relationship, achievement, or success—compares to the peace found in Jesus.

The world tells us to create our own "truth," but we know there is only one Truth—Jesus. Just as we don't question the existence of our earthly fathers, we have no need to question the presence of our Heavenly Father. We wouldn't exist without Him. That's not an opinion; that's reality.

Jesus + nothing = everything. When we have Him, we have all we truly need.

Don't let fear or social pressure silence you. Jesus gave His life for us, and He calls us to share His love boldly. Stay anchored in His truth, knowing He loves you beyond measure. And remember—**Jesus is coming back.** We must be ready—not just for ourselves, but so others can come to know the incredible peace that only He provides.

Today's Verse:

"But he was pierced for our transgressions, he was crushed for our iniquities; the punishment that brought us peace was on him, and by his wounds we are healed."

—Isaiah 53:5

GOD IS SPEAKING—ARE YOU LISTENING?

"But we have this treasure in jars of clay to show that this all-surpassing power is from God and not from us."

2 Corinthians 4:7

God is not limited by human expectations. His ways are beyond our understanding, and His plans for us are limitless because He is a God of unlimited resources. Often, He speaks through unexpected moments—a scripture, a conversation, or a quiet nudge in our spirit.

Recently, I experienced this firsthand when several friends—some of whom I hadn't spoken to in years—reached out with words I desperately needed to hear. One friend told me, *"Wendi, I just want to thank you for being so brave and bold in your faith. Your openness encourages me to share my faith, too."* Her words weren't just encouragement—they were confirmation. God was making it clear: standing boldly for Him is exactly where I need to be.

That moment reminded me why I refuse to stay silent about my faith. God has done too much in my life for me to keep it to myself. I remember when I was lost, searching for something more but unsure of where to turn. I longed for someone to show me Jesus without judgment or condemnation. Now, I want to be that person for someone else—to share the truth of Christ with love, compassion, and unwavering boldness.

There are people right now who feel hopeless, longing for peace. If my testimony helps even one person find Jesus, then every risk, every moment of courage, is worth it.

John 8:47 reminds us, "*Whoever belongs to God hears what God says. The reason you do not hear is that you do not belong to God.*" If we aren't hearing Him, maybe it's because we haven't truly surrendered. But God is always inviting us closer. When we seek Him, we begin to recognize His voice—not as a distant echo, but as a steady, guiding presence.

So stand firm. Speak boldly. Live unashamed. God is moving through you in ways you may not even realize. Trust that He will place you exactly where you're meant to be, equipping you for every step. You don't need to have all the answers—you just need a willing heart.

The world needs the light of Christ, and you were made to shine.

Today's Verse:
"*No one can come to me unless the Father who sent me draws them, and I will raise them up at the last day.*"
—John 6:44

RESTORING GOD'S DESIGN FOR FAMILY

> *"So God created mankind in his own image, in the image of God he created them; male and female he created them."*
>
> Genesis 1:27

S ociety often tells us to "live your truth," but we know that God is truth. In today's culture, there is a growing push to undermine biblical roles—especially the role of men as leaders in the home. Masculinity is often shamed, and the family structure that God designed is being redefined and distorted. This shift away from God's blueprint for family has led to confusion, disorder, and unrest in many households. But how did we lose our way?

The law of "first mention" in Scripture teaches that the first time something is mentioned, it sets a pattern for how that idea unfolds throughout the Bible. And when we look at the Garden of Eden, the very first thing satan attacked was the family unit. When Adam and Eve listened to the serpent instead of God, the family suffered (Genesis 3:6). That attack didn't stop in Eden—satan's war on the family has continued ever since. And it's no surprise that today, he still seeks to divide, distract, and distort God's design.

Our children are growing up in a world full of mixed messages. If we as adults, leaders, and parents don't step in and teach them about Jesus, they will be influenced by everything else. Proverbs 22:6 calls us to *"train up a child in the way he should go,"* reminding us that from a young age, we are to lay a foundation of God's truth in their lives. It is through God's Word that they learn their identity and purpose. Without this foundation, families risk losing their connection to God's vision.

The good news is that God has equipped us for this calling. Parents are not alone—Jesus has given us everything we need to teach, guide, and protect our families. And as a community of believers, we are called to support one another in these roles. We must lift up and encourage men who are faithfully leading, serving, and protecting their families. We must also celebrate the compassion, wisdom, and strength of women who reflect the heart of God in the home.

When we honor God's design for the family, we stand firm against the voices that try to tear down what He has established.

Today, let's commit to reclaiming our families for God. Let's seek His guidance, trust in His strength, and stand firm against the noise of the world. We are equipped to teach the next generation about His love, truth, and grace. And as we lean into His design, we will see His peace and purpose restored—in our families, our homes, and our communities.

Today's Verse:
"But as for me and my household, we will serve the Lord."
—Joshua 24:15

FUEL YOUR BODY, HONOR YOUR TEMPLE

"Then God said, 'I give you every seed-bearing plant on the face of the whole earth and every tree that has fruit with seed in it. They will be yours for food.'"
Genesis 1:29

God designed our bodies to be cherished, cared for, and enjoyed. Just like we invest time and energy into growing spiritually, caring for our physical health is another way we honor the Creator who made us. And one of the simplest (and most practical) ways to do that? Fuel your body with wholesome, energizing foods that prepare you for whatever adventures God places in your path!

Here's a list of Nutrition With Wendi's favorite grab-and-go snack combos. Each one pairs protein, fiber, quality carbs, and essential vitamins to keep you feeling fueled, focused, and ready to thrive:

- **Grapes + Jerky:** A perfect mix of sweet and savory, packed with protein and antioxidants.

- **Hummus + Celery:** Crunchy, refreshing, and loaded with fiber and healthy fats.

- **Greek Yogurt + Berries:** Creamy and satisfying, this combo provides probiotics and a burst of antioxidants. -*It is also my favorite daily snack!*

- **String Cheese + Orange:** Simple yet satisfying with vitamin C and calcium in every bite.

- **Chocolate Milk + Banana:** A science backed 3:1 carb to protein ratio combo packed with calcium, carbs, and protein for post-workout recovery!

- **Cottage Cheese + Cherries:** Tangy and sweet, with protein and antioxidants.

- **Deli Turkey + Cucumber Slices:** Refreshing and light, with protein to keep you full.

- **Hard-Boiled Eggs + Carrot Sticks:** Protein meets crunch, perfect for a quick bite anytime.

Nutrition is your secret weapon against the enemy's attacks—because it's hard to fight back when you're hangry, light-headed, and battling a pounding headache!

Today's Verse:
"At the end of ten days they looked healthier and better nourished than any of the young men who ate the royal food."
—Daniel 1:15

FOR SUCH A TIME AS THIS

"Surely, Lord, you bless the righteous; you surround them with your favor as with a shield."

Psalm 5:12

Have you ever felt that God is positioning you for a purpose you may not fully understand yet?

The book of Esther is a powerful story of courage and divine purpose. Esther was placed in the palace *"for such a time as this"* (Esther 4:14). Her journey wasn't about personal gain—she was positioned to save her people and fulfill God's plan. That same call extends to each of us—men and women alike. God places us in specific situations, families, and communities for His purposes. This could very well be your "Esther season"—a time when God is calling you to step up, stand firm, and make a difference right where He has placed you.

Esther faced fear, uncertainty, and the risk of rejection. But she chose to move forward in faith, trusting that God had equipped her for her calling. You, too, may be facing challenges or feel hesitant about where God is leading you. Maybe He's calling you to take a bold step—in your career, in your family, or in your community. Know this: God doesn't call us without also providing the strength and courage to fulfill that call. His purpose for you in this season isn't accidental. He has handpicked and prepared you for it.

Sometimes we're called to lead from the front; other times, from behind the scenes. Whether you're a parent raising children in faith, a leader in your workplace, or someone quietly supporting others through life's ups and downs—your role is meaningful. God uses each of us uniquely, and no role is too small when it's part of His divine plan.

Trust that God has placed you exactly where you need to be—for such a time as this. Step forward with faith, knowing you are part of a bigger story—His story. Let Christ work through you to make an impact that lasts far beyond this season, because He has chosen you for a purpose only *you* can fulfill.

Today's Verse:
"And Esther won the favor of everyone who saw her."
—Esther 2:15

YOUR LABOR IS NOT IN VAIN

"Therefore, my beloved brethren, be steadfast, immovable, always abounding in the work of the Lord, knowing that your labor is not in vain in the Lord."
1 Corinthians 15:58

God works through His children to fulfill His divine purpose. Our careers, talents, and everyday interactions are opportunities for Him to extend His grace, hope, and strength to those in need. Each of us has unique gifts, and when we offer them in service, God can use even the smallest actions to advance His Kingdom.

As a dietitian, I often share insights and advice, sometimes wondering if they truly make a difference—or if they simply ripple across a vast sea without impact. But in His perfect timing, God sends encouragement to remind us that He is always at work.

One such moment came through an email from Isabella, a college athlete navigating significant health challenges. A freshman at the time, she had been quietly reading my posts and took the time to share her journey—one of resilience, transformation, and gratitude. She expressed how God had used the guidance she found through my content to provide hope and encouragement just when she needed it most.

Isabella's story moved me deeply. She had faced the hardships of Celiac disease, the stress of adapting to college life, and the demands of competing as an athlete—all while managing a strict gluten-free diet. She often felt isolated and exhausted. Yet in her struggle, she chose to trust God, and He faithfully provided the support she needed. One of those provisions was the encouragement she found in the words I had shared—words I had written without knowing who they might reach.

Her testimony was a beautiful reminder that God sees every struggle, every tear, and every act of perseverance. He places people and resources in our lives to uplift and sustain us, often in ways we don't immediately recognize. Even when we don't see the results, He is working beneath the surface—growing something beyond what we could imagine.

Be faithful to God in the small things, trust Him with the results, and let your life be a reflection of His love and hope.

You may never fully know who is watching, who is finding strength, or who is drawing closer to God because of what you share.

Today's Verse:
"For great is your love, higher than the heavens; your faithfulness reaches to the skies. Be exalted, O God, above the heavens; let your glory be over all the earth."
—Psalm 108:4-5

THE BLESSING OF OBEDIENCE

"For this is what the LORD, the God of Israel, says:
There will always be flour and olive oil left in your
containers until the time when the LORD sends rain
and the crops grow again!"

1 Kings 17:14

When God prompts you to pray, give, or make a change, **it's not just about the action—it's about trust.** Every moment of obedience is an invitation to lean deeper into His heart. Obedience isn't just a duty we fulfill; it's a doorway that leads us into His blessings, His provision, and sometimes even His miracles.

We see this clearly in 1 Kings 17. A widow in Zarephath was gathering sticks to prepare her last meal, expecting to die with her son. She had only a handful of flour and a little oil left. Yet when the prophet Elijah asked her to make him bread first, she obeyed, even though it must have felt terrifying. She gave from her lack, not her abundance. Because of her simple, courageous faith, God multiplied her resources. The jar of flour and jug of oil never ran out during the entire drought.

There's a powerful principle tucked inside her story: obedience releases provision. When we step forward in faith, even with trembling hands, God steps in with the miraculous.

I recently experienced this firsthand. I felt a strong prompting from the Lord to give $500 to a friend's charity. Honestly, it didn't feel like a convenient time financially. But I knew God was inviting me to trust Him, so I obeyed. Just hours later, I received an unexpected client purchase totaling $499.99—almost the exact amount! It wasn't just about the money. It was about the reminder that God sees, He provides, and He blesses obedience. That initial step of trust has since turned into a joyful annual donation for me.

One of the greatest joys has been partnering with Future Marriage University, a beautiful ministry based in Franklin, Tennessee, that equips Christians to date well and marry well. Beyond their mission, they often send personal emails full of encouragement and prayers over me and my business. It's been a tangible reminder that when you sow into good ground, God multiplies the blessing in ways you don't expect.

Whatever God is prompting you to do today—whether it's giving, forgiving, stepping out, or letting go—take the step. Obedience always leads to more of His presence and provision. Trust that even if you can't see the whole story yet, God is already at work on the other side of your yes.

Weekly Challenge:

This week, choose one act of obedience that stretches your faith. It might be giving more than feels comfortable, reaching out to someone you've avoided, or finally saying "yes" to something God has been stirring in your heart. Don't wait until it makes perfect sense—trust Him enough to move now. Write down what happens, even if the results are small at first, and celebrate the fact that every step of obedience draws you closer to His heart.

LIVING WITH KINDNESS

"Rejoice in the Lord always.
I will say it again: Rejoice."

Philippians 4:4

At 4:48 a.m., I found myself wide awake, lying in the still-ness of a hotel room in Savannah, Georgia. No alarm. No noise. Just me and the quiet. I tossed and turned, but sleep would not come back. Finally, I gave in and whispered, "Alright, God. What do You want me to know?"

As I lay there, I glanced at the clock and looked for a Bible verse that matched the time. I opened my Bible and found myself in Philippians 4:4–8. *"Rejoice in the Lord always. I will say it again: Rejoice... Do not be anxious about anything... And the peace of God, which transcends all understanding, will guard your hearts and minds in Christ Jesus."*

I sat with those words for a while. I prayed them back to God, feeling His nearness in the quiet, and soon enough, a deep peace washed over me. I fell back asleep.

A few hours later, coffee was calling my name. As I headed out, I noticed an older couple walking hand in hand, laughing softly to each other. Their joy was unmistakable. We ended up in the same coffee shop, and as I stood behind them, I felt that familiar nudge in my heart. *Bless them.*

I did not even hesitate. I paid for their order and whispered a prayer that God would bless their marriage and their trip. When they turned around to thank me, I smiled and said, "It's my gift. But really, you should thank the Lord. It's His money. You two look so happy. I hope you enjoy your trip. Now go and pay it forward."

The gentleman chuckled and told me they were visiting from Michigan. As they left, the joy lingered in the air like a sweet fragrance.

That $25 was one of the best investments I could have made. Kindness is contagious. In a world that often feels heavy, even small acts can light up someone's whole day.

Today, ask God to open your eyes to someone you can bless. It might be a stranger, a coworker, or someone in your own home. It does not have to cost much. Sometimes, a kind word or simply being present for someone is enough to remind them that they are loved and seen by God.

Do not just read about kindness. **Live it.** And when you do, take a moment to thank Jesus for giving you the privilege of carrying His love into the world.

Prayer:

Lord, open my eyes today to the people You've placed around me. Help me see with Your eyes, love with Your heart, and give with open hands. Make me sensitive to Your nudges, even in the smallest moments. Thank You for the privilege of carrying Your kindness into the world. Thank You also for the wisdom of the older generation who show us, through their joy, endurance, and love, what it means to walk faithfully with You. Use me today to be a glimpse of Your goodness to someone who needs it. Amen.

ATMOSPHERES OF FAITH OR DOUBT?

"He could not do any miracles there, except lay his hands on a few sick people and heal them. He was amazed at their lack of faith."

Mark 6:5-6

Have you ever considered how your environment might be shaping your faith?

Not just the physical space around you, but the emotional, relational, and even digital atmosphere you live in each day. When Jesus returned to His hometown of Nazareth, He came with the power to heal and restore. But the people's lack of faith created an environment that limited what He could do (Mark 6:5-6). It wasn't that Jesus lost His power—it was that the atmosphere didn't make room for Him to move.

The same can be true in our own lives. If our surroundings are filled with constant negativity, doubt, fear, or distraction, it becomes harder to sense God's presence or receive what He wants to do in us. Scripture shows us that Jesus was intentional about where He spent His time. He often withdrew to quiet places to pray (Luke 5:16), and He sometimes removed people from a room before performing a miracle (Mark 5:40). He understood that faith creates space for the supernatural.

So what about your atmosphere? Are the people and influences in your life helping you draw nearer to God—or quietly pulling you away? Are your thoughts being shaped by truth or by fear? Romans 12:2 reminds us to renew our minds and resist conforming to the world around us. That might mean setting boundaries, choosing encouraging voices, or spending more time in God's Word.

Ask the Lord to show you anything that may be cluttering your spiritual space. He is faithful to lead you in love. As you create an environment of faith, you may begin to see God move in ways you never imagined.

Today's Verse:

"But when you pray, go into your room, close the door and pray to your Father, who is unseen. Then your Father, who sees what is done in secret, will reward you."

—Matthew 6:6

TURNING THE WORLD UPSIDE DOWN

"These who have turned the world upside down have come here too."

Acts 17:6

I magine living out your faith so boldly that people can't ignore it—even if their reaction is negative.

That's exactly what happened to Paul and Silas in Acts 17. They weren't just preaching—they were sparking a revolution! Frustrated by the impact, their opponents accused them of *"turning the world upside down."* What was meant as an insult became proof that the gospel was alive, powerful, and impossible to silence!

The Gospel was never meant to leave the world unchanged. Jesus didn't come to blend in with the status quo—He came to transform it. When His truth collides with a broken world, everything shifts. Love replaces hate. Forgiveness triumphs over bitterness. Peace overcomes chaos. This is the power you carry when you choose to boldly live out your faith.

But let's be honest—this kind of boldness isn't easy. Standing for truth in a culture that thrives on compromise can be draining. You may face criticism, rejection, or even hostility. Yet opposition is often confirmation that you're right where God wants you.

The gospel is countercultural because it calls people higher—to something greater than themselves.

So, are you ready to turn the world upside down? It doesn't require perfection—just a willing heart. Start small: share your story, extend radical love, stand firm in your convictions. Trust that God will use your obedience in ways beyond what you can imagine. The same Spirit who empowered Paul and Silas is alive in you today.

And who knows? The very people who resist you now may one day thank you for the way you changed their world.

Today's Verse:
"For in Him we live and move and have our being."
—Acts 17:28

GUARD YOUR HEART, PROTECT YOUR PEACE

"Above all else, guard your heart, for everything you do flows from it."

Proverbs 4:23

Early in my business, I faced rejection after rejection. Many teams and schools dismissed me. Former professors told me I would fail—that I'd never make it in sports nutrition, let alone become a dietitian. As I tried to grow my business, their words began to creep in. Clients backed out of agreements. Competitor dietitians seemed to thrive while I struggled to make ends meet. I was gaining clients and working with teams, but the financial and emotional strain was heavy. I went without a lot. The weight of failure settled in, and I began to question if I was even capable.

The voices around me—some well-meaning, others not—whispered discouragement: *Maybe this isn't for you. Maybe you're not strong enough. Maybe you should just go work for the Mayo Clinic. Don't worry—most businesses fail in the first year. It would be more comfortable to work for someone else.* And for a moment, I almost believed them. *But God.*

Instead of feeding my spirit with His truth, I had been absorbing fear, doubt, and comparison. I realized I had to make a decision: if I wanted to guard my heart, I had to unplug from the dead outlets I was drawing energy from.

So I made a shift. I replaced negativity with God's promises. I began reading Scripture morning and night, letting His Word renew my confidence. I set boundaries with people who drained my energy and surrounded myself with those who spoke life and faith over my calling. Most importantly, I prayed—every day—asking God to guard my heart from discouragement and to fill it with His wisdom, strength, and peace.

Philippians 4:8 became my anchor: *"Whatever is true, whatever is noble, whatever is right, whatever is pure, whatever is lovely, whatever is admirable—if anything is excellent or praiseworthy—think about such things."*

As I chose to dwell on truth instead of failure, my heart began to heal. And as I guarded my heart, both my business and my faith began to flourish.

If I've learned anything, it's this—God's voice is the only one that truly matters. Don't let the critics, the doubters, or even well-meaning friends and family steer you off course. Their opinions might be loud, but they're not always right. To protect your peace and your purpose, you have to guard your heart above all else—just like Proverbs 4:23 says. Stay close to the One who called you. The Holy Spirit will never lead you astray.

Today's Verse:
*"Create in me a clean heart, O God,
and renew a right spirit within me."*
—Psalm 51:10

DAY 179

DISCOVERING YOUR SPIRITUAL GIFTS

"There are different kinds of gifts, but the same Spirit distributes them."

1 Corinthians 12:4

Have you ever asked yourself, **"What is my purpose in life?"** For many, this question lingers unanswered. As a dietitian, I've found clarity in my calling: to point people to Christ through my work. But over the years, I've met many who struggle to define their purpose. Do you know yours?

Each of us is uniquely created with talents, passions, and life experiences that shape how we serve in God's Kingdom. When we embrace these gifts, we begin to understand our role in His greater plan—not just for our own fulfillment, but to bless and uplift others.

I once asked a man, *"What are your spiritual gifts?"* He paused, unsure how to answer. It reminded me that many believers either don't know their gifts or underestimate them. Yet Scripture tells us clearly that we've all been equipped. In 1 Corinthians 12:8–10, Paul lists gifts such as wisdom, knowledge, faith, healing, miracles, prophecy, and discernment. Romans 12:6–8 adds serving, teaching, encouragement, giving, leadership, and mercy.

These aren't just qualities—they're spiritual tools, given by God to build up the body of Christ.

Some are gifted in leadership, inspiring and guiding others. Others carry mercy, offering comfort to the hurting. Some teach, while others quietly serve behind the scenes. Each gift matters. When we recognize and use them, we not only fulfill our purpose—we reflect God's glory.

If you're unsure of your gifts, start with this: *What comes naturally to you? What brings you joy and energy? What do people consistently come to you for—wise advice, help, encouragement?* Sometimes, our gifts are revealed through trials, life experiences, or divine nudges we can't ignore. Ask God to show you. He promises wisdom to those who seek it (James 1:5).

So if you're searching for purpose, start here: seek the Holy Spirit, ask Him to show you your gifts, and be willing to use them—even if it feels small. Because in God's hands, even the smallest offering can change the world.

Today's Verse:
"For we are His workmanship, created in Christ Jesus for good works, which God prepared beforehand, that we should walk in them." —Ephesians 2:10

YOU'RE AN ANSWER TO SOMEONE'S PRAYER

"A spiritual gift is given to each of us so we can help each other."

1 Corinthians 12:7

Yesterday, we explored how God gives each of us unique spiritual gifts and aligns us with others who may carry strengths we don't. Today, let's go a little deeper: *why* did God design it this way? The answer is simple—yet profound: **you were never meant to do life alone.** Your gifts were never meant to sit on a shelf. They were created to serve, encourage, and build up others within the body of Christ.

You are an answer to someone's need.

That natural ability you've always had? The thing that feels "too easy" to be special? That might be the exact way God wants to move through you. Maybe you have a calming presence that brings peace to chaos. Or a deep compassion that leads you to care for others without hesitation. Perhaps your strength is in offering wise advice, organizing what feels overwhelming, or simply showing up when others can't.

You might wonder why others don't think the way you do, or why they struggle with something that feels second nature to you. That's the beauty of spiritual gifts—they're not universal. **They're personal, intentional, and given "for the common good."** (1 Corinthians 12:7)

God designed you with a purpose. He knit your gifts into your personality, your life story, and even your trials. The very things you've walked through have prepared you to carry what someone else needs. And when we each bring our gifts to the table—whether it's teaching, serving, encouraging, leading, or showing mercy—the Church becomes whole. Strong. Alive.

So today, take a moment to ask the Lord: *"What have You placed in me that You want to use for others?"*
And then be bold. Use it. Share it. Don't hide the light He's placed within you.

Because when you walk in your gift, you're not only glorifying God—you're helping His people flourish.

Challenge for This Week:

Ask five people from different areas of your life—friends, family, coworkers, or mentors—what they think your gift might be. Choose a diverse group to get a well-rounded perspective. Write down what each person shares with you. Then, set aside time to sit with the Lord, asking Him to highlight areas that might be your strongest gifts. For example, those with the gift of mercy may naturally provide comfort to others, while those with the gift of wisdom often bring clarity in decision-making. Let this week's exercise be a step in discovering how God has uniquely equipped you!

GOD IS RESTORING YOU

'But I will restore you to health and heal your wounds,' declares the LORD, 'because you are called an outcast, Zion for whom no one cares.'
Jeremiah 30:17

Today, God wants you to know that He sees your wounds—both the visible and the hidden. You may feel overlooked, forgotten, or even cast aside, but God calls you His own. His promise of restoration isn't just physical; it's emotional, spiritual, and relational. He desires to bring wholeness where there's been brokenness, comfort where there's been rejection, and strength where there's been weariness.

I once struggled with pride, though I didn't recognize it at first. I thought I had to be strong, capable, and self-sufficient—never needing help, never admitting weakness. But deep down, I was carrying wounds I refused to acknowledge. I believed seeking healing meant exposing my flaws and weaknesses, and that terrified me. Then, through a difficult season of rejection, God revealed my pride. I had placed my worth in my own strength rather than in Him. Slowly, He showed me that true strength comes from surrender, not self-sufficiency. As I laid my wounds before Him, He replaced my pride with peace and my self-reliance with trust in His grace.

God's healing is deeply personal. He sees the pain of betrayal, the disappointment of missed opportunities, and the wounds of feeling misunderstood. Like Zion, once called an outcast, He transforms what the world disregards into something treasured. His restoration reaches beyond the surface, bringing lasting freedom and peace.

But healing requires honesty and repentance. God calls you to sit with Him, to let Him reveal the wounds you've buried under busyness or pride. He isn't a distant healer—He walks with you, gently uncovering what needs restoration. As you surrender, you'll begin to see your purpose in a new light. Often, our greatest calling is birthed from our deepest wounds. Our brokenness can become a source of strength, light, and ministry to others. God longs to turn what once marked you as an outcast into a testimony of His power and grace. Will you let Him?

Today's Verse:
"He heals the brokenhearted and binds up their wounds."
—Psalm 147:3

WHEN GOD CALLS YOU TO SPEAK

"If we are out of our mind, as some say, it is for God; if we are in our right mind, it is for you. For Christ's love compels us, because we are convinced that one died for all, and therefore all died. And He died for all, that those who live should no longer live for themselves but for him who died for them and was raised again."

2 Corinthians 5:13-15

Real love tells the truth. And sometimes, that truth is hard to say. There will be moments when God nudges you to share a word with someone you care about—a word that may gently challenge them or lovingly point out something that's not fully aligned with Him. These moments stretch us. They pull us into the tension between obedience to God and the fear of how the other person might react. But when God asks you to speak, He's not asking you to fix people. He's simply asking you to love them enough to tell the truth—with *humility*, not judgment.

The Apostle Paul knew this tension well. He often had to deliver hard truths to the early churches, confronting divisions, sin, and wrong thinking. Yet even when Paul's words were firm, they were never fueled by anger or pride. He urged believers to, **"Do everything in love"** (1 Corinthians 16:14). Paul understood that truth without love can crush a soul, but love without truth can leave a soul wandering. It's not one or the other—it's both. Real love speaks because it cares too much to stay silent, and real truth flows from a heart anchored in Christ's compassion.

I've experienced this firsthand. There was a time when God put a difficult message on my heart for someone close to me. I wrestled with it for days. What if it ruined our relationship? What if they got angry or pushed me away? The fear was real, but after a lot of prayer, I knew I couldn't let fear have the final word. Obedience had to. So I spoke the truth as gently as I could. At first, it didn't go over well. They resisted. But later, they admitted others had noticed the same thing. God had been speaking all along—I was just one small voice He used to confirm what He was already stirring in their heart.

That experience taught me something I'll never forget: our responsibility is not to control the outcome. It's simply to be faithful. As 2 Corinthians 5:14 reminds us, **"Christ's love compels us."** Not fear. Not pride. Just His love, moving through imperfect people like you and me.

If God is putting someone on your heart today, don't stay silent out of fear. Pray first. Speak with humility. Trust that He's already working behind the scenes. Your obedience might be the very encouragement—or gentle course correction—that helps lead someone closer to Jesus.

Today's Verse:
"Instead, speaking the truth in love, we will grow to become in every respect the mature body of him who is the head, that is, Christ." —Ephesians 4:15

TRUSTING GOD WHEN LETTING GO HURTS

"But seek first His kingdom and His righteousness, and all these things will be given to you as well."
Matthew 6:33

S ometimes obedience feels like holding on. Other times, it looks like *letting go.* Recently, God asked me to release a friendship that had once been very dear to me. It wasn't something I wanted. I wrestled with it, questioning why He would lead me to walk away from something so meaningful. But beneath the questions, there was a quiet certainty stirring in my spirit: *This is what I'm asking you to do.*

Maybe you've felt that too. Maybe you're standing in a place where something once good no longer fits the season you're stepping into. In moments like these, it's easy to wonder if letting go means failure or loss. But often, it means trust. It means believing that God sees further than we can.

When God invites us to release something—or someone—it's never random. He moves with purpose. His direction usually comes gently: through His Word, through a series of confirming moments, or through that persistent stirring in your spirit that you just can't shake. 1 Thessalonians 5:21 reminds us to **"test everything; hold fast to what is good."**

For me, God confirmed His leading in different ways—through dreams, conversations I wasn't expecting, and through the steady peace that came once I surrendered. That's one of the marks of true obedience: it may feel hard at first, but His peace eventually follows.

Letting go makes room for what's ahead. It creates space for the new things God has prepared—things we might not even know to pray for yet. Sometimes the release isn't even about us; it's about what God is doing in someone else's story.

Romans 8:38–39 reminds us that nothing—*not sorrow, fear, mistakes, or missed timing*—can separate us from God's love. His love is the safe place we return to every time He asks something hard of us. And when we say yes, even through tears, we open ourselves to be transformed by that love in ways we never imagined.

If you feel God stirring your heart to release something today, trust Him. You may not understand it all yet—but obedience always positions you for God's best.

Going Deeper:

Sometimes, letting go isn't about walking away from something bad. It's about trusting God when He asks you to release something good, too. It could be a close friendship, a work partnership, a church relationship, or even a small group that once felt like family. But seasons change, and sometimes the Holy Spirit gently moves us on because He sees growth ahead that we can't yet imagine. It doesn't mean the connection was wasted or wrong; it means He is writing a new chapter. When you feel the Lord leading you to release something precious, it can break your heart a little—but it will also prepare you for new beginnings in your life.

STAY AWAKE: GOD IS WHISPERING

"Be sober-minded; be watchful. Your adversary the devil prowls around like a roaring lion, seeking someone to devour."
1 Peter 5:8

In seasons where blessings begin to flow, it can be easy to assume that every open door is from the Lord. But not every "good thing" is a "God thing." The enemy often wraps distractions in attractive packages, hoping to lure you off course. Yet the Holy Spirit, in His deep love for you, is drawing near—sharpening your discernment and inviting you to trust Him with fresh sensitivity.

You may begin to feel a quiet stirring, a gentle uncase in certain conversations, decisions, or relationships. Don't ignore that nudge. That "holy agitation" is often God's whisper, softly asking you to pause and lean in closer. Just as Joshua was instructed to meditate on God's Word day and night, you too are being called to stay grounded—to guard your heart and renew your mind in truth.

This isn't a call to be afraid—it's an invitation to deeper intimacy. God is not trying to overwhelm you; He's protecting you. He sees what you can't, and He is patiently teaching you to see with spiritual eyes. As 1 Samuel 16:7 reminds us, **"Man looks at the outward appearance, but the Lord looks at the heart."**

Now is the time to be still before Him and test everything by the light of His Word. His wisdom, as James 3:17 tells us, is *"pure, peace-loving, considerate, and full of mercy."* If something unsettles your spirit, take a step back. Ask the Lord to clarify. He is faithful to respond.

You are deeply loved, and God's plans for you are sacred. Don't rush ahead. Stay near. Let God's voice lead you—not through pressure, but through *peace*. In every decision, in every moment, let His gentle presence be your guide.

Today's Verse:
"Therefore let us not sleep, as others do,
but let us watch and be sober."
— 1 Thessalonians 5:6

FROM SURVIVING TO THRIVING

"In all these things we are more than conquerors through him who loved us."

Romans 8:37

I spent much of my life in survival mode. Growing up without a mother, I often felt like I was just trying to get by—longing for the guidance and love that so many of my friends had. My dad did his best, and our relatives helped, but nothing could replace a mother's presence. Seeing others with their moms stirred a deep sadness in me, and it hurt even more when I was teased for not having one and for being a tomboy. I learned early how to be strong, how to push through, and how to survive. But God never intended for me to stay in survival mode. He calls us not just to endure—but to thrive.

When Paul says we are *"more than conquerors"* (Romans 8:37), he isn't talking about barely making it—he's declaring a victory so complete that it transforms the way we live. God never intended life to be easy or that pain won't touch us, but He promised to help us through everything. With Jesus at the center of our lives we can rise with joy, strength, and peace instead of fear.

For years, I wrestled with the questions that had no easy answers. *Why didn't God heal my mother so she could stay and be part of my life? Why didn't she fight harder to hold on?* As I got older, the questions grew quieter, but the ache remained. Instead of staying stuck in what I could not change, I began asking God a different question — *What do You want me to know from this?*

Through it all, God met me in my brokenness and gently began to rewrite the story. Thriving doesn't mean avoiding pain—it means letting God fill the empty places with His love, replacing bitterness with peace and survival with purpose.

Maybe you're still asking, *Why?* That's okay. But don't stop there. Ask, *God, what do You want me to see in this? What victory are You revealing?* Thriving starts with surrender—trusting that God's love is enough to carry you through.

You were not created just to survive. You were made to overcome. To rise. To thrive. In Christ, the victory is already yours.

Today's Verse:
"I have told you these things, so that in me you may have peace. In this world, you will have trouble. But take heart! I have overcome the world."
—John 16:33

OPEN THE DOOR TO FREEDOM

"Those whom I love, I rebuke and discipline. So be earnest and repent. Here I am! I stand at the door and knock. If anyone hears my voice and opens the door, I will come in and eat with that person, and they with me."

Revelation 3:19-20

For a long time, I stayed in a place that was breaking me—hoping, praying, and believing it would get better. I thought if I just held on longer, gave more, forgave more, or prayed harder, the pain would eventually pass. I convinced myself that staying was the right thing to do. But no matter how much effort I gave, something deep inside whispered: *This isn't what I have for you.*

What I didn't understand then was that I had slipped into survival mode—trying to hold everything together while silently falling apart. I thought enduring hardship made me strong. I thought staying quiet made me faithful. But God never asked me to carry the weight of something He didn't place on my shoulders.

Eventually, through prayer, Scripture, and quiet nudges from the Holy Spirit, I began to see the truth. God wasn't calling me to stay where I was being emotionally and spiritually diminished.

He was calling me out—to walk away from what was harmful and to step into the life He had been preparing for me all along. It wasn't easy. Leaving meant facing fear, uncertainty, and the grief of letting go. But with each step, God met me—with peace, with provision, and with the reminder that His love for me was not dependent on my ability to endure suffering.

Revelation 3:18 says, "Buy from Me gold refined in the fire." God's refining fire isn't meant to destroy us—it's meant to reveal what's pure and lasting. In that season, He burned away lies I had believed for years: that I wasn't worthy of more, that suffering proved loyalty, that love had to hurt. And in their place, He planted truth: that I am seen, chosen, and deeply loved.

Jesus said, "Here I am! I stand at the door and knock" (Revelation 3:20). He had been knocking all along. But I had to be willing to open the door—to surrender what I thought I needed in order to receive what He had prepared for me.

If you're in a place where you're just surviving, I want to remind you: God didn't create you to live in constant pain, fear, or confusion. He calls you into freedom. Into healing. Into a life that reflects His love and goodness.

Open the door. Let Him in. And trust that what He's calling you into is far more beautiful than anything He's asking you to leave behind.

Today's Verse:
"So, because you are lukewarm—neither hot nor cold—I am about to spit you out of my mouth. Those whom I love, I rebuke and discipline. So be earnest and repent."
—Revelation 3:16, 19

TRUSTING GOD WITH EVERY STEP

"The Lord your God will drive out those nations before you, little by little."

Deuteronomy 7:22

There was a time when I felt stuck in my business—operating, but not truly thriving. I had dreams of expansion, of landing bigger school contracts, of stepping into the full potential I believed God had placed before me. But fear and self-doubt crept in. *Will these programs trust me with their athletes? Will they be willing to pay the fee for my services? What if I fail?* It was easier to stay where I was—hosting solo talks here and there, doing 1:1 coaching, writing a few blog posts. But deep down, I knew I had to take the leap and trust that God would catch me.

Then came the opportunity. Multiple schools wanted to partner for 6 to 12 months at a time—and they were happy to pay the fee I quoted. It was bigger than anything I had pursued before, and with it came uncertainty. *Could I handle the workload? Was I truly equipped for this?* I was already working 12-hour days. I wrestled with doubts, but deep down, I sensed God's voice saying, *"The settling season is over."* It was time to stop circling the same safe places and step forward in faith. Soon after, I was able to hire a few new dietitians and began scaling my private practice by year three.

Like the Israelites standing on the edge of the Promised Land, I had a choice. They had spent years wandering, often looking back to Egypt in fear, even though God was calling them forward. The land was theirs—but possessing it required faith, courage, and action. And just like them, I realized that stepping into God's promises doesn't mean the road will be easy—it means trusting Him to provide along the way. The moment I let go of fear and said yes to His leading, He opened doors I never could have opened on my own.

If you've been hesitating, wondering if it's time to step into something new, hear this: *Do not settle here.* God has more for you. The path may not be easy, but He is with you. His promises are not just for survival—they are for abundance, for growth, for thriving. Trust Him. Take the step. And watch how He leads you into a land flowing with His blessings.

Today's Verse:
"Go in and take possession of the land..."
—Deuteronomy 1:8

GOD SEES MORE IN YOU THAN YOU SEE

"Trust in the Lord with all your heart and lean not on your own understanding; in all your ways submit to him, and he will make your paths straight."

Proverbs 3:5-6

Pastor Craig Groeschel once shared a powerful thought: *"What you worry and stress about most in your life is where you trust God the least."* This statement resonated deeply with me, especially when I began reflecting on areas of my life where I clung to control—relationships being one of the most significant.

For many, dating is a complex and often confusing part of life, especially when we consider that the Bible doesn't provide a detailed roadmap for modern relationships. But while the Bible may not specifically address dating, it offers profound wisdom on how to love, communicate, and honor God in our relationships. The principles of love, trust, and honor are woven throughout Scripture, giving us everything we need to approach relationships with intention and faith.

I came to realize that the foundation of any meaningful relationship—whether dating, marriage, or even friendships—must be built on a shared love for Christ. *Without that common faith, the foundation is shaky.* This truth has become even clearer in my own journey: If I'm going to invest my heart, it must be in a relationship where Christ is the cornerstone. This principle extends beyond dating—it applies to all relationships in our lives. Whether you are single, dating, married, or healing from a breakup, God's call is the same: trust Him fully with your relationships.

If you find yourself feeling uncertain or anxious about a relationship, remember that God's intervention is always timely and trustworthy. His guidance brings the peace and clarity that worry can never offer. He knows the desires of your heart, and His plan for your relationships is always better than anything you could orchestrate on your own. The moments when we feel the need to control and worry often reveal areas where we're not fully trusting God. Yet, He gently invites us to release that control into His hands.

When we place our trust in His plan, rather than trying to control the outcome, we open ourselves to a peace, love, and security that only He can provide. Let go of the need to control, and let His hand lead you through every relationship.

Today's Verse:

"Do not be anxious about anything, but in every situation, by prayer and petition, with thanksgiving, present your requests to God." —Philippians 4:6

TRUSTING GOD WHEN YOU FEEL UNQUALIFIED

"But the Lord said to me, 'Do not say, "I am too young." You must go to everyone I send you to and say whatever I command you."

Jeremiah 1:7

Throughout Scripture, we see God calling people to extraordinary purposes—and almost every time, they respond with doubt about their abilities. We often feel too weak, too flawed, or simply *not enough* to carry out what God is asking of us. Yet in those very moments of self-doubt, God steps in and begins to reveal a version of ourselves we didn't even know existed.

I experienced this firsthand when people told me I would fail. I was "too young" to start a business, and sports nutrition was considered too competitive for someone like me. The message was clear: I didn't have what it took to succeed in an industry that felt daunting and oversaturated. But God had a different perspective.

Like Moses, I found myself focused on my limitations. When God called Moses to lead Israel out of Egypt, his immediate response was, *"Pardon your servant, Lord. I have never been eloquent... I am slow of speech and tongue"* (Exodus 4:10). Moses saw himself as inadequate—yet God saw a leader. I, too, saw myself as too young and inexperienced. But God saw someone He could use.

God doesn't call us based on our weaknesses or the doubts others place on us. He calls us according to His power, His purpose, and His plan. I came to understand that it wasn't about proving myself or meeting worldly standards—it was about trusting God and taking the next step in faith. And as I did, God began to uncover strength and boldness within me that I hadn't seen before.

Here's what I've learned: **God sees a version of you that you may not see yet.** He has uniquely equipped you to serve His Kingdom in a way no one else can. When doubts arise—and they will—remember that God has already chosen, empowered, and equipped you for the purpose He placed before you.

Don't let the voices of fear, insecurity, or comparison hold you back from becoming the person He created you to be. Trust Him. Step forward. And watch Him do more through your life than you ever imagined possible.

Today's Verse:
But he said to me, 'My grace is sufficient for you, for my power is made perfect in weakness.' Therefore I will boast all the more gladly about my weaknesses, so that Christ's power may rest on me.—2 Corinthians 12:9

LOVE WITHOUT CONDITIONS

"'Which of these three do you think was a neighbor to the man who fell into the hands of robbers?' The expert in the law replied, 'The one who had mercy on him.' Jesus told him, 'Go and do likewise.'"

Luke 10:36-37

Since truly surrendering my life to Christ, I've found so much joy in giving to others—whether it's buying someone lunch, paying for a homeless person's meal, or donating to a charity. Generosity flows more freely when you realize everything you have belongs to God. He calls us to be a "good neighbor," just as Jesus described in the parable of the Good Samaritan in Luke 10:30–35. The Samaritan didn't walk past the person in need. He stopped, helped, and showed compassion. As followers of Jesus, we're called to do the same.

During a trip to Pensacola, Florida, I passed a group of homeless men while out on a walk. I felt a gentle nudge from the Lord: *Buy them donuts.* My first response was hesitation—*What if they respond poorly? What if they don't want them?* But then I remembered that every gift, every dollar I have, is God's. So I said a quick prayer for courage and protection, walked to a nearby bakery, and brought back a box of donuts.

To my surprise, they received them with joy. That small act of kindness brightened their day—and mine. But during the interaction, I noticed some of them had iPhones and even an iPad. Instantly, judgment crept in: *Why not sell those and use the money to get off the streets?* But I caught myself. Who am I to judge their situation? I don't know their stories, the battles they've faced, or the reasons they're in that place. God didn't ask me to investigate or evaluate—He simply asked me to love.

We often form opinions based on what we see, forgetting that God sees the whole picture. He sees the pain, the private battles, the humanity. And let's be honest—every one of us has needed mercy. We've all fallen short. Jesus has extended us grace and kindness time and time again, even when we didn't deserve it.

When we encounter someone in need, our job isn't to assess whether they're "worthy." Our job is to reflect the heart of Christ—to give, to serve, to love.

So let me ask you: **How can you show mercy and kindness to someone today, remembering the mercy Jesus has shown to you?**

Today's Verse:
"Do not judge, or you too will be judged."
—Matthew 7:1

JESUS IS CALLING YOU

"Return to Me, and I will return to you," says the Lord Almighty.

Malachi 3:7

I f you've ever drifted away from someone you love, you know it rarely happens all at once. Distance builds quietly—through distractions, misunderstandings, or simply neglect. One day you look up and realize something precious has grown distant.

That's what happened between God and His people. In Malachi 3:7, God isn't shouting at them. He's appealing to their hearts. He's not focused on everything they did wrong—He's focused on restoring what was lost. *Return to Me*, He says. *And I will return to you.*

It's easy to think this verse is only for people who are in full rebellion, but the truth is, all of us have places in our hearts where we drift. Maybe it's a slow loss of passion for prayer. Maybe it's compromise creeping into small decisions. Maybe it's the fear or disappointment that made us subtly pull back from trusting God fully.

The beauty of God's call is that it doesn't come with shame. It comes with open arms. God doesn't say, *"Clean up first, and then come back."* He simply says, *"Return to Me."* His invitation is about relationship, not performance.

The Hebrew word used for "return" carries the idea of turning back, like a traveler realizing they're on the wrong road and making a full-hearted decision to go home. It's not just feeling sorry. It's about realigning your heart and your steps with Father God.

I can think of seasons in my life when I got so busy—even doing "good things"—that I didn't realize how far my heart had drifted. Outwardly, everything looked fine. Inwardly, I was tired and disconnected. It wasn't until I stopped and responded to God's gentle tug that I found my way back to His presence—and with it, the deep peace my soul had been missing.

Wherever you are today, hear God's heart: He's not distant because He's mad at you. He's near, waiting for you to turn back. Jesus desires closeness with you more than you even realize. If you've drifted, don't stay away out of guilt. Come back. Come back quickly! His arms are already open.

Today's Verse:
"Draw near to God and He will draw near to you. Cleanse your hands, you sinners; and purify your hearts, you double-minded."
—James 4:8

GOD DOESN'T JUST LOVE YOU—HE LIKES YOU

"We love because He first loved us."

1 John 4:19

For years, I struggled to grasp the depth of God's love. I knew, in theory, that He loved me—after all, *He is love*. But did He actually *like* me? Did He delight in me, flaws and all? It took me far too long to realize that the answer is yes. God didn't choose me because He needed me; He chose me because He wanted me. And He wants you too.

When we fully embrace the truth that we are loved—not in a distant, obligatory way, but with deep affection and joy—everything shifts. The moment I accepted that God not only loves me but *likes* me, my entire perspective changed. Joy began to fill even the most ordinary moments. I no longer felt the pressure to earn my worth or prove myself, because the God of the universe delights in me. And He delights in you.

In 1 John 4:19, the word "loved" in the original text refers to the highest form of love. It's not driven by emotion or performance, but by choice and commitment. It goes beyond affection—it moves into action. This is a sacrificial, unwavering love that remains constant no matter what. It's the kind of love that makes the first move, without waiting for us to be "good enough" in return.

That's what John is saying: *You are loved with a love that came first.* Before you knew God. Before you did anything for Him. Before you changed, matured, or healed—He loved you. When this truth begins to sink in—not just intellectually, but into your *heart*—everything shifts. You stop living to earn love, and you start living from a place of already being loved. You begin to realize that your identity is not based on your past, your performance, or people's opinions. It's rooted in the unshakable, unconditional love of God.

And here's the beautiful part: God's love doesn't just rescue—it also *empowers*. Because we are loved first, we are now able to love others. When we receive God's love, it spills out into our relationships—not as obligation, but as overflow.

But to love others well, we must first receive love well. Have you fully received the love God has for you? Not just believed it in theory, but soaked in it—let it cover the places you've hidden, the wounds you carry, the parts of yourself you've struggled to accept?

You are loved with a love that is deep, steady, and unconditional. A love that doesn't shift with your performance or disappear when you fall short. Not because of who you are, but because of who He is. The pressure's off. You're not working for love—you're already held by it. And that changes everything.

Today's Verse:
"Be still, and know that I am God."
—Psalm 46:10

SATISFIED IN HIM

"For he satisfies the longing soul, and the hungry soul he fills with good things."

Psalm 107:9

If you've ever struggled with your relationship with food—eating too much, too little, or turning to it for comfort—you're not alone. So many of us carry silent burdens when it comes to our bodies and our eating habits. We know what we should do. We know what is "healthy." But knowledge and willpower alone don't heal the heart.

The Bible speaks of gluttony, a word that can carry guilt and shame if misunderstood. But God never brings up gluttony to condemn you. He brings it up to gently lead you toward healing. In Greek, the word often translated as "glutton" means someone given over to indulgence—someone who eats beyond what is needed or is ruled by appetite. But this word points more to the condition of the heart than just the action of eating. It speaks to what we run to when we're hurting, empty, or overwhelmed.

Maybe food has become that place for you—your escape, your reward, your comfort when life feels heavy. And maybe you've tried countless times to "fix it," only to end up in the same cycle. But here's the good news: Jesus doesn't stand at a distance, waiting for you to get it right. He comes close, right into the struggle, and offers grace, not guilt.

God knows your story. He knows your pain. He knows the moments when you've reached for food not because you were hungry, but because your heart ached. And He doesn't shame you for it—He invites you into something deeper. *Into wholeness.*

The real issue isn't just food—it's the hunger of the soul.

This journey isn't about strict rules or perfection. It's about learning to turn to Christ before turning to anything else. It's about asking Him to sit with you in the craving, the sadness, the stress—and learning that He truly is enough. He gives strength when you have none. He gives gentleness when your inner critic gets loud. And He offers freedom, one day, one choice, one prayer at a time.

You don't have to do this alone. Jesus wants to help.

Prayer:

Jesus, I invite You into my relationship with food. You know where I struggle. You see the times I've turned to food to soothe what only You can heal. Teach me to receive Your love in those moments. Help me walk in freedom—not by my strength, but by Your grace. Satisfy my soul in ways nothing else can. Amen.

DIVINE PROVISION

"I was young and now I am old, yet I have never seen the righteous forsaken or their children begging bread."

Psalm 37:25

God works in mysterious ways. A friend shared about a series of setbacks—his car had broken down, and a close friend had been unexpectedly hospitalized. It was one of those days where everything seemed to go wrong at once. As he shared his frustration, I listened, but more importantly, I reminded him of something greater: *God's love, power, and provision are never out of reach.*

I prayed with him, encouraged him to hold on to faith, and spoke life over his situation. I told him, *"God can step in at any moment—He can provide for you in ways you never expected. He can replace what's been lost, restore what's broken, and turn your situation around in the blink of an eye."*

Just one week later, he came to me with a huge smile. *"You were right!"* he said excitedly. *"God did something amazing—I just got a $2,000 tax refund out of nowhere!"* His joy was contagious, and I couldn't help but praise God with him.

This testimony is a powerful reminder that our prayers don't go unanswered! *Prayer aligns us with His heart and opens our* eyes to His *faithfulness already at work.* God answers our prayers and He does so in ways that are divinely appointed!

One of the best ways to strengthen our faith is by keeping a *victory journal*—a record of God's faithfulness in our lives. When we take time to remember what He has done, it builds confidence in what He *will* do. Gratitude has a way of shifting our focus from what's missing to the abundance of blessings already around us.

Philippians 4:19 reminds us, *"And my God will meet all your needs according to the riches of his glory in Christ Jesus."* Notice that it doesn't say God will give us *everything we want*—but everything we *need!*

Today's Verse:
"Consider it pure joy, my brothers and sisters, whenever you face trials of many kinds."
—James 1:2

LACING UP FOR THE JOURNEY

"And, as shoes for your feet, having put on the readiness given by the gospel of peace."

Ephesians 6:15

As a runner, I know the power of a good pair of shoes. I bet you do too. The wrong pair or worn out pair leads to back and foot pain. However, the right shoes provide support, stability, and protection, helping us push forward through any terrain. Without them, we would be vulnerable to pain, setbacks, and slower progress.

Paul understood this when he urged believers to put on the *shoes of readiness* (Ephesians 6:15). Just as runners rely on quality footwear, we are called to rely on the gospel to stand firm and move forward in faith. The gospel isn't just our foundation—it's our source of peace, keeping us steady in life's challenges and equipping us to share God's love with others.

Every day, we must "lace up" with Christ's peace, trusting Him to guide our steps. When trials come, His peace keeps us from stumbling. When opportunities arise, it gives us the boldness to share His truth.

Challenge: This week, as you put on your shoes, ask God to strengthen your spiritual readiness. Pray for His peace to ground you and His courage to lead you. Keep a journal of moments when He helps you stay steady or opens a door for you to share His love.

Like any athlete, let's train daily—walking in faith, standing firm in truth, and running our race with endurance. I always like to picture Jesus running next to me, telling jokes and reminding me that our Father is at the finish line—and we're headed there together.

FINISH STRONG!

Today's Verse:

"I run in the path of your commands, for you have broadened my understanding."
—Psalm 119:32

REMEMBER GOD'S RECORD

"Being confident of this, that he who began a good work in you will carry it on to completion until the day of Christ Jesus."

Philippians 1:6

Reflecting on God's past work in our lives can bring fresh confidence, reminding us that His track record is flawless—He's shooting 10/10 in faithfulness! When we take time to recall the miracles He's already performed, we're reminded that God hasn't changed. He's still the same loving Father who delights in helping us through. Our situations may change, but His power to sustain and deliver us never wavers. He will always provide the person, provision, or perspective needed to carry us where He wants us to go.

One example of this truth came from a client who came to me feeling defeated. She had lost fifty pounds on her own but hit a plateau—and even gained some of the weight back. Discouraged and unsure if she could keep going, she felt stuck. I reminded her that her progress didn't happen by accident. She had made intentional changes—nutritionally, physically, emotionally. And the same God who gave her strength and wisdom then hadn't left her now.

We adjusted her plan—more protein, more veggies, more intentional workouts, and strategies to reduce stress. Not only did she lose the next fifty pounds, but she kept it off! Even more amazing? She became a coach herself, now empowering women in their fifties to overcome their own obstacles. God used her breakthrough to become someone else's encouragement. Her victory became a testimony.

Reflection: Take a few moments to make a list of how God has shown up in your life—answered prayers, unexpected provision, moments of strength when you felt weakest. Keep that list somewhere visible. Let it remind you: the God who began a good work in you is faithful to bring it to completion.

Today's Verse:
"*Let us hold unswervingly to the hope we profess, for he who promised is faithful.*"
—Hebrews 10:23

PROTECTED BY GRACE

"The Lord will keep you from all harm—he will watch over your life."

Psalm 121:7

Growing up in a family of hard workers taught us the value of grit, discipline, and perseverance. We learned to push through challenges, often working long hours and tackling tough tasks on our own. But even with determination and effort, life sometimes presents moments beyond our control—situations where we need help greater than our own strength.

Years ago, I remember the night my brother was working late on his '88 SS Monte Carlo in my dad's shop when the car suddenly slipped off its blocks and trapped him underneath. By God's grace, his friend Sam was there and quickly called my dad for help. Miraculously, my brother emerged without a scratch. That night became a powerful reminder of God's unseen protection—always present, even when we don't ask for it.

Looking back, I realize how deeply God's love and care were woven into our lives, even when we didn't recognize it. Though we weren't actively following Him in our youth, His hand was still over us. Guardian angels were around us, and His grace was at work. God's protection isn't reserved only for the faithful—it's offered to all, waiting patiently for us to see that He's been near all along.

This experience reminds me that while hard work has its place, there are moments only God can carry us through. Today, take a moment to thank Him—for the times you knew He showed up, and for the countless times you didn't. The same God who protected my brother is protecting you too, surrounding you with mercy, ready to lead you through whatever lies ahead.

Today's Verse:
"For he will command his angels concerning you to guard you in all your ways" —Psalm 91:11

STEP INTO THE UNKNOWN WITH CONFIDENCE

"The LORD himself goes before you and will be with you; he will never leave you nor forsake you. Do not be afraid; do not be discouraged."

Deuteronomy 31:8

L et's be real—stepping into the unknown can shake even the strongest of us. Fear, self-doubt, and all the "what ifs" start to creep in, and suddenly, we're questioning whether we have what it takes. But here's the truth: **you're not walking blind**. God goes *before* you, paving the way, preparing every step, and making sure you're not alone in any of it.

Everything changed for me when I stopped obsessing over the size of my problems and started focusing on the size of *our God*. He doesn't just walk beside you—He leads, equips, and strengthens you.

The Holy Spirit isn't some vague comfort; He's your real-life helper, coach, and guide. I've seen God show up in too many ways to count—moving me across the country with nothing but faith, launching a business that looked impossible, rescuing me from a toxic relationship, renewing my mind, and igniting a ministry in my heart. If He can do all that for me, **what makes you think He can't do it for you, too?**

Remember Joshua? He was stepping into a leadership role that came with massive shoes to fill—and a lot of uncertainty. But God didn't leave him hanging. He said, "*Be strong and courageous. Do not be afraid; do not be discouraged, for the Lord your God will be with you wherever you go*" (Joshua 1:9). And that same promise still stands. The same God who walked Joshua into the Promised Land is walking *with you*—into your new season, your next step, your big decision.

So the next time you feel anxious about what's ahead, remind yourself: God's already there. He's pulling strings behind the scenes, opening the right doors, closing the wrong ones, and lining things up in ways you don't even see yet. You're not behind. You're not lost. You're being *led*.

Every step you take is wrapped in His love and guided by His promises. Keep moving forward—you've got heaven's backing.

Today's Verse:
"The LORD is my light and my salvation—whom shall I fear? The LORD is the stronghold of my life—of whom shall I be afraid?" —Psalm 27:1

BUILDING IN FAITH LIKE NOAH

"By faith Noah, when warned about things not yet seen, in holy fear built an ark to save his family."
Hebrews 11:7

Big tasks require big faith. Like Noah, you may find your-self working on a vision that seems far-fetched—a plan that feels impossible or a dream that doesn't make sense to those around you. But God is calling you to trust Him, to listen closely to His voice, and to act in obedience—even when the skies are clear and no rain is in sight.

Noah endured years of waiting, working, and believing in what God had spoken. Every plank he laid on the ark was an act of obedience—a bold testimony of faith. God sees that same heart in you. He knows the sacrifice, the persistence, and the courage it takes to keep building when others don't understand. Don't let their confusion become your discouragement.

The ark you're building isn't just for you. It's for those who will come after you. Your obedience is laying a foundation of hope, peace, and salvation for others who may one day find shelter in what you're preparing. God has appointed you to build something that will endure storms and offer safety to those in need.

There may be moments when you question whether you heard God correctly. But remember—Noah stood under blue skies, hammer in hand, trusting the word God had spoken, even when it looked senseless to the world. God sees your long nights, your faith-filled prayers, and the hope you're clinging to. **Keep building. Your work is not in vain.**

If I had listened to the voices of doubt—the ones that said I would fail as a dietitian or never succeed as a business owner—Nutrition with Wendi would have never existed. Thousands of lives wouldn't have been impacted, dietitians wouldn't have been employed, and families and teams across the nation wouldn't have received the guidance they needed. But God's plan was greater than the doubts of others, and I chose to trust Him.

To my fellow believers: Noah looked foolish—**until it started to rain**. Obedience to God often looks unconventional to the world. Ignore the noise, trust His plan, and keep your eyes on the mission. God provides. And the impact of your faithfulness will reach further than you can imagine.

Don't quit. Keep building. The rain is coming—and so is the harvest.

Today's Verse:
"The one who calls you is faithful, and he will do it."
— 1 Thessalonians 5:24

WHEN GOD SAYS "NOT THIS"—TRUST HIM FOR WHAT'S NEXT

"For my thoughts are not your thoughts, neither are your ways my ways," declares the Lord. "As the heavens are higher than the earth, so are my ways higher than your ways and my thoughts than your thoughts."

Isaiah 55:8–9

Rejection is redirection—so don't panic when the plan changes. You ever have one of those days where your big idea flops, the client ghosts you, or the relationship you were sure was *it*... isn't? Yeah. Been there. It's like you're holding the blueprint of your dreams, and suddenly someone spills coffee all over it.

But here's the thing: God isn't scrambling. He's not up in heaven saying, "Whoa, didn't see that coming!" Nope. He's rerouting you with precision. Because sometimes that "no" is actually a *better yes* in disguise.

Think about it: that business deal falling through might've saved you from future stress. That relationship ending might be clearing space for one that actually honors who you are becoming in Christ. That door that closed? Yeah, it was probably attached to a hallway full of distractions anyway.

Proverbs 16:9 puts it perfectly: "*In their hearts humans plan their course, but the Lord establishes their steps.*" Translation? You can plan all day (and hey, planning is good!), but God's the one driving—**and He has premium GPS with zero glitches.**

So keep building, keep dreaming, and keep laughing a little when things go sideways. God's not derailing your life—He's *protecting* it. Redirecting it. Upgrading it. Sometimes the blessing is in the break, and the breakthrough is hidden in the *bloopers*.

Let this be your reminder today: When it doesn't go your way, smile anyway. God's got something better cooking. And spoiler alert—it's going to be *amazing!*

Go ahead, thank Jesus now for the closed doors. They're leading to the right ones!

Today's Verse:
"*And we know that in all things God works for the good of those who love him, who have been called according to his purpose.*"
—Romans 8:28

WHEN TRUST COSTS EVERYTHING

> "Then God said, 'Take your son, your only son—yes, Isaac, whom you love so much—and go to the land of Moriah. Go and sacrifice him as a burnt offering on one of the mountains, which I will show you.'"
>
> Genesis 22:2

Abraham had waited his entire life for Isaac. The promised son. The miracle child. The one through whom God had vowed to establish a great nation. Isaac was the embodiment of everything Abraham had trusted God for—and then came the unthinkable request: sacrifice him.

There are moments in every believer's life when God will ask for the very thing He once gave. Not because He wants to take it away, but because He wants to see if our hearts are still fully His. Abraham didn't delay. The next morning, he got up early, saddled the donkey, split the wood, and began the three-day journey to Mount Moriah. Three days. Three nights. Each step a test. Each moment a battle between fear and faith.

Yet Abraham kept walking. Not because he wasn't afraid, but because he believed that even if he had to sacrifice Isaac, God could raise him from the dead (Hebrews 11:19). That's the kind of trust God is after—faith that believes in resurrection even when faced with the grave.

When they reached the place of sacrifice, Isaac noticed there was no lamb. "God will provide," Abraham said with trembling assurance. And just when the knife was raised, heaven interrupted. "Do not lay a hand on the boy." A ram was caught in the thicket. Provision was waiting—Abraham just had to walk in obedience to see it.

We serve a God who provides, but sometimes provision only shows up on the other side of surrender. That's why we must ask ourselves: *Is there anything we love more than God? Is there anything we've made into an idol, even if it once came from His hand?*

Abraham passed the test not because he was perfect, but because he was willing. And because of that, God reaffirmed His covenant and blessed Abraham's descendants forever.

Today, if God is asking you to lay something down—a dream, a relationship, a job, or even a deeply personal desire—don't assume He's trying to take from you. He may be preparing to reveal Himself in a deeper way. He may be leading you to a place where your trust is stretched, your faith is refined, and your eyes are opened to His perfect provision.

Trust doesn't always make sense, but it always makes way for miracles.◻

Today's Verse:
"And without faith it is impossible to please God, because anyone who comes to him must believe that he exists and that he rewards those who earnestly seek him."
—Hebrews 11:6

GUARD YOUR CIRCLE

Do not be misled: "Bad company corrupts good character."

1 Corinthians 15:33

Who you allow close to your heart will shape the direction of your life. Sometimes, it's easy to spot harmful influences. Other times, it's harder—because the people pulling us off course aren't necessarily enemies. They may be well-meaning friends, mentors, or even family members who care about us but don't always speak from a place of spiritual wisdom. The Bible reminds us that even good intentions can lead to dangerous paths if they aren't aligned with God's truth. Remember when Peter, out of love, tried to prevent Jesus from going to the cross? Jesus had to correct him sharply: **"You do not have in mind the concerns of God, but merely human concerns"** (Matthew 16:23).

It doesn't always happen overnight. Sometimes the drift is slow—a slight compromise, a softening of conviction, an emotional attachment that clouds our discernment. Over time, even loving voices can become louder than the voice of God if we're not careful. Good intentions are not a substitute for God's direction. That's why Scripture tells us to guard our hearts diligently, because from it flow the issues of life (Proverbs 4:23). You weren't created to absorb every opinion, no matter how kindly delivered.

You were created to walk in truth, led by the voice of the Good Shepherd.

Ask yourself: "Is this relationship, conversation, or influence pushing me closer to Christ or gently pulling me away?" Be honest. Honor those who love you, but honor God more. Some people, even without meaning to, will project fear instead of faith, or comfort over calling. It doesn't mean you reject their love—it means you anchor yourself first in God's love, where perfect wisdom flows. Some doors must close, and some voices must be quieted, so you can fully walk into the next season God has prepared for you.

Following Christ often means making hard decisions, even when they confuse others. Trust that the right relationships will strengthen your walk, not hinder it. The people God ordains for your life will encourage your faith, sharpen your purpose, and stir up your devotion—not dilute it. Today, make space for God's voice to be the loudest in your life. Guard your heart not out of fear, but out of wisdom. You are too precious, too called, and too deeply loved by God to let even well-meaning distractions detour your destiny.

Today's Verse:
"The thief comes only to steal and kill and destroy; I have come that they may have life, and have it to the full."
—John 10:10

WHEN YOU FEEL SMALL, REMEMBER THIS

"So is my word that goes out from my mouth: It will not return to me empty, but will accomplish what I desire and achieve the purpose for which I sent it."

Isaiah 55:11

Have you ever wondered if what you're doing for God is actually making a difference?

Maybe you've shared a Bible verse on social media, prayed quietly for a coworker, or sent an encouraging text to someone on your heart—but you never heard how it landed. No feedback. No visible fruit. Just silence. And in those moments, it's easy to wonder, *Did that even matter?*

But Isaiah 55:11 is a beautiful reminder that *every single time* God's Word goes out, it does something. Even when you don't see the ripple effect, *Heaven does.* God promises that His Word never returns void. It always hits the target—even if that target is hidden from you.

Not long ago, a coach reached out to me. He shared that one of his athletes had been struggling with anxiety, depression, and major marriage issues. Quietly, behind the scenes, this coach had been sending him my Scripture-based posts—just simple words of encouragement. That young man never commented or responded. But something was happening. Today, he's walking in healing. He's stepping into purpose. God was moving long before any of us knew.

That's how the Kingdom works. What feels small in your eyes—one verse, one prayer, one post—can be a lifeline in someone else's storm. You may never know the full outcome, but God does. Your obedience is never wasted.

So if you've been showing up—posting, praying, encouraging others—but feel like no one's listening, don't stop. Your words may feel like whispers, but in God's hands, they're arrows. Scripture isn't just ink on paper—it's alive. And when you speak His Word, something always shifts, whether you see it or not.

You don't have to be loud. You don't have to be famous. You just have to be faithful.

Keep planting seeds. Keep speaking life. Keep trusting that Jesus is weaving your small acts of obedience into someone else's breakthrough.

Today's Verse:
"Let your light shine before others, that they may see your good deeds and glorify your Father in heaven."
—Matthew 5:16

GRACE FOR YOURSELF

"What do you think? If a man owns a hundred sheep, and one of them wanders away, will he not leave the ninety-nine on the hills and go to look for the one that wandered off?"

Matthew 18:12

Sometimes, we need to offer ourselves the grace we so easily extend to others. Many of us are our own harshest critics—constantly focused on what we haven't accomplished, what we could have done better, or how far we still have to go. We set impossible standards for ourselves, forgetting that God never called us to be perfect in our own strength. He isn't measuring your worth by your productivity or performance. He sees you through eyes of love, mercy, and deep compassion. His heart delights in you simply because you are His.

Matthew 18:12 reminds us of the Good Shepherd who leaves the ninety-nine to find the one. That's how precious you are to Jesus. He doesn't love you based on your achievements; He loves you because you belong to Him. When you feel like you're falling short, remember: He's not condemning you—He's celebrating your progress, even if it feels small to you. Heaven rejoices over your return, your surrender, your heart's posture toward Him. Your small steps are mighty victories in the eyes of the Lord.

Take a moment today to slow down and list all the things God has helped you overcome. Reflect on the debts that were paid off when you didn't know how you would make it. Think about the healing that came after seasons of deep pain. Remember the character growth, the battles you've conquered, and the prayers you almost forgot you prayed—but God answered anyway. That's not luck—that's the evidence of Jesus' faithfulness written all over your story. You are not the same person you were a year ago, or even a month ago. Grace has been working in you even when you couldn't see it.

Perfection isn't the goal. Progress is. Growth is messy. Healing is layered. But every step closer to Jesus matters. In Christ, you're already enough—not because of what you've done, but because of what He's done for you. Rest in that today.

You are not behind. You are not forgotten. You are on the exact path God laid out for you before the foundation of the world. Keep trusting Jesus. Keep showing up. Embrace His grace—and with boldness and gratitude, keep moving forward.

Today's Verse:
"*The LORD is compassionate and gracious, slow to anger, abounding in love.*"
—Psalm 103:8

HOLD ON TO YOUR CONFIDENCE

"So do not throw away your confidence; it will be richly rewarded."

Hebrews 10:35

Dear friend, confidence is a gift from God—but the enemy works hard to steal it. When you feel small, uncertain, or question your worth, remember: it's often because the enemy is trying to measure you by the world's ever-changing standards. But the truth is, **your worth was settled forever on the cross.** You don't have to hustle to earn it. You don't have to strive to deserve it. In Christ, you are already enough.

I understand how you feel. I've wrestled with seasons of discouragement too. I've believed the lie that my value depended on my performance, my achievements, or how others viewed me. But God, in His relentless love, interrupted my striving. He showed me that my identity is not rooted in my success—**it's rooted in Jesus**. And because of Him, my value is secure. Nothing and no one can change that.

When Hebrews 10:35 urges us to hold onto our confidence, the word used in the original Greek speaks of much more than surface-level boldness. It reflects a ***fearless trust*** and *freedom* to stand openly before God without shame!

God sees your quiet obedience. He hears every whispered prayer. He catches every tear. Even when you feel unseen, you are deeply known by Jesus. Nothing you do for the Lord is ever wasted.

So hold on, dear one. You are closer than you think. What feels like a painful delay is often divine preparation. God is building a strength in you that will sustain you for the blessings ahead. He's cultivating wisdom, depth, and endurance inside of you—things the world can't see yet, but heaven is already celebrating.

You are not forgotten. **You are not behind.** You are walking the exact path God prepared for you before you even took your first breath. Every day you keep trusting, you are moving forward—even when it feels slow. Stand firm. Keep your head up. Rejoice even in the midst of setbacks and delays!

God finishes what He starts—and, beautiful friend, He's not finished with you yet.

Today's Verse:

"The LORD himself goes before you and will be with you; he will never leave you nor forsake you. Do not be afraid; do not be discouraged."—Deuteronomy 31:8

SPIRITUAL WARFARE IS REAL

"You will not need to fight in this battle. Stand firm, hold your position, and see the salvation of the Lord on your behalf..."

2 Chronicles 20:17

Spiritual warfare is not just something we read about—it's **something we live through.** I've encountered evil directly, and it taught me a lesson I will never forget: listen when God warns you. Jesus said, *"My sheep listen to my voice; I know them, and they follow me"* (John 10:27). I didn't know how to listen then. But now I do. And I want you to hear this clearly: **discernment is not optional in this world—it's vital.**

In 2019, I had one of my most vivid encounters with spiritual darkness. I entered a relationship with a man who, at first glance, seemed like the perfect partner—smart, charming, and supportive. He was eleven years older than me, carrying an air of wisdom and maturity that I thought would anchor me. We shared pain from our pasts, and that trauma-bond felt powerful. I clung to the hope that our wounds could somehow heal each other. But the truth? That relationship became a trap.

Maybe you've been there—bound to someone by pain instead of purpose. The enemy often uses our vulnerabilities to get a foothold. And that's exactly what happened to me. My ex came into my life when support from my family was limited, and I was easy prey for emotional manipulation disguised as love. I wanted so badly to be loved that I ignored the signs until I had no choice but to listen.

One weekend, this man booked a beautiful cabin for my birthday in northern Michigan, where we stayed in separate rooms. But that first night, a terrifying encounter happened. In my sleep, I turned over to see his face close beside me, but it twisted into something else—a red, demonic face. I awoke startled, screaming, but quickly rationalized it away, thinking maybe it was just a bad dream. But it wasn't just a bad dream; it was all real, and the gut-wrenching feeling from that night would haunt me for the next 18 months.

Friend, I'm here to tell you: don't ignore the signs. I now realize that night was a major warning from the Holy Spirit! The man's family visited mediums, he was drawn to darkness, and he spoke spiritual words to maintain control.

When I left, something broke off of me. My healing journey began. People noticed how much healthier I looked—physically, emotionally, and spiritually. That's the power of deliverance. Today, I live in the freedom Jesus died to give me. But I don't take it lightly. **If you're in a toxic relationship, I pray you'll begin to write things down, track what you feel in your spirit, and ask God for clarity.** Cognitive dissonance can trick your mind, but the Holy Spirit will always tell you the truth. Abuse and trauma distort our perception—but Jesus reveals. And when He reveals, He *heals.*

Today's Verse:
"So if the Son sets you free, you will be free indeed."
—John 8:36

STAY IN YOUR LANE

"We do not dare to classify or compare ourselves with some who commend themselves. When they measure themselves by themselves and compare themselves with themselves, they are not wise."

2 Corinthians 10:12

Each of us is running a unique race. Some of us are on a quick sprint, while others are tackling a marathon. Too often, though, we get caught up comparing our race to someone else's.

We see someone else further along, and envy creeps in, robbing us of the joy of our own journey. But remember, God has set each of us on our own course, and Jesus is with us from start to finish. Instead of focusing on the distance others are running, fix your eyes on your path and allow Jesus to guide you step by step.

I've had the privilege of coaching athletes from all walks of life, from young amateurs to seasoned elites. One thing that remains true across all levels is this: the best athletes compete out of love for the game, not to outdo others. In the same way, let your love for Jesus be your motivation, not a desire to match someone else's "personal best." God's love for you isn't based on your pace or distance but on His unwavering presence with you. When we run for Jesus, His love becomes the fuel that keeps us moving forward.

As you begin your race, Jesus has already provided you with everything you need to finish strong. You don't have to worry about getting tired if you let Him set the pace. The temptation to sprint ahead or lag behind fades when we trust in His timing. At mile 5 or mile 100, God has the strength you need to keep going. Comparison, however, will drain your energy, sap your joy, and blur your vision. Keep your eyes on Jesus, for He knows the best path for you, and He is there to renew your endurance.

Contentment comes when we focus on Jesus, not on the distance others have covered. In this race, your worth is not in your performance but in His presence.

Today, take a deep breath. Walk at God's pace, and let Jesus' love be enough. Trust that He is giving you everything you need for each step. He knows your heart, He sees your needs, and He will get you to the finish line at just the right time. Let His strength be your confidence, and remember—He has already won the victory for you.

Today's Verse:

"Therefore, since we are surrounded by such a great cloud of witnesses, let us throw off everything that hinders and the sin that so easily entangles. And let us run with perseverance the race marked out for us."

—Hebrews 12:1

TELL THE TRUTH, EVEN WHEN IT'S HARD

"The Lord detests lying lips, but He delights in people who are trustworthy."

Proverbs 12:22

It's the little lies that chip away at our character. Have you ever said something like, "I didn't see your text," when really you just forgot to respond? Or maybe you told someone you were "five minutes away," even though you hadn't left yet.

These may seem like harmless white lies, but over time, even small dishonesty can build up—and begin to distance us from God and from our true identity in Him.

God cares deeply about truth because He is Truth. When we lie, no matter how small, we don't just mislead others—we misalign ourselves with the nature of our Father. Jesus said the enemy is the "father of lies" (John 8:44), so each time we choose deception, we're agreeing with the wrong voice. But when we choose honesty, even when it's uncomfortable, we reflect the heart of God.

I remember lying to my dad when I was sixteen. It wasn't a massive lie, but it broke his trust. I told him I was somewhere I wasn't. At the time, it seemed easier to lie than face consequences. But the guilt stuck with me. That one moment taught me a powerful lesson—our words carry weight. That lie lingered in our relationship, and it took intentional steps to rebuild trust. I wasn't just lying to protect myself; I was lying out of fear, insecurity, and a desire to be seen as better than I was.

Why do we do this? Often, it's because we haven't dealt with something deeper—shame, rejection, fear of disappointing others. But Jesus invites us to bring all of that into the light. He doesn't expect perfection; He longs for honesty. When we walk in truth, we walk in freedom. Lies create confusion and distortion, but truth brings peace, clarity, and healing.

So I want to challenge you today—ask God to reveal any areas in your life where you've been less than honest. Maybe with others. Maybe with yourself. Maybe even with God. He already knows everything, and He's not looking to punish you—He wants to restore you. Write it down. Confess it. And let God begin the work of realigning you with who you truly are in Him.

Today's Verse:
"Do not lie to each other, since you have taken off your old self with its practices and have put on the new self, which is being renewed in knowledge in the image of its Creator."
—Colossians 3:9–10

HOLD ON—YOU'RE CLOSER THAN YOU THINK

"So do not throw away your confidence; it will be richly rewarded. You need to persevere so that when you have done the will of God, you will receive what he has promised."

Hebrews 10:35–36

Sometimes God sends a reminder just when you need it most. That's what happened one morning when I woke up, grabbed my coffee, and opened my Bible. I whispered, "Lord, I could use some wisdom today."

Later that day, I found myself overwhelmed—worrying about my business, my living situation, and all the unknowns ahead. Have you ever felt like you were holding on by a thread? That was me. I left for a meeting at my favorite coffee shop, still heavy-hearted, when I ran into an old friend—Coach John. He had written a book years ago called *Don't Throw Away Your Confidence*, and wouldn't you know it, he sat down to talk.

For over an hour, we shared tears and testimonies. Coach looked me straight in the eye and said, "You can't throw away your confidence. God is going to bless you. He's going to send a windstorm of blessings. But the enemy wants to break you. Don't let him win. You're too close. Don't quit."

His words felt like a message from Heaven. Paul wrote in Hebrews 10:35, "So *do not throw away your confidence; it will be richly rewarded.*" He was reminding believers that endurance in the face of hardship brings a reward that God Himself promises. Confidence, in this sense, is not about self-reliance—it's about clinging boldly to God's faithfulness, trusting that His promises are still alive even when circumstances look bleak.

My dad used to say, "We don't quit." And here was Coach, at eighty-five years old, reminding me that God still has a plan—and it's worth persevering for.

So, friend, hear this: **Do not throw away your confidence**. You may be closer than you realize to the very thing you've been praying for. God sees every sacrifice, every tear, every moment of silent perseverance. He sends help in the form of people, prayers, Scripture, and reminders like this one.

Jesus is faithful. And He will finish what He started in you.

Today's Verse:

"*And without faith it is impossible to please God, because anyone who comes to him must believe that he exists and that he rewards those who earnestly seek him.*"

—Hebrews 11:6

THE WORDS YOU WRITE MATTER

And the LORD answered me: "Write the vision; make it plain on tablets, so he may run who reads it."
Habakkuk 2:2

Journaling is more than just writing—it's an act of worship. When we write by hand, we're not just recording thoughts; we're slowing down long enough to process emotions, hear from God, and remember what He's doing in our lives. Science backs this up—handwriting has been shown to engage the brain differently than typing, helping us reflect, retain information, and reduce stress. But for the believer, journaling is even more powerful. It becomes a sacred space to meet with the Lord, pour out our hearts, and receive His truth in return.

The Bible offers many examples of people writing down what God revealed to them. The prophet Habakkuk was told to write the vision so that it could be shared clearly and quickly. Paul often mentioned writing his letters by hand to express his personal connection to the churches. David poured out prayers, praises, and even his anguish in the Psalms, calling himself *"the pen of a ready writer"* (Psalm 45:1 KJV). Throughout Scripture, we see God partnering with people through the written word—and He still does today.

Journaling creates a personal archive of God's faithfulness. It allows us to track His answers to our prayers, record the whispers of the Holy Spirit, and document the growth of our faith over time. When doubt creeps in or discouragement hits, flipping through past entries can reignite hope. Just like the Israelites built altars and memorials to remember God's miracles, your journal can become a testimony of His goodness and nearness in your life.

It's also a powerful way to discern His voice. Sometimes when we write, clarity comes mid-sentence, and the Holy Spirit brings a scripture to mind or unveils a truth we hadn't noticed before. Journaling allows us to engage in a two-way conversation with God—one where we listen more deeply. In moments when prayer feels hard or life feels loud, writing helps us filter through the chaos to find the still, small voice of the Lord.

Let this be the season you start journaling consistently. Grab a hardcopy Bible and a notebook dedicated to your time with God. There's something beautifully grounding about underlining a verse, writing a date next to it, and journaling what the Lord speaks to you through that moment. These aren't just notes; they're the record of your walk with Him.

Practical Challenge: Before reaching for your phone, reach for your Bible. Start your day with a short prayer, read a passage of Scripture, and write what stands out. Then journal what you're feeling, what you're praying for, or what you're sensing God is saying. Over time, your journal will become more than a collection of pages—it will be a living testimony of God's hand in your life.

Today's Verse:
"I will remember the deeds of the Lord; yes, I will remember your miracles of long ago" —Psalm 77:11

HEARING GOD IN UNEXPECTED WAYS

Whether you turn to the right or to the left, your ears will hear a voice behind you, saying, 'This is the way; walk in it.'

Isaiah 30:21

God is always speaking—we just need to learn how to listen. Many people believe that God doesn't give signs to guide us anymore, but this overlooks the love and intentional care our Heavenly Father has for His children. The Holy Spirit is still actively communicating.

In fact, one of the ways God trained the prophet Jeremiah was through what he *saw* with his eyes—ordinary things like an almond branch or a boiling pot. God used these visuals to teach him how to discern spiritual meaning in everyday life. In the same way, the Holy Spirit speaks uniquely to each of us, in ways we'll recognize.

In biblical times, God often spoke through the land and seasons, as people lived in harmony with nature. Today, we live in a fast-paced digital age, where we might notice patterns in numbers, words, or recurring symbols. While the New Age has tried to hijack this idea with things like "angel numbers," God remains the true Author of all creation—including numbers. There's even a book in the Bible called *Numbers*! His signs aren't mystical gimmicks; they are invitations to draw closer and seek clarity in His Word.

God especially speaks when it's time for a change. I remember when I was debating a move from Michigan to Nashville. After praying for clarity, I had a close encounter with a car—and noticed it had a Tennessee license plate. That wasn't a coincidence—it was confirmation. Years later, as I prayed about a possible move to Texas, I began seeing Texas plates and even a bumper sticker in the shape of Texas with the word "home" across it. That was my answer. God responds to specific prayers, and when we pray with expectation, He makes His direction clear.

Throughout Scripture, God guided His people to new places—Abraham, Ruth, the disciples, Paul, and more. Every move came with a promise, a purpose, and a deeper relationship with Him. When Jesus called His followers, He didn't give them a roadmap. He simply said, *"Follow Me."* And their lives were never the same.

God might be calling you to move—physically, emotionally, or spiritually. Don't let fear of the unknown keep you stuck. Just because something is unfamiliar doesn't mean it's unsafe. God is already there, preparing the way. So, listen closely—not just with your ears, but with your heart and eyes too. He's always speaking.

Today's Verse:
"My sheep listen to my voice; I know them, and they follow me."—John 10:27

BUILDING FAITH ON PURPOSE

"And if we know that he hears us—whatever we
ask—we know that we have what we asked of him."
1 John 5:15

I often remind our teams, clients, athletes, and anyone chasing a goal that success does not happen by accident. No one simply shows up to a championship game by chance, gains 10 pounds of muscle overnight, or stumbles into publishing a book without effort. Success requires work. It requires dedication, discipline, focus, consistency, structure, and repetition.

The same principle applies to our faith. No one accidentally grows closer to Jesus; it requires intentional, daily pursuit. If you want to deepen your relationship with the Lord, consider these four foundational steps:

Pray and Devote Time: Schedule a morning devotional before checking your email, scrolling your phone, or letting the world rush in. That quiet space is sacred. It is often where God whispers truth and peace into your day before the noise begins. A simple principle worth repeating is this: *Scripture before screens.*

Inquire of God First: Ask Jesus how to live, what to choose, and where to go. Seek direction from God before seeking advice from others. People may change or let you down, but Jesus never will. Make Him your first point of reference, not your last resort.

Pursue Community: Surround yourself with people who are also pursuing God. Join a small group, attend in-person worship, and engage actively in a faith community. Without community, it becomes easier to drift. That said, there may be seasons when community feels out of reach—when you are grieving, ill, recovering, or mentally struggling. In those moments, take comfort in this truth: you are not alone. The Father, Son, and Holy Spirit are present with you.

Prioritize Your Health: Your spiritual walk is closely tied to your physical well-being. When you are well-rested, nourished, and energized, you are more likely to walk in the Spirit and resist temptation. Your body is a temple; care for it intentionally and diligently.

Faith does not grow by accident. Like success in any other area of life, it is the result of purposeful pursuit. The beautiful truth is this: as you seek Jesus, He is already running to meet you.

Today's Verse:

"In the same way, the Spirit helps us in our weakness. We do not know what we ought to pray for, but the Spirit himself intercedes for us through wordless groans."
—Romans 8:26

EMPOWERED TO MOVE FORWARD

"For God has not given us a spirit of fear, but of power, love, and a sound mind."

2 Timothy 1:7

There's a unique power within you, one that's not rooted in your own abilities or confidence but in the Spirit of God. God has called you to live boldly, stepping into each day empowered by His love and strength, without fear or hesitation. Sometimes, though, we feel hesitant or even held back by doubt, insecurity, or past failures. But these feelings can't hold us back because God is so much bigger.

Think about Moses. He was called by God to confront Pharaoh, the most powerful ruler of his time, and lead an entire nation to freedom. But Moses felt inadequate, asking God, "*Who am I, that I should go?*" God's response wasn't to reassure Moses of his abilities but to promise His presence: "*I will be with you*" (Exodus 3:11–12). God reminded Moses that the power wasn't in himself—it was in the God who went before him.

In the same way, God goes before you. He has equipped you with a spirit of power, not of fear. This isn't a spirit that cowers or shies away; it's one that stands tall, confident in the love and guidance of a mighty God. When you step out in faith, God moves on your behalf. He fills in the gaps of your weaknesses with His strength, His wisdom, and His peace. The Spirit of power, love, and a sound mind empowers you to push past whatever's holding you back.

Maybe there's something God is nudging you toward—a new job, a conversation, a step into ministry, or a change in your lifestyle. Don't let fear or insecurity stop you. Remember, God has already equipped you. Your calling isn't about your own ability but about His power working through you. He's given you His Spirit—one of love that drives out fear, a sound mind to make wise decisions, and power to step out in faith.

Today, take hold of this truth: you are empowered by God Himself. Step forward boldly, knowing that God has not given you a spirit of fear but a spirit of strength and courage. Whatever lies ahead, God is with you, and His power is working through you. Stand confidently in that truth, and watch Him open doors and make a way as you walk in faith.

Today's Verse:
"Be strong and courageous. Do not be afraid; do not be discouraged, for the LORD your God will be with you wherever you go."—Joshua 1:9

THE POWER OF YOUR ENVIRONMENT

"Take no part in the unfruitful works of darkness, but instead expose them."

Ephesians 5:11

The environment we live in greatly shapes the person we become. If we're surrounded by negativity, it's only a matter of time before that negativity seeps into our mindset and choices. I've seen this in a client of mine who works in a high-pressure corporate setting. It's an environment where everyone is constantly on the go, chugging energy drinks, and pushing for ever-higher sales numbers.

She doesn't even like energy drinks, but since everyone around her relies on them, she finds herself reaching for one in the afternoon just to fit in—despite the fact that it disrupts her sleep, drains her bank account, and isn't a habit she even enjoys.

Breaking habits tied to our environment can be challenging. Sometimes we need to change the environment itself, and other times, we need to change our response to it. In this case, I suggested she try replacing the energy drink with something like sparkling water or a caffeine-free alternative. She's made the switch, but it's still hard to stick with it because everyone around her continues with the same routine. Her situation is a powerful reminder that we often mirror the behaviors of those around us—sometimes for good, sometimes for harm.

This principle applies directly to our walk with Jesus. If we surround ourselves with people who aren't pursuing Christ, who don't value His Word or His ways, it's only a matter of time before we find ourselves drifting. Our environment and our relationships influence us more deeply than we realize. If the people closest to us are pulling us away from God, staying anchored in our faith becomes much harder.

But the opposite is also true. When we intentionally spend time with believers who are actively chasing after the heart of Jesus, our own faith is strengthened. We begin to hunger for truth, to desire righteousness, and to become more like Him. God often uses other people to sharpen and shape us. When we surround ourselves with a Christ-centered community, we're more likely to become the people God designed us to be—anchored in truth, filled with peace, and grounded in purpose.

Today, take an honest look at your surroundings. Are you being supported in your walk with Jesus, or are you in an environment that's subtly pulling you away from Him? You don't have to settle for a space that stifles your faith. Choose to cultivate an environment that draws you closer to Christ, and trust that He'll meet you there.

Today's Verse:
"Walk with the wise and become wise, for a companion of fools suffers harm."—Proverbs 13:20

CHOOSING PEACE OVER PLEASURE

"Do not be yoked together with unbelievers. For what do righteousness and wickedness have in common? Or what fellowship can light have with darkness?"

2 Corinthians 6:15

Just because something or someone feels good in the moment doesn't mean it's healthy for you. Sometimes, letting go of a toxic person, place, habit, or even certain foods can actually improve your life significantly. When something is removed and you find your heart and mind at peace, that's a sign it wasn't meant to be in your life. We're often drawn to things that give us temporary pleasure or "dopamine hits," but these things can ultimately lead us into pain, regret, and heartbreak.

Sin often disguises itself as something appealing and easy. It might look like a charming relationship or an activity that feels rewarding at the moment but leads to harm. God cautions us about being "yoked together with unbelievers," a phrase that reminds us to consider who we align our lives with. Dating someone who isn't following Jesus might feel exciting or fulfilling at first, but ultimately, it can steer you off the path God intends for you. When you're in a relationship with someone who doesn't share your faith, it becomes challenging to walk fully with God.

We can't ignore the tug of their influence on our choices, atti-tudes, and even our purpose.

Jesus calls us to love others, but this doesn't mean we need to enter into romantic relationships with people who aren't fol-lowing Him. The Bible's guidance is clear: don't try to change someone's heart—that's God's work, not ours. We can pray for others, care for them, and point them toward Jesus, but only they can choose to open their hearts to Him. Entering a relationship with the hope of changing someone leads to frustration and pain, as this isn't the role God calls us to play.

It takes strength and discernment to resist the appeal of rela-tionships or activities that don't align with God's will. But when you choose God's path, you're saving yourself from unnecessary pain and regret. True peace and joy come from relationships rooted in Christ, where both people are walking in faith and supporting each other's growth in Him.

Today, take a moment to reflect on your relationships and habits. Are there people or things in your life that might be pulling you away from God? Remember, it's okay to let go of what doesn't bring you closer to Jesus. By following God's wisdom, you're allowing Him to shape your future, filled with love, pur-pose, and true peace.

Today's Verse:
"Above all else, guard your heart,
for everything you do flows from it."
—Proverbs 4:23

GOD IS NEAR TO THE BROKENHEARTED

"The LORD is close to the brokenhearted and saves those who are crushed in spirit."

Psalm 34:18

When we look at the world around us, it's easy to feel overwhelmed by the brokenness, evil, and suffering that seem so widespread. It can leave us questioning how to pray or where to start when there's so much pain and injustice. The world's burdens can weigh heavily on our hearts as we witness financial struggles, danger, and children suffering at the hands of evil. But today, take comfort in this: God is near to the brokenhearted.

He is not distant from the pain you see or the burdens you carry in prayer. The same God who created the universe also holds your personal concerns close to His heart. He hears your cries for your family, community, those serving in the military, people suffering with illnesses, the financially stressed, and the children living in danger. He listens when you beg for change and ask for your family members' and friends' hearts and minds to be transformed.

Sometimes we may feel like our prayers aren't being heard, that we didn't ask God in the proper way, or that we simply can't

434   WENDI A. IRLBECK

find the right words to say. But God's power is not limited by our words. He is a God who turns messes into miracles, and He can take even the most broken situations and bring redemption, healing, and hope. Our role is to keep coming before Jesus in faith, knowing that He is good and that His plans are far greater than what we can see.

As you pray today, remember that God's love and forgiveness have no limits. Change begins with having the right heart posture and aligning our spirit with the Father's perfect and pleasing will. When we allow Jesus to transform us, we become His vessels of change and reflect His glory in the world.

Reflection: Ask God to align your desires with His desires. Be honest with the areas you feel discouraged and over-whelmed—even if that means admitting you're upset with Him. He can handle it. The more honest you are with yourself, the more God can help you. Pray for a renewed sense of hope, trusting that Jesus is still at work, even in the darkest situations. As you surrender your burdens to Him, believe that He is more than capable of bringing miracles out of messes.

Today's Verse:
"The LORD will fight for you; you need only to be still."
—Exodus 14:14

LOVE THAT LIFTS

*"Be devoted to one another in love. Honor one an-
other above yourselves."*

Romans 12:10

God often calls us to love and serve in challenging situations, offering us the chance to lean on His strength
and wisdom. Loving difficult people isn't easy, especially
when we feel hurt, undervalued, or unappreciated.

Early in my business, I took on a family who needed my
services, but the experience was far from ideal. They were
wealthy, demanding, and resistant, yet I felt called to help
their daughter. After one especially tough session, I left feeling frustrated and unappreciated. I had to pause, repent for
my anger, and remind myself that I was here to serve—just as
Jesus would.

Later that day, while filling up with gas, I saw an elderly
woman walking with a limp. I felt a strong pull to talk with
her. Her name was Maria. During our conversation, she said
I did "so much good work with children." I had never told her
anything about my job—her words were a clear confirmation
from God. We prayed together, and as she cried, my own
discouragement lifted. I bought her a meal and a gift card,
and I left with a peace no difficult client could take from me.

In the past, I may have numbed that kind of discouragement with habits like overworking or restrictive eating. We all have unhealthy coping mechanisms—some isolate, some overeat, some drink—but God invites us to something better. That day with Maria reminded me that when we pour out love, even when we feel drained, God fills us back up.

The joy of serving others has a healing power. If you're feeling discouraged or depleted, try reaching out to someone in need. God often refreshes us as we refresh others.

Today's Verse:

"Carry each other's burdens, and in this way, you will fulfill the law of Christ."—Galatians 6:2

THE SPIRIT OF EXCELLENCE

"Then this Daniel was preferred above the presidents and princes, because an excellent spirit was in him; and the king thought to set him over the whole realm."
Daniel 6:3

T here's a difference between striving for perfection and walking in excellence. Perfectionism can wear us down, leaving us anxious, burnt out, and afraid of making mistakes. But a spirit of excellence flows from a different place—it's about doing our best not to prove something, but to honor God. It's rooted in worship, not worry. It reflects the heart of someone who knows who they are in Christ and chooses to steward their gifts with intention and care.

Daniel is a powerful example of someone who carried this spirit. The Bible tells us that he was preferred by the king because *"an excellent spirit was in him."* Daniel didn't rise to leadership because he was the most talented or had the flashiest accomplishments. He stood out because his work, attitude, and decisions consistently honored God. He carried himself with integrity, wisdom, and humility—and that excellence opened doors no man could shut.

Today, God is still looking for people like Daniel—those who will approach their work, relationships, and calling with excellence. This doesn't mean being flawless. It means being faithful. It means letting our love for Jesus show up in how we serve, lead, speak, and show up. When we live this way, we not only stand out—we give glory to God.

Here are three hallmarks of a spirit of excellence:

1. Diligence and Dedication: Those who walk in excellence are deeply committed to giving their best, regardless of who is watching or whether they receive praise. They approach their tasks with care and follow through with consistency. They pay attention to detail because they know their work is ultimately an offering to God, not just a task to complete. *"Whatever you do, work at it with all your heart, as working for the Lord, not for human masters"* (Colossians 3:23).

2. Integrity in All Things: Integrity is non-negotiable for someone with an excellent spirit. They refuse to cut corners or compromise their values for the sake of speed, success, or convenience. Even when it's hard or unnoticed, they choose what is right. Proverbs 22:1 says, *"A good name is more desirable than great riches; to be esteemed is better than silver or gold."* They understand that *who* they are matters just as much as what they do.

3. Purpose-Driven Focus: Excellence flows from clarity. People who operate in excellence know *why* they do what they do. They aren't tossed around by distractions or comparison because their motivation is anchored in purpose. They pursue their calling with focus and intentionality, allowing God to guide their decisions and direct their steps.

Today's Verse:
"Commit to the LORD whatever you do, and he will establish your plans."
—Proverbs 16:3

WHO YOU WALK WITH MATTERS

"Walk with the wise and become wise; associate with fools and get in trouble."

Proverbs 13:20

The people we surround ourselves with shape the direction of our lives. Proverbs 13:20 reminds us that wisdom is often contagious—but so is foolishness. God designed us for relationships that sharpen us, not distract or drain us. When we walk with people who revere God, speak life, and live with integrity, we naturally grow stronger in our faith and purpose.

God desires to place us among Kingdom-minded people—those who pursue His heart and reflect His character. These are the voices that help us stay grounded in truth, challenge us to grow, and stir up the gifts God has placed within us. If you've felt the nudge to step back from relationships that no longer align with your walk, it may be the Lord inviting you into something deeper.

This is a season of alignment. God is calling His people to rise above distractions and link arms with those who carry His wisdom and strength. He wants you surrounded by *winners* in the Spirit—people who will lift you up, speak prophetic encouragement, and help you stay rooted in His Word.

Take time today to pray over your relationships. Ask God for discernment—who should be speaking into your life? Who helps you walk closer to Jesus? Be open to new, divine connections and willing to release those that hinder your growth. Wise relationships aren't just about avoiding trouble—they help position you to walk in the fullness of God's calling on your life.

Today's Verse:
"Two are better than one, because they have a good return for their labor: If either of them falls down, one can help the other up. But pity anyone who falls and has no one to help them up."
—Ecclesiastes 4:9–10

SHARPENED BY PURPOSE

"As iron sharpens iron,
so one person sharpens another."

Proverbs 27:17

S ometimes God creates divine encounters in the most unexpected places. I recently had one of those moments with a new client at a café inside my gym. As we spoke, he picked up my business card and pointed to the verse printed on it—Proverbs 27:17. "What does this mean?" he asked. I always welcome these conversations because they open the door to share God's heart in a natural, meaningful way.

What made this encounter even more special was that the man was Hindu, but his 15-year-old son, a rising basketball player, is a Christian. Despite their different beliefs, this father has been fully supportive of his son's faith—attending church, youth groups, and standing respectfully in the back of the room while his son worships. That kind of unconditional support immediately reminded me of the heart of Jesus.

I explained that Proverbs 27:17 speaks to the power of relationships to refine and strengthen us. It means we grow when we encourage, challenge, and support one another. I shared how, in my work in health and fitness, I aim to help others grow physically, mentally, and spiritually. We can sharpen one another regardless of our backgrounds by calling out the best in each other with love, wisdom, and truth.

His response moved me. He told me he may not share his son's beliefs, but he would never stop standing by him. That loyalty and fatherly love spoke volumes. It was a reminder that God's love works through people in all kinds of ways. This dad's heart reflected Christ more than he realized—an unwavering, faithful love that stands close, no matter what.

As believers, we carry the Spirit of Christ into every room we enter. You don't have to preach a sermon to share the gospel—sometimes, it's as simple as showing up with integrity, compassion, and readiness to listen. This moment also reaffirmed the importance of standing firm in faith. Though others have questioned my decision to include Proverbs 27:17 on my card, I'm thankful I didn't compromise. That verse, that moment, may have been the very thing God used to plant a seed. Every act of obedience matters. When we honor God, He shows up—sometimes quietly, sometimes unexpectedly—but always with purpose.

Keep showing up, even when it feels like no one sees. Keep loving people well, even when it's not returned. Stay faithful, even when it's hard. You never know who's watching or how your quiet obedience is speaking louder than words. Someone might find Jesus just by watching you stay steady.

Today's Verse:
"We have different gifts, according to the grace given to each of us. If your gift is prophesying, then prophesy in accordance with your faith; if it is serving, then serve; if it is teaching, then teach." —Romans 12:6–8

THE GOD WHO SEES YOU

She gave this name to the Lord who spoke to her: 'You are the God who sees me,' for she said, 'I have now seen the One who sees me.'"

Genesis 16:13

Today, God wants you to know that He is with you, rejoicing over you, and ready to fill every anxious or empty space in your heart with His love. Maybe you've been feeling unseen or overlooked, carrying silent burdens that no one else seems to notice. But take heart—God sees you. Not from afar, not passively, but with deep compassion, love, and attention. His presence surrounds you, and His eyes are never off of you.

One of the most comforting stories in Scripture that illustrates this truth is found in Genesis 16—the story of Hagar. Hagar was a servant in the household of Abram and Sarai (later Abraham and Sarah). When Sarah could not conceive, she gave Hagar to her husband in hopes of building a family through her. But when Hagar became pregnant, tension grew, and Sarah treated her harshly. Feeling rejected and mistreated, Hagar ran away into the wilderness, alone and overwhelmed.

But in that desolate place, the Angel of the Lord found her. God didn't ignore her pain—He came to her, spoke directly to her, and gave her a promise for the future. Hagar was so moved by the encounter that she gave God a name: *El Roi*, meaning "*The God who sees me*." She realized that even when no one else seemed to care, **God did**. He saw her heart, her hurt, her situation—and He responded.

Maybe today you feel like Hagar—wandering through your own emotional or spiritual wilderness. Maybe you've felt invisible in your relationships, unnoticed in your efforts, or alone in your pain. But just as God saw Hagar, He sees *you*. He knows your story, your struggles, and your strength. He's not only aware—He's present, and He cares deeply.

God's love is personal. He's not just the God who sees people in general—He sees **you**. He rejoices over you, He walks beside you, and He sings over you with gladness (Zephaniah 3:17). Even when the world is loud with distractions or silent in support, His voice whispers peace and His presence remains faithful.

Let today be a reminder that you are not forgotten. You are fully known, fully loved, and never out of God's sight. Lean into that truth. Rest in it. Let it strengthen your faith and still your heart.

Today's Verse:

"You are my hiding place; you will protect me from trouble and surround me with songs of deliverance."

—Psalm 32:7

WHEN FAITH MEETS THE MOMENT

"Before he had finished praying, Rebekah came out with her jar on her shoulder..."

Genesis 24:15

Rebekah's story is a powerful reminder that God often answers our prayers through ordinary moments that turn into divine appointments. Found in Genesis 24, her story unfolds as part of God's plan to provide a wife for Isaac, the promised son of Abraham. Abraham, full of faith, sends his servant on a mission to find the right woman—believing God would guide him to her.

Before the servant even finishes praying, Rebekah arrives. She's carrying a jar on her shoulder—just another day in her life, just another routine task. But in God's plan, it was a pivotal moment. The servant had prayed a very specific request: that the right woman would offer him a drink *and* also offer to water his camels. Rebekah's willingness to go above and beyond what was asked revealed the kind of heart she had. Without hesitation, she offered the drink—and then took on the exhausting task of watering ten camels. That wasn't quick or easy. Yet she did it joyfully, with no idea that her obedience would become the very answer to someone's prayer.

This act alone revealed her generosity, strength, and servant-hearted nature. But Rebekah's story doesn't stop with that moment of kindness. When the servant explained why he had come, and how God had answered his prayer through her, she didn't pause. She agreed to leave everything familiar—her home, her family, her culture—to follow a path of faith. She said "yes" to a future she couldn't see because she trusted the God who was writing her story.

Rebekah shows us that you don't need to be in the spotlight to be in the center of God's will. She was simply living her life with kindness and integrity when God brought His purpose to her doorstep. Her faith, her willingness to serve, and her readiness to follow God's leading became part of a much bigger story—one that would shape the future of Israel and the lineage of Christ Himself.

Maybe you're in a season where your life feels ordinary. But never underestimate what God can do through your faithfulness in the day-to-day. One small act of obedience can open the door to something extraordinary. God still honors the willing heart—just like Rebekah's. So carry your jar, serve with love, pray with expectancy, and walk forward in faith.

Today's Verse:
"Isaac brought her into the tent of his mother Sarah, and he married Rebekah. So she became his wife, and he loved her; and Isaac was comforted after his mother's death."
—Genesis 24:67

DAY 223

GROUNDED IN PEACE

"God is our refuge and strength, an ever-present help in trouble."

Psalm 46:1

Last night in the sauna, I had no idea God was setting me up for a divine appointment. I noticed a woman with a beautiful tattoo on her foot that read *"hope."* I'll call her Jane. She smiled and said, "You're that dietitian, right? We met here a few months ago." I remembered her—we had chatted about fasting and gut health. She mentioned she had two children under two and was feeling overwhelmed. I told her I love kids and even offered to babysit one Saturday so she could sleep in. She smiled, thanked me, and said she'd been in the sauna a bit too long and needed to head home. I wished her a Happy Mother's Day as she walked out.

I planned to stay another 15 minutes but felt a strong prompting to leave. I didn't overthink it—I simply obeyed. As I exited, I found Jane looking disoriented. She walked up to me and whispered, "Wendi, I don't feel so good. Will you help me?" Moments later, she collapsed into my arms and began vomiting. Instinctively, I acted. I called out for help—asking for someone to call 9-1-1 and grab juice or electrolytes—but everyone froze.

With no help coming, I leaned into God's peace. I laid her on her side to keep her airway clear. She kept trying to roll onto her stomach, but I gently held her steady. I remembered she was breastfeeding and hadn't eaten much that day—this looked like heat exhaustion. When her eyes rolled back and she lost consciousness for a few seconds, I quietly prayed, "Lord, help." Seconds later, she sat up suddenly, clear-eyed and steady.

"You saved me," she said, still weak. "I was coming back to find you because I knew you would help me." While we waited for EMTs, Jane kept thanking me. But the truth is—I didn't save her. **Jesus did.** I just listened to the Holy Spirit, who told me to leave the sauna. He gave me peace in the chaos, clarity in the moment, and compassion to respond with love.

Later, Jane texted me, thanking me again for "saving her life." But what I felt most was gratitude—for God's presence, His promptings, and the reminder that He's always near. It stirred a fresh desire in me to be more like Jesus—to live ready to respond when He calls.

God wants to use you like that too. He wants to place you in someone's path to be their answered prayer. When you open your heart to His guidance, He'll equip you with the wisdom, strength, and love to make a difference.

Today's Verse:
"Praise be to the God and Father of our Lord Jesus Christ, the Father of compassion and the God of all comfort, who comforts us in all our troubles, so that we can comfort those in any trouble with the comfort we ourselves receive from God."
—2 Corinthians 1:3–4

STAND STRONG

"Put on the whole armor of God, that you may be able
to stand against the schemes of the devil."
Ephesians 6:11

Here's a powerful truth to remember: if the devil can't take you out, he'll try to wear you out. He may not be able to stop your purpose, but he'll aim to drain your joy, peace, and strength. The pressures of life, constant responsibilities, and unexpected struggles can leave us feeling depleted. And when we're weary, we're vulnerable—making it easier for the enemy to plant seeds of doubt, discouragement, and distraction.

But God hasn't left us defenseless. In Ephesians 6:11, Paul reminds us to *put on the full armor of God*—a daily, intentional act that equips us to stand firm when life gets hard. This isn't just spiritual language; it's a survival strategy. Each piece of the armor—truth, righteousness, peace, faith, salvation, and the Word—protects us from spiritual fatigue and real-life breakdowns. It reminds us that our strength doesn't come from ourselves, but from the One who never grows tired.

The enemy will try to wear us down through stress, fear, and exhaustion. But when we're filled with God's presence—through prayer, worship, and time in the Word—we're strengthened from the inside out. God's peace protects our hearts, His truth renews our minds, and His power sustains our steps. In Him, we find real rest and resilience.

Think of God's armor like a spiritual recharge. Just like we plug in our phones to power through the day, we must "plug in" to God's truth, love, and presence to be spiritually strong. Without His armor, we're left to rely on our limited strength. But when we suit up, we're covered—ready to stand no matter what comes our way.

Today, ask God to clothe you in His armor. Let His truth guide your decisions, His peace guard your heart, and His Word light your path. With Christ's strength, you can stand firm—unshaken, unworn, and fully equipped to walk in victory.

Today's Verse:
*"Therefore take up the whole armor of God, that you may be able to withstand in the evil day,
and having done all, to stand firm."*
—Ephesians 6:13

FASTING THAT FILLS

"Then Jesus declared, 'I am the bread of life. Whoever comes to me will never go hungry, and whoever believes in me will never be thirsty.'"

John 6:35

This morning, I felt a strong pull to fast and pray—to shut out the noise and draw closer to God. Fasting isn't just about abstaining from food; it's a posture of the heart. It reminds us that our true hunger is spiritual and that Jesus alone satisfies. In Isaiah 58, God reveals His heart for fasting—it's about compassion, freedom, and care for others, not just self-denial.

"Is not this the kind of fasting I have chosen: to loose the chains of injustice... to share your food with the hungry... to clothe the naked?" (Isaiah 58:6–7). True fasting draws us closer to Jesus while also turning our hearts toward the needs of others.

After praying, I went for a walk around Lipscomb Academy's football field in Nashville. As I circled the track, I saw a group of athletes finishing their training. I sensed God prompting me to quicken my pace—maybe there was a reason. In the parking lot, one of the athletes smiled and said, "Happy Mother's Day if you're a mom!" I responded, "Not a mom, but thank you—that's sweet." That small exchange opened a 45-minute conversation.

The man, a 27-year-old minor league player, shared about his life, and I handed him my card. He looked down and noticed the verse: "*Iron sharpens iron.*" Instantly, he rolled up his sleeve to show me the exact same verse tattooed on his arm. He shared about losing his brother and how God had used that pain to help others. I quoted Romans 8:28—"*God works all things for the good...*"—and he immediately pulled up his pant leg to reveal yet another tattoo: Romans 8:28.

We both stood in awe of God's divine orchestration. These weren't coincidences—they were reminders that when we fast, pray, and remain open to the Holy Spirit, God aligns our steps with purpose. Right there in the parking lot, we prayed—asking God for strength, healing, and clarity. It was holy ground.

Fasting sharpens your spiritual senses. When you set aside physical cravings, your awareness of God increases. You begin to see people more clearly, hear God more distinctly, and feel His presence more deeply. Fasting aligns your heart with Jesus and positions you to be His hands and feet in unexpected places.

If God prompts you to fast, don't fear it—embrace it. It's not punishment; it's an invitation. When we fast with the right heart, we're filled with something far greater than food: God's presence, power, and direction.

Today's Verse:

"But when you fast, put oil on your head and wash your face, so that it will not be obvious to others that you are fasting, but only to your Father, who is unseen; and your Father, who sees what is done in secret, will reward you."

—Matthew 6:17–18

SPIRITUAL STRENGTH TAKES INTENTION

"In the same way, the Spirit helps us in our weakness. We do not know what we ought to pray for, but the Spirit himself intercedes for us through wordless groans."

Romans 8:26

No one becomes strong by accident—not athletes, business owners, or believers. Athletes don't get faster and stronger without training. Businesses don't become successful by chance. Degrees aren't earned without late nights and sacrifice. So why do we sometimes assume spiritual growth will just happen? The truth is, growing close to God takes effort, consistency, and intention. You don't become spiritually strong by mistake—you have to show up, seek Him, and be willing to grow.

One of the most powerful ways to grow is through prayer. But let's be honest—there are times we don't know what to say or where to begin. Romans 8:26 gives us comfort and assurance: *"The Spirit helps us in our weakness."* When we don't have the words, the Holy Spirit steps in, interceding for us with groans too deep for words. Even when your mind feels scattered or your heart feels heavy, God hears you. He knows your need before you speak it—and He responds with love.

In seasons of grief, uncertainty, or emotional exhaustion, your prayers might feel like little more than tears or silence. That's okay. God doesn't require perfect words—He wants a present heart. The Holy Spirit is your helper, praying with you and for you, translating your deepest emotions into divine communication. This means you're never alone in your prayers. Even in the quiet, heaven hears.

Just like an athlete begins with simple routines—stretching, drills, discipline—your spiritual strength begins with daily moments in God's presence. Start with what you have. Set aside time each day to talk to God. Begin by thanking Him. Invite the Holy Spirit to guide your thoughts. If you don't know what to say, sit quietly. Trust that He's working even in the silence.

Over time, this daily rhythm becomes your source of peace and strength. It builds spiritual endurance. You'll begin to recognize the Holy Spirit's voice more clearly and sense His promptings more strongly. You'll also start to walk in greater confidence because you're relying on the Lord's strength.

Going Deeper: One of the names for the Holy Spirit means "Helper" or "Advocate." He is the precious gift Jesus promised. He dwells within your heart and guides you in righteousness. The Holy Spirit fights for you and loves you dearly. He will always draw you nearer to Jesus.

Today's Verse:

"But the Advocate, the Holy Spirit, whom the Father will send in my name, will teach you all things and will remind you of everything I have said to you."
—John 14:26

PRAYING WITHOUT SHAME

"I tell you, whoever publicly acknowledges me before others, the Son of Man will also acknowledge before the angels of God."

Luke 12:8

I always pray before meals, no matter where I am. One time at Whole Foods, I bowed my head to pray and a woman leaned over, saying, "Good for you. I always try to pray discreetly." Curious, I asked why. She replied, "I'm from New York. I just don't want to upset anyone."

I gently challenged her, "Why would praying upset someone? Jesus died for our sins—are you ashamed of that?" She quickly said, "No, of course not." I then asked, "So why hide it? Don't you want people to know about Jesus? If they see you pray, it might open the door for them to know Him too." She paused, shrugged, and walked away. As she left, I felt a deep sadness—not just for her, but for how often we allow fear of others' opinions to silence our faith.

Here in North America, we are blessed with the freedom to express our faith publicly. In many parts of the world, doing so could mean imprisonment—or worse. Jesus understands that some face persecution for their beliefs. He sees the risk and honors the heart behind every act of courage, even when it can't be expressed openly.

Still, for those of us who *can* speak freely, why wouldn't we? Jesus went to the cross openly, unashamed, for all the world to see. If we truly believe in Him, shouldn't our lives reflect that boldly, even in simple acts like bowing our heads before a meal?

That day in Whole Foods, I was reminded of Matthew 10:33: *"But whoever disowns me before others, I will disown before my Father in heaven."* It's not meant to guilt us, but to stir us toward courage. Our faith is meant to be lived out loud—not for show, but as a witness to the world.

Some may point to Matthew 6:6, where Jesus says to pray in private. But He was addressing hypocrisy—not sincere believers living out their faith with integrity. There's a difference between praying to be seen and praying while not being afraid to be seen.

Your quiet prayer in public may seem small, but it could be the spark that leads someone else to seek Jesus. Our everyday boldness—spoken with grace, lived with love—is one of the simplest ways to reflect the light of Christ.

Today's Verse:
"Whoever acknowledges me before others, I will also acknowledge before my Father in heaven."
—Matthew 10:32

ROOTED IN HIS WORD

"Keep my words and store up my commands within you. Keep my commands and you will live; guard my teachings as the apple of your eye. Bind them on your fingers; write them on the tablet of your heart."

Proverbs 7:1–3

"If you want to establish God's reputation, you must be willing to risk yours."

I wrote those words on January 24, 2023, and taped them to my bathroom mirror. Every morning, they remind me of something foundational: my identity is in Christ—not in people's opinions or the world's approval. That little note challenges me to walk in bold obedience, even when it feels uncomfortable or when others might not understand. It reminds me that courage in faith often looks like standing alone in the world's eyes, but never in God's.

Like anyone else, I have moments of weakness and doubt. But I've learned to lean hard on Christ during those times. When life feels uncertain or overwhelming, it's often God calling us to deeper trust and surrender. Growth rarely happens in ease—it happens in the tension, in the letting go, and in the leaning in.

When something is from God, it carries peace—even in the unknown. When confusion, fear, or anxiety dominate, it's often the enemy trying to derail what God is building in you. Satan's goal is always the same: to steal, kill, and destroy. But Jesus came so we could live free, healed, and whole. That freedom starts when we allow God to prune and shape our hearts.

His refining process may be uncomfortable, but it's always for our good and His glory. When we say "yes" to His leading, even when it's hard, we begin to see the fruit of obedience—peace, purpose, and a deeper walk with Him. God's Word becomes our anchor in a shifting world, and His Spirit becomes our guide when clarity feels out of reach.

Every decision to follow Him—even the quiet, private ones—transforms us from the inside out. Don't be ashamed of where you've been. God can take the broken pieces of your story and turn them into something beautiful. As Romans 8:28 says, *"God works all things for the good of those who love Him."*

So today, surround yourself with truth. Keep God's Word near—on your heart, in your mind, even posted on your mirror. Let it renew your thoughts and shape your choices. As you write His Word on the tablet of your heart, you'll find the strength to walk boldly, live fully, and bring Him glory in everything you do.

Today's Verse:
"I have hidden your word in my heart that I might not sin against you."
—Psalm 119:11

GET UP, WARRIOR

"The Lord said to Joshua, 'Stand up! What are you doing down on your face?'"

Joshua 7:10

You weren't created to live in defeat. You were made to RISE.

Life is hard. The setbacks are real, and sometimes they cut deep. Maybe you've recently failed, lost something precious, or made a decision you regret. But hear this today: **you are not meant to stay down.** Just like God called Joshua to rise after a painful defeat, He is calling you, too. The Lord told Joshua, "*Do not be afraid; do not be discouraged. Take the whole army with you, and go up and attack Ai*" (Joshua 8:1). In other words—get up, take your people, and go again. **Your comeback starts now.**

There's a principle I teach to my athletes and clients: **the 24-hour rule.** After a tough loss or failure, you get 24 hours. Feel the frustration. Let yourself process the disappointment. Cry, pray, write it down—do what you need to do. But then, you get up. You don't camp out in the pain. You rise from it. Growth happens when you reflect, reset, and move forward with purpose.

God doesn't want you to carry the weight of failure. He wants to strengthen you through it. The pain you're feeling? It's not your identity. It's a part of your journey. You're being *sharpened*. You're being *refined*. You're being *prepared*.

When Joshua was faced with defeat, God didn't coddle him. He didn't tell him to sit longer and feel bad. He said, **"Stand up!"** God was telling Joshua to stop dwelling in what went wrong and start moving toward what was still possible. And He's saying the same to you: *Get up, warrior! It's time to fight again!*

Start by renewing your mind. Speak truth over yourself. God is with you, and you are not defined by your lowest moment! You are only defined by who Jesus says you are! Beloved, you are a child of the Most High. Redeemed. Equipped. Anointed. Capable. Called. Like David, sometimes we do have to strengthen ourselves in the Lord (1 Samuel 30:6).

You may have lost a round, but the battle isn't over—and the victory still belongs to the Lord. Today is the beginning of your bounce-back season!

Let this be your turning point. Get back in the game with boldness. Sharpen your mindset. Attack the process. And trust that God is leading you every step of the way.

Today's Verse:
"Do not gloat over me, my enemy! Though I have fallen, I will rise. Though I sit in darkness, the Lord will be my light."
—Micah 7:8

PURE JOY

"This is the day the Lord has made; let us rejoice and be glad in it."

Psalm 118:24

Today is a gift. Yes—this day, right here, right now! Whether the sun is shining or clouds are rolling in, whether the to-do list is long or your heart feels light, *this* is the day the Lord has made, and you are invited to rejoice in it. That doesn't mean everything has to be perfect. It simply means you've been given a chance to live, laugh, love, and reflect God's goodness in your own unique way.

Sometimes we think joy is reserved for big moments—weddings, birthdays, vacations, or breakthroughs. But joy is also found in the little things: the sound of your favorite song, an unexpected message from a friend, a walk outside, or the first sip of coffee in the morning. Joy is built into the ordinary when we pause long enough to notice it.

Here's the truth: **joy is a fruit of the Spirit**, not a result of perfect circumstances. It's not something you have to chase—it's something you can *choose*. When we set our eyes on Jesus and remember who we are in Him, joy naturally rises up. Even in hard seasons, you can hold onto the kind of joy that anchors your soul and lifts your spirit.

Take a moment today to smile. Laugh out loud. Do something that makes your heart feel light. Dance in the kitchen. Send a funny meme. Sing in the car—even off-key. Jesus delights in seeing you enjoy your life. He came that you may have life—and have it *abundantly* (John 10:10). That means a life marked not just by surviving, but by thriving. A life full of joy, even when things aren't perfect.

Let go of the guilt that tells you you need to earn rest or joy. God is not a taskmaster—He's a Father. He wants you to enjoy the beauty He's placed around you. You weren't created to just push through—you were created to live fully and joyfully in His love.

So take a deep breath. Soak in this moment. Laugh a little louder. Thank God for something small and beautiful today. There's joy waiting for you right here, in the midst of the ordinary.

Today's Verse:
"You make known to me the path of life; you will fill me with joy in your presence, with eternal pleasures at your right hand."
—Psalm 16:11

THE BEAUTY IN THE WAIT

"Wait for the Lord; be strong and take heart and wait for the Lord."

Psalm 27:14

As I write these words, I'm a single woman who deeply desires to be a wife and mother, but even more than that, I long to chase after the will of my Heavenly Father. I want to point people to Christ and rest in His perfect timing, trusting that He knows the desires of my heart and will fulfill them in the way that aligns with His plan for my life.

Still, if I'm honest, that trust isn't always easy. There are days when I would love nothing more than to share my life with someone and raise children of my own to walk in the ways of Jesus. Yet, over and over again, God gently reminds me: **His timing is always perfect—even when it feels slow or hard to understand.**

Maybe you can relate. Perhaps there's a longing in your own heart—something you've prayed over, wept over, and waited for—but the promise still feels distant. In those moments, questions creep in: *Has God forgotten me? Are His plans for me still in motion?* Friend, don't lose heart. Jesus gave us a powerful reminder in Matthew 6:33: *"Seek first His kingdom and His righteousness, and all these things will be given to you as well."* When we seek Him first, we can rest knowing that He is working behind the scenes in ways we can't always see.

I've seen this truth lived out in the lives of others. One of my former clients walked through years of disappointment and failed IVF treatments. Her heart ached with the desire to be a mother. But just days after Mother's Day, she sent me a photo—her and her husband holding their beautiful newborn daughter. It was a sacred reminder that **God had not forgotten her.** He was just working according to His perfect timeline, and the joy she now holds in her arms far outweighs the sorrow she once carried.

If you find yourself in a season of waiting, I want to encourage you today: **God sees you.** He knows the deepest desires of your heart, and He is not indifferent to your prayers. You are not overlooked. Every tear, every whispered hope, every moment of surrender matters to Him. His timing is not a delay—it's divine preparation for something greater.

Hold on. Take heart. And keep trusting. Because when God fulfills His promises, it will be more beautiful, more complete, and more meaningful than anything you could have orchestrated on your own.

Today's Verse:
"The Lord is good to those who wait for Him,
to the soul who seeks Him."
—Lamentations 3:25

KEEP BUILDING

"By faith Noah, when warned about things not yet seen, in holy fear built an ark to save his family. By his faith he condemned the world and became heir of the righteousness that is in keeping with faith."

Hebrews 11:7

God meets us right where we are—whether in our pain, confusion, or discouragement. Yesterday, I had one of those moments while stuck in Dallas traffic. Out of nowhere, my radio switched to a Christian station, and just as it did, a bright red cardinal flew across my windshield.

I felt the Holy Spirit nudge me: *Be still and listen.* Earlier that day, I saw a license plate that said *"My Plan."* I hadn't thought much of it at the time, but as I listened to a pastor talk about Noah's obedience in building the ark, everything clicked. God was reminding me to stay faithful and trust His plan—even when my own feels like it's falling apart.

Lately, I've been discouraged. I've poured my heart into building a health, fitness, and nutrition coaching business, but lately the doors seem to be closing. New clients aren't coming in, partnerships are fading, and the excitement of our new membership program has cooled. Despite years of hard work, I've felt stuck. Maybe by the time this devotional is released, things will look different. But today? Things are tough. And still—I choose to share the real, raw journey.

As I sat there in traffic, that message about Noah hit me deeply. Noah didn't see results right away. He didn't get applause. He was building something massive in obedience to a God-sized assignment, even while others laughed or questioned him. Yet Noah remained faithful. **He trusted what God had spoken over what he saw.** That's the kind of faith we're called to walk in too.

The next morning, God reminded me He sees every ounce of effort. While grabbing coffee at a hotel cafe, I met a baseball coach who recognized me from social media. He told me how much he appreciated my nutrition content and how it's helped his players. It was a simple moment—but it was God's way of saying, *Keep going. You're making an impact, even when it doesn't feel like it.*

If you're in a season that feels fruitless, friend, know this: **God sees you.** Keep showing up. Keep being faithful. Keep building your "ark" with what He's put in your hands. Just like Noah, your obedience will lead to something far greater than you can see right now. The rain *will* come. The breakthrough *will* happen. And when it does, you'll be ready—because you never stopped building.

Today's Verse:
"Noah did everything just as God commanded him."
—Genesis 6:22

MOUNT UP

"But those who wait on the Lord shall renew their strength; they shall mount up with wings like eagles, they shall run and not be weary, they shall walk and not faint."

Isaiah 40:31

The Lord is saying to you today: *This is your season to mount up!*

For too long, you may have felt grounded—held down by delays, disappointments, or discouragement. But God is calling you higher. He's inviting you to let go of what's been weighing you down and to trust that He's giving you fresh strength to soar. Just like an eagle spreads its wings to catch the wind and rise above the storms, the Lord is preparing you to rise into a new level of clarity, purpose, and breakthrough.

This is not the time to shrink back or stay stuck. God is renewing your strength even now. Where you've felt too tired to try again or too weary to hope, He is breathing new life into your spirit. He is restoring your endurance, filling you with boldness, and equipping you to run with fresh determination. **You may not feel strong, but that's okay—His strength is made perfect in your weakness.**

Let this be your reminder: the waiting season wasn't wasted. God has been preparing you, pruning you, and positioning you. And now, it's time to rise. Fix your eyes on Him—not on the obstacles around you or the doubts within you. Keep your focus on the One who lifts you up. His ways are higher. His plans are better. And His timing is never off.

You are being called into a new rhythm—a season not of striving, but of **soaring**. That doesn't mean everything will be easy, but it does mean you'll walk with the assurance that **God is carrying you.** You're being led forward by His peace and surrounded by His joy. The winds of His Spirit are beneath your wings, and He is guiding every step you take.

So today, mount up. Rise with hope. Run without fear. Walk with purpose. And know that the Lord is right beside you—empowering, uplifting, and sending you forward into all He's prepared for you. **You're not just stepping into a new season—you're rising into it.**

Today's Verse:
"You will go out in joy and be led forth in peace; the mountains and hills will burst into song before you, and all the trees of the field will clap their hands."
—Isaiah 55:12

DAY 234

STEP INTO ALIGNMENT

"The steps of a good man are ordered by the Lord, and He delights in his way."

Psalm 37:23

I t's the 234th day of the year—and here's what God wants you to know: You're not behind. You're not too late. You're exactly *where you need to be to align with His next move.*

This is a divine checkpoint. A holy pause. A moment where God is saying, *"Look how far we've come together—and just wait until you see where I'm taking you next."*

Maybe the year hasn't unfolded the way you thought it would. Maybe you've faced delays, detours, disappointments—or maybe you've made decisions you regret. But friend, today is not about looking back in shame. Today is about realignment. It's about stepping back in sync with the rhythm of God's heart and receiving fresh instruction for what's ahead.

God is saying, *"If you let Me lead, I'll take you somewhere better than you imagined."* He doesn't need a perfect path—He just needs your willing heart. The journey is not about speed; it's about *surrender*. And when your steps are ordered by the Lord, even the slow seasons serve a purpose.

This is a season of reordering. Just like the numbers 2-3-4 move forward in sequence, the Lord is bringing **order to what's**

felt out of place in your life. Where there's been chaos, He's bringing peace. Where you've been uncertain, He's releasing clarity. God's not asking you to figure everything out—He's simply asking you to follow Him step by step.

Today, take one bold step toward obedience. Maybe it's forgiving someone, starting something new, returning to a promise you put down, or simply getting quiet with God again. Small steps in the right direction make big impact over time.

You've come this far not by accident, but by divine design. And there's still time left in this year for God to surprise you, bless you, and launch you into something brand new. **Stay close. Stay ready. Stay aligned.**□

Today's Verse:
"Commit to the Lord whatever you do, and He will establish your plans."—Proverbs 16:3

DIVINE CONNECTIONS

"Therefore encourage one another and build each other up, just as in fact you are doing."

1 Thessalonians 5:11

G od often places people in our path for a reason—and when we respond to His nudges, something beautiful happens. I met a flight attendant named Matthew on my flight from Dallas to Nashville. From the moment I saw him, something about him stood out.

About twenty minutes into the flight, I looked toward the front of the plane and felt a sudden, overwhelming awareness of Jesus' presence. It was as if He were standing right there—comforting, near, and undeniably real. Tears filled my eyes. I sensed God prompting me to talk to Matthew, yet I hesitated. "Lord, I don't want to bother him. He's working. What if it's awkward?" But the nudge persisted, and eventually, I smiled and thought, *Well, making friends with strangers is what I do best.*

With a deep breath, I walked to the front and asked, "Is there something going on in your life that you've been praying about, but feel unsure if God hears you?" His eyes widened. "Yes," he said. "You're spot on. How did you know?" I replied, "God told me to speak with you. I didn't know what I'd say, but I trusted He'd give me the words."

Matthew then opened up about his painful struggles—his ex-spouse, concerns about his kids, and a growing sense of doubt. He had been praying, but felt unheard. I reminded him of Romans 8:28, that *God works all things together for good for those who love Him,* and assured him that **God hears every word** and is working behind the scenes even now.

We prayed together in the galley, two strangers bonded by the Spirit of God at 30,000 feet. He showed me his bracelet—a symbol from the Book of Acts—and we exchanged contact info so I could continue encouraging him.

When I returned to my seat, my heart was full. There was a peace and joy I can't quite describe—the kind that only comes from knowing you've walked in step with the Spirit. I opened my Bible app and saw the verse of the day:"*Everyone was filled with awe at the many wonders and signs performed by the apostles*" (Acts 2:43).

Another confirmation. God was at work.

Let this be your reminder: **you don't have to be in a pulpit to minister. Just be** *available.* When the Holy Spirit nudges you, trust that He's setting up divine appointments. Your obedience may be the answer to someone's silent prayer.

Today's Verse:
"*Now to each one the manifestation of the Spirit is given for the common good. To one there is given through the Spirit a message of wisdom, to another a message of knowledge by means of the same Spirit.*"
—1 Corinthians 12:7-8

COMFORTED TO COMFORT

"Praise be to God...who comforts us in all our troubles, so that we can comfort those in any trouble with the comfort we ourselves receive from God."
2 Corinthians 1:3–4

God never wastes our pain—He uses it to help others heal. After a workout, I headed to Whole Foods to get some work done. As I sat in the café, I noticed a young girl—thin, quiet, and visibly burdened—being tutored nearby. There was a sadness in her eyes I recognized. As she got up to leave, I smiled and gently invited her to sit down. I didn't know exactly what I'd say, but I knew I was supposed to ask if she was okay.

She introduced herself as Sara and said she was stressed, studying hard for her SATs. We connected over her dream of becoming a physician assistant. But I sensed God nudging me to go deeper, so I asked again—this time with more intention—if she was truly okay.

Tears filled her eyes as she admitted she was recovering from an eating disorder and that the journey had been painful. I told her I understood and that I, too, had battled those same lies. I looked her in the eyes and reminded her she is strong, loved, and not defined by what the enemy says. God's truth speaks a better word.

Then she shared something that confirmed this divine appointment—she had just left an abusive relationship. I told her that I, too, had once walked that path, and God helped me find freedom. I reassured her that our meeting was no accident—that God had brought us together for a reason. Before she left, I gave her my card and offered support. She lit up and even mentioned wanting to share my story with her school, where speakers talk to girls about health and self-worth.

That moment reminded me that God uses our past pain to become someone else's breakthrough. Every time I follow His nudge, I watch Him do what only Jesus can—heal, restore, and redeem.

If you're in a hard season right now, don't give up. It's not the end of your story. God is preparing you to comfort others with the same hope He's pouring into you. Someone needs the light you carry—your testimony may be the very thing that sets them free.

Today's Verse:
"Then they cried out to the Lord in their trouble, and He delivered them from their distress."
—Psalm 107:6

FRIENDS OF GOD

"I no longer call you servants, because a servant does not know his master's business. Instead, I have called you friends, for everything that I learned from my Father I have made known to you."

John 15:15

Faith isn't about religion or rules—it's about a personal relationship with Jesus.

I first heard about Jesus in my small-town Lutheran church, but even as I attended Bible classes, I didn't truly feel the love of God people talked about. My family was going through a lot, and I struggled to believe Jesus cared for me in the middle of all the pain. My dad taught us to pray, and my grandmother encouraged us to turn to God, but I often found myself praying to angels just to feel safe—especially during the constant back-and-forth between my mom and dad after their divorce.

As a child, I couldn't reconcile the idea of a loving God with the reality of innocent children going through loss and instability. My older sister stepped in as a caretaker at a young age, sacrificing so much for me and my brother. Now, I see how God used her strength—and even our pain—to shape something bigger. He was there, even when I couldn't feel it.

When I truly encountered Christ later in life, everything changed. I came to understand that God hadn't abandoned me—He had been patiently walking with me the whole time, preparing my heart for a deeper relationship with Him. What once felt like abandonment, I now see as preparation. The pain had purpose.

Today, I'm passionate about sharing the gospel, not from a place of religious tradition, but from personal experience. I don't talk about God as a list of rules—I talk about Him as a friend. A Savior. A healer. I wish someone had helped me understand that growing up—that Jesus meets us in our brokenness, and through the Holy Spirit, gives us power to live with courage, compassion, and conviction.

Now, I wake up every day with the intention to show someone who Jesus really is. If I don't reach them with God's love, who will? Whether through a kind word or simple act of service, each of us has the power to reflect God's heart to the world.

Today's Verse:
"He has made us competent as ministers of a new covenant—not of the letter but of the Spirit; for the letter kills, but the Spirit gives life."
—2 Corinthians 3:6

YOU BELONG

"Now you are the body of Christ, and each one of you is a part of it."

1 Corinthians 12:27

G ood morning, friend. I don't know where this message finds you today—maybe on the mountaintop, or maybe deep in the valley.

Maybe you're clinging to hope with everything you have, or maybe it feels like hope is slipping right through your fingers. Life has a way of pressing in, doesn't it? *The disappointments, the heartbreaks, the slow, steady ache of feeling unseen.*

But hear this today: **you are not forgotten. You are not alone.**

God, in His great love, chose *you* to be part of His family. You're not just another face in the crowd—you're a vital part of the body of Christ. That means your life carries weight, your story has purpose, and your presence leaves an impact. Whether you feel like the strong one or the struggling one today, you belong.

Jesus never promised a life without trials. But He *did* promise His presence—and that changes everything. When you say "yes" to Him, you don't just get a Savior—you gain a Companion. A Helper. A Father. A Friend. Jesus walks with you when you're weary and lifts you up when your knees buckle. His arms are wide enough to hold your questions, your silence, your heartbreak, and even your doubt.

Faith doesn't mean you'll never struggle. It means you'll never have to struggle alone.

So if you're hurting today, lean in a little closer. Let God's presence wrap around you like a blanket. Remember this: the same God who spoke galaxies into existence thought the world needed one of *you*. You are uniquely made, purposefully placed, and fully loved—not because of what you do, but because of *who* you are.

We are the Church—not buildings, but people. And that means wherever you are right now, God can meet you there. Your car, your kitchen table, your office, your lunch break—that's holy ground. Your smile, your kindness, your story—they all point people to Jesus.

Today, take just one small step closer to Jesus. Whisper a prayer. Crack open your Bible. Or simply sit still and let Him speak to your heart.

You belong. You're part of something bigger than you can see. And the world wouldn't be complete without you.

Today's Verse:
"The Lord your God is with you,
the Mighty Warrior who saves."
—Zephaniah 3:17

SPIRITUAL VITAMINS FOR THE SOUL

"Dear friend, I pray that you may enjoy good health and that all may go well with you, even as your soul is getting along well."

3 John 1:2

Don't forget to take your spiritual vitamins each day! Just as we nourish our bodies with the right nutrients, we also need to care for our spiritual health. As a Christian dietitian and sports nutritionist, I emphasize a balanced approach to well-being—one that supports mental, physical, and spiritual health.

Here's a fun and refreshing checklist to help give your soul a daily boost.

Daily Spiritual Vitamin Checklist

Morning Praise Shot: Start your day with a burst of gratitude. Always prioritize *Scripture before screens*. Thank God for three things. This "gratitude shot" sets the tone for a joyful and centered day.

Scripture Smoothie: Blend in some Word. Choose a Bible verse to meditate on throughout your day. Write it on a sticky note or save it as your phone wallpaper. Let the truth of God's Word nourish your thoughts.

Prayer Power-Up: Take a moment (or several) to talk to God. It doesn't have to be long or formal—just heartfelt. Prayer fills you with peace, strength, and divine direction.

Faith-Fiber Check-In: Call or text a friend for a quick faith boost. Share something you're thankful for or encourage each other with a verse or prayer. This spiritual "fiber" strengthens the Body of Christ.

The "No" Nutrient: Say *no* to one thing that doesn't serve your purpose today. Each "no" makes room for a "yes" to what truly matters—God's will and your well-being.

Joy Jumpstart: Add joy to your routine. Whether it's dancing to your favorite worship song, walking outside, or laughing with a friend, joy is one of God's most healing vitamins for the soul.

Evening Reflection & Recharge: Wind down with gratitude. Ask: Where did I see God today? Thank Him, release any worry, and rest in His peace. Set a calming atmosphere for sleep, and aim for 7–11 hours to allow your body and spirit to renew.

Today's Verse:
"Praise the Lord, my soul, and do not forget how kind he is. He forgives all my sins and heals all my diseases."
—Psalm 103:2–3 (GNT)

FIGHT WITH PURPOSE

"I have fought the good fight, I have finished the race, I have kept the faith."

2 Timothy 4:7

Life can feel like a fight—swings thrown at the air, hoping to land a hit. The Apostle Paul understood this. In 1 Corinthians 9:26-27, he says, "*I do not run like someone running aimlessly; I do not fight like a boxer beating the air.*" Paul wasn't interested in flailing faith. He trained his spiritual life with discipline, self-control, and focus—like a champion athlete preparing for a prize.

Why did Paul use such physical imagery? Because he lived in a culture that celebrated athletic competition. Sports were everywhere—Olympics, races, boxing, gladiators. Paul used what people understood to teach what they needed: that faith is not passive. It's a race to be run with endurance. A fight to be fought with purpose.

Just as an athlete doesn't win by accident, neither does a believer walk in victory without training. Paul wasn't shadowboxing. *He struck with intention.* That's the call for us too: to pursue Jesus with clarity, not chaos. We must set boundaries, focus on Scripture, pray consistently, and reject distractions that disqualify us from the prize.

Ask yourself: *Am I running aimlessly? Or am I pressing forward with intention?*

The Christian life isn't about comfort—it's about commitment. Like an athlete enduring workouts and setbacks, we grow stronger through discipline and resistance. When trials hit, we don't quit. We press on because we know the crown of life awaits those who endure.

So fight. Train. Run. Whether you're in a valley or climbing uphill, God is working in the effort. The Holy Spirit is your coach, your power, and your endurance. Don't waste your punches on things that don't matter. Don't run aimlessly through life. Aim your steps toward Christ and finish your race well.

You were never meant to shadowbox your way through this journey. With God by your side, **you are equipped to fight—*and win*—the good fight of faith.**□

Today's Verse:
"No discipline seems pleasant at the time, but painful. Later on, however, it produces a harvest of righteousness and peace for those who have been trained by it."
—Hebrews 12:11

KEEP YOUR AX SHARP

"If the ax is dull and its edge unsharpened, more strength is needed, but skill will bring success."
Ecclesiastes 10:10

L et's be honest—praying for wisdom or strength often comes with unexpected challenges. You ask for patience, and suddenly you're sitting in bumper-to-bumper traffic. You pray for strength, and God hands you a trial. Ask for wisdom? Don't be surprised when He starts revealing areas where you're swinging with a dull ax.

Ecclesiastes is filled with straightforward truth, like this zinger in 10:3: *"Even as fools walk along the road, they lack sense and show everyone how stupid they are."* Harsh? Maybe. But also accurate. We've all had those moments where we said too much or spoke too soon and instantly wished we could rewind.

Early in my career as a dietitian, I believed I had to know everything and speak on everything—nutrition tips, trends, even unsolicited advice. I thought being helpful meant always having an answer. But I learned the hard way that wisdom isn't found in having the loudest voice—it's found in knowing when to speak and when to stay silent. Ecclesiastes 10:20 reminds us, *"Be careful what you say. Word does get around."*

And then there's this: "*If the ax is dull... more strength is needed.*" That hits deep. A dull ax requires more force. Translation? When you're relying on your own strength without spiritual sharpness, you wear yourself out fast. Whether it's your words, your decisions, or your energy—if you're swinging aimlessly, you're going to burn out.

So, what sharpens your ax? Time in God's Word. Listening more. Speaking less. Humbling yourself enough to ask God for the wisdom to know what to say, when to say it, and when to stay quiet.

Another gem from Ecclesiastes: "*If a snake bites before it is charmed, the charmer receives no fee*" (10:11). In other words, timing matters. Rushing into conversations or decisions without seeking God's wisdom first can leave you with unnecessary consequences—metaphorical snake bites included.

Today, take a step back and ask: *Where am I swinging harder than I need to? Where is God asking me to slow down, sharpen up, and trust Him?*

Let your words reflect Heaven. Let your actions reflect wisdom. And let God be the one who sharpens your edge—so you can live with purpose, precision, and peace.

Today's Verse:
"*The one who has knowledge uses words with restraint, and whoever has understanding is even-tempered. Even fools are thought wise if they keep silent, and discerning if they hold their tongues.*"
—Proverbs 17:27-28

DAY 242

THE HUMBLE CARPENTER

"Isn't this the carpenter? Isn't this Mary's son and the brother of James, Joseph, Judas and Simon?" And they took offense at him.

Mark 6:3

Isn't it beautiful that the Savior of the world was once known simply as a carpenter?

In a culture that often measures success by titles, status, and accolades, Jesus turns everything upside down. He wasn't born in a palace. He didn't grow up with earthly riches or social prestige. He was known in His hometown not as a king, but as a carpenter—someone who worked with His hands, built with care, and quietly honored Father God through everyday labor.

And yet, it was this same Jesus who would walk on water, heal the sick, raise the dead, and ultimately conquer sin and death. His humble beginnings didn't disqualify Him—they were a part of God's plan.

If you've ever felt overlooked, underestimated, or dismissed because of your background, your job, or your past, let this truth wash over you: **God delights in using what the world sees as "ordinary" to bring about the extraordinary.**

Jesus' life is a reminder that the work you do matters, not because of who sees it, but because of *who you're doing it for.*

Whether you're leading a company, running a household, cleaning rooms, or quietly encouraging others—you are seen. And just like Jesus, you carry divine purpose in everything you do.

He didn't choose status; Jesus chose regular people. He sat with the lonely, spoke hope to the broken, and looked past appearances to see hearts. He showed a love that didn't depend on what people could give, but on who they were: deeply loved by God.

Let today be a fresh reminder that greatness in the Kingdom isn't about rising to the top—it's about going low. Serving. Loving. Being faithful where God has placed you. **You don't need a platform to reflect Christ. You just need a heart willing to love like Christ.**

So keep building, keep showing up, and keep loving well. You are not invisible. Heaven sees you, and the Carpenter calls you His own.

Today's Verse:
"The Lord does not look at the things people look at. People look at the outward appearance, but the Lord looks at the heart."
—1 Samuel 16:7

CREATIVITY IS A SPIRITUAL GIFT

"I have filled him with the Spirit of God, with wisdom, with understanding, with knowledge and with all kinds of skills..."

Exodus 31:3

T he first time Scripture mentions someone being filled with the Spirit of God might surprise you. It wasn't a prophet or a king. It wasn't a warrior or a priest. It was a man named Bezalel—a skilled **craftsman**, chosen by God to help build the Tabernacle. He wasn't leading revivals or parting seas. He was sketching blueprints. Melting gold. Carving wood. And yet, God said: *"I have filled him with My Spirit."*

Bezalel was an artist—and God called him to create something sacred. The Tabernacle would become the very place where God's presence would dwell among His people. And Bezalel? He was entrusted with shaping that space. This moment changes everything. It tells us something we don't hear enough in church culture: **God loves creativity.** Not just platform creativity—like singing on stage or preaching from a pulpit—but real, tangible, hands-on creativity.

Yes, the Holy Spirit inspires sermons. But He also inspires interior designers, architects, editors, coders, carpenters, stylists, bakers, and teachers. If it reflects beauty and order, it reflects the heart of our Creator. Even formatting this book required perseverance and diligence, leaning heavily on the Holy Spirit to guide every decision—not just about the words, but the design of the pages themselves. Every single day had to be prayerfully ordered to align with what God wanted to speak into your life.

Jesus is in the details. When we put on clothes, someone stitched together the design. When we eat at restaurants, someone put in their effort to prepare that meal. God's creativity and excellence are all around.

You don't need a title to be used by God. You don't need a microphone to minister. Your art can speak. Your business plan can build the Kingdom. Your cooking, your painting, your organizing, your storytelling—it all matters to Him. Bezalel didn't need a spotlight to be significant. He just needed a willing heart, skilled hands, and the breath of God upon his work.

Maybe you've felt overlooked. Maybe you've wondered if your gift is "less spiritual." But that's not the voice of God. That's the voice of culture. If God breathed on Bezalel's work, He can breathe on yours. You don't have to separate your creativity from your faith. You were designed to design.

So the next time you write that article, decorate that room, brainstorm that logo, or bake that sourdough loaf—invite the Holy Spirit into it. Jesus delights in your details. He empowers your excellence. He honors your offering. When God fills you, everything you touch can become holy.

Today's Verse:
"Let the favor of the Lord our God be upon us; establish the work of our hands for us—yes, establish the work of our hands."
—Psalm 90:17

TRANSFORMED, NOT CONFORMED

"Do not conform to the pattern of this world, but be transformed by the renewing of your mind. Then you will be able to test and approve what God's will is—His good, pleasing and perfect will."

Romans 12:2

Reading God's Word isn't just a habit—it's a holy encounter. Every time we open the Bible, we give God a chance to speak directly to our hearts, to renew our thinking, and to guide our steps. Romans 12:2 is one of those cornerstone verses that invites us into a different way of living—a way marked by surrender, renewal, and transformation. It challenges us not to fall in line with the values and pressures of this world but instead to let God reshape us from the inside out.

The world says, "Fit in." God says, **"Stand apart."** The world says, "Follow your truth." God says, **"Be transformed by My truth."**

Today's verse reminds us that transformation doesn't happen in one moment; it's a daily choice to renew our minds with His Word, to allow Scripture to shape our perspectives, and to let the Holy Spirit lead. As we do this, we begin to discern God's will—not just the big-picture plans, but the daily steps, the quiet nudges, and the divine opportunities that unfold when we're walking closely with Him.

One of the most powerful practices I've developed in my walk with God is dating the scripture passages He highlights to me during my quiet time. Every time a verse jumps out, brings conviction, or feels like a direct message from heaven—I write the date in the margin or blank space next to it. Why? Because that date becomes a marker of God's faithfulness. It becomes a timestamp of His voice in my life. Months or years later, when I flip through my Bible, I see those dates and remember exactly what He spoke, how He comforted me, or how He confirmed something I needed.

It's a beautiful way to track the personal journey of faith and to reflect on how God's Word has been active and alive in real time. Dating your Bible is like leaving breadcrumbs of divine encounters—it turns your Bible into a living testimony.

So today, as you read Romans 12:2, ask the Lord: "*What do You want to renew in me?*" If He gives you something, date it. Mark the moment. That small act may one day remind you just how far He's brought you—and how faithful He's always been.

Today's Verse:
"Your word is a lamp to my feet and a light to my path."
—Psalm 119:105

FREELY RECEIVE, FREELY GIVE

"Freely you have received; freely give."
Matthew 10:8b

We cannot give what we have not first received. It sounds simple, but it holds a profound truth. When Jesus sent out His disciples in Matthew 10, He gave them clear instructions: heal the sick, raise the dead, cleanse the lepers, drive out demons. But tucked into His command was this reminder—*"Freely you have received; freely give."*

Before they were sent out, they had spent lots of time with Jesus. They had walked with Him, listened to Him, and received His power and authority. Their ability to minister did not come from their natural talents. It came from the overflow of what Jesus had already deposited in them.

Sometimes we rush to give because we think that is what faithfulness looks like. We give our time, our energy, our emotions, even our money. But if we are not careful, we can end up giving from an empty place. Jesus never asked His disciples to manufacture miracles or force compassion. He asked them to *freely* give what they had *freely* received.

That is the rhythm of Kingdom life: Receive first, then give.

Receiving is not a passive act. It is *intentional*. It is opening your heart daily to the presence of God, allowing His love to re-

WENDI A. IRLBECK

fresh you, His wisdom to guide you, and His Spirit to strengthen you. It is acknowledging your complete dependence on Him.

When you have truly received from Jesus, giving becomes natural. You do not have to force generosity. You do not have to pretend to have joy. You do not have to fake compassion. What has been poured into you will naturally pour out of you.

Freely received means there were no strings attached. God did not ask you to earn His love. He simply gave it. In the same way, we are called to give to others without expecting anything in return.

Maybe today the Lord is inviting you to pause and ask: "Am I *giving from overflow—or am I running on empty?"* The best thing you can do for the people around you is not to give them your last drop of strength. It is to stay connected to the Source, so you can overflow with life, love, and power that points them straight to King Jesus.

Today's Verse:
*"I am the vine; you are the branches. If you remain in me and
I in you, you will bear much fruit;
apart from me you can do nothing."*
—John 15:5

YOUR FATHER LOVES YOU

"See what great love the Father has lavished on us, that we should be called children of God! And that is what we are!"

1 John 3:1

When you think about God, do you picture Him as a Father? For some, that image brings warmth and comfort—a strong, safe protector. For others, it stirs up pain or distance, shaped by earthly fathers who were absent, harsh, or just didn't know how to love well. But no matter your story, Scripture is clear: God is not just *like* a father—He *is* our Father. And He is a perfect one.

God's not distant. He's not disinterested. He's not waiting for you to earn His love. He is deeply involved in your life, present in every breath, every battle, and every breakthrough.

Jesus taught us to pray, "Our Father," not just to remind us of who God is—but to remind us of who *we* are. Loved. Chosen. Seen. Sons and daughters of the Most High. That truth changes everything.

When you stumble, your Father doesn't withdraw—He leans in. When you weep, your Father doesn't say, "Get over it"—He gathers your tears. When you succeed, your Father rejoices with you—not because of your performance, but because you're His.

Maybe you didn't grow up with someone cheering you on, protecting you, or teaching you how to walk through life with wisdom and grace. But your Heavenly Father longs to do that now. He wants to walk with you, speak to you, guide you, and remind you again and again: *you are Mine.* Let His love re-father the parts of you that still feel unloved. Let the Holy Spirit's presence fill the gaps of your story. You are not fatherless—you are fully and forever His.

And Father God is not going anywhere.

Today's Verse:
"As a father has compassion on his children, so the Lord has compassion on those who fear him."
—Psalm 103:13

YOU WILL BEAR FRUIT

"They are like trees planted along the riverbank, bearing fruit each season. Their leaves never wither, and they prosper in all they do."

Psalm 1:3

The season you're walking into will look nothing like the one you've just walked out of. If the last chapter felt like drought, get ready—God is sending the rain.

There's a shift happening in the Spirit, and I believe the Lord wants you to know this: **you will bear fruit in this next season.** Not just any fruit—but fruit that *lasts.* Fruit that brings glory to His name. The kind of fruit that proves you were faithful in the hidden place.

God saw you when you kept sowing in silence. He watched as you obeyed without applause, forgave without fanfare, and kept showing up even when nothing seemed to be growing. He saw every tear, every sacrifice, every moment of surrender—and He did not forget.

In John 15:5, Jesus says, *"If you remain in me and I in you, you will bear much fruit."* Fruitfulness isn't the result of striving—it's the result of *abiding.* When your roots go deep into the presence of God, the harvest will come.

You don't have to force it. Just stay close. Stay faithful. Stay planted.

The enemy may have tried to convince you that your time has passed or that your obedience didn't matter. But here's the truth: **the seeds you planted in obedience are about to break through the soil.** God is breathing on your efforts, watering your faith, and commanding growth in dry places. The waiting wasn't wasted—it was preparing you for what's coming.

Lift your eyes and believe again. Start thanking God now, because He is already at work behind the scenes. Soon, your hands will be overflowing! They will be filled with new hope, joy and assignments that prove you are deeply rooted in Christ!

Today's Verse:

"You did not choose me, but I chose you and appointed you so that you might go and bear fruit—fruit that will last."
—John 15:16

THE APPLE OF HIS EYE

"Keep me as the apple of your eye; hide me in the shadow of your wings."

Psalm 17:8

You are more protected, more cherished, and more guarded by God than you realize. In Psalm 17:8, David prayed one of the most beautiful and vulnerable prayers in Scripture. He asked God to keep him as the *"apple of His eye"* and to hide him under the shadow of His wings. This was not a prayer from a place of weakness—it was a prayer rooted in deep *trust.*

The phrase "apple of your eye" in Hebrew literally refers to the pupil, the most delicate and protected part of the eye. Think about it. Our instinct is to shield our eyes from any threat without even thinking. That is the level of care and vigilance God has toward you. You are not overlooked. You are not forgotten. You are precious to Him, guarded with the deepest love.

When David asked to be hidden in the shadow of God's wings, he was using imagery of a mother bird sheltering her young under her feathers. It speaks of nearness, tenderness, and fierce protection. In ancient times, the idea of wings also symbolized the covering of God's presence, like the wings over the mercy seat in the Holy of Holies.

What David understood—and what we sometimes forget—is that our strength is not in striving harder. It is in staying hidden in God. His covering is our confidence. His care is our courage. His love is our safety net when life feels uncertain.

Today, the Lord is inviting you to live fully aware of His protection over you. Not as someone scrambling to earn it, but as someone who simply receives it.

When you walk into new territory, remember—you are the apple of God's eye. When fear tries to rise up, remember—you are sheltered under His wings. When the enemy whispers that you are vulnerable or alone, remember that you are fiercely guarded by the Most High.

You do not have to fight for God's attention. *You already have it*. His eye is on you. His wings are over you. Walk boldly today, not because you have everything figured out, but because you are hidden in the shadow of the Almighty.

Today's Verse:
*"God is love. Whoever lives in love lives in God,
and God in them."*
—1 John 4:16

REJECTION ISN'T THE END OF THE STORY

"If anyone will not welcome you or listen to your words, leave that home or town and shake the dust off your feet."

Matthew 10:14

When Jesus sent out the disciples, He prepared them for both miracles and rejection. In Matthew 10, He commissioned them to go town by town, declaring that the Kingdom of Heaven had come near. But He also gave them a sobering instruction: if any home or town wouldn't receive them or listen to their message, they were to *shake the dust off their feet and move on.*

This wasn't a gesture of anger—it was one of release. It meant they had done their part. The rest was up to God.

This principle still applies today, especially when sharing our faith with people we deeply love. And sometimes, the ones hardest to reach are the ones closest to us—family.

You might be walking through this right now. You've shared your testimony. You've planted seeds. You've loved consistently. And yet, someone in your life just doesn't seem open to Jesus. It's heartbreaking. But Jesus understands.

Even His own brothers didn't believe in Him during His ministry (John 7:5). He shared meals with them, grew up in the same home—but they couldn't see who He truly was. And still, Jesus didn't force it. He kept obeying the Father. He kept loving them.

And after the resurrection? Everything changed.

James, the brother who once doubted, became a pillar of the early church and wrote the Book of James. Jude, another brother, penned a letter that's now part of the New Testament. What made the difference? **A personal encounter with the risen Jesus.**

That's the kind of transformation you can't manufacture. Only God can do that.

So if you've been carrying the weight of trying to convince someone, release it. That doesn't mean you give up on them—it means you entrust them to God. Keep loving. Keep praying. Keep living your faith with quiet strength and deep joy. And when it's time, shake the dust—not from your heart, but from your feet.

Rejection doesn't mean failure. It means it's time to let God do what only He can do.

Today's Verse:
"They all joined together constantly in prayer, along with the women and Mary the mother of Jesus, and with his brothers."
—Acts 1:14

WHEN GOD PAYS IN THE MOST UNEXPECTED WAYS

"But so that we may not cause offense, go to the lake and throw out your line. Take the first fish you catch; open its mouth and you will find a four-drachma coin. Take it and give it to them for my tax and yours."

Matthew 17:27

If you've ever prayed, *"Lord, I don't know how I'm going to pay for this,"* you're in good company. Peter was probably thinking the same thing. The temple tax was due, and they didn't have the money just lying around. But instead of sending Peter into a financial panic, Jesus sends him fishing. Not to escape his problems—but to find the provision.

Today's verse is one of the quirkiest, most creative miracles in the Bible! A *coin inside a fish*? Come on, that's next-level God stuff. But here's the lesson we sometimes miss: Jesus didn't just hand Peter the coin. He told him where to go, what to do, and to trust that the provision would be there when he *obeyed*.

Sometimes we pray for a miracle but sit on the shore, waiting for God to drop the fish at our feet. But often, He invites us to *move* in faith—to cast our line even when it doesn't make sense.

That business idea you've been nervous to launch? *Cast the line.* That resume you've been hesitating to submit? *Cast the line.* That call you've been afraid to make? Yep—*cast the line.*

Take the first thing that rises to the top!

God already knows where the coin is. He's not scrambling to figure it out. He's just waiting on your yes. This miracle also shows us something sweet about Jesus' heart. He didn't only provide for Peter—He included *Himself* in the miracle. He said, "Give it for *my* tax and *yours*." Jesus wasn't removed from Peter's stress—He stood in it with him.

So if you're feeling overwhelmed by bills, deadlines, or unexpected expenses, take heart. God's provision might not look like a check in the mail or a surprise bonus (although it could)! It might come through something so ordinary—so small—that it takes faith to see it for the miracle it really is.

Trust Him. Obey. Cast your line. The first fish is coming.

Today's Verse:
"And my God will meet all your needs according to the riches of his glory in Christ Jesus."
—Philippians 4:19

YOUR BREATH IS A GIFT

"Let everything that has breath praise the Lord."
Psalm 150:6

If you've got breath, you've got a reason to praise. Sometimes we wait for the big breakthrough to lift our hands. We think worship only happens when life feels good or when everything's in place. But God says if you're breathing, that's reason enough. Your breath is evidence of the Father's mercy. It's the rhythm of His presence sustaining you moment by moment. Praise doesn't have to be loud. It can be quiet gratitude. A whispered *"thank You."* A heart that stays open, even in the struggle.

Today, don't let your circumstances dictate your worship. Let your breath be your offering. Praise Jesus for air in your lungs and purpose in your steps. Because if you're still breathing, He's not done.

Today's Verse:
"I will bless the Lord at all times;
His praise shall continually be in my mouth."
—Psalm 34:1

YOU MARCH UNDER LOVE

"His banner over me was love."
Song of Solomon 2:4

You don't walk through life invisible. You march under a banner—and that banner boldly reads: LOVED.

Think of the opening ceremony of the Olympics. Nations parade in, athletes energized, heads held high. They walk under their flags—symbols of identity, unity, and honor. The flag declares to the world: *I belong. I represent something greater than myself.*

Now imagine this: Heaven's banner waving above you. But instead of the name of a nation, it carries a declaration far greater—**LOVE**. Not just any love. **God's love.** Unconditional. Unshakable. Unstoppable.

Song of Solomon 2:4 paints a vivid picture: "*He brought me to the banqueting table, and His banner over me was love.*" This isn't a hidden, whispered kind of love. This is bold. Visible. Unapologetic. God doesn't love you quietly. He announces it. Over you, above you, around you.

That means you don't have to prove your worth to be accepted. You don't have to hustle for God's affection or strive to be "enough." You already are. Your identity is not based on your resume, past mistakes, or Instagram following. It's rooted in the love of a King who calls you His.

When the enemy whispers, "You're unworthy," look up—there's a banner above you shouting, **"LOVED."** When life makes you feel small or unseen, remember—you walk under a covering that says, **"This one belongs to Me."** Even in your hardest moments, His banner never comes down. It flies high in failure and victory, in tears and triumph.

So today, walk differently. Stand taller. Speak with courage. Why? **Because you're carrying the banner of Heaven.** You're marked by Jesus who sees you, knows you, and still chooses you. Let that truth silence the lies and awaken your spirit. You're not just surviving—you're marching under love! And that makes you unstoppable.

Today's Verse:

"See, I have engraved you on the palms of my hands; your walls are ever before me."

—Isaiah 49:16

STEP INTO THE PROMISE

"How long will you wait before you begin to take possession of the land that the Lord, the God of your ancestors, has given you?"

Joshua 18:3

In Joshua 18, we find a powerful moment of hesitation among the Israelites. Seven of the twelve tribes had yet to claim the land God had already promised them. They had journeyed through the wilderness, crossed the Jordan, and witnessed God bring victory after victory. Yet, even with the promise right in front of them, they lingered in a state of waiting. Joshua's question to them was simple but convicting: *How long will you wait?*

So many of us live in that same space—standing at the edge of what God has already declared ours, but hesitant to step forward. Maybe it's fear of the unknown, doubt in our own ability, or uncertainty about what happens next. We pray for open doors, for God to move, for clarity—but sometimes, the Lord is waiting on *us* to move. The promise is there, but it takes faith-filled action to walk into it.

God had already given the Israelites their inheritance—they just needed to go and possess it. Likewise, Jesus has given *you* access to every spiritual blessing (Ephesians 1:3). The Holy Spirit empowers you to step into your calling, to claim the healing, freedom, peace, and purpose that Christ already secured. The question is: are you still waiting when God has already said *go*?

Writing this devotional book has been one of those promises for me. It had been stirring in my heart for years, but I faced every kind of setback you can imagine—even in the final stages. Delays, distractions, doubts, and moments when I questioned if it would ever be completed. But what God taught me through it all is this: obedience is often the first step to breakthrough. He never asked me to have it all figured out—just to trust Him enough to keep going. And in the process, He deepened my faith and showed me that the journey *is* part of the promise.

If you feel like you're standing at the edge of a promise, wondering when things will shift, ask yourself: *Is God waiting on me to move?* Sometimes faith isn't about waiting for one more confirmation—it's about taking the next step boldly, knowing the Lord has already gone before you.

Today, don't stay stuck in indecision. Take a bold step forward. Trust that God is with you, and move into what He has already prepared. The land is yours. The promise is real. Go and take possession of it.

Today's Verse:

"Go and make a survey of the land and write a description of it. Then return to me, and I will cast lots for you here at Shiloh in the presence of the Lord."
—Joshua 18:8

JOY IS YOUR SUPERPOWER

"A cheerful heart is good medicine, but a crushed spirit dries up the bones."

Proverbs 17:22

God delights in your joy—even your laughter. Somewhere along the way, many of us began to believe that spiritual maturity looks serious all the time. We think God only shows up in quiet devotionals, long prayers, or solemn worship moments.

Here's the truth: the same God who designed galaxies, oceans, and the intricate details of your DNA also created smiles, humor, and those deep belly laughs that leave your face sore and your soul refreshed!

Joy is not a surface emotion. **It's a spiritual weapon.** It disarms anxiety. It disrupts heaviness. It reminds your heart that even if everything isn't perfect, God still is. Scripture says laughter is good medicine—not just figuratively, but spiritually too (Proverbs 17:22). It lifts what weighs you down and gives your spirit space to breathe.

So let go today. Let yourself laugh. Let joy in. Watch something that makes you laugh. Call a friend who fills your heart. Dance in the kitchen. Smile at strangers. Thank God for the warmth of sunshine, the sound of music, or a really good cup of coffee.

These little moments matter more than you think. They reconnect your heart to the goodness of God and awaken gratitude.

Action step: Do one joyful thing today—*just because.* Set aside the pressure to be productive, and choose to be present. Your joy honors God. Your laughter reflects Heaven. You *were* made for joy. So smile big. Laugh loud. Dance with all your might before the Lord. Let joy be part of your worship today.

Today's Verse:

"You make known to me the path of life; in your presence there is fullness of joy, at your right hand are pleasures forevermore."
—Psalm 16:11

RELEASE THE WEIGHT

*"Cast all your anxiety on him
because he cares for you."*

1 Peter 5:7

You **weren't designed to carry what only God can handle.** Think about that for a moment. We carry so much—expectations, deadlines, worries, "what ifs." We try to juggle it all, convincing ourselves that if we don't, everything will fall apart. But here's the truth: your nervous system wasn't made to bear the weight of constant anxiety. That's why God gives us a divine invitation—to *cast* it all on Him. Not just some of it. *All* of it.

The word "cast" in this verse isn't passive. It doesn't mean to gently set something down. It means to *hurl* it, to *throw* it forcefully onto someone else. Imagine physically removing a heavy load from your shoulders and tossing it into God's capable hands. He isn't surprised by your stress. He doesn't scold you for being overwhelmed. He simply says, "*I care for you. Let Me carry this.*"

If you've ever struggled with anxiety, you know it can feel like a fog, a tightness in your chest, or a restless mind that won't quit. But anxiety doesn't disqualify you from peace—it actually invites you closer. God's care isn't conditional. You don't have to get everything together before approaching Him. You just have to come.

Sometimes, the most spiritual thing you can do is *exhale.* Surrender. Let go. Say, *"God, this is too much for me—but it's not too much for You."* And then, actually picture yourself throwing it—yes, imagine it. See yourself holding your fear, your financial worry, your relationship stress, and *literally tossing it* into God's open hands. Let that visual remind your heart of what your spirit already knows: God's got this.

Here's a practical step: write down what's been weighing on you. Then read it aloud in prayer and, when you're done, crumple it, shred it, or throw it in the trash—as a physical sign of releasing it to the Lord. He never meant for you to carry it alone.

And when the weight tries to creep back in, come back to this promise: *He cares for you.* Not just in theory—but in real, tangible, every-hour-of-the-day ways.

Today's Verse:
"Do not be anxious about anything, but in every situation, by prayer and petition, with thanksgiving,
present your requests to God."
—Philippians 4:6

THE RIPPLE EFFECT OF OBEDIENCE

"Therefore go and make disciples of all nations, baptizing them in the name of the Father and of the Son and of the Holy Spirit, and teaching them to obey everything I have commanded you. And surely I am with you always, to the very end of the age."

Matthew 28:19–20

You never know how one simple act of encouragement can multiply. A few months ago, I encouraged a man I had never met, unaware that our paths would cross again. But today, while I was working at a café, he approached me with a story I didn't expect to hear. "Wendi," he said, "remember when we met and you encouraged me? You gave me a new perspective during a tough time. That boldness helped me speak up in my men's group that night. I was able to encourage someone else because you encouraged me. Thank you."

His words struck me—not because of what I said, but because of what God did with it. That moment reminded me how powerful it is to say "yes" to the Holy Spirit's promptings. What feels like a small nudge to speak, pray, or smile could actually be the beginning of someone else's breakthrough. And sometimes, we never get to hear the impact—but this time, I did. It reminded me that obedience doesn't end with us. It multiplies.

When Jesus gave the Great Commission, He didn't say to go with a polished sermon or a perfect plan. He simply said to go—to make disciples, to baptize, to teach, and to trust that He would be with us. That means each one of us is invited into this mission, whether we're in a café, at work, at home, or across the globe. It's not about titles or training—it's about love, obedience, and being present when the Spirit moves.

If the Lord nudges you to encourage a stranger, pray with someone, or speak life into a hard situation, don't hold back. The Kingdom grows in quiet, beautiful ways—through conversations, encouragement, and bold moments of faith.

You may never know the full impact of your obedience. But you can trust that God does—and He is multiplying it for His glory.

Today's Verse:
"Let us consider how we may spur one another on toward love and good deeds."
—Hebrews 10:24

THE WIND OF MOMENTUM

"The wind blows wherever it pleases. You hear its sound, but you cannot tell where it comes from or where it is going. So it is with everyone born of the Spirit."

John 3:8

I believe I'm supposed to speak this over you today: a wind **of momentum is coming over your life.** There are days when the Spirit whispers, and then there are days when He moves like a rushing wind. Today is the latter. As I sat with the Lord, I felt Him place this on my heart for you: *"Tell them the wind is shifting. Tell them I'm stirring something new."*

You may have felt stuck lately—like your feet are planted but nothing is moving. Or maybe you've been faithful, showing up, praying, working, sowing—but the harvest hasn't come. The waiting has felt long. Heavy. Quiet. And perhaps you've wondered if you missed something... or if God forgot your name.

But hear this: **You haven't missed it. God hasn't overlooked you. He's been preparing you for the momentum that's coming.**

When the wind of the Spirit blows, it's not chaotic—it's purposeful. God breathes life into dry places. He fills sails and moves things forward with ease and power. And today, I believe the Spirit of God is breathing fresh wind over your purpose. New connections. Rekindled dreams. Open doors. Healing in places that once felt stagnant. A shift in your situation.

This isn't hype—it's Heaven reminding you that your story is still being written. You're not behind. You're not forgotten. And your obedience has not gone unnoticed.

So, lift your eyes. Strengthen your posture. Get ready. Because where you once felt stuck, you're going to feel carried. Where you once felt delayed, you're going to feel propelled. It's not because of your own striving—but because of God's divine momentum at your back.

Today, receive this as a prophetic promise: the wind of the Spirit is moving in your life. Step forward in faith—and let Him carry you.▫

Today's Verse:

"Forget the former things; do not dwell on the past. See, I am doing a new thing! Now it springs up; do you not perceive it?"
—Isaiah 43:18–19

LAY DOWN YOUR PRIDE

"But Samuel replied: 'Does the Lord delight in burnt offerings and sacrifices as much as in obeying the Lord? To obey is better than sacrifice, and to heed is better than the fat of rams.'"

1 Samuel 15:22

S ometimes we do things "for God," but they're really more about us.

Saul was chosen by God to be king, but somewhere along the way, his confidence turned into pride. In 1 Samuel 15, God told Saul to destroy everything related to the Amalekites. But Saul didn't follow through. He spared their king and kept the best animals. Why? He claimed it was for God—he said he wanted to offer sacrifices. But the truth? Saul didn't fully obey. And God saw right through it.

How often do we do the same thing?

Maybe we give generously but secretly want others to notice. Maybe we volunteer at church but avoid doing what God really asked us to do—like forgiving someone or walking away from something He's told us to let go of. We justify it with good intentions, but partial obedience is still disobedience.

God doesn't want our impressive efforts—He wants our surrendered hearts.

Saul's issue wasn't just that he disobeyed. It was that he let pride get in the way. He wanted to look good to the people more than he wanted to be faithful to God. That hits close to home, doesn't it? Many of us wrestle with wanting to be liked, approved, or applauded. We say we're doing it "for the Lord," but we're also checking who's watching.

The truth is, God isn't impressed by our sacrifices if our hearts aren't fully His. He's not looking for perfect performances. He's looking for real obedience. And real obedience is often quiet, unseen, and uncomfortable.

So, what does obedience look like for you today? Maybe it's having a hard conversation. Maybe it's walking away from something you know isn't right. Maybe it's doing something small and unseen that no one will ever thank you for—but God sees it.

Here's what we learn from Saul's story: you can't fake obedience. And you don't have to. God's love isn't based on your performance—it's based on your relationship with Him. Jesus just wants your yes.

Let's not give God what we think looks good. Let's give Him what He actually asked for.□

Today's Verse:
"The fear of the Lord is the beginning of wisdom, and knowledge of the Holy One is understanding."
—Proverbs 9:10

BOLD FAITH, HUMBLE HEART

"He began to speak boldly in the synagogue. When Priscilla and Aquila heard him, they invited him to their home and explained to him the way of God more adequately."

Acts 18:26

Apollos was a passionate and gifted teacher—bold, eloquent, and eager to share what he knew about God. But as we see in Acts 18, he didn't yet have the full picture of the gospel. He only knew about John's baptism and hadn't heard the complete message of salvation through Jesus Christ. Still, his willingness to step out with what he *did* know opened the door for God to use him in powerful ways.

What makes Apollos' story so beautiful isn't just his boldness—it's his humility. When Priscilla and Aquila, two mature believers, heard him preaching, they didn't tear him down or call him out. Instead, they gently pulled him aside and invited him into their home, where they explained the gospel more thoroughly. And here's the best part: Apollos *received* their correction. He didn't let pride get in the way. Because of that teachable spirit, he went on to become one of the most influential voices in the early church.

There's so much we can learn from Apollos. First, don't wait until you feel like you have it all figured out before stepping out in faith. God honors your willingness, not your perfection. If you've been holding back because you think you're not ready—start where you are. Share your story, speak life, encourage someone. God will grow you as you go.

Second, stay teachable. God often sends people to help shape and sharpen us—mentors, friends, or even strangers who lovingly speak truth into our lives. When correction comes, don't shut down. Receive it with grace. God uses these moments to prepare us for greater impact.

So today, ask yourself: Am I willing to be bold like Apollos? Am I humble enough to learn from others? Let God use your voice *and* your willingness to grow. The Kingdom needs people who are brave enough to speak and humble enough to listen.

Today's Verse:
*"I planted the seed, Apollos watered it,
but God has been making it grow."*
—1 Corinthians 3:6

A GIFT THAT BUILDS OTHERS

*"Follow the way of love and eagerly desire gifts of the
Spirit, especially prophecy."*

1 Corinthians 14:1

God wants to speak *through* you. Yes—*you.*

In 1 Corinthians 14, Paul urges us to *eagerly* desire spiritual gifts, and he highlights one in particular: prophecy. Why? Because prophecy builds people up. It strengthens, encourages, and brings comfort. It's not about predicting the future or sounding spiritual—it's about revealing God's heart for someone in real-time. And when rooted in love, it becomes one of the most beautiful ways we can reflect Christ to the world.

That's why Paul begins this verse by saying, **"Follow the way of love."** Love is the filter for everything. Prophecy, when driven by love, isn't about platform—it's about people. It's not performance—it's *presence.* It's about showing up, listening to God, and delivering a word that breathes life into weary hearts.

One of the best modern examples of this is Sarah Young, the late author of *Jesus Calling.* She was never chasing influence or recognition—only the heart of Jesus. Her quiet time with God turned into one of the best-selling books of our generation. I often find myself sharing her daily words on X (formerly Twitter), because they remind us of something essential: **God still speaks, and He deeply cares about every detail of our lives.** Her writing is soaked in Scripture and intimacy, and every time I share it, I'm reminded of how prophecy looks like encouragement wrapped in love.

What started as a private journal in the quiet moments of Sarah's day has reached millions of people. She faced plenty of criticism for her approach—some thought her conversational tone with God was too bold. But she pressed on, undistracted by man's opinion, focused instead on her quiet obedience to Christ. Her impact lives on because she listened—and she shared what she heard.

Prophecy isn't reserved for pastors, authors, or people with microphones. It's for *you*. Maybe God's been nudging you to encourage a friend, pray for someone, or share a verse that's been on your heart. That's prophetic in action. You never know how one word spoken in love might shift someone's entire day—or life.

So ask God today, "Who needs a word of hope from You?" Then be bold. Follow the way of love, and speak with courage.

Today's Verse:

"But the one who prophesies speaks to people for their strengthening, encouraging, and comfort."
—1 Corinthians 14:3

IS THIS DOOR FROM GOD?

"Trust in the Lord with all your heart and lean not on your own understanding; in all your ways submit to him, and he will make your paths straight."
Proverbs 3:5-6

We've all faced decisions that make us stop and wonder: *Is this from God... or is this just me?* Whether it's a new job, a relationship, a move, or even a ministry opportunity, it can be hard to know which path to take. But the Bible promises that when we trust in the Lord and seek Him with all our heart, He will make our path clear. Here are three simple checks to help you figure out if the door in front of you is truly from God:

1. It won't go against God's Word. God will never ask you to do something that contradicts Scripture. If the opportunity requires you to compromise your values, lie, cut corners, or make excuses for sin—it's not from Him. That includes relationships that pull you away from God or jobs that feed pride, greed, or deceit. God's will always aligns with His Word. Period.

2. It comes with peace and clarity—not pressure and confusion. God doesn't speak through panic. When He opens a door, you'll usually experience confirmation—through Scripture, wise counsel, or a sense of peace that settles in your spirit. If you're feeling rushed, overwhelmed, or like something's "off," that's a sign to slow down and seek Him more. The Holy Spirit is never pushy. He leads gently, not with chaos or fear.

3. It draws you closer to Jesus—not farther away. God's open doors often require faith. They might stretch you or take you out of your comfort zone, but they'll always pull you toward dependence on Him. If you find yourself thinking, *"This is bigger than me—I need God for this,"* you might just be on the right track. His plans always draw us nearer, not farther.

So here's the question: **Is there a door in your life you need to walk away from—or one you're afraid to walk through?**

Don't rush your decision. Ask God for wisdom. He promises to guide you when you submit your plans to Him. You're not meant to figure everything out on your own—He's already gone ahead of you. Trust the Lord's timing, lean into His peace, and take the next step in faith.

Today's Verse:
"Whether you turn to the right or to the left, your ears will hear a voice behind you, saying, 'This is the way; walk in it.'"
—Isaiah 30:21

WHEN GOD REDEEMS A MESSY STORY

"When the time came for her to give birth, there were twin boys in her womb."

Genesis 38:27

Tamar's story is one of the most unexpected and powerful redemptions in all of Scripture. Her life didn't unfold like a fairytale. In fact, if you've ever felt overlooked, mistreated, or like your story has gone off the rails, you'll find comfort in hers.

Tamar was the daughter-in-law of Judah, one of Jacob's sons. She married his firstborn son, but when he died, Jewish custom required the next brother to marry her and carry on the family line. That brother also died, and Judah, fearing she was bad luck, refused to give her his youngest son. Tamar, left in limbo and unjustly treated, took matters into her own hands. Disguised as a prostitute, she tricked her father-in-law into sleeping with her—and from that union came twins: Perez and Zerah.

Messy? Yes. Scandalous? Definitely. But here's the incredible part: God didn't cancel Tamar. He didn't erase her from the narrative. **Instead, He included her—by name—in the lineage of Jesus (Matthew 1:3).**

God isn't afraid of your mess. He doesn't skip over the complicated chapters of your story. In fact, He often works through them in the most astonishing ways. Tamar's name is etched into the genealogy of the Messiah to remind us that no situation is too far gone for God to redeem. Her twins, Perez and Zerah, symbolized a turning point—not just in her life, but in God's unfolding plan for redemption. *So what does this mean for us?*

It means your story matters, even the chapters you'd rather skip. It means God sees what's been done to you and what you've done—and He still calls you chosen. Tamar's boldness to fight for justice, even imperfectly, positioned her to be part of something greater than she could have imagined.

Where others saw scandal, *God saw purpose.* And through her, a lineage was born that would lead to the Savior of the world.

Don't count yourself out. Don't write off your story. Like Tamar, you might be holding the birth of something powerful—even in a messy place.

Today's Verse:

"This is the genealogy of Jesus the Messiah the son of David, the son of Abraham...
Judah the father of Perez and Zerah, whose mother was Tamar, Perez the father of Hezron..."
—Matthew 1:1,3

WHEN DESIRE BECOMES AN IDOL

"You shall have no other gods before me."
Exodus 20:3

I've noticed a shift in the Kingdom lately—one that's subtle, yet deeply significant. More and more people are getting married later in life, and with this cultural and spiritual delay has come an unintended consequence: the temptation to idolize marriage.

Marriage, in itself, is a beautiful gift from God. It's a reflection of Christ and His bride. But like all good gifts, it can become misplaced when it becomes the ultimate thing we're chasing. When our prayer life becomes consumed by timelines and relationship status updates, when disappointment in singleness becomes despair, and when marriage becomes the central measure of God's goodness—it's time to pause and ask ourselves, "*Has this become an idol?*"

Idolatry doesn't always look like golden calves or false religions. Sometimes, it looks like obsession with a good thing—just elevated to a place it was never meant to occupy. **The delay in receiving a promise can sometimes expose what our hearts have started to rely on more than God.**

The enemy is clever. He'll whisper, "God is withholding," or, "Everyone else is moving forward but you," in order to cultivate bitterness and comparison. But God is after something deeper in you. He's shaping a trust that isn't tied to whether a ring is on your finger—but whether your heart is fully His.

Singleness isn't a holding pattern or a punishment. It's a season that carries its own powerful purpose. **Paul even called it a gift (1 Cor. 7:7), not because it's easy, but because it can create undivided devotion to Christ.** There are things God can do in your life now that won't look the same later—and Jesus knows exactly what He's doing.

Let this be a loving reminder: you are not behind. You are not forgotten. You are not defined by whether you wear a wedding dress or stand beside someone at an altar. You are defined by Christ. And your value is not delayed just because your relationship status is.

Sometimes what feels like a longing for a relationship is really a deeper cry for connection with Jesus—the only One who can truly satisfy our souls. If you're finding yourself worn out or caught up in dreams of marriage, don't beat yourself up. Instead, let it draw you closer to Him. God isn't frustrated with your heart—He's inviting you to let Him be enough right here, right now. When your joy is rooted in Him, waiting doesn't feel like losing. It feels like living.

Today's Verse:

"Those who look to Him are radiant; their faces are never covered with shame."
—Psalm 34:5

FAITH LIKE AN ATHLETE

"Do you not know that in a race all the runners run, but only one gets the prize? Run in such a way as to get the prize."

1 Corinthians 9:24

As a former college softball player, I've always loved a good sports analogy—because sports teach us about life in powerful ways.

The discipline. The grind. The teamwork. The setbacks. The come-from-behind wins. It's all there. And one of my favorite things about the Bible? God wove those same lessons into the pages of Scripture.

Paul often used athletic metaphors to teach spiritual truths. He talked about running races, training with purpose, finishing well, and fighting the good fight. *Why?* Because the life of faith is a lot like training for a championship. It requires commitment, endurance, and a clear focus on the prize.

I work with athletes every day in my career, and they're some of my favorite people to coach. They're driven, disciplined, and not afraid to be stretched. But one thing I always remind them: **Your identity isn't found in stats or a scoreboard.** You may be a competitor, but more importantly—you're a child of God. And in God's Kingdom, the greatest victories aren't measured by stats but by how well we loved, how boldly we believed, and how faithfully we ran our race.

Spiritual endurance looks a lot like athletic training. You show up daily. You press in, even when it's hard. You fuel your body—and your soul—with what strengthens you. You surround yourself with a team that sharpens you. And you listen to your Coach's voice above the noise of the crowd.

If you've been in a spiritual slump lately, maybe it's time to get back in the game. Dust off your cleats. Recommit to training. Fix your eyes on Jesus, the author and perfecter of your faith (Hebrews 12:2). Your race matters. Your fight is worth it. And the prize? Eternal life, unshakable peace, and the joy of knowing you played your part for the Kingdom.

So today, run with purpose. Train like it counts—because it does. God's not just cheering you on... He's running right alongside you.

Today's Verse:
"I have fought the good fight, I have finished the race,
I have kept the faith."
—2 Timothy 4:7

FEELING DEEPLY ISN'T A FLAW—IT'S A REFLECTION

"Jesus wept."

John 11:35

Emotions are not the enemy. They're actually one of the clearest signs that we're made in the image of a feeling, relational God.

We sometimes get the idea—especially in church culture—that spiritual maturity means suppressing our feelings or pushing past them with "faith." But if we look at Jesus, we see something refreshingly human and beautifully divine: He *felt* deeply. He *wept, groaned in anguish, flipped tables in righteous anger,* and *rejoiced* with His friends. He didn't hide His emotions. He expressed them in holy, honest ways.

In John 11, when Jesus approached the tomb of His dear friend Lazarus, He stood beside grieving people—and He *wept*. Even though He knew resurrection was moments away, Jesus allowed Himself to feel the weight of human sorrow. That's not weakness. That's compassion. **That's love.**

Jesus wasn't afraid of emotion, and you don't have to be either. Maybe you've been told your emotions are "too much" or that you need to "toughen up." But the truth is, emotions are a gift when they're rooted in truth and surrendered to the Holy

Spirit. Anger can point us toward injustice. Grief can lead us to deeper compassion. Joy can spark gratitude. Even sadness can draw us into intimacy with God.

Your feelings aren't a failure—they're a signal. What you do with them is what matters. When emotions are handed to God, they become tools for healing, connection, and discernment.

If Jesus cried, then crying doesn't mean you're weak. If Jesus got angry at injustice, then righteous anger isn't sinful. If Jesus rejoiced, then celebration is holy.

Let this free you: You don't have to pretend to be okay when you're not. You don't have to numb what you feel to be "strong." God isn't asking for polished perfection—He's asking for *honest hearts*. So today, feel what you need to feel. Don't stuff it down—bring it to Jesus. He understands. He's been there. And He promises to sit with you, walk with you, and heal you through the heartache.

Today's Verse:

"The Lord is close to the brokenhearted and saves those who are crushed in spirit."
—Psalm 34:18

100 DAYS LEFT

"Being confident of this, that he who began a good work in you will carry it on to completion until the day of Christ Jesus."

Philippians 1:6

If you're reading this right now, guess what? There are 100 days left in the year! I believe God wants to mark these next 100 days with fresh strength, renewed vision, and divine acceleration over your life.

Let's be real—this year may not have looked how you thought it would. Maybe you started out strong, full of goals and momentum, only to hit some bumps, disappointments, or delays along the way. Maybe you've accomplished some things... but other dreams still feel like they're stuck on the shelf. But here's what I feel the Lord speaking over you right now: **He's not finished.** He didn't bring you this far just to leave you. He's still writing your story. These next 100 days? They're going to matter.

The number 100 in Scripture is often tied to fullness, completion, and promise. It reminds me of Abraham, who was 100 years old when God fulfilled the promise of Isaac (Genesis 21:5). What felt "too late" was actually *right on time* in God's eyes. That same promise-keeping God is with you now.

So here's my challenge for you: Don't check out. Don't coast through the rest of the year. Ask God, "*What do You want to complete in me before this year ends?*" Whether it's a healing journey, a step of obedience, a new habit, or a promise you're still believing for—God is in it. And He's faithful to finish what He started.

If you're still reading, I want to hear from you. Seriously—send me a message or a tweet today. Let's encourage one another. Let's link arms in faith. Let's run the last leg of this year strong, together.

You've got 100 days. Not to earn God's love—but to *walk in it.* Not to strive for approval—but to *live from it.* Not to panic about the time left—but to *press into what's possible* when you trust Jesus with all of it. Your best days are ahead!

Today's Verse:
"Let us not become weary in doing good, for at the proper time we will reap a harvest if we do not give up."
—Galatians 6:9

THE ART OF "TREASURING"

"But Mary treasured up all these things and pon-
dered them in her heart."

Luke 2:19

I f Mary lived today, she wouldn't have been scrambling for the perfect Instagram caption after Jesus was born. There would be no boomerangs of angels singing, no selfies with shepherds, no hurried birth announcement for the world to double-tap.

Instead, Mary chose something far rarer—she tucked the moment away in her heart. She didn't rush to explain it or prove it. She let it breathe. She let it be sacred.

In a world where everything begs to be posted, shared, and seen, Mary's quiet reverence reminds us: not everything God gives you is meant to be public right away. Some miracles are meant to stay hidden for a time, held close between you and Him.

When I was writing this book, it wasn't a public journey—it was private. It started with a journal stained with tears, whispered prayers in the dark, and moments of wondering if what I carried would ever be ready for the world. I didn't rush to tell anyone. I just kept showing up with Jesus, letting Him shape it in the secret place.

And what most people don't realize about doing a Kingdom project like this is that writing was only the beginning. *It was the easy part.* The real stretching came after—the formatting battles, the technical glitches, the software that refused to cooperate no matter how hard I tried. It tested my patience, my perseverance, and my faith in ways I never expected. There were days it felt like the enemy was fighting me at every turn, just to get these words into the world.

But looking back, the real treasure wasn't finishing the manuscript or even overcoming the technical mountains—it was the time spent clinging to Jesus through it all. Even if not a single person ever reads a word, I wouldn't trade the sweetness of those hidden moments for anything.

Maybe you're carrying something too—a dream, a word, a hope—that feels tender and small. Maybe it's not ready for the world's eyes yet. That's not weakness. *That's wisdom.* Like Mary, you're honoring the holy hush before the trumpet blast.

It's okay to treasure what God is doing in silence. It's okay to ponder. It's okay to keep it tucked in the secret place a little longer. Jesus' public ministry would come, but first, He went through years of hiddenness.

So today, don't rush. Don't feel pressured to turn God's whispers into headlines. Some of the most sacred things begin in the secret place with King Jesus. God delights when you hold His treasures close until the time He says, "Now."

Today's Verse:
"There is a time for everything, and a season for every activity under the heavens... a time to be silent and a time to speak."
—Ecclesiastes 3:1,7

WHEN GOD SAYS GO

*"By faith Abraham obeyed when he was called to go
out to a place that he was to receive as an inheritance.
He went out, not knowing where he was going."*

Hebrews 11:8

I've moved to new cities more times than I can count—often
with no connections, no backup plan, and no roadmap—just
a word from the Lord. And every single time, it was enough.

When God speaks, it doesn't always come with a five-year plan
or a safety net. Sometimes, He simply says, "Go," and expects us
to trust that He will meet us there. That's been my story. From
big cities to small towns, I've packed up my life, stepped into
the unknown, and landed in places where I didn't know a single
soul—but I knew Jesus had gone ahead of me.

Maybe you're preparing for a move right now—or maybe you've
just arrived in a new city and feel overwhelmed, unsure, or alone.
If so, I want to remind you that if God called you there, He has a
reason—and a plan.

Here are a few ways I've learned to settle in and align with what
God is doing when He sends me somewhere new:

Start with prayer and posture. Before you network or find a
local spot for coffee, posture your heart before the Lord. Ask
Him, *"Why did You bring me here?"* and *"What do You want to do*

in and through me in this city?" Let your first step be spiritual before it's social.

Seek out a spiritual community. Find a local church—even if it's your first Sunday in town. Join a small group, sign up for a class, or serve in an area that matches your gifts. The quickest way to meet like-minded people is to step into the places where faith is already active.

Sow into your season. Don't just treat this move as a transition—treat it as a mission. Ask God what He wants you to build or plant here. Whether it's relationships, creative work, or simply prayer, what you sow now will produce fruit later.

Walk in obedience and peace. Even when you feel unsure, remember: obedience always leads to purpose. You may not see the full picture now, but God does—and every step you take in faith is a step toward your calling.

Wherever Jesus sends you, He's already there. And if you're standing in a new place with a promise in your pocket, that's more than enough to start.

Today's Verse:
"Trust in the Lord with all your heart and lean not on your own understanding; in all your ways submit to him, and he will make your paths straight."
—Proverbs 3:5-6

DIVINE APPOINTMENTS

"I can do all things
through Christ who strengthens me."
Philippians 4:13

God has a way of orchestrating encounters that remind us He sees us—and others—deeply.

Not long ago, I had just finished stretching at the gym when a young woman approached me with a nervous smile. "Is your name Wendi?" she asked. A bit surprised, I said yes. She reminded me of a conversation I had with her mom over a year ago. They had hoped to work with me as a dietitian, but finances made it impossible. I remembered praying for them and sending some free resources—but I hadn't thought about it since.

God had.

Now, here we were—face to face again. She'd recently undergone surgery and was struggling with recovery and nutrition. As we talked, I realized she didn't just need advice; she needed truth. Like so many female athletes, she was caught in the pressure of performance and body image. I gently explained how skipping meals, under-eating, and overtraining don't just hurt performance—they can lead to stress fractures, hormone imbalances, and long-term health issues.

But more importantly, I reminded her who she is.

I opened her notebook and wrote: *You are strong. You are beautiful. You are not defined by a number on the scale. You are a temple of the Holy Spirit. Carbs are fuel. You need food. You need healing. And most of all—God loves you, and you are enough.* I closed with Philippians 4:13.

As she read my words, her eyes filled with tears. It hit me again: people need to be reminded of who they are in Christ. We underestimate how much power there is in simply showing up, speaking truth, and offering compassion.

God often uses the ordinary to accomplish the extraordinary—conversations at the gym, moments in passing, people we thought we'd never see again. Your kindness, your words, your time—it matters.

Challenge for Today: Write a note—yes, an actual handwritten one—to someone who needs encouragement. Ask God who needs to hear, "*You are seen. You are loved. You are not forgotten.*" It doesn't have to be long. Just let it be sincere. You never know how your simple act of obedience can become someone else's turning point.

Today's Verse:
"Love is patient, love is kind..."
—1 Corinthians 13:4

THE HAND-SHOOTER-UPPER

"Then I heard the voice of the Lord saying, 'Whom shall I send? And who will go for us?' And I said, 'Here am I. Send me!'"

Isaiah 6:8

Ever been in class when the teacher asked for a volunteer? You know the moment—half the room freezes, eyes locked on the desk, while one bold soul shoots their hand up like it's a race to the ceiling. That bold kid? That was Isaiah.

God asked, "Who will go for us?" and Isaiah didn't wait to find out the job description. He didn't ask for salary details or PTO. He just said, "Here I am. Send me!" That's *faith*. That's availability. That's trusting God enough to volunteer for an adventure without seeing the map first.

Now, if you're more of the "look away and hope the teacher skips me" type when God nudges, you're not alone. Most of us feel a little unqualified, a little unsure, and a lot like someone else could do it better. But guess what? God's not looking for perfect résumés—He's looking for willing hearts.

He's the One who equips you. If He calls you to it, He'll see you through it.

So, what's your "send me" opportunity today? It might not look like preaching to thousands (yet). It could be praying for a coworker, mentoring a younger person, or simply saying "yes" to something that stretches you out of your comfort zone. Spoiler alert: that's usually where God does His best work.

Today, be the hand-shooter-upper. Even if your voice shakes or your knees knock, raise your hand and say, *"I'm in, God."* Because He's not just calling the brave—He makes you brave *after* you say yes.

Don't wait for all the pieces to fall into place before you move. Obedience comes before clarity. God reveals the next step *after* you start walking. Heaven is looking for volunteers—not the most polished, but the most surrendered. So stand up, speak up, show up. Make the enemy nervous and make God's name known.

This is your moment to stop spectating and start participating. Burn the excuses. Silence the fear. Write down your yes today—and then go live it. Text the person. Apply for the opportunity. Pray the bold prayer. Sign up, step out, and trust that Jesus will meet you there.

Today's Verse:
"I will hurry, without delay, to obey your commands."
—Psalm 119:60

THE FIRE OF YOUTH, THE FATIGUE OF MIDLIFE

"Don't let anyone look down on you because you are young, but set an example for the believers in speech, in conduct, in love, in faith and in purity."

1 Timothy 4:12

I **love working with young people.** There's something so electric about their energy, their hope, and their fearless desire to change the world. Whether it's in health coaching, mindset training, or spiritual growth, young clients show up hungry to learn and willing to risk. They haven't been told "no" a thousand times yet. They're not as afraid to fail. They're dreamers, doers, and wide-eyed believers in what *could be*. And that lights something up in me every single time.

But as a business owner who works with all age groups, I've also noticed a pattern: when people hit midlife, many of them start to drift. They lose the spark. The courage. The curiosity. They stop asking, "What's possible?" and start settling for what's predictable. Somewhere between the pressure of responsibilities and the scars of past failures, they trade in their God-given vision for survival mode.

I'm not saying this to shame anyone—it's something I've had to fight off myself. Because the truth is, we all hit crossroads where we're tempted to shrink back, play small, and stop dreaming. But God never meant for us to live life on autopilot. He designed us to grow, evolve, and walk in faith at *every stage* of life.

Young people remind me of that. They reflect a hunger that's biblical—full of wonder, risk, and radical trust. And older people? They remind me how deeply we need to *protect* that hunger, even as life adds layers.

So wherever you are today—whether you're in your twenties or your fifties—I want to challenge you: **don't let your age determine your fire.** Ask God to reignite the parts of you that have grown weary. Surround yourself with dreamers, risk-takers, and believers. And be willing to pour into the next generation, even as you keep growing yourself.

It's never too early—or too late—to burn bright for the Kingdom.

Today's Verse:

"Even to your old age and gray hairs I am he, I am he who will sustain you. I have made you and I will carry you; I will sustain you and I will rescue you."

—Isaiah 46:4

FUEL FOR THE BODY, FUEL FOR THE SOUL

*"So whether you eat or drink or whatever you do, do
it all for the glory of God."*

1 Corinthians 10:31

Transformation doesn't start with a massive overhaul. It begins with one obedient, consistent step in the right direction. I recently had a 45-year-old client whose journey reminded me just how powerful these small choices can be.

He started by prioritizing protein in the morning—something simple, yet effective. It broke his cycle of stress eating after work. Then, he upped his water intake from 50 ounces to 90 ounces a day, which helped eliminate daily migraines. These weren't flashy changes, but they were intentional. And over five months, he didn't just lose eight inches—he gained clarity, discipline, and a sustainable lifestyle that honored his body and his God.

It was a living picture of 1 Corinthians 10:31: **whatever you do—eat, drink, exercise, rest—do it all for God's glory.**

Physical transformation is deeply tied to spiritual transformation. Just as we hydrate and fuel our bodies, we're also called to nourish our spirits. Jesus said, "*I am the bread of life. Whoever comes to me will never go hungry, and whoever believes in me will never be thirsty*" (John 6:35). When we make Christ the foundation of our routines—body and soul—He provides strength for real, lasting change.

This client's story is also a powerful reminder of stewardship. We are not our own; our bodies are temples of the Holy Spirit (1 Corinthians 6:19-20). Honoring our health, practicing discipline, and showing up for our own healing is a form of worship. It's not about perfection—it's about progress. And when we stay faithful, God multiplies our efforts.

So, *how are you stewarding what God has given you?* It doesn't have to be dramatic. It just has to be **consistent.**

Today's Verse:

"Do you not know that your bodies are temples of the Holy Spirit, who is in you, whom you have received from God? You are not your own."

—1 Corinthians 6:19

DAY 273

WHEN GOD WHISPERS BACK

"The Lord is near to all who call on Him, to all who call on Him in truth."

Psalm 145:18

God is always speaking—are you slowing down enough to hear Him? We often expect to hear God in big, dramatic ways, but more often, He speaks in gentle whispers, quiet nudges, and divine interruptions disguised as everyday moments. Whether it's through a verse that leaps off the page, a song lyric that lands right on time, or the stillness that draws your heart to pause—God is near, and He is personal. He desires to speak *with* you, not just *to* you.

Yesterday, I experienced one of those "God moments" that stopped me in my tracks—literally. I was out for a walk in the woods when I passed a woman on the trail. On my second loop, I noticed a bright red cardinal flutter into view. For me, cardinals are personal reminders of God's presence and often a sign of Heaven's nearness. As I paused to take it in, that same woman passed by again and asked what had caught my attention.

That simple question turned into a sacred moment. She confided in me that her late husband had passed and shared her deep longing to know if he was in Heaven. In that moment, I silently asked God for guidance. And He whispered to my heart, "Yes, he is with Me."

When I told her what I felt the Lord had spoken, her entire countenance shifted. Tears welled in her eyes, and she said, "That's what I've been praying for—that someone would confirm it." We stood in the middle of the woods, two strangers wrapped in God's presence, overwhelmed by His kindness.

Sometimes, obedience is just *being available*. Saying hello. Stopping for a moment. Choosing to believe that the small thing on your heart might just be the *big thing* someone else is praying for.

So today, pay attention to the promptings. Don't ignore the nudge to pause, to speak, to ask the deeper question. God may be using you to whisper hope to someone else. And if you're the one waiting for an answer—take heart. Jesus hears you. He is near. And He *will* speak.

Today's Verse:
"Call to me and I will answer you and tell you great and unsearchable things you do not know."
—Jeremiah 33:3

A FAMILY THAT STARTS WITH JESUS

"Train up a child in the way he should go; even when he is old he will not depart from it."

Proverbs 22:6

This morning, I saw something that stopped me in my tracks—in the best way.

At a local coffee shop, tucked into a corner booth, sat a father and his young son. Their Bibles were open. No screens. No distractions. Just Scripture, conversation, and intentional time together. The boy, maybe nine years old, wore an oversized Cubs cap and read aloud with focus and reverence. His father gently asked him questions about what he thought the passage meant, encouraging him to think, reflect, and apply God's Word.

They had arrived before I did—bright and early at 7:30 a.m.—and had chosen to start their summer day not with cartoons or games, but with Christ. It was one of the most beautiful things I've witnessed in a long time.

In a culture where so many families are pulled in a hundred different directions, seeing this kind of intentional parenting was powerful. It reminded me of what's missing in so many homes today: a consistent commitment to putting Jesus at the center—not just on Sundays, but every day.

I couldn't keep quiet. I walked over to tell them how encouraged I felt by their example. The father, it turns out, is a local pastor. His son, polite and wise beyond his years, even started talking to me about carbs and protein—clearly, Mom and Dad are teaching him well on more than one front!

As we talked, a group of men sitting nearby chimed in, echoing our shared longing to see more families rooted in faith. In a world filled with noise and darkness, this father and son were a reminder that the light still shines—and it often begins at home, around an open Bible and an open heart.

If you're a parent, a mentor, or simply someone with influence over the next generation, let this be your reminder: what you model matters. When you prioritize time with God, they'll notice. When you speak life and truth, they'll remember. And when you plant seeds of faith early, those roots will run deep.

Today's Verse:
"Children are a heritage from the Lord,
offspring a reward from him."
—Psalm 127:3

WHEN YOU DON'T FIT IN

"By faith Moses, when he had grown up, refused to be known as the son of Pharaoh's daughter."

Hebrews 11:24

Moses grew up in a palace, but his heart beat for a people he didn't fully know. Born a Hebrew but raised Egyptian, Moses lived between two worlds. He had the education, the clothes, and the customs of royalty, but he never truly belonged.

When Moses saw an Egyptian beating a Hebrew, something inside him stirred. Though he had lived his whole life surrounded by the luxury of Pharaoh's household, he knew deep down that he was Hebrew by birth. He couldn't ignore the injustice happening to his own people. But when he tried to step in, everything unraveled. The Hebrews didn't rally around him. They questioned his authority and intentions, asking, *"Who made you ruler and judge over us?"* Pharaoh, hearing what Moses had done, sought to kill him.

Moses fled to the wilderness, carrying a heart divided between two worlds. He was too Hebrew to be fully Egyptian, but not yet embraced by his own people. He belonged everywhere and nowhere all at once.

Maybe you know that feeling too. Maybe you've felt caught in between—too "churchy" for your non-believing friends, yet too honest and raw for spaces that prefer polished appearances over real faith. You're too bold to stay silent at work. Too passionate to settle in environments that choose comfort over conviction. Maybe it happens in the cafeteria, on your sports team, or even in your own family. Standing for Jesus can sometimes make you feel exposed when all you want to do is blend in.

Moses' life reminds us that our identity is not rooted in where we came from, but in who *God* says we are. His assignment was not based on his upbringing or his acceptance by the crowd. It was based on God's calling. Moses was chosen to lead not because he had all the right credentials, but because **God delights in using those who walk in obedience despite feeling out of place.**

If you feel like you don't fit neatly into any box, you're not alone—and you're not off track. You were not made to blend in. You were made to stand out. You were made to carry the light of Christ into dark places, to lead others out of bondage into freedom.

So if you're feeling misunderstood or stuck in the middle, take heart. God specializes in using the "in-between" people for His greatest missions. Just like Moses, He is preparing you to walk in authority that comes from Him alone.

Today's Verse:

"You did not choose me, but I chose you and appointed you so that you might go and bear fruit—fruit that will last."
—John 15:16

GOD IS IN THE MIDDLE

"The Lord will fight for you; you need only to be still."
Exodus 14:14

Y ou don't have to fix everything.

That pressure you feel to have all the answers, to mend every broken piece, to push forward when you're exhausted? Lay it down. When the Israelites stood trapped between Pharaoh's army and the Red Sea, they panicked—but God had already made a way. He didn't ask them to come up with a plan. He asked them to trust.

You may not see the full picture yet, but God is working behind the scenes. His power shows up in the middle—between your problem and your breakthrough.

So breathe. Let God be your defender. He hasn't forgotten you. He's just preparing the waters to part.

Today's Verse:
"He makes a way where there is no way."
—Isaiah 43:16

CHOOSING FRIENDS WISELY

"A friend loves at all times, and a brother is born for a time of adversity."

Proverbs 17:17

Not every connection is a covenant. In a world filled with followers, likes, and quick connections, true friendship can feel rare. The Bible teaches that Godly friendship goes far deeper than shared interests or convenience—it's rooted in love, loyalty, and spiritual alignment.

One of the most beautiful examples of biblical friendship is between David and Jonathan. Their relationship was not built on status, benefits, or even longevity—it was based on deep mutual respect, shared faith, and unwavering loyalty. Jonathan, the son of King Saul, risked his own position and safety to protect David, knowing God's hand was on his friend. That's the kind of friend who's sent by God.

But here's the truth: not every person in your life is meant to stay forever. Some are acquaintances, some are seasonal, and a few are covenant. Part of spiritual maturity is learning how to discern which is which.

Here are three questions to help you weigh your friendships this season:

1. **Do they draw you closer to God?** A friend sent by God will encourage your faith, not distract you from it. Like Jonathan did for David, they'll remind you of who you are and what God has called you to do.

2. **Do they show up when it costs them something?** A Godly friend won't just be around when it's easy or exciting. They'll get in the trenches with you when the road gets hard. They'll cover you in prayer, sit with you in the waiting, and remind you of God's promises when your hands grow tired. The people God sends won't pressure you to move faster than His timing. Real love honors the quiet work God is doing, even when no one else can see it yet.

3. **Do they speak truth with love?** A good friend is not just a cheerleader—they're also a truth-teller. They won't flatter you into destruction. They'll love you enough to speak life and correction when needed.

When you find a friend like Jonathan—a person who celebrates your calling, strengthens your spirit, and walks in truth—cherish them. That's a gift straight from God.

Today's Verse:
"Jonathan said to David, 'Go in peace, for we have sworn friendship with each other in the name of the Lord.'"
—1 Samuel 20:42

THE GOD OF SURPRISES

*"See, I am doing a new thing! Now it springs up; do
you not perceive it?"*

Isaiah 43:19

If you've been waiting, wondering, or just plain weary—get ready! We serve a God of SURPRISES!

He doesn't always move how we expect Him to. Just ask Moses, who never imagined a burning bush would change his whole life. Or Mary, who wasn't planning on carrying the Messiah. Or Peter, who thought he was just casting nets, only to be called a fisher of men. Over and over, Scripture reminds us that God loves to move in unexpected ways, at unexpected times, through unexpected people.

Maybe you've been walking through a season that feels silent. Maybe you've done everything you know how to do, and the door still hasn't opened. But here's what I feel led to speak over you today: **God is not done surprising you.**

He still parts seas. He still heals broken hearts. He still makes water flow from rocks and multiplies what little you have into more than enough. You don't have to have it all figured out. You just need to stay available. Because often, it's when we least expect it that He does something we couldn't imagine.

That job you weren't looking for? That person you just happened to sit next to? That unexpected check, call, open door, new opportunity? Don't count it as coincidence. Count it as **God.**

Jesus is still speaking. He's still shifting things. He's still making rivers in deserts and roads through impossible places. And sometimes, the reason it hasn't looked how you thought it would is because He's doing something *better* than you expected.

Today, I believe He wants you to release your timeline, your plan, and your need to see every detail. Trade it for trust. Hold your hands open and your heart expectant. You serve a God who delights in exceeding your expectations—not just meeting them.

Your assignment? Stay ready. Stay faithful. Stay soft. The surprise might be closer than you think.

Today's Verse:
"Now to him who is able to do immeasurably more than all we ask or imagine, according to his power that is at work within us."
—Ephesians 3:20

BUT SERIOUSLY, WHY AM I LIKE THIS?

"I do not understand what I do. For what I want to do I do not do, but what I hate I do."

Romans 7:15

There's something oddly reassuring about Paul—the spiritual giant who wrote half the New Testament—basically saying, "I can't get my life together."

In Romans 7:15, Paul admits, "*I don't really understand myself, for I want to do what is right, but I don't do it.*" Translation? "*Why am I like this?!*" If you've ever sworn off late-night scrolling only to end up deep in a rabbit hole of pasta-making videos at 2 a.m., Paul would be nodding with you in solidarity.

This tension he describes? We all feel it.

We want to speak life, but our words come out sharp. We want to trust God, but fear keeps creeping in. We want to walk in freedom, but shame still lingers like a shadow.

Here's the beautiful truth: **Paul's struggle didn't disqualify him—it made him relatable.** He didn't pretend to have it all figured out. And that honesty? That's what makes his words powerful. God didn't choose perfect people—He chooses real ones. People who mess up, get up, and try again.

The fact that you *feel* the struggle is actually a sign that the Holy Spirit is at work in you. Before Jesus, you didn't wrestle with sin—you just lived in it. Now you notice it. You feel convicted. That's growth.

So what do we do in the "messy middle" of our faith walk? What happens when we want to do good but we keep slipping and falling short?

We run back to grace. We ask Jesus for help. We choose the Spirit over the flesh even when it's hard.

And here's the mic-drop moment: Romans 7 is followed by Romans 8. The very next breath Paul takes, he writes, *"There is now no condemnation for those who are in Christ Jesus."*

So take a breath. Laugh a little. Get back up. God isn't asking for perfection—He's asking for surrender. And He's not done with you. *Not even close.*

Today's Verse:
"The Spirit helps us in our weakness... And we know that in all things God works for the good of those who love him."
—Romans 8:26, 28

WHEN GOOD GETS EXHAUSTING

"Let us not become weary in doing good, for at the proper time we will reap a harvest if we do not give up."

Galatians 6:9

Let today's verse sink deep into your soul—because it's one you'll need to revisit often. Doing good, day in and day out, can be draining. Whether you're serving others, giving generously, showing up consistently, or simply choosing to respond with grace when it's easier to walk away, the weight of faithfulness can feel heavy—especially when there's no visible reward in sight.

I'll be honest: as I write this, it's Saturday morning, and I'm tired. I'm showing up for others, pouring out in ministry and work, but emotionally, I'm drained. And in that vulnerable space, satan tries to sneak in with whispers like, *"Is this even worth it?"* or *"Why does it feel like no one sees what you're doing?"*

But those thoughts aren't from God. They're the enemy's subtle attempt to take your eyes off the harvest and onto your weariness.

Here's the truth: You don't have to pretend you're fine. God never asked you to put on a brave face and power through. He asked you to *come to Him*. And when you do—when you bring your tired heart, your doubts, and your emotions—He meets you there. He doesn't shame your struggle. He strengthens you in it.

God sees your obedience, even when no one else does. He sees you staying up late to finish what no one thanked you for. He sees the gentle answer you gave when anger would've been easier. He sees you serving, showing up, praying, hoping, and trusting. And He's not just watching—He's working. Behind the scenes, He's preparing a harvest, and in due time, you *will* reap it.

So today, give yourself permission to rest—but don't give up. Surrender your weariness. Tell God how you really feel. Then let Him fill you up again. Keep sowing seeds of goodness, even when it's hard. Because the promise still stands: the harvest *is* coming.

Today's Verse:
"Cast all your anxiety on him because he cares for you."
—1 Peter 5:7

GOD SETS THE TABLE

"You prepare a table before me in the presence of my enemies. You anoint my head with oil; my cup overflows."

Psalm 23:5

David today's words as a declaration of God's personal favor and protection. In ancient culture, to be invited to someone's table was not just a casual gesture—it was a profound act of friendship, honor, and covenant. When a host prepared a table for you, it signified that your safety, provision, and well-being were now their personal responsibility. It meant you belonged in their care.

David, a seasoned warrior who knew the constant threat of enemies and betrayal, wasn't celebrating a life free from trouble. He was exalting the faithfulness of God to provide, protect, and promote him even when opposition surrounded him.

Psalm 23:5 is a powerful reminder that God's blessings are not postponed until life becomes perfect. He doesn't wait until your enemies disappear or your problems resolve. Right in the middle of conflict, uncertainty, and attack, God spreads a table before you—a table overflowing with peace, strength, joy, and provision. It's a public display of His love for you. Your enemies may watch, but they are powerless to stop the hand of God moving on your behalf.

This verse teaches us something profound: spiritual maturity doesn't mean the absence of battles. It means learning to feast in the presence of the One who has already secured the victory. It's the confidence to sit down at God's table even when arrows are flying, trusting that you are covered, protected, and honored by the King Himself.

Today, lift your eyes above the noise. Refuse to focus on who is against you. Focus instead on who is with you. Your Shepherd offers you His peace, His strength, and His dignity. He anoints your head with oil, reminding you that you are chosen and set apart. Your cup overflows not because the battle isn't real—but because God's goodness is greater.

You are safe at His table. You are seen. You are protected. You are celebrated by Heaven. So take your seat boldly and receive everything your Good Shepherd has prepared for you.

Today's Verse:
*"Surely your goodness and love will follow me
all the days of my life..."*
—Psalm 23:6

EMPOWERED TO GO

"But you will receive power when the Holy Spirit comes on you; and you will be my witnesses in Jerusalem, and in all Judea and Samaria, and to the ends of the earth."

Acts 1:8

Have you ever felt like you're not qualified to do what God is asking of you? You're not alone. The disciples probably felt the same way. Right before Jesus ascended into Heaven, He gave them a mission—to be His witnesses, not just in their hometown, but in distant, unfamiliar places too. It must have felt overwhelming. But Jesus didn't expect them to do it in their own strength. Instead, He gave them a promise: *"You will receive power when the Holy Spirit comes on you."*

That word "power" comes from the Greek word *dynamis*, which is where we get the word *dynamite*. It's not just a gentle push or a boost of confidence—it's explosive, life-changing strength from Heaven. It's the kind of power that enables you to speak boldly, love deeply, endure trials, heal the sick, and walk in supernatural courage.

And that promise wasn't just for the disciples back then. It's for you too.

If you've received the Holy Spirit, you already carry everything you need to walk out your calling. That doesn't mean you'll never feel afraid or unsure. It simply means you're never walking alone. The same Spirit who empowered Peter to preach, Paul to endure persecution, and countless believers to carry the Gospel across continents is the same Holy Spirit who lives and reigns within you.

You might not be called to a foreign country, but you are absolutely called to the people around you. Your "Jerusalem" might look like your family. Your "Judea" could be your workplace. Your "Samaria"? Maybe it's that difficult relationship you've been trying to avoid. And the "ends of the earth"? That could even be the digital spaces where your words and your witness reach people you may never meet in person.

God's plan has always included you. His Spirit empowers you to go—not in your own strength, but in His. All He asks is for your willingness to say "yes."

So today, stop waiting until you feel ready. The Holy Spirit makes you ready. Start right where you are. Use what's already in your hands. Speak life. Show love. Be bold in your faith, even if your voice shakes. The power isn't in your personality—it's in the presence of God inside you. Now go and be His witness—right where you are!

Today's Verse:
"For the Spirit God gave us does not make us timid, but gives us power, love and self-discipline."
—2 Timothy 1:7

NO MORE SHAME

"Therefore, there is now no condemnation for those who are in Christ Jesus."

Romans 8:1

Have you ever looked at someone who seems joyful and thought, *They must have it all together?* Maybe you've even been that person—smiling on the outside while hiding deep sadness within. I've been there. For years, I wore a happy mask, not wanting to burden anyone with my struggles. But beneath the surface, I carried a heavy weight of shame and self-doubt that I couldn't shake.

No matter how much I achieved or how "successful" I appeared, I woke up most days disliking who I was. The enemy used my own thoughts and words against me, whispering lies like, "You'll never be enough," or "You don't deserve happiness." For a long time, I believed him. I had been believing lies since I was young: "Your family is cursed," "You'll never be free from the brokenness you were born into," "Joy is for other people, not for you."

Even though I believed in Jesus, the truth of His love hadn't fully set me free. I knew the Scriptures in my head, but I hadn't allowed them to penetrate my heart. That started to shift the day I made a decision: I was done agreeing with satan. I was done giving my voice to the lies that kept me bound. I began to speak life, even when I didn't feel it. I dove into the Word like it was oxygen—because it was.

I discovered that every time I criticized myself or replayed old shame, I was giving the enemy ground in my life. But when I began to declare God's Word out loud—truth like Romans 8:1, that *there is now no condemnation for those who are in Christ Jesus*—my inner dialogue started to change. I stopped handing satan the microphone and started worshiping with my words instead.

Was it easy? No. It took daily, intentional practice. But day by day, I learned to view myself through the lens of God's love, not through the filter of my past or my pain. His love is not performance-based. It doesn't rise or fall with our mistakes. It's steadfast. It's free. And it's yours.

If you're struggling with shame or self-hatred, hear this: God isn't waiting for you to clean yourself up before He loves you. He loves you right now, fully and completely. Jesus died to free you not only from sin but from the voice of shame. So stop agreeing with the lies. Start agreeing with your Savior.

You are chosen. You are redeemed. You are enough in Christ.

Today's Verse:
"The Lord is compassionate and gracious, slow to anger, abounding in love."
—Psalm 103:8

BREAK A SWEAT, BUILD YOUR FAITH

"I run in the path of your commands, for you have broadened my understanding."
Psalm 119:32

Breaking a sweat isn't just about physical exercise—it's an act of stewardship, worship, and renewal.

When we move our bodies and engage in an activity that makes us sweat, we're doing more than strengthening muscles or burning calories; we're releasing built-up tension, clearing mental fog, and aligning ourselves with the way God designed us. Physical movement has profound effects on our spiritual and mental health, and in many ways, it mirrors the discipline and intentionality required for spiritual growth.

Sweat is often the result of exertion, of pushing past what is comfortable. In the same way, spiritual growth often comes through seasons of effort—like praying when we're tired, fasting when we crave comfort, or showing up for others when we feel depleted. Each time we "sweat" spiritually or physically, we shed the weight of what holds us back. It's not just a physical release—it's symbolic of breaking through resistance and getting stronger.

As you break a sweat today—whether through exercise, a long walk, or any form of movement—remember that it's not only for your body but also for your mind and spirit. Movement releases endorphins that help combat stress and anxiety, which often cloud our ability to hear from God. When you move, you create space for clarity, focus, and gratitude. It's in these moments that God can speak, renewing your mind and filling you with His peace.

And here's the prophetic part: I sense someone reading this has been feeling stuck—spiritually, mentally, or even physically. You've been waiting for a breakthrough, but God is saying, "*Move.*" This isn't just about exercise; it's about stepping out of stagnation and embracing the discipline of action. Whether it's a commitment to regular exercise, a deeper prayer life, or pursuing a calling you've been hesitant about, God is asking you to trust Him with the process. He's saying, "If you'll move, I'll meet you there."

So today, take a step if you can—literally and spiritually. Move your body as an act of obedience, and move your heart closer to God's will. Let the sweat remind you that transformation takes work, but the growth is holy. You're not just working out—you're working within.

Best of all? The Holy Spirit, your Comforter and Encourager, will be running with you every step of the way!

Today's Verse:
"Therefore, strengthen your feeble arms and weak knees."
—Hebrews 12:12

DISCIPLINE IS A SIGN OF LOVE

"My son, do not regard lightly the discipline of the Lord, nor be weary when reproved by him. For the Lord disciplines the one he loves, and chastises every son whom he receives."
Hebrews 12:5–6

T oday, I skipped a summer citrus cookout with friends to catch up on work. It's not the first time, and I know it won't be the last. Building two nutrition-based private practices has required over a decade of focused discipline and countless sacrifices. When I left the comfort of a corporate wellness job, I knew the road would be harder—but I also knew I was following a vision from God. That made the choice worth it.

Was it hard to say no to an afternoon of laughter, food, and friends? Absolutely. But I've learned that success—both in business and in spiritual growth—requires delayed gratification. It's doing the behind-the-scenes work when no one's watching. It's choosing purpose over popularity. And most importantly, it's honoring the gifts God has given you by stewarding them well.

Discipline isn't glamorous, but it's holy. Hebrews 12 reminds us that God disciplines those He loves. His discipline shapes us, strengthens us, and calls us higher—not to punish us, but to prepare us. If you've ever felt like you're in a season of pruning, correction, or refinement, remember: it means you're His.

When aspiring dietitians or entrepreneurs ask how I've built my platform, my answer is never about going viral—it's about grit, consistency, integrity, and a heart that doesn't quit. It's learning to show up day after day, doing excellent work when no one applauds, trusting that God sees every seed sown.

So let me ask you—where do you need more discipline in your life? Your eating habits? Your work ethic? Your quiet time with the Lord? Discipline is more than saying no—it's saying yes to something greater.

Whatever the area, know this: you're not doing it alone. God is with you. His Spirit will guide you. And if you keep showing up with a heart to honor Him, He will bless your efforts. Stay the course. What feels like sacrifice today will become fruit in the season to come.

Today's Verse:

"Go to the ant, you sluggard; consider its ways and be wise! It has no commander, no overseer or ruler, yet it stores its provisions in summer and gathers its food at harvest."
—Proverbs 6:6–7

CLIMB YOUR TREE

"So he ran ahead and climbed a sycamore-fig tree to see him, since Jesus was coming that way."

Luke 19:4

Zacchaeus wasn't letting a crowd—or his height—stop him from seeing Jesus.

Let's set the scene: the streets are packed, the buzz is electric, and Jesus is on His way into town. Everyone is jockeying for position, craning their necks, hoping to catch a glimpse. And then there's Zacchaeus—wealthy, not exactly well-liked, and vertically challenged. But instead of grumbling about his lack of height or letting his reputation get in the way, this guy *runs* ahead of the crowd and *climbs a tree.*

Imagine that. A grown man in fine robes shimmying up a tree like a kid chasing a squirrel—all because he wanted to see Jesus! That's bold. That's gutsy. That's the kind of hunger God honors.

And guess what? Jesus noticed. He didn't walk past. He stopped, looked up, and called Zacchaeus by name. He basically said, "Hey Z, I'm coming to your house today!" That's the power of pursuit. When you go out of your way to see Jesus, He goes out of His way to meet you.

Now, let's bring it home: What's your sycamore tree? What's something you can *run toward* to get a better view of Jesus?

Maybe it's waking up a little earlier to pray, turning down the volume of your distractions, or saying no to something so you can say yes to Him. It might feel awkward. It might go against your usual rhythm. But if it brings you closer to Jesus, it's worth it.

Don't let the crowd (opinions, busyness, comparison, doubt) block your view. Push past it. Climb something. Do something bold. Jesus loves when we chase after Him—even when it looks a little messy.

And spoiler alert: He's already looking for you. He's ready to meet you in the middle of your pursuit and call you by name.

Today's Verse:
*"You will seek me and find me when you
seek me with all your heart."*
—Jeremiah 29:13

THE WORLD CAN'T GIVE WHAT ONLY GOD CAN

"Do not love the world or anything in the world. If anyone loves the world, love for the Father is not in them. For everything in the world—the lust of the flesh, the lust of the eyes, and the pride of life—comes not from the Father but from the world."

1 John 2:15–16

The world loves ambition, but God loves *surrender*.

Ambition, vanity, materialism, and self-promotion are celebrated almost everywhere you turn. Culture teaches us to climb the ladder, secure the spotlight, and build a life that looks impressive from the outside. The trouble is, those same attitudes have crept into the Church—and sometimes, without realizing it, we start chasing after things that aren't eternal.

It starts subtly. Ambition seems harmless—even noble—when it's about growth and goals. But when ambition becomes self-focused and rooted in pride, it shifts from purpose to performance. Vanity follows closely behind, whispering that your value is in how polished, popular, or perfect you appear. Then materialism joins the chorus, convincing you that more—more stuff, more status, more success—is the key to peace.

But none of it satisfies. In fact, the more you chase what the world values, the more distant you feel from the One who created you. That's why Scripture says that if love for the world fills your heart, love for the Father cannot. These things don't come from Him—and they certainly don't lead to Him.

Jesus asked a soul-searching question: "*What good is it for someone to gain the whole world, yet forfeit their soul?*" (Mark 8:36). It's not that God is anti-success. He just wants your heart more than He wants your resume. He cares about who you're becoming more than what you're building. He's looking for hearts fully surrendered to Him—not chasing after counterfeit fulfillment.

So today, ask the Holy Spirit to search your heart. Is there anything you've been holding onto that the world celebrates but God wants you to release? He doesn't expose things to shame you—He reveals them to heal you. Your identity isn't found in what you have or how you look. It's found in who you are: chosen, seen, loved.

Don't trade the eternal for the temporary. What the world promises can never compare to what the Father freely gives.

Today's Verse:
"*But seek first his kingdom and his righteousness, and all these things will be given to you as well.*"
—Matthew 6:33

LET'S DRINK TO THAT

"Whoever drinks the water I give them will never thirst. Indeed, the water I give them will become in them a spring of water welling up to eternal life."

John 4:14

At the beginning of this devotional journey, I included weekly challenges to help you build habits that honor **your whole self—body, mind, and spirit.** Today, I feel led to bring one back. It's simple but powerful: *drink more water.*

Most people underestimate how much water their body truly needs. The common advice of six to eight glasses a day isn't sufficient for everyone. Many people—especially those with higher body weight, active lifestyles, or high sweat rates—require significantly more. In my nutrition practice, we recommend that most clients and athletes aim for a minimum of 80 to 100 ounces of water per day. For athletes or those in intense training, that number often jumps to 90 to 120 ounces.

How do you know if you're getting enough? Your body gives clues. One of the easiest ways to gauge your hydration status is to check your urine color. A pale yellow usually means you're well hydrated. Anything darker is a clear sign you need more fluids. One practical tip: drink 10 to 20 ounces of water right when you wake up. It jumpstarts your system and sets a tone for the day.

The science is clear. Dehydration—just a 1–2% loss of body weight from fluid loss—can impair your mood, performance, focus, and even lead to more serious consequences. Add under-fueling to the mix, and the risk of injury, poor performance, and even muscle loss increases dramatically. Staying hydrated is not just a wellness trend—it's a spiritual discipline of stewardship.

In the same way physical dehydration wears you down, spiritual dehydration leaves your soul weary. But Jesus invites you to come and drink deeply of Him. He doesn't just satisfy—He fills, restores, and overflows.

So here's your challenge: drink water with intention this week. Carry a water bottle, track your intake, and if needed, add electrolytes or lemon to make it more enjoyable. Let every sip be a reminder that just as your body needs water, your soul needs the Living Water—Jesus Himself.

Today's Verse:
"Blessed are those who hunger and thirst for righteousness, for they will be filled."
—Matthew 5:6

WRITE THE VISION

"Then Moses summoned Bezalel and Oholiab and every skilled person to whom the Lord had given ability and who was willing to come and do the work."

Exodus 36:2

We need more Kingdom content. More books. More podcasts. More devotionals. More art, music, videos, and conversations that point people back to Jesus. In a culture saturated with noise, opinions, and distractions, the world is starving for truth. And maybe—just maybe—God is calling *you* to create it.

Writing this book wasn't easy. It cost me time, focus, and more than a few moments of self-doubt. But in every chapter, God reminded me: *"This isn't about being perfect. It's about being faithful."* Obedience is what moves Heaven. And when God gives a vision, He also gives the grace to carry it out.

But here's the fresh perspective—Kingdom content isn't just about writing devotionals or launching podcasts. It could be building a garden with your family and using that time to speak life into your kids. It could be sending a heartfelt email to a friend who's struggling, or writing a prayer in a notebook that someone will one day discover. It's creating beauty, peace, and meaning wherever you are, with whatever you have.

You may not be called to write 365 devotionals, but you *are* called to steward what's in your hands. That might look like journaling your story, writing a children's book, or even baking with scriptures taped to your cookie boxes. Don't overlook the power of your daily acts of creativity—Heaven certainly doesn't.

God isn't asking you to go viral. He's asking you to be *available*. Sometimes the content He calls us to create isn't for the masses—it's for the *one*. For your child. For your neighbor. For the weary friend scrolling at midnight. Jesus always had time for the one.

Your voice matters. Your story matters. You don't need a platform. You need a *yes*. A heart willing to show up, even when it's messy. Even when you feel unqualified. Your obedience could unlock someone else's healing, clarity, or breakthrough.

Maybe you've been waiting for a sign. *This is it.* The world is hungry for hope—and you carry that hope. So write the blog. Plant the garden. Send the text. Tell the story. Don't wait for perfect conditions. Start now.

Because obedience doesn't require perfection. It just requires your YES!

Today's Verse:
"Write the vision and make it plain on tablets,
so he may run who reads it."
—Habakkuk 2:2

STOP FIGHTING THE NUDGE

"I am Jesus, whom you are persecuting," the Lord
replied. "It is hard for you to kick against the
goads."

Acts 26:14

When Jesus appeared to Saul (later Paul) on the road to Damascus, He asked a powerful question—and used **a picture Saul would understand.** He said, "It's *hard for you to kick against the goads.*" Back then, a *goad* was a sharp stick farmers used to gently poke oxen and keep them moving in the right direction. If the ox kicked against it, it only hurt more. In other words, Jesus was saying, "*Saul, why are you fighting Me? You're only making it harder on yourself.*"

The same thing can happen in our lives. God nudges us—through His Word, the Holy Spirit, or even people around us—and we resist. We feel a pull in one direction, but we want to go another. Maybe you've felt it too. God is leading you to let go of something, take a leap of faith, forgive someone, or change a habit—but instead of surrendering, you dig in your heels. You argue. You delay. You kick.

But here's the truth: the longer we fight God's direction, the more frustrated and tired we become. Kicking against the goads doesn't just slow us down—it steals our peace. God isn't trying to hurt us; He's trying to guide us into the best possible life. His nudges are always for our good.

Take a moment today and ask yourself: *Where might I be resisting God?* Is it in a relationship? A career decision? A daily habit or attitude? Be honest with Him. You don't have to keep fighting. You can stop kicking—and start walking with Him in peace.

Remember, Jesus didn't confront Saul to condemn him. He did it to transform him. And He wants to do the same for you.

Today's Verse:
"Trust in the Lord with all your heart and lean not on your own understanding; in all your ways submit to him, and he will make your paths straight."
—Proverbs 3:5–6

YOU ARE DEEPLY LOVED

"I have loved you with an everlasting love; I have drawn you with unfailing kindness."

Jeremiah 31:3

God's love for you isn't fragile—it's forever. On the days you feel overlooked, unseen, or not enough, come back to this truth: you are deeply, wildly, endlessly loved by your Creator. It's not because of what you do, but because of who He is. Jesus wants you to remember that you DO belong. He has marked you with His mighty love. You are His. Regardless of how others treat you, God sees you. And that's enough.

Today's Verse:
*"For we are God's handiwork,
created in Christ Jesus to do good works,
which God prepared in advance for us to do."*
—Ephesians 2:10

THEY HAD BEEN WITH JESUS

"When they saw the courage of Peter and John and realized that they were unschooled, ordinary men, they were astonished and took note that these men had been with Jesus."

Acts 4:13

I've always had a deep love and respect for blue-collar workers. I love those who get up before the sun, lace their boots, pack their lunch, and show up—rain or shine. My dad is one of them.

I grew up around people who didn't need to say much because their lives spoke volumes. They worked hard. They were loyal. And though they didn't always have college degrees or polished words, they had wisdom—and grit—that could never be taught in a classroom.

That's why I love this verse in Acts 4. Peter and John weren't scholars. They weren't dressed up with religious robes or degrees. They were fishermen—hardworking, hands-in-the-net, dirt-under-the-fingernails kind of men. And yet, when they spoke, even the religious elite were stunned. Why? Because it was clear they had *been with Jesus.*

That's it. That was the credential. The difference. The thing that turned heads and opened hearts.

There's something so beautiful and powerful about this. Because it means your influence for the Kingdom isn't tied to your education, your eloquence, or your social status. It's tied to your time with Jesus.

Maybe you're like my dad. Maybe you work with your hands. Maybe you've never stood behind a pulpit or written a devotional—but your life is a sermon. Your faithfulness, your integrity, your quiet prayers, your kindness in the break room—they preach. And the world takes note.

If people can look at your life and see the fingerprints of Jesus all over it, then you're exactly the kind of "ordinary" God loves to use. You don't need to be impressive. You just need to be *with* Him.

So today, whether you're in steel-toe boots, scrubs, or behind a desk—walk in that same boldness. Let your life reflect who you've been with. And may others see it and be amazed—not at you, but at the One who's walking with you.

Today's Verse:
"Those who look to him are radiant; their faces are never covered with shame."
—Psalm 34:5

LOCKED-IN HOPE

*"Let us hold unswervingly to the hope we profess,
for he who promised is faithful."*

Hebrews 10:23

Sometimes, right before the breakthrough, comes the biggest wave of discouragement.

You've prayed. Waited. Worked. Believed. And yet, it still feels like nothing is shifting. If you've ever felt like quitting right before the finish line—this is for you. Don't let go now. You're closer than you think.

Faith isn't just about trusting when everything is clear—it's about trusting when everything is quiet. God doesn't tease or trick His children. He's not dangling a promise in front of you just to take it away. If He gave you a word, He's going to fulfill it. But sometimes, the silence before the miracle is the space where our roots grow deeper, where trust is solidified, and where we discover what kind of faith we actually carry.

There's a reason Scripture reminds us to *"hold unswervingly."* **The Greek word carries the meaning of being *firm*, *unmoving*, *unwavering*, and *without giving up*.** It's a strong word. It doesn't imply holding on with a loose grip—it means gripping with everything you've got! *White knuckles. Steady heart. Locked-in* *hope.* This kind of holding on says, *"I may not see it yet, but I know Who holds the future, and I'm not letting go!"*

That's the kind of perseverance Hebrews is calling out in you—not because you're strong, but because *He who promised is faithful.* Your grip isn't what secures the promise—His character is. But that firm grip anchors you through the waiting, reminding your soul who your God is.

You're not failing. You're not forgotten. You're not off track. You're being refined. Strengthened. Prepared. So if you're tired today, let this be your reminder: Don't stop here. Take one more step. Say one more prayer. Praise one more time.

You're closer than you think!

Today's Verse:
"You need to persevere so that when you have done the will of God, you will receive what he has promised."
—Hebrews 10:36

DAY 294

GOD SEES WHAT OTHERS MISS

> "But the Lord said to Samuel, 'Do not consider his appearance or his height, for I have rejected him. The Lord does not look at the things people look at. People look at the outward appearance, but the Lord looks at the heart.'"
>
> 1 Samuel 16:7

If you've ever felt overlooked, underestimated, or disqualified because of what others see—today's verse is for you.

In 1 Samuel 16, the prophet Samuel is sent to the house of Jesse to anoint the next king of Israel. Saul had fallen out of favor with God, and now a new leader was to rise. Naturally, when Jesse's oldest son, Eliab, walks in—tall, strong, and kingly—Samuel assumes, *"This must be the one!"* But God stops him in his tracks.

God's response is both gentle and firm: *"Do not consider his appearance... the Lord looks at the heart."*

It was David, the overlooked one, who had the heart God was after. Not because he had it all together, but because his heart was tender, surrendered, authentic, and devoted to the Lord. David even showed great potential through the way he cared for his father's sheep. He fought off lions and bears to protect them. That pet you have at home? God sees how you love what's entrusted to you. Those little things matter more than you know.

This one moment reshaped the way we understand God's value system. While the world measures status, beauty, talent, and performance, God is weighing something deeper: the heart. Jesus goes further than appearances. He's drawn to purity, humility, and a willingness to follow Him, even when no one is watching.

Maybe you're not the loudest in the room or the most polished speaker. Perhaps you don't have a platform, and sometimes feel invisible. **In the Kingdom of God, visibility isn't the requirement—*availability* is. God isn't looking for impressive résumés. He's looking for *open hearts*.**

David wasn't chosen because he was the most visible. He was chosen because he was available—worshipping in the field, faithfully tending sheep, unseen by man but fully seen by God. And that's where God found him.

Here's the lesson: Don't be discouraged when others pass you by. Don't disqualify yourself because you don't match the world's version of success. You don't have to be seen by everyone to be chosen by God.

Keep tending your field. Keep showing up with a pure heart. Keep worshipping in the quiet places. God sees—and when the time is right, He will call your name.

Today's Verse:
"Humble yourselves before the Lord, and he will lift you up."
—James 4:10

WHEN IT FEELS LIKE GOD FORGOT

"But when all goes well with you, remember me and show me kindness; mention me to Pharaoh and get me out of this prison."

Genesis 40:14

There's a man in the Bible named Joseph, and his story is one of the most remarkable examples of waiting with faith. As a teenager, he had vivid dreams about his future—visions that hinted he would one day lead and influence others. But shortly after, everything in his life seemed to fall apart. He was betrayed by his own brothers, sold into slavery, falsely accused of a crime, and thrown into prison for something he didn't do.

And then came the waiting.

While in prison, Joseph helped someone who promised to remember him—but didn't. Days turned into weeks. Weeks into years. Two full years went by. No word. No change. Just silence. Can you relate? That place where you've done your best, stayed faithful, trusted God... but nothing seems to move? You wonder, *Does God see me? Did He forget me?*

But here's what Joseph didn't know: God was not ignoring him—He was *preparing* him. The delay wasn't random; it was right on time. Because when Joseph was finally remembered, it wasn't just to get out of prison. It was to step into a position of influence where he could help save thousands of lives during a coming famine—including the very family that had betrayed him.

Sometimes the seasons of waiting feel the hardest—especially when you don't see what's coming next. But Joseph's life shows us something powerful: God can use delays to build character, refine purpose, and set the stage for something greater than we imagined.

If you feel stuck, overlooked, or uncertain about what God is doing, don't give up. You are not forgotten. You are being formed. And when the time is right, God will open the door—not just to set you free, but to fulfill the reason you were placed there to begin with.

God sees you. He's writing your story. And He never wastes a delay.▫

Today's Verse:
"The Lord is good to those whose hope is in him, to the one who seeks him; it is good to wait quietly for the salvation of the Lord."—Lamentations 3:25–26

WHEN YOU FEEL BEHIND

"But many who are first will be last, and the last first."

Matthew 19:30

It's easy to feel forgotten when it seems like everyone else is getting ahead. In a world obsessed with status, achievement, and recognition, it's tempting to measure success by how quickly or visibly it comes. But Jesus flips that thinking upside down. He reminds us that in His Kingdom, the ones who seem overlooked today may be honored tomorrow. The last will be first, and the first will be last.

Maybe you've been faithfully serving behind the scenes, with no applause. Maybe you've watched others step into dreams you're still praying for. It's easy to wonder if you've missed your moment or if God somehow skipped over you. But friend, God's timeline isn't like ours. His promotions come from a place of perfect wisdom, not popularity. His rewards are eternal, not based on fleeting praise.

The disciples themselves wrestled with this. In Matthew 19, Peter asked Jesus what reward they would receive for leaving everything to follow Him. Jesus assured them that their sacrifices were seen—and would be honored far beyond anything they could imagine. But He also issued a gentle warning: don't get caught up in comparing places or positions. In God's Kingdom, it's not about who gets there first—it's about faithfulness.

If you feel last in line today, remember: God hasn't forgotten you. Sometimes the ones who are hidden the longest are the ones He's preparing for the greatest impact. Your story isn't delayed; it's being developed.

Stay faithful. Keep loving. Keep serving. Keep showing up, even when no one else notices. Heaven's rewards are not measured by earthly timelines.

Today's Verse:
"Humble yourselves before the Lord, and he will lift you up."
—James 4:10

THE DOOR OF HOPE IN YOUR VALLEY

*"I will give her back her vineyards, and will make the
Valley of Achor a door of hope."*

Hosea 2:15

What if your darkest valley could become your greatest doorway?

The *Valley of Achor* first appears in the book of Joshua. It's a place of deep pain and consequence, named after Achan's sin against God when he took what was forbidden during the battle of Jericho. His actions brought judgment not just on himself, but on all of Israel. The name "Achor" means *trouble*—and that's exactly what it represented: a place of sorrow, discipline, and heartbreak.

But our God is a Redeemer.

Centuries later, in the book of Hosea, God references this same valley—not as a reminder of punishment, but as a **promise of restoration**. He says He will *make the Valley of Achor a door of hope*. The very place that once symbolized sin and sorrow would now become a gateway to redemption and fresh beginnings.

God doesn't waste pain. He repurposes it.

That valley you're walking through? The one filled with trouble, regret, or unanswered questions? God can transform it. In fact, He often meets us most powerfully in the places we least expect. The Valley of Achor reminds us that even in our mess, our mistakes, and our mourning—God is already preparing a door of hope.

You might be feeling stuck in your own "Valley of Achor" right now. Maybe you're facing the consequences of a poor decision. Maybe you've been carrying guilt, shame, or sorrow that feels too heavy to bear. Don't believe the lie that it ends here. What feels like a dead end might actually be the place where hope begins to rise.

Today, ask the Lord to open your eyes to the door of hope He's placed in front of you. It may not look like you expected—but it will lead to peace, healing, and restoration.

God doesn't leave us in the valley.

He leads us through it.

Today's Verse:

"Even though I walk through the darkest valley, I will fear no evil, for you are with me; your rod and your staff, they comfort me."—Psalm 23:4

WHEN WEAKNESS MEETS GRACE

"But he said to me, 'My grace is sufficient for you, for my power is made perfect in weakness.' Therefore I will boast all the more gladly about my weaknesses, so that Christ's power may rest on me."

2 Corinthians 12:9

Perfectionism nearly broke me. For much of my youth, I lived under the weight of trying to be perfect. I wanted to be seen as capable, strong, and accomplished—someone who could handle anything life threw at her. From academics and athletics to my social life and physical appearance, I wore performance like armor. But underneath all the accomplishments was a wounded heart, quietly wondering if love could really be unconditional.

What I didn't realize back then was that I wasn't running toward success—I was running away from pain. My mother's absence left a deep hole in my heart, and instead of processing it, I buried it under busyness. Without a strong relationship with God in those early years, I tried to earn worth through hard work, thinking if I could just do enough, maybe I would finally feel enough.

That ache followed me into adulthood. I smiled on the outside but wrestled with self-worth on the inside. I believed lies the enemy whispered: "You weren't worth staying for," "You'll never be enough," and "Your story disqualifies you." Like many, I used strength as a survival tool. But survival isn't the same as healing.

Everything began to shift when I met Jesus in a real way. He didn't scold me for striving. He didn't wait until I had it all figured out. He met me right in the mess of my weakness. The very things I was ashamed of became the places where His grace rushed in.

I started to see that His strength didn't require my perfection—it required my surrender. Slowly, I began to lay down the need to impress and started picking up the truth of who I really was: loved, chosen, and enough in Christ. My broken story didn't disqualify me. It was the very soil God used to grow compassion, resilience, and purpose.

Through my grandmother's love, my sister's sacrifices, and God's unrelenting faithfulness, I learned that even the most painful parts of our stories can be redeemed. God used people around me to reflect His nurturing nature, filling the gaps left by others. What the enemy tried to twist into shame, God used to write a testimony.

If you are tired from striving or weighed down by wounds from your past, know this: God's grace is sufficient. You don't have to earn it, prove yourself, or hold it all together. Let Him meet you in your weakness. He is not repelled by your brokenness—He's drawn to it.

Today's Verse:
"Those who sow with tears will reap with songs of joy. Those who go out weeping, carrying seed to sow, will return with songs of joy, carrying sheaves with them."
—Psalm 126:5–6

REST FOR THE WEARY

"Come to me, all you that are weary and are carrying heavy burdens, and I will give you rest."
Matthew 11:28

A **few weeks ago, I found myself pushing for something I knew God had planted in my heart.** But instead of trusting His timing, I tried to control the outcome. I overanalyzed. I *obsessed*. I made plans God hadn't greenlit.

As a result, I opened the door for the enemy to whisper lies that sent me into a spiral of discouragement. I spent an entire day in a fog, moping and questioning everything. I knew James 4:7 said to resist the devil and he would flee, but I didn't. I surrendered my peace instead.

The next morning, I made a different choice. I had gotten ten hours of sleep and decided to realign my mind with the truth. I reminded myself: I am a daughter of the Most High God. I don't belong to fear, shame, or striving. And then, something unexpected happened. My dad—who never calls me that early—rang my phone at 7:30 a.m.

I almost didn't answer. I was ashamed. I thought he might sense that I'd spent the day before in defeat, which would disappoint him. But I picked up. And what he said brought me to tears.

He said, "Wendi, I woke up at 1:30 a.m. to the sound of your voice calling, 'Dad, Dad, Dad,' in fear. I thought you were warning me of something, so I got up and checked the house. Nothing was wrong. But I knew I had to call you this morning."

Right then, I knew: the Holy Spirit had intervened. God saw me in my weakness and used my dad's obedience to encourage me. I told him everything, and he laughed and said, "See? God knew you needed someone."

This moment reminded me that even when we try to carry things ourselves, God doesn't let go. He sees. He responds. He sends help in ways we don't expect. And often, the first thing He offers is rest. Not the kind of rest the world gives—but the deep, healing kind that only Jesus provides.

If you're weary, stop striving. Rest in God's arms. Trust His timing. He's not disappointed in you—He's drawing near.

Today's Verse:
"Cast all your anxiety on him because he cares for you."
—1 Peter 5:7

YOU ARE MORE THAN ENOUGH

"I have been crucified with Christ. It is no longer I who live, but Christ who lives in me. And the life I now live in the flesh I live by faith in the Son of God, who loved me and gave himself for me."
Galatians 2:20

The most powerful thing you can know about yourself is this: *Christ lives in you.* This changes *everything.* Your identity is not rooted in your past, your paycheck, your popularity, or your performance—it's rooted in a Person. And His name is Jesus.

When the world tries to label you by your mistakes, God calls you redeemed. When culture says your value comes from what you produce, God says your worth was settled at the cross. You don't need to earn His love. You just need to receive it—and live from it.

We often spend years trying to prove ourselves—grinding, striving, hustling for a sense of "enough." But Galatians 2:20 gives us freedom from that cycle. The old you is gone. The insecure, uncertain, unqualified version? Crucified. What remains is a life empowered by the very Spirit of God.

You are not powerless. You are not too late. You are not less-than. You are full of divine potential, because Christ Himself dwells in you. And that makes you bold, brave, and beloved.

So, the next time you find yourself shrinking back, questioning your worth, or wondering if you're "doing enough"—stop. Look in the mirror and remind yourself of what's true: **"I am who God says I am. I am His. And Christ lives in me."**

Let that truth shape how you walk into rooms, how you face hard days, how you speak to yourself and others. The same power that raised Jesus from the dead is alive in you—and it's more than enough for every challenge you face.

Today's Verse:

"The Spirit you received does not make you slaves, so that you live in fear again; rather, the Spirit you received brought about your adoption to sonship. And by him we cry, 'Abba, Father.'"
—Romans 8:15

WHEN GOD STEPS INTO THE IMPOSSIBLE

Jesus looked at them and said, "With man this is impossible, but with God all things are possible."

Matthew 19:26

Sometimes life confronts us with situations that seem insurmountable and downright impossible to our human eye. We look at the mountain in front of us and think, "There's just no way." Whether it's a financial burden, a broken relationship, or a calling that feels way too big, our limited perspective often stops us before we even begin. But Jesus offers us a different lens—one that shifts our focus from what we can't do to what He can.

In today's passage, Jesus is speaking to His disciples after a rich man walks away sorrowful, unwilling to let go of his possessions to follow Him. The disciples, confused, ask, *"Who then can be saved?"* And Jesus responds with a truth that still echoes today: salvation, like every part of this faith journey, isn't something we accomplish by human effort—it's made possible through Jesus alone. What feels unreachable to us is always within reach for Him.

God has a track record of showing up in impossible situations. Moses stood at the edge of the Red Sea with Pharaoh's army charging behind him—and the sea split. Sarah laughed at the idea of becoming a mother in her old age—and held Isaac in her arms. David, a shepherd boy, ran toward a giant with only a sling—and won. God didn't need perfect circumstances; He just needed willing hearts.

What impossible situation are you facing right now? Maybe it's a health battle, a prodigal child, or a dream you've tucked away because it feels too far gone. Don't give up. Don't count God out. He is still the God of miracles, and He still moves mountains.

Take your situation to Him in prayer. Ask boldly. Trust fully. And remember—what seems impossible for you is entirely possible for the One who holds the world in His hands.

Today's Verse:
"Now to him who is able to do immeasurably more than all we ask or imagine, according to his power that is at work within us."
—Ephesians 3:20

DIVINE DIRECTION IN UNEXPECTED MOMENTS

"The Lord directs the steps of the godly. He delights in every detail of their lives."

Psalm 37:23 (NLT)

I was stretching after a workout when a kind man nearby said, "You look like an athlete." I smiled, a little surprised, and replied, "I try to be. I like to stay in shape to keep up with the athletes I work with—and let's be honest, it wouldn't make sense to give nutrition advice if I didn't take care of myself too." I shared that I played college softball and returned the compliment, telling him he looked fit himself.

As we talked, something about him seemed familiar, but I couldn't place it—until he extended his hand and said, "Reggie Jackson."

I blinked for a moment, realizing it really was that Reggie Jackson—14-time All-Star, five-time World Series champion! We ended up chatting for a few minutes about youth athletes and how important it is to encourage them. I pulled up my website to show him a resource he might pass along to his grandkids. That's when he handed me a business card with his name, the title "Mr. October," and the Houston Astros logo. "Why don't you just send me an email," he said.

What struck me most about the encounter wasn't who he was—it was how God used that moment to gently encourage my heart. For months, I'd been praying about whether or not I should move to Texas. The idea has been in my heart, but I've hesitated, not wanting to make a decision outside of God's will. Receiving a card with "Houston Astros" written on it felt less like a career clue and more like a quiet whisper from the Lord: I see you. I know your thoughts. I'm guiding you.

God is so kind to meet us in small, personal ways. He didn't give me a loud answer or a lightning bolt. He simply used a stranger, a small interaction, and a tiny logo to remind me He's present in the details.

If you're in a season of decision or transition, be encouraged. You don't have to have it all figured out. Stay open. Keep seeking. And be ready—sometimes God answers with a whisper when you're expecting a sign.

Today's Verse:
"Your word is a lamp to my feet and a light to my path."
—Psalm 119:105

PRAY SPECIFICALLY, TRUST PATIENTLY

"If you remain in me and my words remain in you, ask whatever you wish, and it will be done for you."
John 15:7

God answers prayers—sometimes in the most personal and specific ways. You might be thinking, *He doesn't answer mine*, or *I've been praying for something for years and there's still no response.* But His answers are always rooted in what is best for us. Sometimes the answer is *yes*, sometimes *no*, and other times it's simply *wait*.

John 15:7 reminds us of something powerful: when we abide in Christ and His words live in us, our desires begin to align with His. Our prayers become shaped by His heart. It's not about asking for anything and getting it on demand—it's about communion with Jesus. From that place of closeness, our prayers shift, and transformation follows.

This truth became real to me when I started seriously praying about relocating to Dallas, Texas—something that had been stirring in my heart for years. I've always been sensitive to how the Holy Spirit speaks to me through personal and subtle confirmations. So, I got specific. I asked the Lord, *If Dallas is truly where You want me to go, will You show me a Texas license plate with the letters* SWW? Those letters had personal meaning to me, and I knew only God could arrange something like that.

Weeks passed. Plenty of Texas plates came and went—but never SWW. I began to wonder if I had made the whole thing up. Was I asking for too much? Did I need to let it go?

Then one quiet evening, while sitting outside reading Scripture with my friend Morgan, a car pulled into the lot. As it got closer, I squinted to see the plate. My heart started pounding. SWW. I jumped to my feet, laughed, cried, and praised God right there in the parking lot. Morgan watched the whole thing unfold, stunned at the Lord's perfect timing.

It was more than just a plate—it was confirmation. The kind only the Holy Spirit gives when you're preparing to make a major move. God didn't give me that sign early on because I wasn't ready yet. He needed to prepare my heart, teach me to trust, and help me release things in Tennessee first. Isaiah 60:22 came alive for me: "*When the time is right, I, the Lord, will make it happen.*"

If you're in a season of waiting or seeking clarity, don't be afraid to pray specifically. God isn't intimidated by your requests. He delights in the details and confirms with care. And when the time is right, He'll show you—clearly and personally—that He's been leading all along.

Today's Verse:
"*The Lord is good to those who wait for him, to the soul who seeks him.*"—Lamentations 3:25

HE'S STILL CARRYING YOU

"I have made you and I will carry you; I will sustain you and I will rescue you."

Isaiah 46:4

I **was sitting outside, enjoying the sunshine and reading a book, when I noticed a little boy having a full-on meltdown on the sidewalk.** He was crying, visibly upset, and to make matters worse, he flopped down dangerously close to where cars were speeding by.

I expected his mom to react with frustration or urgency, but instead, she calmly knelt beside him. She didn't scold him or pull him up. She simply scooped him into her arms and carried him to the safety of the grass. There, she rubbed his back gently while he cried. After a few moments, he reached for her and gave her a hug. She hugged him back. Then, hand in hand, they walked across the parking lot to their car.

Watching this unfold, I felt a lump in my throat. I couldn't help but think, "This is exactly what God does with us."

So often we collapse under the weight of life. Maybe we're anxious, burnt out, afraid, or just overwhelmed. Our version of lying in the street might look like shutting down emotionally, isolating ourselves, or trying to carry more than we were meant to hold. And yet, God doesn't turn away. He doesn't say, "Get it together." He comes close. He kneels beside us. He picks us up, carries us to safety, and stays with us while we process what we're feeling.

That little boy didn't fight his mom's help. He rested in her arms, and eventually he stood up again. What a picture of child-like trust. Jesus said unless we become like little children, we can't enter the Kingdom of Heaven. Being childlike means we know who to run to, who to cry to, and who to trust when life feels too big for us.

If you're feeling overwhelmed today, remember that your Heavenly Father loves you deeply. You don't have to carry the weight alone. Let Him take over and walk with you through this hard stage. Like that little boy, you can rest in the arms of a Savior who longs for you to lean into His love. James reminds us that *"Draw near to God, and He will draw near to you"* (James 4:8). The Lord comes with compassion, not condemnation.

Today's Verse:
"The LORD himself goes before you and will be with you; he will never leave you nor forsake you.
Do not be afraid; do not be discouraged."
—Deuteronomy 31:8

DAY 305

WISDOM FROM THE SMALL THINGS

"Four things on earth are small, but they are exceedingly wise..."

Proverbs 30:24

God is the best storyteller, and sometimes His most powerful lessons come from His tiniest creatures. In Proverbs 30, Solomon points us to four small animals that live with big wisdom—wisdom we can apply right now. Let's break it down.

The ant is all about preparation. These little workers don't wait for winter to panic. They gather what they need in the summer so they're ready when things get tough. Spiritually, that means filling your heart with truth now—before the storm hits. Are you consistently spending time in God's Word, even when life feels "easy"? Because when the pressure comes, what you've stored up is what you'll draw from.

The rock badger (a little, furry cliff-dweller) knows where to hide. It's not strong, but it's smart. It builds its home high up in the rocks where predators can't easily reach. Your security doesn't come from your strength—it comes from where you choose to dwell. Is Jesus your safe place? Are you making decisions from a place of refuge in Him?

The locust is a picture of unity. No one's in charge, but they move in sync. There's power in community. Are you isolated, trying to handle life alone? Or are you marching with others in faith—supporting, sharpening, and walking together in step with God's Spirit?

And finally, the lizard. It's small. Easy to miss. But somehow it ends up in royal places. That's a picture of access—of how God uses the unlikely to show up in unexpected rooms. Don't count yourself out just because you feel ordinary. God can place you anywhere for His purpose.

These four creatures live with intention. They remind us that wisdom isn't about status or size—it's about how you respond to your season. Be prepared like the ant. Be grounded like the badger. Be connected like the locust. And be bold like the lizard.

Small doesn't mean insignificant. When we live with Godly wisdom, even the smallest life becomes mighty in the hands of our Creator.

Today's Verse:

"The ants are a people not strong, yet they prepare their food in the summer; The rock badgers are a people not mighty, yet they make their homes in the cliffs; The locusts have no king, yet all of them march in rank; The lizard you can take in your hands, yet it is in kings' palaces."

—Proverbs 30:25–28 (ESV)

THE LORD DELIGHTS IN YOU

"For the LORD takes delight in his people; he crowns the humble with victory."

Psalm 149:4

Did you know that God delights in you? Not just tolerates you, not just watches over you from a distance—but truly *delights* in you.

Psalm 149:4 is a beautiful reminder of God's affection for His people. He doesn't see you as a burden or a disappointment. He rejoices over who you are and takes pleasure in working in your life.

Still, this can be hard to believe. We often feel too flawed, too broken, or too behind to imagine God would take joy in us. But this verse isn't directed at the perfect—it's for the *humble*.

Humility is not about thinking less of yourself; it's about knowing your deep need for God. When you surrender your heart, trusting in His strength rather than your own, He doesn't just meet you—He crowns you with victory.

Think about that for a second. A crown symbolizes honor, identity, and purpose. When God places a crown on your life, He is not just lifting you up; He is affirming who you are in Him. That crown doesn't always look like success the way the world defines it.

Sometimes it's quiet peace when everything feels uncertain. Sometimes it's resilience in the face of disappointment. But it always means you are walking in the fullness of His love.

Take a moment today to really let this truth sink in: The Lord delights in you. He sees your effort, your growth, your desire to draw near. And He calls it *beautiful*. You don't have to earn His love—it's already yours. Walk forward today with confidence, not in your perfection, but in His delight. You are crowned, cherished, and fully seen.

Today's Verse:

"You will be a crown of splendor in the Lord's hand, a royal diadem in the hand of your God."
—Isaiah 62:3

THE QUIET STRENGTH OF HUMILITY

*"Now Moses was a very humble man, more humble
than anyone else on the face of the earth."*

Numbers 12:3

Moses wasn't known for his charm, charisma, or eloquence—he was known for his humility. And in God's eyes, that made him one of the greatest leaders of all time.

The word "humble" might sound soft or timid to modern ears, but it's anything but weak. Humility is one of the most powerful postures a person can take. It's not thinking less of yourself—it's choosing not to make yourself the center of everything. It's giving God the microphone instead of trying to hold it all the time. It's the courage to say, "I don't have it all figured out, but I know the One who does."

Moses wasn't always that way. When God first called him, he argued. He doubted. He even tried to pass the assignment to someone else. But over time, through wilderness seasons and mountaintop moments, Moses learned to depend on God. He let go of trying to prove himself. And in doing so, he made space for God's presence to move through him.

That's what humility looks like—it's not self-deprecation, **it's God-exaltation.**

In today's world, humility doesn't always get applause. It's countercultural. While others climb ladders, humility *kneels*. While others shout to be heard, humility *listens*. It doesn't need to win every argument or be the most important person in the room. **Humility just needs to stay close to the Father.**

And that's where the real strength is.

So if you feel small today, perhaps overlooked, underappreciated, or just tired of trying so hard—*you're not alone*. Moses knew what that felt like too. But God chose him anyway. Not because he was confident or had it all together, but because he had a heart that was willing. God still loves to use the ones who make space for Him to move.

May we be the kind of people who don't need the spotlight to feel seen. The kind who trust God to open the right doors, defend our names, and guide our every step. Humility won't always make headlines—but it always catches Heaven's attention.

Today's Verse:

"He has shown you, O mortal, what is good. And what does the LORD require of you? To act justly and to love mercy and to walk humbly with your God."

—Micah 6:8

THE GIFT OF ENJOYING YOUR LIFE

"When God gives someone wealth and possessions, and the ability to enjoy them... this is a gift of God."
Ecclesiastes 5:19

Life is short. And while we know that in theory, most of us live as if we'll have all the time in the world. In the U.S., the average life expectancy hovers around 73 for men and 79 for women. With retirement often beginning in our mid-60s, that leaves only a handful of years to enjoy the fruits of our labor. Yet too many spend those years recovering from the toll that unbalanced striving took on their health, relationships, and peace of mind.

Solomon's wisdom in Ecclesiastes is a timely reminder: it is not only okay to enjoy life—it's God's idea. Finding joy in your work, taking time to eat, laugh, rest, and be with those you love isn't indulgent. It's spiritual. When you slow down to enjoy what God has placed in your hands, you are actually honoring Him.

Yes, the Bible calls us to work diligently, but hustle without heart can drain your soul. If you're burning the candle at both ends to prove something, achieve more, or build your future alone, pause and ask—what's the cost? God wants you to work with joy, not exhaustion. He wants your life to be full, not just busy.

Taking care of your body, resting well, and nurturing meaningful relationships is not weakness—it's wisdom. You can glorify God with your hands and also with your Sabbath. You can build a career and still care for your health. You can chase dreams and still pause for dinner around the table. That's the kind of life God desires for you—one where balance, gratitude, and gladness of heart aren't rare luxuries but daily rhythms.

So today, take inventory. What small shift could help you live more intentionally? Where can you let go of unnecessary striving and embrace the joy of enough? Ask God to help you number your days—and enjoy them.

Today's Verse:
*"Teach us to number our days,
that we may gain a heart of wisdom"*
—Psalm 90:12

A SHIFT IS HAPPENING

"See, I am doing a new thing! Now it springs up; do you not perceive it?"

Isaiah 43:19

You are stepping into something new, even if you don't feel it yet. The Lord is preparing a shift in your life—quietly, intentionally, and powerfully. It may feel like you're still in the in-between, waiting for the page to turn. But Heaven wants you to know: the shift has already started.

God is not looking for perfect vessels. He's looking for available ones. You don't have to have it all figured out to walk in what He's calling you to. You just have to say yes. He's taking what seemed dry and forgotten and breathing life into it again. Some doors are closing—not because you failed, but because you've outgrown them. You've been faithful in the hallway, and now the next door is unlocking.

You've asked for confirmation, for clarity, for peace. And here it is: **you're not late. You're right on time.** God has not overlooked you. He's been pruning you, not punishing you. You were hidden, not buried. And now He's about to reveal what He's been doing behind the scenes.

There is an anointing on your obedience. Even in your quiet "yes," He's been building something eternal. That friendship you walked away from, that job you turned down, that step you took without applause—He saw it all. And He's going to honor it in ways you didn't expect.

Lift your head, beloved. Get your hopes up again. Speak life over the dry bones in front of you. The wilderness season was real—but so is the river God is bringing into it.

Today's Verse:
"Those who sow with tears will reap with songs of joy."
—Psalm 126:5

HEARTS THAT REMAIN STEADY

"They will have no fear of bad news; their hearts are steadfast, trusting in the Lord. Their hearts are secure, they will have no fear; in the end they will look in triumph on their foes."

Psalm 112:7–8

Election season in the United States brings a storm of emotion, passion, and division. It's easy to become swept up in debates, policies, and predictions, but as followers of Christ, we're called to fix our eyes higher—on the King who reigns above all earthly leaders.

Recently, I shared something simple but convicting online: *"Don't be so concerned with who's in the White House that you forget to tend to your own house."* It sparked all kinds of reactions, but the heart behind it remains true. Yes, leadership matters. But our peace doesn't depend on who wins an election. Our peace comes from knowing who holds eternity in His hands.

As believers, we're not called to idolize nations or political parties. Patriotism is not a sin, but when love for country overshadows love for Christ, it becomes a distraction. Can you picture Jesus walking around with Caesar's emblem or pledging loyalty to Roman politics? He didn't. He made it clear: *His kingdom is not of this world* (John 18:36).

The enemy loves using politics to divide the body of Christ. And sometimes, we play right into it—choosing sides and slinging words that hurt our witness. We start representing a party more than we represent the gospel. This isn't about disengaging from important issues—it's about making sure our highest allegiance is to Jesus. Always.

So here's a question to consider: *are you more passionate about national headlines than the condition of your own heart or household? Are you raising your children to know and love the Lord? Are you praying over your home, your community, and your church family?* Change starts there. Not in Congress, but in the kitchen. Not on a debate stage, but at the dinner table.

Each election season, resist the temptation to spiral into fear or division. Ground yourself in God's Word. Serve your neighbor. Take a walk with your kids. Bake something for a family in need. Choose peace when the world chooses panic. Why? Because your heart is secure in the One who never changes. You are not shaken by bad news when your hope is anchored in Christ. The world may shift, but His Kingdom stands forever.

Today's Verse:
"But seek first his kingdom and his righteousness, and all these things will be given to you as well."
—Matthew 6:33

BEAUTY TAKES TIME

"He has made everything beautiful in its time. He has also set eternity in the human heart; yet no one can fathom what God has done from beginning to end."

Ecclesiastes 3:11

You might not see it yet, but God is making something beautiful out of your life.

There are moments when everything feels unfinished—like your story is stuck in the messy middle. You wonder when the breakthrough will come, or why the waiting feels so long. But the truth is, God is not done. He's still painting, still pruning, still preparing. And His timing is not a delay—it's an act of love.

Ecclesiastes 3:11 reminds us that beauty is part of God's plan, not just at the end, but in the making. He's not waiting until your life is perfect to make it beautiful. He's forming something radiant right in the middle of the waiting, the wondering, and the growing.

Maybe you're healing from something heavy. Maybe you're rebuilding hope after disappointment. Maybe you're still praying for something you haven't seen. Wherever you are, know this: Jesus hasn't forgotten you. You are not behind. You are not too late. You are right on time in His hands.

The eternal God is doing an eternal work in you. And what He's building won't just shine for a season—it will shine forever.

So when life feels out of sync, lean into the truth that God makes everything beautiful—in its time.

GOING DEEPER

Hope deferred can feel like a weight on the soul—like something good is always just out of reach, and your heart can't help but ache from the waiting. Proverbs 13:12 says, *"Hope deferred makes the heart sick, but a longing fulfilled is a tree of life."*

Today, take a few moments to write down where you feel that ache—where hope feels delayed, where the wait has worn you thin. Be honest with God. Then, right beside it, write what it would look like if that longing was fulfilled. Picture it. Speak life over it. Let yourself dream again.

This is where faith breathes—between the ache and the answer. And Jesus, the One who never forgets a seed sown in faith, delights in turning deferred hope into fulfilled joy.

Today's Verse:
"The Lord will fulfill his purpose for me;
your steadfast love,
O Lord, endures forever."
—Psalm 138:8

SAFE IN HIS ARMS

"My sheep hear my voice, and I know them, and they follow me. I give them eternal life, and they will never perish, and no one will snatch them out of my hand."

John 10:27–28

There's something so comforting about being known—*truly known*—and still loved. That's the kind of love Jesus has for us. He calls us His sheep, and not in a distant, impersonal way. He knows each of us by *name*.

He recognizes your voice, tears and even the things you haven't told anyone else. Jesus knows your *heart*. And when you belong to Jesus, He promises something the world can't offer: you are safe in His care.

I remember sitting in church one day, listening to a message about John 10. The pastor painted the picture of a shepherd lying across the entrance of the sheep pen at night, becoming the gate. That image stuck with me. Jesus Himself becomes our protection. No danger can slip past Him. No thief can steal us away. He's not just watching over us—He is with us, always.

There are days when we feel scattered and unsure, when the world feels like too much. But even then, Jesus is whispering, "I've got you." His sheep know His voice. And even if life feels noisy, His voice still cuts through with peace, gentleness, and love.

The best part? He says no one can snatch us from His hand. Not fear. Not failure. Not the mistakes of yesterday or the worries of tomorrow. You are held tightly by the One who loves you most. And *nothing* can pull you away.

So today, breathe a little deeper. Let your shoulders drop. You don't have to figure everything out. Just listen for the voice of your Shepherd. He's guiding you. He's holding you. *And He's not letting go.*

Today's Verse:

"I am the gate; whoever enters through me will be saved. They will come in and go out, and find pasture."

—John 10:9

THE MEANING BEHIND MILK AND HONEY

"So I have come down to rescue them from the hand of the Egyptians and to bring them up out of that land into a good and spacious land, a land flowing with milk and honey."

Exodus 3:8

When God described the Promised Land to Moses, He didn't just call it "good." He said it was *flowing with milk and honey.* That phrase wasn't random. It was deeply intentional and deeply prophetic.

Let's unpack why this matters. Milk symbolizes nourishment. It's a staple food, especially for the young and growing. In the Promised Land, there would be plenty of livestock, pastureland, and resources to produce milk. Spiritually, milk represents God's provision for daily needs and growth. It tells us that He would take care of His people—not only physically, but also spiritually. He would feed their souls with His truth, just like a newborn depends on milk to thrive.

Honey, on the other hand, represents sweetness, pleasure, and delight. In a time when refined sugar didn't exist, honey was the sweetest thing you could taste. It was also rare and valuable. Honey points to the richness of God's presence and the joy of living in a place where His abundance is evident. It tells us that God doesn't just provide—He satisfies.

Together, milk and honey form a picture of *nourishment and delight*. God was saying, "I am not just bringing you to a land where you'll survive—I'm bringing you to a land where you'll *flourish*." He was offering a life that would fill their bodies and souls.

But here's the deeper truth for us today: the Promised Land is a foreshadowing of life in Christ. Jesus is the true Milk and Honey. In Him, we find everything we need to grow and be sustained. In Him, we find unmatched sweetness, joy, and delight. And just like the Israelites, we have to journey through wilderness seasons to get there.

If you're in a waiting season, hold on to the promise. God doesn't just want to rescue you from something—He wants to bring you *into* something. A good, spacious, satisfying place. One that flows with everything your soul has been craving.

Today's Verse:
"Taste and see that the Lord is good;
blessed is the one who takes refuge in him."
—Psalm 34:8

RECOGNIZING THE ENEMY'S TACTICS

"We wanted very much to come to you, and I, Paul, tried again and again, but Satan prevented us."
1 Thessalonians 2:18

Have you ever had a door slam shut that felt like it *had to* be from the enemy? Paul knew that feeling. He longed to visit the church in Thessalonica, but satan kept getting in the way. This wasn't just bad luck or poor timing—it was spiritual warfare. And the same is true in our lives. Not every delay or obstacle is from God. Sometimes, it's the enemy working overtime to derail the mission.

To walk in victory, we need to understand who our enemy is. The Bible gives us several names and descriptions for him, each revealing how he operates.

Satan means "adversary." He stands in opposition to the purposes of God. Paul felt that resistance. So did Job. So do you. But here's the truth: even when satan tries to block the way, *God will still make a way if it's in His will.* You might face delays, but you will not be denied what God has for you.

The devil is a slanderer. He twists your words, distorts your character, and attacks your name. He thrives in confusion and gossip. When you're misunderstood or falsely accused, remember—you're in good company. Jesus was slandered too. He teaches us what to do. He often stayed silent, secure in who He was.

The accuser whispers lies in your ear: "You're not worthy. God can't use someone like you." Don't listen. Those are not the words of your Shepherd. They are the schemes of your enemy. Revelation 12:11 says we overcome by the blood of Jesus and the power of our testimony. Speak truth over the lies.

Sometimes, you'll need to ask God, *Is this You correcting me or the enemy attacking me?* Jonah faced a storm because he was *running* from God. The disciples faced a storm because they were *following* Jesus. The difference? One storm was discipline. The other was resistance from the enemy. Jesus rebuked the waves in Mark 4:39. In the original language, He spoke with authority, like someone commanding an unruly servant to stand down.

And finally, **the thief** comes to steal your joy, kill your peace, and destroy your purpose. If you're in a season where you feel drained, defeated, or distracted, pause. Pray. Ask the Holy Spirit to restore what's been stolen. God is not only your Protector—He is your Redeemer.

Don't fear the enemy. Be aware, be wise, and be rooted in truth. You are not alone in this battle, and God's plans for your life cannot be stopped.

Today's Verse:
"The Lord is faithful, and he will strengthen you
and protect you from the evil one."
—2 Thessalonians 3:3

YOU BELONG IN GOD'S HOUSEHOLD

"You are no longer foreigners and strangers, but fellow citizens with God's people and also members of his household."

Ephesians 2:19

The day after I posted a devotional video to my *Devotions with Wendi* Instagram page, I received the kindest message from a single dad. He said, "Thank you for being a light in a dark world." His words truly touched my heart. What he didn't know was that the night before, I had received a cruel message from someone trying to tear me down. But that's just how God works—He sends the right encouragement at just the right time.

There was a season when something like that mean message would've shaken me. But now, I know who I am. My identity isn't in what people say—it's in Christ. The enemy loves to try and silence us, especially when we're shining for Jesus. He wants us to shrink back, stay quiet, and stop sharing the truth. But here's the good news: when we know we belong to God's family, we can keep going no matter what comes against us.

That single dad's message reminded me how powerful encouragement is. Maybe today, you're the one who needs a reminder—or maybe God is nudging you to be the reminder for someone else. Don't hold it back. Your kind words might be exactly what someone needs to hear.

If you've ever felt like you don't belong, let this verse settle deep in your heart: You are not a stranger to God. You are part of His household. You're family. And not only that—He delights in you, and He's placed His light inside you for a reason.

So let's keep shining, even when it's hard. Let's keep loving and speaking life. The world can be loud and unkind, but our God is louder with His love. He sees you, He knows you, and He is so proud that you're His.

Today's Verse:
"The light shines in the darkness,
and the darkness has not overcome it."
—John 1:5

DAY 316

GOD GETS THE GLORY

"And if we know that he hears us—whatever we ask—we know that we have what we asked of Him."

1 John 5:15

Before every meeting or presentation, I always pause to **pray.** I ask God to help me be a light, to guide my words with love and clarity, and to use my role in sports nutrition as a platform to reflect His heart. I pray that I can encourage every person in the room, even if just one heart truly hears.

At my most recent presentation, something powerful happened. The words flowed, the message resonated, and I felt completely in my element. I know without a doubt—it was the Lord. From my opening line, where I gave Him credit for shaping my career, to my closing gratitude, His hand was all over it.

But I haven't always lived with this kind of humility or dependence. For a long time, I carried pride like a hidden weight, thinking my success was solely the result of hard work and perseverance. Pride whispered, "You did this," while quietly burdening me with anxiety and the fear of messing up. Maybe you've felt that tension too—the pressure to perform, succeed, or prove yourself. Here's what I've learned: surrender changes everything.

When I finally gave everything to Jesus, I began to see that none of it was mine to begin with. Not my abilities, not my title, not even the breath in my lungs. Every skill I have is a gift from God, and returning the glory to Him is not only right—it brings peace.

I used to struggle deeply with reading as a child. Some teachers labeled me a "slow learner," and it wounded me. But my dad stepped in and taught me to read. It was a hard season, but it planted seeds of perseverance and compassion. Today, God uses those very roots—once seen as weaknesses—as strengths that allow me to speak, teach, and write in ways I never imagined.

Because Jesus gave His life for me, I now live every day for Him. That fuels everything I do. And you know what? It's freeing. When God gets the glory, the pressure falls away. He hears our prayers. He responds in love. And He turns our offerings—whether simple or bold—into something far greater than we could produce alone.

So if you're facing something today that feels big, nerve-wracking, or uncertain, pray. Ask. Trust. And then give Him the credit. You won't believe what He can do with a surrendered heart.

Today's Verse:
"*Commit your work to the LORD,*
and your plans will be established."
—Proverbs 16:3

HEARTS THAT LISTEN HEAR HEAVEN

"My dear brothers and sisters, take note of this: Everyone should be quick to listen, slow to speak and slow to become angry, because human anger does not produce the righteousness that God desires."

James 1:19–20

There's an old saying: **"God gave us two ears and one mouth for a reason."** It's funny, but there's wisdom in it. Listening well is something we often overlook—especially when we're rushing to be heard or to get our point across. And if we're honest, this applies to our conversations with God too. How often do we bring Him our lists, our worries, and our frustrations, but forget to pause and simply listen?

Listening creates space. It invites God to speak, to guide, and to settle our hearts. Yes, He wants us to pour everything out before Him. He loves when we talk to Him. But He also wants us to be still long enough to hear His response. His voice is often gentle—a nudge in Scripture, a whisper in your spirit, a word through someone else. When we slow down enough to truly listen, we begin to hear those quiet, powerful whispers of truth and direction.

This kind of listening is just as important in our relationships with others. Sometimes, people don't need advice or a solution. They just need someone to be present—to hear them without judgment or interruption. Listening is an act of love. It communicates, "You matter to me." When we're quick to listen and slow to speak, we create space for peace, empathy, and healing.

God's Word reminds us that listening is deeply connected to righteousness. When we're quick to anger or quick to speak, we often miss the heart of the moment. But when we practice restraint, humility, and attentiveness, we allow room for God's wisdom to shape our responses.

So today, let this be your challenge: slow down. Listen longer than feels natural. Pause before you respond. In prayer, in conversation, and even in conflict—give space for God to move. You may be surprised at what you hear when you finally stop to listen.

Today's Verse:
"There's a time to be silent and a time to speak."
—Ecclesiastes 3:7

THE ENEMY IS ALREADY SPOOKED

"I know that the Lord has given you this land and that a great fear of you has fallen on us, so that all who live in this country are melting in fear because of you."

Joshua 2:9

If today's verse was a movie, Rahab would've been the unexpected plot twist! She was a woman with a past, living in a city destined for destruction, and she ends up being the one who confirms to the Israelites what they didn't even know yet: *the enemy was already shaking in their boots!*

Before a single trumpet blasted or a stone from Jericho's wall cracked, God had already gone ahead and stirred fear into the hearts of Israel's enemies. They were "melting in fear"—not because of Israel's military skills, but because of what they'd *heard* about *Israel's God!*

Here's your reminder for today: **the same God who caused enemies to tremble back then is still fighting for you now.** Whatever you're stepping into—whether it's a new job, a hard conversation, or a bold dream—the opposition is not as fearless as it looks. In fact, the enemy is often more afraid of you stepping into your calling than you are of the resistance.

Rahab's faith was wild. She hadn't seen the Red Sea part with her own eyes, but she believed the stories. She knew something bigger was at work, and she wanted in. Her bold move to protect the spies didn't just save her—it secured her legacy. She went from "that woman on the wall" to being part of the very bloodline of Jesus!

So don't let fear hold you back. When you show up with the Spirit of God inside you, you're not just walking into the room—you're shifting the atmosphere. You don't need to be perfect, polished, or powerful by the world's standards. You just need to believe that the Holy Spirit is watching over you!

And next time you hear doubt whisper, "*Who do you think you are?*" just smile and say, "*One of God's kids—and the enemy already knows it!*"

Today's Verse:
"*The Lord your God, who is going before you, will fight for you, as he did for you in Egypt, before your very eyes.*"
—Deuteronomy 1:30

DAY 319

THE LONG WAY IS STILL GOD'S WAY

"When Pharaoh let the people go, God did not lead them on the road through the Philistine country, though that was shorter. For God said, 'If they face war, they might change their minds and return to Egypt.' So God led the people around by the desert road toward the Red Sea."

Exodus 13:17–18

When God freed the Israelites from Egypt, they left looking strong and ready. They were organized like an army. But God knew something they didn't—deep down, they weren't truly ready to fight. So instead of taking them the fastest way to the Promised Land, God took them on a longer path through the desert.

Why? Because He loved them. If they had faced a battle too soon, they might have panicked and wanted to go back to Egypt, even though Egypt was where they were mistreated and enslaved. God didn't want that. He wanted to protect them—not just physically, but emotionally and spiritually, too.

Honestly, I had to learn this lesson while writing this book. I wanted it done much sooner. I had goals and deadlines. However, I kept running into roadblocks. At times, I felt discouraged and questioned if I'd ever finish it. Looking back, I now see that God was using the slower pace to teach me. He wasn't withholding progress; He was building depth, healing wounds, and shaping me for the message He wanted to come through.

Sometimes we think we're ready for something big—maybe a new job, relationship, move, or opportunity—but God knows when our hearts need more time with Him. He's not punishing us by making us wait. He's preparing us so that when we do arrive, we're strong enough to stay and thrive.

Later in Deuteronomy, God says He will drive out the enemies in the land **"little by little."** That means God often works in steps, not all at once. He knows what's best, even when it's slower than we want. It's not about delay—it's about growth.

If you're feeling like things are taking too long, remember: God hasn't forgotten you. He's protecting you, preparing you, and walking with you. The long way may feel hard, but it's still His way. And it will always lead to His promises.

Today's Verse:
"The Lord will fight for you; you need only to be still."
—Exodus 14:14

MORE THAN YOU IMAGINED

"Now to him who is able to do immeasurably more than all we ask or imagine, according to his power that is at work within us."

Ephesians 3:20

Day 320 brings us face to face with one of the most stunning promises in all of Scripture. Ephesians 3:20 is a declaration of God's ability to do the impossible—far beyond what we can ask, dream, or even imagine! When Paul wrote this, he wanted believers in Ephesus (and us today) to understand that God's power has no ceiling, and His desire to bless His children is expansive and full of wonder.

Paul doesn't end his prayer with a simple amen. Instead, he transitions into a proclamation that points us back to God's greatness. The same power that raised Jesus from the dead is alive and active in you right now. Not someday. Not in a vague, distant way. Today. His Spirit is at work in your life, moving in ways you may not even see yet.

So often, we come to God with limited expectations, unsure if He'll come through. But what if God's plan isn't just to answer your prayer—but to exceed it? What if the dreams in your heart are only shadows of what He truly wants to do in and through you?

This is your 320 season. I feel the Lord is saying, *"Watch what I can do. What you thought would take years, I can do in a moment. What looked impossible, I will make possible. What you released to Me in faith, I will return to you in abundance. This is not the season to shrink back. It's the time to believe boldly again, to pray with expectancy, and to surrender your timeline for My schedule!"*

Ephesians 3:20 calls us higher. It invites us to let go of small thinking, to trust that God sees the whole picture, and to believe that He is able. Not just willing—*able*. He's not trying to figure out how to make things work. He already has a plan, and it's immeasurably more than you can imagine.

If you're feeling discouraged or stuck, let this verse breathe life back into your heart. God is not finished. He's just getting started. Keep dreaming, keep asking, and above all, keep trusting. His power is at work in you, and He's writing a story that's more beautiful than anything you could write on your own.

Today's Verse:
"For we are God's handiwork, created in Christ Jesus to do good works, which God prepared in advance for us to do."
—Ephesians 2:10

WHEN TRUST FEELS HARD

"Though he slay me, yet will I trust in him."
Job 13:15 (KJV)

Let's be real for a minute. Trusting God when life is smooth? That's simple. But when things fall apart—when the prayers go unanswered, the diagnosis stings, or the door slams shut—that's when trust becomes a choice. That's when Job's words hit differently: *"Though He slay me, yet will I trust in Him."*

Job wasn't pretending everything was fine. He was grieving, questioning, and hurting. And still, his heart clung to hope. That kind of trust is raw and honest. It's not about having the answers. It's about knowing who God is—even when life doesn't make sense.

I once walked a hiking trail shouting my frustrations to God. I was tired, angry, and questioning everything. Years later, I found myself back on that same path—only this time, I was *worshiping*. Something had shifted in *me*. I had learned that God doesn't abandon us in our pain. He walks with us through it. His presence is constant, even when our feelings aren't.

You don't need to have perfect faith to be held by a perfect God. You just need to keep showing up. Keep trusting. Keep whispering, *"I don't understand, but I believe You're still good."*

Because here's the truth: God is not afraid of your questions. He can handle your doubts. But He also wants to remind you—He's not done with your story. He's still writing. He's still working. And even if it feels like the end, it's not.

So if today feels heavy, take a breath. **You're not alone.** God sees you. He's not disappointed in your weariness. Jesus understands it. Keep trusting Him—not because it's easy, but because He's worthy.

Today's Verse:

"I know that my redeemer lives, and that in the end he will stand on the earth. And after my skin has been destroyed, yet in my flesh I will see God."
—Job 19:25–26

STRENGTH IN THE SACRIFICE

"Do not fear, for I am with you; do not be dismayed, for I am your God. I will strengthen you and help you; I will uphold you with my righteous right hand."

Isaiah 41:10

Growing up with a single dad gave me a front-row seat to what real love and sacrifice look like. He worked hard—sometimes too hard—to make sure I had what I needed. It wasn't flashy or perfect, but it was real. And looking back, those quiet acts of provision and protection taught me more than any sermon ever could.

If you're a single parent reading this, I just want to say: I see you. And more importantly, **God sees you.** All the long days, the late nights, the quiet prayers, the decisions you make that no one claps for? He sees all of it. And He's walking with you through every moment. You're not just holding your family together—you're planting seeds of legacy.

And if you were raised by a single parent like I was, maybe today's a good day to pause and really think about all the ways they showed up for you. Not perfectly, maybe not always how you hoped—but consistently, in their own way. That kind of love changes a person.

I've come to learn that God often uses the hard and hidden places in our stories to reveal just how near He really is. For many single parents and their kids, God becomes the One who fills in the gaps—bringing comfort, provision, strength, and hope in the places that felt like lack.

This is also your gentle nudge if you know a single parent: reach out. Say something kind. Drop off a coffee. Offer to watch the kids or just check in. You have no idea how much that might mean to them.

Whatever season you're in—parenting solo, missing a parent, or just carrying something heavy—know this: God hasn't left your side. He promises to strengthen and help you. He promises to hold you up when you don't feel strong enough to stand. And He always keeps His promises.

Today's Verse:

"Honor your father and your mother, so that you may live long in the land the Lord your God is giving you."
—Exodus 20:12

WHEN HIS WAYS DON'T MAKE SENSE (YET)

"For my thoughts are not your thoughts, neither are your ways my ways," declares the LORD. "As the heavens are higher than the earth, so are my ways higher than your ways and my thoughts than your thoughts."

Isaiah 55:8–9

I recently sat down for coffee with a new friend and by the end of our conversation, I knew I had to include her story in this devotional. It was one of those raw, honest testimonies that speaks to the very heart of God's mysterious and beautiful timing.

She told me that for most of her life, running was everything. It wasn't just a sport—it was her identity. She ran through high school, college, and even became a collegiate cross-country coach. But she admitted something that struck me deeply: running had become an idol. It gave her worth, structure, and control—until injury after injury forced her to stop altogether.

In the midst of that loss and identity crisis, she tried something new: swimming and biking. She joined a new gym. She was frustrated, uncertain, and healing in more ways than one. And then, in that place of discomfort, she met someone. Not just anyone—the man she's now engaged to. Her eyes lit up as she told me, "*I knew right away he was going to be my husband.*" What had felt like a painful detour turned out to be the path to something sacred.

It's easy to trust God when life feels clear and our plans go the way we hoped. But what about when things are confusing or painful? What about when doors close, dreams die, or we're forced into places we never planned to go? That's where this verse in Isaiah becomes real. God's thoughts are not our thoughts. His ways are higher. And while we don't always understand what He's doing, we can trust that He is doing something good.

Her story reminds us that sometimes God allows things to fall apart—not to hurt us, but to rebuild us for something better. If she hadn't been injured, she never would've stepped into that gym. She never would've met the man she'll now build a life with. And she wouldn't have discovered how much more there is to her story than running.

If you're in a season that feels confusing or off-course, let this be your encouragement: God hasn't forgotten you. He's rerouting you for something beautiful. What feels like a setback could be the exact step that leads you into your next chapter.

Today's Verse:
"*Then the LORD God made a woman from the rib he had taken out of the man, and he brought her to the man.*"
—Genesis 2:22

HOW TO KNOW IF SOMEONE IS FROM GOD

"By their fruit you will recognize them. Do people pick grapes from thornbushes, or figs from thistles? Likewise, every good tree bears good fruit, but a bad tree bears bad fruit."

Matthew 7:16–17

How do you really know if someone is from God? It's not always obvious—especially when they speak the right language or know all the Christian answers. But Jesus didn't say we would know people by their knowledge. He said we would know them by their **fruit**.

Fruit is what naturally grows from someone's life. You can't fake it for long. Eventually, what's inside will come out.

Recently, I had a heart-to-heart with a friend about a new guy she's been seeing. On the surface, he seemed like a strong believer. He could quote Scripture, talked about God, and had impressive church connections. But the more she described him, the more something didn't sit right in my spirit. There was no mention of humility, servanthood, or consistent fruit. He kept people at a distance. There was charm—but no character. That matters.

So how can we know if someone is really from God?

1. Do they walk in love?

Not just say it, but show it. Are they kind to people who can't offer them anything? Do they love sacrificially or selfishly?

2. Do they bear the fruit of the Spirit?

Galatians 5:22–23 lists the fruit of the Spirit: love, joy, peace, patience, kindness, goodness, faithfulness, gentleness, and self-control. These qualities are evidence of the Holy Spirit working in someone's life.

3. Are they submitted to Christ in their lifestyle?

Do they honor purity, integrity, and accountability? Or do they hide their habits, avoid conviction, and justify sin?

4. Does being around them push you closer to Jesus?

Do they challenge your faith in a healthy way? Or do they distract you, create confusion, or cause compromise?

5. Do they repent when they're wrong?

No one is perfect, but someone who walks with Christ is willing to admit their faults, seek forgiveness, and grow. Pride resists correction. Humility welcomes it.

If someone checks all the spiritual boxes outwardly but is cold, controlling, easily angered, or dismissive of conviction, it's a red flag. Don't ignore that still, small voice. God will never lead you into confusion. His wisdom is gentle, peaceable, and pure (James 3:17).

You don't have to figure it all out alone. Ask the Holy Spirit to guide you and confirm truth through His Word and godly counsel. God is not trying to trick you—He longs to protect you.

Today's Verse:
"The righteous choose their friends carefully, but the way of the wicked leads them astray"
—Proverbs 12:26

DISCERNMENT IN RELATIONSHIPS

"But when he, the Spirit of truth, comes, he will guide you into all the truth."

John 16:13

Not every connection is God-ordained, and when it comes to friendships or relationships, discernment is essential.

Here's a Spirit-led checklist to help you evaluate:

1. **Bears Good Fruit:** Is this person consistently showing love, joy, peace, patience, kindness, goodness, faithfulness, gentleness, and self-control? (Galatians 5:22–23)

2. **Aligns with God's Word:** Does this relationship pull you closer to obedience—or closer to compromise? (2 Corinthians 6:14)

3. **Brings Peace, Not Confusion:** Do you feel clarity and peace in their presence, or does the relationship stir up constant anxiety and uncertainty? (1 Corinthians 14:33)

4. **Leads You Closer to Christ:** Do they encourage your walk with Jesus? Are you growing in your faith through their presence in your life? (Hebrews 10:24–25)

5. **Reflects Selfless Love:** Is the relationship built on respect, patience, and humility—or is it fueled by selfishness and pride? (1 Corinthians 13:4–7)

6. **Confirmed by Wise Counsel:** Have spiritually mature mentors or friends affirmed this relationship? (Proverbs 11:14)

7. **Convicted by the Holy Spirit:** Do you sense peace from the Holy Spirit—or do you keep feeling a quiet warning to slow down or step away? (John 16:13)

8. **Purpose for God's Kingdom:** Does this relationship help fulfill God's bigger purpose in your life and glorify Him? (Matthew 6:33)

9. **Honors Purity:** In a romantic relationship, do they honor your body as a temple and pursue purity alongside you? (1 Corinthians 6:18–20)

10. **Called to Encourage or Disciple:** Is this someone God is asking you to walk with and encourage, especially if they're not yet a believer? Are you spiritually anchored enough to pour in? (2 Corinthians 5:20; Matthew 5:16).

Today's Verse:
"Above all else, guard your heart, for everything you do flows from it."—Proverbs 4:23

THANKFUL FOR THE SCARS

"He was pierced for our transgressions, he was crushed for our iniquities; the punishment that brought us peace was on him, and by his wounds we are healed."

Isaiah 53:5

Your scars tell a story—not just of pain, but of survival. Others may not see them, but you remember where they live. You know the nights you cried yourself to sleep, the moments you wondered if you would ever feel whole again. You know the strength it took just to keep breathing when it felt like everything inside you was breaking. Abuse and mistreatment leave invisible wounds that can take a lifetime to heal—but you need to know: **Jesus bears His scars too.** Not as a symbol of defeat, but as a reflection of how much He loves you and what He endured to set you free.

He didn't hide His scars after rising from the dead—He revealed them. He showed them to His disciples as proof: *"I was wounded for you, and I overcame. So will you."* (John 20:27). His scars weren't erased—they were redeemed. And yours will be too. Your scars are not shameful; they are sacred. They whisper of the grace that held you through the darkest seasons, the strength that carried you when you thought you couldn't take another step. They tell the truth: you are still here, and God is not finished with you.

If you have been mistreated, abused, or made to feel small, hear this today: **you are not the sum of what was done to you.** You are the beloved child of a God who binds up the broken-hearted and gives beauty for ashes. The evil that was meant to destroy you will never have the final word. God will use even this to write a story of redemption so powerful that it will bring healing not only to you, but to others who will one day hear your testimony.

God has never wasted a single tear you cried. Every moment of pain, every prayer you prayed through trembling lips, every silent scream of your heart—Jesus saw it all, and He is holding you still. So today, breathe deep. Let gratitude rise like a quiet song in your chest. You are not broken—you are becoming. And your scars? They are not signs of defeat. They are evidence that you fought hard, you survived, and God is still telling your story—one chapter at a time.

Today's Verse:
"The Lord is close to the brokenhearted
and saves those who are crushed in spirit."
—Psalm 34:18

THE GOD OF ALL COMFORT

"Praise be to the God and Father of our Lord Jesus Christ, the Father of compassion and the God of all comfort, who comforts us in all our troubles, so that we can comfort those in any trouble with the comfort we ourselves receive from God."

2 Corinthians 1:3–4

Paul doesn't just talk about comfort—he repeats it again and again, like a heartbeat. In 2 Corinthians 1, the word *comfort* shows up repeatedly, and it's not by accident.

Paul knew suffering well. He was beaten, imprisoned, shipwrecked, misunderstood, and burdened beyond his strength. Yet in the middle of those hardships, Paul boldly called God the *"Father of compassion"* and *"God of all comfort."* That's not a description you give unless you've personally experienced it.

Notice the pattern: God comforts *us* so that we can comfort *others*. Our pain is never wasted. The comfort we receive becomes the comfort we extend. Your story, with all its valleys and broken pieces, holds power. Not because it's perfect—but because God met you in it. And now, He wants to use it.

Maybe you're in a hard season right now. You might feel too broken to help anyone else. But here's what Paul teaches us: it's not about fixing others—**it's about showing up with the same**

comfort you've received. Sometimes that means sitting with someone in silence. Sometimes it means sharing a verse that carried you through. Sometimes it's just your presence, reminding them they're not alone.

The Greek word for comfort carries the idea of being called to someone's side to help. That's what the Holy Spirit does. He draws near and walks with you. And when you walk with others, *you reflect that same Spirit.*

So whether you're comforting or being comforted today, know this: you are seen by the Father of compassion. You are held by the God of all comfort. And one day, the comfort He's pouring into you right now will be poured out through you into someone else's life.

Today's Verse:
*"Carry each other's burdens, and in this way you
will fulfill the law of Christ."*
—Galatians 6:2

NO SMELL OF SMOKE

"There was no smell of fire on them."

Daniel 3:27

When God walks you through the fire, you come out without the smell of smoke. That's what happened to Shadrach, Meshach, and Abednego. They were thrown into a blazing furnace, but God didn't just deliver them—**He joined them in the flames.** And when they came out, their clothes weren't scorched, their hair wasn't fried, and the smell of fire wasn't even on them.

That's how our God works. He doesn't always keep us from the fire, but He promises to meet us in *it*. His presence protects us, not just from destruction, but from the residue of bitterness, fear, and hopelessness. He guards your soul even when the battle around you feels relentless. Others may see the fire, but they won't see it on you. What they'll see instead is peace that makes no sense, joy that rises in sorrow, and strength that clearly didn't come from you.

But let's be honest—some seasons feel hotter than others. In Daniel 3:19, the king was so furious that he ordered the furnace to be heated *seven times hotter than usual.* That wasn't symbolic. That was *real* heat—intense pressure, overwhelming odds, and the kind of trial that feels like it might kill you. Maybe that's the season you're in now. The kind where things feel unusually painful, like the fire has been turned up without warning. But even there—*especially there*—God is still with you. The hotter the fire, the greater the glory when He brings you out of it.

You may be walking through something hard right now—loss, rejection, fear—but take heart. Jesus is with you, and He's carrying you like a father carries his child (Deuteronomy 1:31). You may come out with lessons, but you don't have to come out with scars. You'll come out radiant, with a deeper trust, and a testimony of God's faithfulness. The same God who stood in the fire then is standing with you now.

You will not be defined by your fire. You'll be defined by the One who walked with you through it. And when you emerge, others will know it wasn't the furnace that shaped you—it was the presence of God within it. So lift your eyes, even in the heat. You're not alone. You're not forgotten. You're walking with the Fourth Man in the fire, and when you come out, you'll carry His glory—not the smoke.

Today's Verse:
"When you walk through the fire, you will not be burned; the flames will not set you ablaze."
—Isaiah 43:2

WHEN A DOOR CLOSES

"What he opens no one can shut, and what he shuts no one can open."

Revelation 3:7

We've all heard the phrase, **"When one door closes, another opens."** It's often said to bring comfort, but let's be honest—sometimes, when the door slams shut, it doesn't feel like comfort.

It feels like confusion. Maybe the job didn't work out. Maybe the relationship ended. Maybe your dream started to unravel, and you're left standing in front of a door that just won't budge.

But what if the closed door is actually a gift?

When Jesus closes a door, it's always to redirect, protect, or prepare. In Scripture, we see this in Acts 16 when Paul and his companions were *"kept by the Holy Spirit from preaching the word in the province of Asia."* They tried to go a different direction again—and the door closed once more. It wasn't until they reached Troas that Paul had a vision calling him to Macedonia. Only then did the right door swing open. God wasn't rejecting Paul's mission. He was guiding it.

Sometimes the closed door in your life is a sign that something unseen needs healing or development. Maybe your heart isn't ready. Maybe the person or place on the other side isn't either.

God may be strengthening your character, building endurance, or teaching you how to fully rely on Him.

Here are some quiet signs that a door is closing in your life:

- **You feel increasing restlessness or lack of peace, even in things that once felt right.**

- **The opportunities keep drying up, no matter how hard you try to force them.**

- **People who were once part of the journey begin to step back or change.**

- **God's Word starts to highlight different promises or directions than before.**

These aren't always easy to spot, especially when your heart is attached to what was behind the door. But God sees the full picture. He's not asking you to understand every detail—He's asking you to *trust* Him with it.

If a door has closed in your life, don't stand there banging on it in frustration. Step back. Breathe. And ask God what He's doing. Trust that His "no" is always for a greater "yes." He's not punishing you. He's preparing you. And when He opens the right door, it will be one you don't have to force—it'll open with peace, clarity, and divine timing.

Today's Verse:
"In their hearts humans plan their course,
but the Lord establishes their steps."
—Proverbs 16:9

DAY 330

YOU ARE SEEN AND VALUED

"Therefore do not worry about tomorrow, for tomorrow will worry about itself. Each day has enough trouble of its own."

Matthew 6:34

Brothers in Christ, you are not alone. You may carry more than you show. You may lead others while silently fighting your own battles. You may feel like you have to be strong for everyone else—but hear this today: God doesn't ask you to carry the weight of the world. He already carried it to the cross.

We live in a culture that tells men to suppress their emotions, to "man up," and never show weakness. But Jesus redefined strength. He wept openly. He withdrew to pray. He leaned on His Father. And He invites you to do the same.

A few weeks ago, I heard a heartbreaking story that I can't shake. A man took his life near a running trail. My friend happened to be nearby and noticed the signs—his parked car, the stillness, the moment when everything changed. He was in his fifties. A life gone too soon. That man may have felt invisible, unseen, or too burdened to go on. But I believe if someone had reminded him of his worth, his story could have turned out differently.

So to every man reading this—if you are struggling with depression, anxiety, stress, or hopelessness, please know: you are not weak. You are not broken beyond repair. You are a son of the Most High God. He knows your name. He sees your heart. And He is not ashamed of your pain.

Jesus didn't come for the perfect. He came for the weary. He came for the overwhelmed. He came for you.

Reach out. Talk to someone. Message a friend. Let someone pray with you. Your story still matters, and the Kingdom still needs what God placed inside of you. Don't believe the lie that you have to be "fine." You're allowed to need help. You're allowed to cry. You're allowed to rest.

And if you're not struggling right now—be the one who checks in. Be the brother who sends the text, who makes the call, who shows up.

God is with you, and He's not done with you. Let Him walk with you. There is purpose on your life. Keep going, brother.

Today's Verse:
"The Lord is close to the brokenhearted and saves those who are crushed in spirit."
—Psalm 34:18

WHY FISHERMEN?

*"His divine power has given us everything we need for
a godly life through our knowledge of him who called
us by his own glory and goodness."*

2 Peter 1:3

One of the questions I often ask the Lord is, *Why did You choose fishermen?* Out of all the professions, why were those first few disciples people who cast nets, fought storms, and smelled like the sea?

The more I walk with Jesus, especially through my own career in health and fitness, the more I'm beginning to understand.

Fishermen are gritty. They're used to long nights and uncertain results. They know what it means to wait patiently, to work faithfully, and to throw the net one more time even when they're exhausted. They're teachable, observant, and know the rhythm of the water. There's something about the quiet persistence and daily discipline of a fisherman that makes them ready for discipleship.

And maybe that's the point.

Jesus didn't choose polished theologians or powerful kings to launch the Kingdom. He chose ordinary, hardworking people who knew how to show up, get dirty, and follow instructions. He chose people who would listen, fall down, get back up, and try again. He chose those who had been overlooked, because He knew they'd be willing to look up.

Peter's story reminds me of this. He wasn't chosen because he was perfect. He was chosen because he was *willing*. He messed up. He doubted. He even denied Jesus—**but he never quit**. And that's the kind of heart Jesus trains. Not the one that gets it right every time, **but the one that keeps coming back**.

In health and fitness, I've learned that transformation doesn't happen overnight. It's the result of showing up consistently, trusting the process, and being willing to grow through the hard parts. Discipleship is no different. It takes endurance. Humility. Strength. Faith. And just like fishermen, we're called to cast our nets—whether or not we see results—and trust the One who calls us.

So if you're wondering whether you're the "right kind" of person for God to use, take heart. **You are.** God isn't looking for flawless resumes. He's looking for *available hearts*. And He's already given you everything you need to live a Godly life—right where you are.

Today's Verse:

"The Lord makes firm the steps of the one who delights in him; though he may stumble, he will not fall, for the Lord upholds him with his hand."
—Psalm 37:23-24

WHAT YOU FEED WILL GROW

*"So I say, walk by the Spirit, and you will not gratify
the desires of the flesh."*

Galatians 5:16

What you feed grows. What you starve dies.

This isn't just a catchy phrase—it's a spiritual principle that shapes your daily life. Your thoughts, your habits, your emotions, and your desires are all being nourished by *something*. If you keep feeding fear, it will grow louder. If you rehearse offense or bitterness, it will take root and begin to shape how you see the world. But when you feed your spirit—when you nourish your soul with the Word of God, time in His presence, worship, and truth—you begin to change from the inside out.

Paul's words in Galatians aren't a call to strive for perfection. They're an invitation to intimacy. *Walk by the Spirit*, he says—not sprint, not perform, not pretend—but walk. That means step by step, one decision at a time. It's a daily surrender. A quiet choosing of God's voice over the world's noise.

And here's the thing: walking by the Spirit doesn't always look "spiritual." Sometimes it's choosing to hold your tongue. Sometimes it's getting off social media because your peace is too precious to trade. Sometimes it's apologizing first or turning the worship music up in your car instead of venting again. These small choices matter more than we think.

Why? Because what you feed, you become.

You have a choice every day: will you feed the flesh or will you feed the Spirit? Will you reach for a temporary fix or walk in eternal truth? It doesn't happen all at once, but over time, those small Spirit-led choices build a life marked by peace, purpose, and power.

And here's the beauty of it: the more you walk with Jesus, the more your cravings begin to change. What once satisfied you no longer does. Your desires are shaped by His. Your thoughts begin to reflect His heart. You start to want what He wants—not because you *have* to, but because you've been changed.

So today, pay attention to what you're feeding. Your spirit is hungry. Let it feast on what brings life.

The transformation starts with one step.

Today's Verse:
"Set your minds on things above, not on earthly things."
—Colossians 3:2

WHEN YOU SEE A DEER

"As the deer pants for streams of water, so my soul pants for you, my God."

Psalm 42:1

The next time you see a deer, pause. Watch how it moves—quiet, steady, alert. It's not rushing, but it's not aimless either. It's looking for something essential. **Water.**

Psalm 42 opens with that exact image. A deer panting for water. Not casually walking to a stream, but thirsting—urgently, deeply, fully aware that without it, it won't survive. **That's the kind of longing the psalmist uses to describe the soul's need for God.**

And if you've ever felt spiritually dry, emotionally worn out, or disconnected from the Lord's presence, you know exactly what that feels like.

The deer isn't desperate because it's weak. It's desperate because it knows where its strength comes from. In the same way, your hunger for God isn't a sign of failure. It's a sign of life. Your soul remembers where it came from, and it knows what it needs to thrive.

We live in a world that offers all kinds of things to fill the emptiness. Noise. Numbness. Distraction. But just like a deer doesn't drink from muddy puddles, your soul was never meant to settle for substitutes. You were made for living water. For presence that restores. For peace that doesn't depend on circumstances.

Sometimes that longing feels heavy. You may not always have words for it. You may just feel tired, or restless, or like something's missing. That's okay. God understands that language too. The sigh. The silence. The ache. He meets you there.

When the deer finally finds water, it doesn't question if it's worthy to drink. It just drinks. And so can you.

Let this verse be your reminder: God welcomes your longing. He's not intimidated by your thirst. He's not disappointed that you're in need. In fact, Jesus delights in filling the empty places. His presence is your stream. His Word is your refreshment. His nearness is what your soul has been searching for all along.

So come thirsty. Come honest. And trust that God is already drawing near.

Today's Verse:
"You, God, are my God, earnestly I seek you; I thirst for you, my whole being longs for you."
—Psalm 63:1

WHEN GOD WANTS YOUR ATTENTION

"I run in the path of your commands, for you have set my heart free."

Psalm 119:32

Sometimes God whispers. Other times, He speaks through circumstances, conversations, or even dreams—especially when we're too busy to listen any other way.

A few weeks ago, my life felt full but unfocused. I was juggling interviews, travel, a few dates, and managing a busy schedule that looked "good" on the outside. But my soul was restless. I hadn't been as still before the Lord as I needed to be, and in His kindness, He met me in a dream.

In the dream, I was speeding along a mountain road and lost control, flying off the edge of a cliff. As the car flipped and fell, I didn't feel fear or pain—only one strange thought echoed in my mind: *Someone is going to read my journals.* As the dream shifted, I began rising toward Heaven. The clouds opened, light poured through, and God's presence felt near and real. But before I reached the top, I woke up.

That dream stayed with me. I knew it was God nudging me to slow down and realign. So I wrote it down and prayed: "Speak, Lord. I'm listening."

Later that same day, I met a man named Sam. He was in a wheelchair, and we struck up a conversation. It turned out he writes devotional books too. Before we parted ways, he told me, "I asked God this morning to let me encourage someone today—and that person was you." His words brought me to tears. It was confirmation that God had been speaking, and I needed to listen.

That night, I read Psalm 119:32: "*I run in the path of your commands, for you have set my heart free.*" It brought everything into focus. I'd been running, yes—but not in the freedom of His direction. God was inviting me back, not to restrict me, but to free me.

Now, as I write this devotional, that moment in the dream makes even more sense. The journals I once thought were just private reflections have become tools God is using to encourage others. He was showing me that none of it—none of the quiet pages or personal prayers—was wasted. It was preparation.

If you've had a dream that lingers, or a moment that tugged at your spirit, don't dismiss it. Write it down. Pray over it. Ask God to reveal His purpose. Sometimes the meaning unfolds slowly—but when it does, it can change everything.

Today's Verse:

"*For God does speak—now one way, now another—though no one perceives it. In a dream, in a vision of the night, when deep sleep falls on people as they slumber in their beds.*"
—Job 33:14-15

BLOOM WHERE HE PLANTS YOU

"For we are his workmanship, created in Christ Jesus for good works, which God prepared beforehand, that we should walk in them."

Ephesians 2:10

Lately, I've been walking alongside my friend Sarah as she navigates a draining season in her life. She's in a job that wears her down emotionally and spiritually. Each day chips away at her confidence, and she no longer finds meaning in the work she once hoped would fulfill her. It's not about having a more positive attitude—she's simply planted in the wrong soil.

One day she admitted, "I don't fully trust God." That level of honesty is rare, and I encouraged her to bring that exact feeling to Him in prayer. "Ask Him why," I said. Because trust is the foundation. If we don't trust the One who made us, we'll never feel safe enough to follow Him into the unknown.

To help her visualize this, I shared a memory from my childhood. I grew up on a gravel road in southeastern Minnesota, and my sister loved planting flowers. But no matter how much she wanted beauty along that dusty path, petunias wouldn't grow in the middle of the gravel. The soil wasn't meant for it. Instead, she planted them closer to the house where the soil was rich and the sun reached every bloom. Those flowers thrived, not because of the flowers themselves—but because of where they were planted.

In the same way, if you're in the wrong environment—emotionally, spiritually, relationally—you will not thrive. You might survive, but you won't bloom. Some of us are like Sarah, stuck in soil God never intended for us, holding onto what feels safe while drowning in discouragement. It's like being lost at sea with the Coast Guard circling and throwing life preservers—yet we keep refusing the rescue because fear whispers, "You'll sink if you let go."

But here's the truth: *you were created for good works*. God prepared them ahead of time, specifically for you. When we allow Him to replant us—when we say yes to His guidance—He gives us everything we need to thrive. Not just survive. The Holy Spirit is faithful to whisper when it's time to move, time to stay, or time to stretch toward the light.

Let God move you. Let Him grow you. Trust that where He plants you, you'll bloom.

Today's Verse:

"That person is like a tree planted by streams of water, which yields its fruit in season and whose leaf does not wither —whatever they do prospers."
—Psalm 1:3

GOD KNOWS, GOD HEALS

Then Peter came up and said to Him, 'Lord, how many times shall my brother sin against me and I still forgive him? Up to seven times?' Jesus said to him, 'I do not say to you, up to seven times, but up to seventy-seven times.'

Matthew 18:21–22

One afternoon at the gym, I noticed a woman sitting in the sauna with a book titled *God Knows*. I felt a gentle prompting from the Holy Spirit to ask her about it. That one question opened the door to a beautiful, Spirit-led conversation.

As we sat there, I began sharing parts of my journey—the times when God saved me, sustained me, and built something beautiful from the ashes. I talked about how He rescued me from an abusive relationship, helped me start a business from scratch, walked with me through grief, and gave me strength to pass my RDN exam. Each story came with its own pain, but also a purpose. And through every chapter, God remained faithful.

The woman, a former teacher and mother, began to tear up. She shared that the central message of the book she was reading was simple but powerful: *God knows.* He knows what happened. He knows how deeply it hurt. And He's not asking us to pretend it didn't. He's asking us to trust Him with it.

I'll be honest—there were times when I wanted revenge. Times when I held on to bitterness and hoped the people who hurt me would feel it. But that's not the way of Christ. When we choose to forgive, we're not excusing the wrong; we're handing it over to the only One who can truly judge righteously.

Forgiveness is one of the hardest things God asks of us, but it's also one of the most freeing. We don't forgive because people deserve it—we forgive because *we've been forgiven.* Jesus didn't say to stop forgiving after seven tries. He told Peter to forgive *seventy-seven* times, which was His way of saying: keep going. Keep letting go. Keep trusting God with what hurts.

So if you're carrying something today—a betrayal, a harsh word, an old wound—know this: God sees it. He knows. He hears your cry. And He will bring justice in His perfect time. Forgiveness isn't weakness. It's strength. And it's how you'll find peace again.

Today's Verse:
"Father, forgive them, for they do not know
what they are doing."
—Luke 23:34

REACH FOR THE HEM

"Just then a woman who had been subject to bleeding for twelve years came up behind him and touched the edge of his cloak. She said to herself, 'If I only touch his cloak, I will be healed.'"
Matthew 9:20–21

Imagine carrying an invisible burden for over a decade—twelve years of pain, rejection, and isolation. That was the reality for the woman in Matthew 9.

She had a condition that caused her to bleed continuously, and according to Jewish law, this made her ceremonially unclean. It meant she couldn't go to the temple. She couldn't be touched. She couldn't be part of regular community life. She was seen as contaminated. Every relationship, every interaction, was marked by distance.

She went to doctors, but nothing worked. Her body remained broken, and her hope began to fade. Yet when she heard that Jesus was passing through her town, something stirred in her spirit. It was risky, even dangerous, for her to be in a crowd. She wasn't supposed to be there. But she had one goal: to get close enough to touch Him. Not His hand, not His face—just the edge of His garment.

She believed that would be enough. That's the kind of faith that stirs Jesus.

Can you imagine the desperation in that moment? The crowd pressed in. She reached forward, maybe crawling, heart pounding. And then—contact. Immediately, her bleeding stopped. Her body felt whole again. But more than that, Jesus noticed. He stopped. He turned. He called her *daughter.*

This is the only time in the Gospels Jesus uses that word to address someone personally. It happened right in front of the very crowd that once shunned her. Jesus restored not only her health, but her dignity. *Her identity.*

This story is for every person who's ever felt unseen, unworthy, or unclean. Maybe you're carrying something—shame, sickness, trauma—that's caused you to withdraw. Maybe you've been suffering quietly for a long time. Jesus sees you. He knows your story. And even the smallest reach of faith moves His heart.

Let this be your action step this week: Is there an area of your life where you need healing? Be honest with God. Reach for Him in your weakness. Whisper a prayer, open your Bible, ask a friend to pray with you. You don't need to have it all together—you just need to reach. He'll meet you there.

Today's Verse:
"He heals the brokenhearted and binds up their wounds."
—Psalm 147:3

STAY FAITHFUL IN THE PROCESS

"You need to persevere so that when you have done the will of God, you will receive what he has promised."
Hebrews 10:36

So often, people get discouraged when success doesn't come overnight. The truth is, good things take time—and great things take even longer. It took over a decade of showing up, adding value, and building relationships for me to gain trust among families, athletes, and clients. I didn't get here because of one viral moment or one lucky break. It's been years of sowing seeds and staying faithful, even when I didn't see immediate fruit.

People sometimes ask, *"How did you grow your platform? How did you start speaking and getting opportunities?"* And while I'm humbled by the question, the honest answer is simple: consistent, authentic work. Trusting God. Serving when no one clapped. Saying yes to assignments that didn't have a spotlight. Over and over again, I've had to remember it's not about being seen—it's about being obedient.

And yes, it's hard. The enemy will try everything to wear you out, especially when you're walking in purpose. He'll send distractions, discouragement, and delay to get you to stop short of the finish. But you can't stop. You were never meant to carry it all—Jesus is your strength.

When the thoughts come—"*Is this even worth it?*" or "*Am I making a difference?*"—go back to the Word. Fill your mind with what is true. You are called. You are anointed. And God is not finished with you.

I've learned that the work I do only bears real fruit when I keep my heart rooted in Christ. The second it becomes about me, the joy fades. But when it's about Him—His glory, His people, His timing—the peace stays, no matter what the outcome looks like.

It's not about climbing a ladder. It's about building the Kingdom. Stay faithful. Keep trusting. And believe that the same God who called you will complete the good work He started in you.

Today's Verse:
"Commit your work to the Lord,
and your plans will be established."
—Proverbs 16:3

FAMILY WE CHOOSE

*"'Who are my mother and my brothers?' Jesus asked.
Then he looked at those seated in a circle around
him and said, 'Here are my mother and my brothers!
Whoever does God's will is my brother and sister and
mother.'"*

Mark 3:33–35

There's a special saying I often share with my friends, clients, athletes, and those in my social community: 'Family we choose.' While we can't choose our biological family, we can choose the people we surround ourselves with.

That truth carries deep meaning for anyone who has experienced loss, hurt, or disconnection from their blood relatives. I can relate.

Even now, some of my relationships with family members aren't as close as I wish they were. Distance, choices, and beliefs have created space—and yes, I carry my share of that responsibility. But what a gift it is to focus on the people who do choose to show up, rather than grieving those who don't.

It's easy to feel the sting of being overlooked by family while being cheered on by friends, clients, or even strangers. I've felt that ache. But I've also learned that God fills in the gaps. He places people in our lives on purpose—people who support, love, and speak life into us. One of my clients, who has become like family, reminds me of this constantly. Though I've helped her with her health journey, she's poured encouragement right back into mine.

Jesus had a lot to say about family. His earthly father, Joseph, most likely died while Jesus was still young. Some of His own siblings didn't believe in Him during His early ministry. And yet, later, His brother James would become a key leader in the early church. Jesus also taught that whoever does the will of God is His true family. He wasn't rejecting His birth family—He was expanding the definition of what true, eternal family looks like.

Families shift. Some fade. Some hurt. **But God remains.** He calls us His own, and He never walks away. When earthly relationships fall short, God reminds us: you belong.

So don't dwell on the ones who aren't showing up. Celebrate the ones who are. God knows what your heart needs, and He's already placed people in your life who reflect His love. And most of all, He has made you part of His eternal family.

Today's Verse:

"Both the one who makes people holy and those who are made holy are of the same family. So Jesus is not ashamed to call them brothers and sisters."

—Hebrews 2:11

ARE YOU LISTENING?

"I will listen to what God the Lord says; he promises peace to his people, his faithful servants—but let them not turn to folly."

Psalm 85:8

When I was preparing my move to Texas, I found myself in a familiar routine—selling my things, saying **goodbye, and getting ready to start over.** It's a bittersweet rhythm. Building a life in a new place has become more familiar than staying put. As I packed, I couldn't help but reflect on how different my life looks from what I once imagined. At 34, I don't have the husband, home, or family I thought I would by now. But God has given me something far better—opportunities to serve Him, grow deeper in faith, and follow His voice. His plans always exceed our own, even when they don't look like what we expected.

One of my favorite quotes by C.S. Lewis says, *"You are never too old to set another goal or to dream a new dream."* I launched my business at 29, and at the time, I felt too young and unqualified. People told me to wait. Looking back, I actually wish I had started even earlier. God doesn't operate on our timelines. His call comes when we're willing, not when we feel ready.

If you're reading this and wondering why God feels silent, let me reassure you—He's not. He never stops speaking. Sometimes we're just not listening. I've learned this firsthand. When I prayed for direction about moving to Tennessee, I asked God to make it clear. The answer came through a car with Nashville plates that nearly hit me. When I asked for confirmation about moving to Texas, I prayed to see a plate with specific letters. And I did. Not once, but clearly, unmistakably.

Just last night, I sold my swivel chairs to a sweet local couple. They asked why I was selling such beautiful pieces, and that opened the door for me to share my testimony about why I'm moving. That ordinary interaction became a moment of ministry. Their faith was strengthened, and so was mine. God is always working—and always speaking. The question is, are we tuned in?

God doesn't always shout. Sometimes, He speaks through whispers, through people, through unexpected moments, or quiet nudges. But He is never silent. Scripture is full of examples: He spoke through burning bushes, angels, dreams, even a donkey. And today, He still speaks—to you and to me.

So if you're feeling disconnected, take a deep breath. Turn off the noise. Step away from the distractions. He's waiting to meet with you, to guide you, and to give you the peace He promised.

Today's Verse:
"Whether you turn to the right or to the left, your ears will hear a voice behind you, saying, 'This is the way; walk in it.'"
—Isaiah 30:21

RAISING THE NEXT GENERATION

"Train up a child in the way he should go; even when he is old, he will not depart from it."

Proverbs 22:6

This morning, I received an email from a single dad—let's call him Michael—asking for help with his son, James. James is a 16-year-old high school sophomore with a big dream of playing collegiate football. Michael shared how he's doing everything he can to help James gain weight and stay healthy, even while navigating the challenges that come with ADHD medication. His message wasn't just about nutrition—it was full of love, hope, and a father's deep desire to see his son succeed.

What moved me most was Michael's humility. He wasn't afraid to ask for help. His heart was wide open—not just for advice, but for encouragement, for someone to come alongside him. And in that moment, I sensed God speaking.

Michael's story is a powerful reminder that we're not alone in raising the next generation. Whether you're a parent, coach, mentor, teacher, or friend, you've likely felt the weight of trying to get it all right. You want to equip those you love with every tool they need to thrive in life and in faith. But the truth is—we're not meant to do it on our own.

Just like Michael is showing up for his son, God shows up for us. He gives us His Word to guide us, His Spirit to comfort us, and His wisdom when we feel like we're in over our heads. He is the ultimate Provider, and He loves our children even more than we do.

So if you're in a season where you're pouring into someone else—whether it's your child, a student, a mentee, or a team-mate—take heart. God sees your efforts. He honors your prayers. And He promises to fill in every gap with His grace. You don't have to have all the answers. You just have to be willing, and God will do the rest.

Today's Verse:

"He tends his flock like a shepherd: He gathers the lambs in his arms and carries them close to his heart; he gently leads those that have young."

—Isaiah 40:11

STAY CLOSE TO THE SHEPHERD

"I am the good shepherd. I know my sheep and my sheep know me."

John 10:14

There's something sacred about being truly known and still deeply loved. No pretending. No striving. No need to perform. That's what Jesus offers us as the Good Shepherd. He doesn't just lead us. He *knows* us.

In the original Greek, the word "know" speaks of *deep, experiential knowledge*. This isn't surface-level awareness. It's intimate, personal, and rooted in relationship. Jesus knows every part of you including your patterns, fears, failures and dreams. He knows the thoughts you don't say out loud. He knows when your faith feels strong and when you're just barely hanging on.

And still, He chooses to stay close.

Sheep, by nature, are vulnerable. They wander without realizing it. They're easily startled. They need a guide. That's not a weakness—it's a design. And spiritually, we're no different. We all drift at times. We get caught in comparison, tangled in worry, or numbed by distraction. But Jesus isn't surprised by our tendency to stray. He came *because* of it.

As our Shepherd, He doesn't lead from a distance. He walks among us. He calls us by name. His voice is calm, clear, and trustworthy. When God speaks, it's not to shame—it's to steady. He draws near not with a list of demands, but with an invitation: *Come close. Rest here. I know you.*

You don't have to clean yourself up to come back. You don't need to fix everything before He'll receive you. His presence is not a prize for the perfected. It's a refuge for the weary. That means you can come exactly as you are—confused, discouraged, hopeful, hungry—and He'll meet you right there.

Today, maybe your heart has been running. Maybe life feels scattered, noisy, or heavy. But Jesus hasn't moved. He's still right where you left Him, gently calling you back—not to add more to your plate, but to remind you: *You belong to Me.*

You don't need all the answers to walk closely with Him. Just a willing heart. Just a quiet, honest prayer: *"Jesus, I want to know You more."*

And the Good Shepherd will always answer.

Today's Verse:
"The Lord is my shepherd, I lack nothing."
—Psalm 23:1

THE SHIFT INTO JOY

*"You turned my mourning into dancing;
you removed my sackcloth and clothed me with
joy."*

Psalm 30:11

Sometimes we don't realize the season of sorrow has ended until joy quietly slips back in. You laugh at something small, and it surprises you. The tears that used to come daily begin to slow. You find yourself waking up with hope again, even if just a flicker. These are signs that the weight is lifting and the Lord is shifting your season.

Sorrow doesn't always exit loudly. More often, it fades gently, as the presence of God begins to warm places in your heart that had gone cold. Where heaviness once sat, peace begins to take root. It's not that the pain never happened—it's that God, in His faithfulness, has been working behind the scenes to heal what you couldn't.

You may start to feel a desire to dream again, to plan, to engage with life in ways you couldn't before. That's the Spirit's way of telling you, *"The old has passed, and I'm doing something new."* You'll know you're stepping into a new season when what used to break you no longer defines you. The grief loses its grip. The light returns.

If this is you, take a deep breath and thank God. The season of sorrow served its purpose, but it's not where your story ends. Let yourself dance again, hope again, and believe again. God has turned the page, and what's ahead is filled with promise.

Three Signs The Season of Mourning Is Lifting

1. Joy begins to return in small, surprising ways.
You find yourself laughing again—maybe at something simple, maybe without even realizing it. A smile comes easier. Peace slips in during a quiet moment. These small sparks of joy are gentle signs that the sadness is no longer holding center stage, and that the Holy Spirit is renewing your heart from the inside out.

2. What once overwhelmed you now feels lighter.
The memories haven't vanished, but they've lost their grip. You're no longer constantly defined by what happened. The heaviness is lifting, and you're able to breathe deeper. Grief doesn't vanish overnight, but grace softens its edges.

3. You begin to feel hopeful about the future again.
You catch yourself wanting to plan, to create, to show up for life in a new way. You're open to new possibilities—even if they feel fragile. That desire to dream again? It's a holy signpost that God is leading you into something new.

Today's Verse:
"Weeping may stay for the night,
but rejoicing comes in the morning."
—Psalm 30:5

JUST SAY YES

"When the time is right, I, the Lord, will make it happen."

Isaiah 60:22

As we come to the final weeks of this devotional journey, I want to share something honest with you—I was scared to do this. I worried my theology wouldn't be perfect. I feared being misunderstood. I wrestled with the vulnerability of sharing my story, opening my heart only to risk silence or judgment. But underneath every fear, there was one simple prayer that kept rising: *"Lord, I just want to serve You."*

That prayer became my anchor. Even when the words felt heavy. Even when doubt tried to paralyze me. What started as a shaky step of obedience became one of the most intimate and humbling walks with Jesus I've ever experienced.

Isaiah 60:22 carried me through the uncertain days: **"When the time is right, I, the Lord, will make it happen."** Over and over, God whispered that promise into my heart—especially when I wrestled with delays, blank pages, software issues and timelines that didn't unfold the way I imagined. His timing is never off. Jesus doesn't rush. He doesn't forget. And He *certainly* doesn't waste anything.

There were days I sat in front of a blank page, unsure if anything would come. But somehow, God always met me there. It's not because I had it all figured out—but because I was *willing*. And that's the beautiful thing about walking with Jesus: **God doesn't ask for perfection—He asks for surrender.** If you're willing to just try and take one step of faith even when afraid, the Lord will meet you with His strength.

The Holy Spirit will breathe on what you offer and turn even your shaky efforts into something beautiful.

I may not have gotten every word exactly right. I might have missed a few spacing issues or left a random period here or there. My theology is still growing. But I showed up—*with trembling hands, an open heart, and trust that God would do what I couldn't.* I trusted Jesus with the story, and I trusted Him with you. And I pray that somewhere along the way, these pages have helped you feel seen, known, and loved by a God who writes the most powerful stories through the most unlikely people.

So when God places something on your heart—don't wait until you feel ready. Don't wait until you have it all figured out. **Just try.** Say yes with what you have. Because God loves to take small beginnings and turn them into something far greater than we could ever imagine.

Today's Verse:
"The Lord makes firm the steps of the one who delights in him; though he may stumble, he will not fall, for the Lord upholds him with his hand."
—Psalm 37:23–24

RUN LIKE IT MATTERS

> *"Therefore I do not run like someone running aim-lessly; I do not fight like a boxer beating the air. No, I strike a blow to my body and make it my slave so that after I have preached to others, I myself will not be disqualified for the prize."*
>
> 1 Corinthians 9:26-27

There comes a moment when you realize you're not just meant to drift—you're meant to RUN!

Not half-hearted. Not distracted. Not unsure. But with clarity, with focus, and with Heaven's purpose in your stride. That's what Paul is getting at in this verse. He's saying: I'm not shadowboxing. I'm not wasting time swinging at the air. I know what I'm fighting for. I know WHO I'm running toward!

Maybe lately, you've been feeling spiritually tired or scattered. Maybe it's been hard to stay consistent or motivated. That's okay. You're not alone in that. But this is your invitation to pause, reset, and realign with what truly matters. God never called you to run in circles. He called you to run with **vision**.

We live in a world that promotes hustle without purpose—busy schedules, endless striving, constant noise. But the Kingdom of God is built differently. The Holy Spirit trains us to live with

intention. We have to show up when it's hard. To keep pressing forward, even when no one else sees the cost.

Discipline isn't a punishment—it's a gift. It's how God grows us into people who can carry His promises well. That might mean getting up a little earlier to sit with Jesus. Or saying no to what looks flashy so you can say yes to what's faithful. It might look like rest when the world says grind, or obedience when it doesn't make sense yet.

Paul didn't run for applause or platform. He ran to stay close to Jesus. He's the only PRIZE that truly matters!

So here's the fresh word today: Stop running aimlessly. Stop swinging at shadows. Start living like the Holy Spirit is coaching your every move as you run into the arms of your Savior! Now *that's* **a life worth living.** ▫

Today's Verse:
"And let us run with endurance the race God has set before us. We do this by keeping our eyes on Jesus, the champion who initiates and perfects our faith."
—Hebrews 12:1-2

WALKING IN RESPECTED POWER

"No one else dared join them, even though they were highly regarded by the people."

Acts 5:13

There was a holy awe resting on the early church—do you carry that kind of weight?

Imagine this: the early believers in Acts were so full of the Holy Spirit, so set apart in their walk with Jesus, *that no one dared treat them casually*. These weren't just people who attended a weekly gathering. These were vessels of POWER!

Miracles were happening. The presence of God was so real that even those outside the faith held them in high regard. Reverence and honor surrounded them—not because they demanded it, **but because of the way God marked their lives.**

Acts 5 paints a picture of a church walking in purity and fear of the Lord. The chapter begins with Ananias and Sapphira dropping dead after lying to the Holy Spirit. This wasn't just about dishonesty—it was about the sacredness of what God was building. The fear of the Lord spread, and people started to see that this was no ordinary gathering. **These were people who had been with Jesus.**

What would it look like if our lives carried that same kind of weight today? Not fear that drives people away, but a holy reverence that draws people to God through the purity, love, and truth that shines from our lives?

The early church wasn't trying to be famous. *They were trying to be faithful.* Their integrity made them *influential.* They walked in power, but also *humility.* They were approachable in love, but *unshakable in character.* And that combination made the world pay attention.

So here's the challenge: live in such a way that your life demands a question. Let your decisions, your purity, your peace, and your pursuit of God speak for themselves. You don't need to shout to be heard. The fruit of your life will speak volumes.

You are called to be set apart—not to be strange, but to be sacred. When you walk closely with the Holy Spirit, people notice. And when they do, it's not you they admire—**it's Jesus in you.**

Today's Verse:
"In the same way, let your light shine before others, that they may see your good deeds and glorify your Father in heaven."
—Matthew 5:16

YOU MIGHT BE GLOWING TOO

"Arise, shine, for your light has come, and the glory of the Lord rises upon you."

Isaiah 60:1

As I reached the final pages of writing this book, something unexpected began happening—people started telling me I looked different.

"You're glowing," they'd say. At first, it caught me off guard. I figured it was just a kind compliment, but after hearing it again and again, I paused and asked the Lord, "Is this You?" And I believe it was. Not a glow from makeup or sunshine—but something deeper. A spiritual glow that only comes from spending time with Jesus.

Psalm 34:5 says, *"Those who look to Him are radiant."* When you walk closely with God—through fire, tears, steps of faith, and long seasons of waiting—you begin to carry something. His peace. His joy. His light. You may not even realize it, but others can sense it.

As this writing journey came to a close, I stepped into a brand-new season. I moved to Dallas. It's unfamiliar and stretching, but I know I'm where God wants me—for now. I've been meeting new people, settling into a new rhythm, and watching God unfold the next chapter.

My business is blooming in ways only He could orchestrate. And something else beautiful was born out of this obedience—my nonprofit organization, **Devotions With Wendi**, was officially established. What started as a simple desire to write for the Lord has become a growing ministry. I don't share any of this to boast. I share it to glorify **JESUS**. If you've followed my story, you know He's pulled me out of the gutter more times than I can count. And while I often write about the hard stuff, today I want to celebrate the *good*. Because God deserves our praise in both the breaking and the building.

I doubted. I wrestled. I didn't always feel qualified to write a book. But I said yes. I wasn't chasing perfection—I was chasing Jesus. And maybe that's where the glow comes from. Not from striving, but from surrender. Not from having it all together, but from staying close to the One who holds it all.

So if someone tells you you're glowing—believe them. You've been in the presence of the King. And it shows.

Today's Verse:
"Those who look to him are radiant; their faces are never covered with shame."
—Psalm 34:5

JESUS CARES FOR YOU

"Praise be to the Lord, to God our Savior, who daily bears our burdens."

Psalm 68:19

There are some weights we were never meant to carry. Maybe you're trying to hold it all together—keeping up with work, showing up for family, managing the endless to-do lists—but deep down, you're exhausted. Not just physically tired. Tired in your soul.

God sees it. He knows the weight you're carrying, even the parts you don't talk about. And He's not standing there shaking His head in disappointment—He's inviting you to let Him carry it with you.

Sometimes we carry burdens that were never ours to bear. We try to fix everything, help everyone, control outcomes, or hold pain that God's been asking us to lay down. We say we trust Him, but we live like everything depends on us. No wonder we feel drained. You were never designed to do life on your own strength.

Psalm 55:22 says, *"Cast your cares on the Lord and He will sustain you."* Not just tell Jesus about your stress. Not just pray once and take it back. *Cast it*—literally throw it into His hands. Drop the weight you were never meant to hold.

If you've been quietly trying to be strong for everyone around you, here's your permission to stop. You don't have to carry everything. You don't have to prove you're strong enough. You don't have to earn the right to rest. God's shoulders are bigger than yours, and His love for you is not based on your performance.

Take a moment right now and ask Him, "God, *what am I carrying that You never asked me to?*" Sit quietly with that. Let Him show you. Maybe it's fear about the future. Maybe it's shame from your past. Maybe it's pressure you've put on yourself to be perfect. Whatever it is, you don't have to keep dragging it behind you. Jesus is strong enough to carry it—and He's willing.

You are not weak for needing help. You are human. And the good news is, God's power shows up best not when we're crushing it, but when we're willing to say, "*I can't do this alone.*"

Today's Verse:
"Cast all your anxiety on Him because He cares for you."
—1 Peter 5:7

YOUR TEARS MATTER

"You keep track of all my sorrows. You have collected all my tears in your bottle. You have recorded each one in your book."

Psalm 56:8

Tears are not weakness—they're worship. Crying is one of the most sacred, healing responses God created. Whether they come from sorrow, joy, or something in between, your tears matter to Him.

Psalm 56:8 shows us that God doesn't just notice your tears—He collects them. Every drop carries meaning, and not one is wasted in His presence.

Even Jesus cried. He wept at the tomb of Lazarus, and again over Jerusalem's spiritual blindness. He wasn't ashamed of His emotion; it was His compassion in motion. If the Son of God could cry, you can too. In fact, you're invited to.

Jeremiah, the "weeping prophet," poured out tears over a rebellious nation. His weeping was intercession—grief that turned into prayer. Like Jeremiah, your tears can become prayers when you don't have the words. They express what your heart can't say out loud.

But what if you've stopped crying? Emotional numbness is real. Sometimes we've held it together for too long, and our bodies shut down to protect us. Or we've learned to suppress pain so well that we can't feel it anymore. If that's you, be gentle with yourself. God knows. He understands even the tears you haven't cried yet.

Instead of forcing emotion, invite God into it. Ask Him to reveal what you've buried. Journal, sit in stillness, worship, or talk to someone safe. Often, tears return when we stop running and start listening. And if they don't come just yet, that's okay too. God still sees your heart.

The beautiful truth? Tears are a form of surrender. When we cry, we release control. We tell God, "This is too much for me—but not for You." And in return, He promises to restore. The Bible says those who sow with tears will reap with joy (Psalm 126:5). That means your grief today can become your joy tomorrow.

You don't have to hide your tears. Let them fall freely into the hands of the One who holds you.

Today's Verse:
"Those who sow with tears will reap with songs of joy."
—Psalm 126:5

KEEP GOING!

"Therefore, since we are surrounded by such a great cloud of witnesses, let us throw off everything that hinders and the sin that so easily entangles. And let us run with perseverance the race marked out for us."

Hebrews 12:1

YOU ARE NOT RUNNING ALONE! There are moments in this journey when you feel weary—like no one sees your quiet obedience, your daily battles, your faith when it's hard. But Scripture reminds us that we are not running this race unseen.

There is a great cloud of witnesses surrounding you, cheering you on! Saints who have gone before you. Heroes of the faith who endured hardships, heartbreak, prison cells, and rejection—yet stayed the course! And now, they're watching you, urging you to press on!

Think of Abraham, who waited decades to see God's promise fulfilled. Moses, who left behind comfort to lead a stubborn people. Esther, who risked her life to save her people. And of course, Jesus, who endured the cross because of the joy set before Him. You are part of their story now. They're not watching to judge. They're watching with fire in their eyes, cheering, *"Don't give up! You're almost there! This race is worth it!"*

It's easy to feel isolated in your faith. But you are connected to something eternal, something bigger. Heaven leans in when you choose forgiveness. Angels rejoice when you say yes to God. And the cloud of witnesses? They are clapping for you like the finish line is in sight!

So throw off what's been weighing you down. Lay aside the sin that trips you up. Stop looking side to side and lock your eyes on Jesus, the author and perfecter of your faith. Run with renewed strength, knowing you are cheered on, upheld, and empowered.

This isn't just about you—**it's about the Kingdom.** It's about generations yet to come who will walk freer because you chose to keep going.

You're not alone. Heaven is watching. And Heaven is cheering!

Today's Verse:
*"Let us not grow weary in doing good, for at the proper time
we will reap a harvest if we do not give up."*
—Galatians 6:9

FAITH IN THE TRANSITION

"I have been constantly on the move. I have been in danger from rivers, in danger from bandits, in danger from my fellow Jews, in danger from Gentiles; in danger in the city, in danger in the country, in danger at sea; and in danger from false believers."

2 Corinthians 11:26

One day I sat in my favorite Nashville coffee shop, reflecting on what God was asking of me.

I was preparing to leave a beloved Christian community that had become my home. The friendships, Bible studies, and small comforts of routine had filled a season with warmth and growth. Yet, God was clearly closing that chapter and writing a new one. As I stared into my cup of coffee, I felt both grief and anticipation swirling in my heart. If you're facing a similar moment—a shift in job, relationship, calling, or city—know this: you are not alone. Transitions are rarely easy, but they are often sacred.

Leaving something meaningful can feel like a loss. But endings often make room for beginnings. God doesn't ask us to leap blindly—He asks us to trust Him one step at a time. He knows the new place, the new people, the growth that awaits. He is already there, preparing the way.

I've moved more than 40 times. I used to think something was wrong with me because I never quite settled. But I've learned that sometimes God asks us to move—not just physically, but spiritually. To let go of what's comfortable. To release what's good for what's better. And every time I've surrendered, even if reluctantly, God has met me there. He has shown me that my "settled" isn't tied to a zip code—it's tied to Him.

Paul understood this better than most. In 2 Corinthians 11, he recounts his trials—not to gain pity but to show how relentless obedience to God often comes with resistance. He was always on the move, rarely comfortable, but fully rooted in his purpose. Through hardship and danger, Paul remained faithful. He reminds us that even when the path is rocky, God never asks us to walk it alone.

If you're in a season of transition, trust that God has already gone before you. Like a gardener pruning for greater growth, He is shaping you for what's ahead. Don't cling to what was. Instead, open your hands to what's next.

Today's Verse:
*"If I must boast, I will boast of
the things that show my weakness."*
—2 Corinthians 11:30

KNOW YOUR ARMOR

"Then Saul dressed David in his own tunic. He put a coat of armor on him and a bronze helmet on his head... 'I cannot go in these,' he said to Saul, 'because I am not used to them.' So he took them off."

1 Samuel 17:38–39

You don't need someone else's armor to walk into your calling. In fact, trying to wear what was never meant for you will only slow you down.

When David stepped onto the battlefield to face Goliath, King Saul offered him his royal armor. It looked impressive—shiny, heavy, battle-worn. But David had never trained in it. It didn't fit him. It restricted him. And he wasn't called to fight like Saul—he was called to fight like David. So he took it off.

Instead of what looked strong, David chose what was strong for him. He picked up five smooth stones and his sling—the tools that had served him well in secret places when no one was watching. The same God who delivered him from the lion and the bear would now deliver him from the giant.

Maybe you've been tempted to wear someone else's armor. You admire their platform, their style, their voice, their pace. But the truth is, God didn't call you to be them—He called you to be *you*. When you know who you are in Christ and operate in the gifts

He has given you, you move with power and precision. You are not less spiritual because your walk looks different. You are not behind because your process doesn't match theirs.

In your workplace, relationships, ministry, or business—don't mimic what worked for someone else just because it's popular. Ask the Lord, "What fits *me*?" Because the armor that fits will free you. It will make you agile, effective, and powerful in the hands of the Living God.

David's story reminds us that the victory doesn't come from appearances, credentials, or borrowed strategies. It comes from knowing your God, knowing your weapons, and walking confidently in what He has entrusted to *you.*

Today's Verse:
"Not by might nor by power, but by my Spirit,'
says the Lord Almighty."
—Zechariah 4:6

CAST IT ON THE RIGHT SIDE

"He said, 'Throw your net on the right side of the boat and you will find some.' When they did, they were unable to haul the net in because of the large number of fish."

John 21:6

After a long night of fishing, the disciples caught nothing. These weren't amateurs—they were professional fishermen. They knew the waters, the rhythms, the right techniques. But still—nothing. Empty nets. Empty hands. Maybe even some empty hearts.

Then Jesus appeared on the shore, unrecognized at first, and gave them an unusual instruction: *"Throw your net on the right side of the boat."* It seemed almost too simple, even strange. The right side? What difference would a few feet make? But they obeyed. And in that moment of simple obedience, everything changed. The net was so full they couldn't even haul it in.

There's a powerful truth here: when Jesus gives you a right-side instruction, it might not make logical sense—but it always carries supernatural results.

Sometimes we're like the disciples—working tirelessly, doing what we know, and still coming up empty. We think we've exhausted every option. But Jesus isn't asking for hustle; He's asking for surrender. He's not saying, "Try harder." He's saying, "Listen closely."

Has the Lord been prompting you lately with a subtle shift? Maybe He's asking you to speak to someone you've avoided. To apply for that position one more time. To start the ministry. To let go of what's been weighing you down.

Your "right side" might not be about direction—it might be about trust. It might be one step of obedience that unlocks provision, clarity, or breakthrough. The disciples had to pivot. So do we. The miracle wasn't in their strategy—it was in their sensitivity to His *voice*. Today, ask God this simple question: "Lord, what is my right side?"

Be open. He may show you a small adjustment that brings a supernatural shift. The difference might only be a few feet—but when Jesus is in it, it's the difference between empty and overflow.

Today's Verse:

"Blessed are those who listen to me, watching daily at my doors, waiting at my doorway."
—Proverbs 8:34

TRAINED THROUGH TRIAL

"No discipline seems pleasant at the time, but painful. Later on, however, it produces a harvest of righteousness and peace for those who have been trained by it."
Hebrews 12:11

When I think back to packing up my tiny apartment in Nashville before moving to Dallas, I can't help but smile at God's goodness. That old 500-square-foot space wasn't much—but it was my launching pad. It kept me grounded and focused as I worked tirelessly to grow my business and improve my financial situation.

Over the past few years, I've paid off over $80,000 in student loan debt—all while living in less-than-ideal conditions: no washer or dryer, an oven that couldn't fully open, and crime just outside my door. But that little apartment was a place of purpose. Now, here in Dallas, I can open my oven without hitting the fridge. It may seem small, but it feels like a luxury—a sign of answered prayer.

I want to share the wisdom God gave me along the way, in case you're walking through your own financial mountain. These were the steps I took, and I pray they help you, too:

Know where your money is going. Make a clear, honest budget. Track your expenses and assign every dollar a purpose.

Start small. Don't be overwhelmed by the big number. Focus on one debt at a time, even if the progress feels slow.

Live beneath your means. I skipped vacations, dining out, and unnecessary purchases. I hustled, saved, and trusted that the Lord would bless my discipline—and He did!

Sell what you don't need. I sold extra clothes and chose not to buy a TV or new furniture. I kept my 2016 Chevy Malibu instead of upgrading. It wasn't glamorous, but it was faithful.

There were months I paid off $2,000, and some where I paid $5,000. In the final two months, I wiped out the last $9,000 by faith, using savings and trusting God to replenish. He did! He brought new clients and expanded my business right after. Here's what I've learned about how God helps with our finances: Jesus cares about every detail, and He knows exactly what we need before we even ask. When we trust Him with what's in our hands, He proves—*over and over again*—that His hands are bigger, stronger, and always faithful to provide!

Today's Verse:

"Let us not become weary in doing good, for at the proper time we will reap a harvest if we do not give up."
—Galatians 6:9

HUMILITY COMES BEFORE HONOR

"For those who exalt themselves will be humbled, and those who humble themselves will be exalted."
Matthew 23:12

When we choose humility, God has a way of lifting us up in ways we never could have orchestrated ourselves. Lately, He's been reminding me of that in tender and unexpected ways.

As my social media pages started gaining traction, I noticed a shift in my focus. It's been exciting for my business, yes—but also convicting. I found myself spending more time thinking about strategy and growth than guarding my time with Jesus. I had to step back and ask myself, "Lord, am I still doing this for You?" And He gently reminded me—yes, but stay close. Keep Me first.

I never set out to be known. I'm just a small-town girl who wanted to help people, provide for my future family, and walk in freedom from the struggles I've known. My dad used to say, "If my kids have it better than I did, I've done my job." That stayed with me. But as I've grown, I've learned that hard work isn't the whole story—faithfulness is. And sometimes, faithfulness looks like choosing quiet obedience over flashy success.

In the past, I've been driven by the desire to "prove them wrong." Maybe you've been there too. There's something tempting about trying to succeed just to silence the voices of doubt. But that's not the posture Jesus invites us to live from. These days, I want every win to say one thing: "Look at what God did."

One night, while wrestling with doubt about whether to keep writing this devotional, I tweeted from that place of surrender:

"Don't do it to prove them wrong. Do it because you believe God can, and then let others see the glory of what's possible with Him leading the way. It's ALL for HIM!"

That's the place of peace. Not striving. Not comparison. Not self-promotion. Just obedience.

And friend, if He can use someone like me—flawed, learning, growing—He can use you too. Humble yourself under His mighty hand, and in time, He will lift you up. It's never been about perfection. It's always been about proximity to the King.

Today's Verse:
"Do not be wise in your own eyes;
fear the LORD and shun evil."
—Proverbs 3:7

SEEN AND LOVED

"The Lord looks down from heaven on all mankind to see if there are any who understand, any who seek God."

Psalm 14:2

You are not invisible. Jesus sees you—right now, exactly where you are. He sees the effort you're making when no one applauds. He sees the tears you cry when no one else notices. He sees your faithfulness, your longing, your weariness, and your hope.

When others overlook you, God draws near. When you feel like you don't measure up, He calls you chosen. He doesn't look at you the way the world does. Jesus looks at your heart. And what He sees is someone worth dying for.

You don't have to strive for His attention—you already have it. You don't have to earn His love—it's already yours. Rest in that today. Breathe it in. Jesus sees you, and He calls you His.

Today's Verse:
"You are the God who sees me."
—Genesis 16:13

JUST DO IT

His mother said to the servants, 'Do whatever he tells you.'

John 2:5

Sometimes, obedience doesn't make sense—until the miracle comes. In John 2, Jesus is at a wedding in Cana when the hosts run out of wine.

It's a big deal in their culture—running out would've brought shame and embarrassment. Mary, Jesus' mother, turns to Him and says, "*They have no more wine.*" His response? "*My hour has not yet come.*" But Mary, knowing who He is, turns to the servants and says, **"Do whatever He tells you."**

What happens next is wild. Jesus instructs the servants to fill six large stone jars with water. Then He tells them to draw some out and take it to the master of the banquet. No fancy words. No dramatic display. Just simple, quiet obedience. And when they do it—**just do it**—the water turns into wine. Not just any wine, but the *best* wine!

Here's what's powerful: the servants were part of the miracle because **they obeyed without needing all the details.** Jesus didn't explain why, how, or what would happen. He simply gave a directive, and they followed through.

So here's your reminder: sometimes God will ask you to do something that feels small, strange, or unclear. He might prompt you to make a call, send a message, apply for the job, walk away from a relationship, or forgive someone who hurt you. Your obedience might not make sense right away—but your "yes" could unlock the next miracle.

Like the servants, your role isn't to understand—it's to *trust*. Jesus is still turning water into wine. He's still doing the impossible in unexpected ways. But often, it begins with a simple step of faith.

So what has God asked you to do lately? Maybe you've been waiting for confirmation, but deep down, you already know. Don't delay. **Just do it.** The miracle might be on the other side of your obedience.

Today's Verse:
"Blessed are those who hear the word of God and obey it."
—Luke 11:28

YOU'RE GOING TO CROSS OVER ON DRY GROUND

"Then you will know which way to go, since you have never been this way before. But keep a distance... between you and the ark. Do not go near it."

Joshua 3:4

God gave me a word for you today from Joshua 3: **You're about to cross over—and it's going to be on dry ground.**

The Israelites had come to the edge of the Jordan River, right before entering the Promised Land. But it was harvest season, and the Jordan was overflowing—impossible to cross. That's when God gave Joshua instructions that required complete trust. The priests were to carry the Ark of the Covenant, which represented God's presence, and step into the water first. Not after it parted—*before*.

And when their feet touched the edge, the water *stopped*. The riverbed dried up. The entire nation crossed safely—not through mud, not in chaos—on dry ground.

That's the word for you: **God is about to make a way where there is no way.** What looked impossible, overwhelming, or too delayed is going to shift in a moment. But it starts with obedience. You may not have all the answers, but you do have instructions. Step in. Go forward. The waters will part *as* you move.

You're not crazy for believing God will do something new. You're not behind. You're not disqualified. You're standing at the edge of a shift—and He's about to show you which way to go, even though you've never been this way before.

The "dry ground" represents supernatural clarity and ease in places that once looked chaotic. It's not because you've got it all figured out. It's because you're following the Presence. The Ark always goes first.

You may feel the weight of transition or the fear of the unknown, but don't let it stop you. God is already upstream, stopping the flow, making a way, holding it back until you cross completely.

This isn't just a new chapter. It's *a new land*. You're crossing over. And it will be on dry ground!◻

Today's Verse:
"The priests who carried the ark of the covenant of the Lord stopped in the middle of the Jordan and stood on dry ground, while all Israel passed by until the whole nation had completed the crossing."
—Joshua 3:17

RENEW YOUR MIND

"Do not conform to the pattern of this world, but be transformed by the renewing of your mind. Then you will be able to test and approve what God's will is—his good, pleasing and perfect will."

Romans 12:2

Renewing your mind is not a one-time shift—it's a daily **transformation that changes everything.** Paul's words in Romans 12:2 are often quoted, but many don't realize the depth behind them.

The word **"transformed"** comes from the same root word for *metamorphosis*. It describes a radical change, like a caterpillar becoming a butterfly. It's not surface-level or behavior modification. It's an *inward* transformation that reflects *outwardly*. You don't just look different—you *are* different.

The word **"renewing"** means a complete renovation. Imagine gutting a house—ripping out old wiring, worn carpets, and moldy drywall—and rebuilding it with fresh materials. That's what the Holy Spirit does when we yield our thoughts to God's truth. He tears down lies, rewrites mindsets, and builds up a new way of thinking that aligns with Heaven.

When Paul says not to conform to the patterns of this world, he's warning us against passive living. We shouldn't allow ourselves to be influenced by society, the culture, fear or other circumstances. Instead, we must look at everything through the lens of eternity and the Kingdom of God.

Here's the beauty of it: **when your mind is renewed, your life begins to shift**. You start recognizing God's will more clearly. Anxiety loses its grip. Shame begins to crumble. You respond with grace instead of reaction. You begin to see yourself and others the way God does.

But it's not passive. Renewing your mind is a partnership with the Word and the Spirit. It happens when you meditate on Scripture, worship through the hard days, take your thoughts captive (2 Corinthians 10:5), and surrender your inner dialogue to Jesus.

This isn't about pretending to be positive. It's about allowing God to completely rebuild your thought life from the inside out.

Today's Verse:
"Set your minds on things above, not on earthly things."
—Colossians 3:2

FULL CIRCLE FAITHFULNESS

"The Lord will fulfill his purpose for me; your stead-fast love, O Lord, endures forever."

Psalm 138:8

S ometimes God brings things full circle not to remind you of the pain—but to reveal His purpose.

There's something special about a full circle moment. Maybe it's a return to a place you once left in tears, only now you're walking in with joy. Maybe it's reuniting with someone you had to let go of—but this time, your heart is healed. Maybe it's finally using your gifts in a way you only dreamed of years ago. These moments remind us that God was writing a bigger story all along.

This past season has been that for me. As I reflect on the chapters of this book and all the transitions I've walked through—from loss to calling, from silence to purpose—I realize now: nothing was wasted. Every detour had direction. Every delay was a divine setup. And every closed door was part of the preparation.

One day, I found myself standing in a place I had once prayed to leave—this time not in desperation, but with gratitude. That's when I heard the Lord whisper, *"See? I brought you back to show you how far we've come."* It was a full circle moment. Not because everything was perfect—but because He was faithful.

You may not be able to see the full picture yet, but trust this: God finishes what He starts. He is not only the Author of your faith—He is the Finisher (Hebrews 12:2).

If you're back in a season or place you never thought you'd revisit, pay attention. God may be revealing His handiwork in ways you couldn't see before. If you're stepping into something that once seemed impossible, praise Him. That's what redemption looks like.

Today, take a moment and reflect: *Is there anything in your life that's come full circle? A healed relationship? A dream that's being revived? A new level of peace where pain once lived?* If so, rejoice. If not yet, hold on. God is still working.

He's not finished with your story. He's just showing you the arc of His glory.

Today's Verse:
"He who began a good work in you will carry it on to completion until the day of Christ Jesus."
—Philippians 1:6

FAITH THAT FREES

He said to her, 'Daughter, your faith has healed
you. Go in peace and be freed from your suffering.'
Mark 5:34

"**W**endi, our daughter has been struggling with bouts of an eating disorder and a level of perfectionism we have never seen. Please talk to her."

This was the plea of a local client, a father desperate to help his teenage daughter. This request humbled me because this man wasn't a believer. In fact, when we first met, he told me he thought it was nice that I shared my faith, but it wasn't for him. Yet, over months of working together on nutrition and fitness, I witnessed God begin to work in his life. He started making lifestyle changes and, perhaps unknowingly, started getting a taste of what a Christian walk looks like.

The father explained how his family had tried everything, including therapy, but they felt led—after prayer—to ask me to meet with their daughter, Sue. Though Sue wasn't an athlete, her parents trusted that I could help her. We met a few times, simply talking about life, praying together, and sharing our stories. I told Sue about my own struggles with perfectionism and pain, and how I had found healing in Christ.

Sue, at 15, was remarkably good at hiding her pain—just as I had been for years. I asked her one day, "Are you sick and tired of being a victim, and a prisoner to this pain? Are you ready to get well?" Tears flowed, hugs were exchanged, and Sue said, "Yes." We prayed together that day, and though her life didn't change overnight, a transformation began. With time, Sue overcame her disordered eating, let go of the need to be perfect, and even joined a sports team.

Today, Sue is the captain of her volleyball team, and her family attends church regularly. What's more, her parents' faith has grown and flourished in ways they never thought possible. This is the miracle-working power of God! He takes our past pain and brokenness and redeems it to help others in ways we could never imagine.

I didn't save Sue—**God did**. But He used me, a woman once broken and now healed, as a vessel for His love and grace. That is one of the greatest joys of following Christ: seeing how He works through our lives to bring hope and healing to others.

Today's Verse:
"LORD my God, I called to you for help, and you healed me."
—Psalm 30:2

LAUGH A LITTLE

"A cheerful heart is good medicine, but a crushed spirit dries up the bones."
Proverbs 17:22

Let's be honest—sometimes we take ourselves way too seriously. Life can feel like one long to-do list mixed with a never-ending loop of "Am I *doing enough?*" "Am I *holy enough?*" "Did I *drink enough water today?*"

But I believe Jesus had a sense of humor. You can't tell me He doesn't have a playful side. I bet the disciples shared inside jokes and laughed around the campfire after a long day of walking through dust and dodging Pharisees. Joy was never meant to be separate from the sacred. It *is* sacred.

Sometimes the most spiritual thing you can do is laugh. If your week has felt heavy, this is your permission slip to take a deep breath, laugh at something silly, and remember that joy is holy. God isn't annoyed when you smile—He's the source of that joy. **He wired us to laugh, not just to survive but to actually *enjoy* this life.**

And science backs this up. Laughter reduces stress hormones, increases endorphins (your brain's "feel-good" chemicals), and even boosts your immune system. It improves circulation, relaxes the body, and protects your heart—literally. Studies show that people who laugh regularly have lower levels of anxiety and depression. Isn't that just like God? He built a medicine right into our bodies, and it sounds like laughter.

Proverbs knew what psychology would later confirm—a cheerful heart really is good medicine. And that medicine doesn't come with side effects, only side-splitting joy. When we choose to embrace lightness, even for a moment, we give our souls a chance to breathe again.

So today, go ahead and laugh a little. Watch that ridiculous TikTok. Dance in the kitchen while you wait for your toast. Tell your dog about your dreams. Tell someone about something silly you did this week. The joy of the Lord really *is* your strength.

Let's not be people who only cry in God's presence. Let's be people who laugh there too. He's not just the God who heals wounds—He's the God who makes our hearts light again.

Today's Verse:
*"You make known to me the path of life;
in your presence there is fullness of joy;
at your right hand are pleasures forevermore."*
—Psalm 16:11

LOVE YOUR NEIGHBOR (EVEN IF HER DOG BITES)

"Wake up! Strengthen what remains and is about to die, for I have found your deeds unfinished in the sight of my God."

Revelation 3:2

L et me tell you about a neighbor I had when I lived in Nashville. From day one, she was... a challenge. Her personality was intense, her dog bit me (yes, *bit* me), and let's just say our interactions were less than warm and fuzzy. I love dogs—but this dog? We were not friends. I avoided her like expired milk in the fridge.

Fast forward a year, and something unexpected happened. We both found ourselves annoyed about the same thing: our apartment complex's lack of action when it came to safety. The broken gate, sketchy trespassers, and nonexistent response from management gave us something to unite around. Surprisingly, this shared frustration opened the door to civility, even a little neighborly camaraderie.

Looking back, I laugh because God definitely used that situation to stretch me. I mean, what if she ends up being my neighbor in Heaven someday? It kind of changes your perspective, doesn't it?

Revelation 3:2 urges us to *"wake up and strengthen what remains."* Sometimes what remains is a relationship we've given up on or a mission we left half-finished—like loving that difficult person we're convinced God must have accidentally placed in our lives. (Spoiler: There's a purpose even in difficult relationships. God is often using them to teach us something we couldn't learn any other way).

The truth is, Jesus doesn't give us a pass to love only the easy people. He calls us to love like He loves. That includes the dog-owning, gate-complaining, nerve-touching neighbors next door.

So today, ask yourself: *Who have I been avoiding that I'm actually called to love?* It could be a coworker, a family member, or yes, even your literal neighbor. Don't wait for Heaven to get it right. Start now—with grace, with humor, and with the love of Christ.

Today's Verse:
"A new command I give you: Love one another. As I have loved you, so you must love one another."
—John 13:34

DAY 364

KEEP JESUS AT THE CENTER

"I have fought the good fight, I have finished the race,
I have kept the faith."

2 Timothy 4:7

If you knew your time on earth was coming to a close, **what would you say?** What would you leave behind? For the apostle Paul—a man who wrote over half the New Testament, who planted churches, mentored leaders, and endured beatings, shipwrecks, prison, and persecution—the message was simple: **Keep Jesus at the center.**

In 2 Timothy, believed to be Paul's final letter before his death, you can feel the weight of urgency and love. These are the words of a spiritual father passing the baton to the next generation. And what does he emphasize most? Not fame, not church growth strategies, not accolades. **But Christ.**

Paul urges Timothy: *"Preach the word... keep your head in all situations... endure hardship... discharge all the duties of your ministry"* (2 Timothy 4:2–5). In other words: *Don't lose sight of Jesus. Stay the course. Keep the faith.* And then Paul adds his own reflection: *"I have fought the good fight, I have finished the race, I have kept the faith."*

That's the goal, isn't it? Not just to start well, but to finish well. Not just to follow Jesus when it's easy, but to stay anchored to Him when it's hard. Paul knew that what matters most is a life rooted in Christ. When everything else fades—platforms, influence, recognition—it's Jesus who remains.

As I reflect on my own life, and even this devotional journey we've taken together, I'm reminded that all the writing, serving, speaking, and ministering mean nothing if Jesus isn't at the center. He's *the reason*. He's *the message*. Jesus is the prize.

Friend, you may not write half the New Testament like Paul did, but your story still matters. Your life, your choices, your legacy—it all counts. Let it be said of you that you kept Jesus first. There will be distractions, no doubt. But don't let them pull you off course. Keep your eyes on Him. Keep running your race. Keep believing, even when it's hard.

Finish well. Jesus is worth it.

Today's Verse:
"But as for you, continue in what you have learned and have become convinced of, because you know those from whom you learned it."
—2 Timothy 3:14

FOR SUCH A TIME AS THIS

"For if you remain silent at this time, relief and deliverance for the Jews will arise from another place... And who knows but that you have come to your royal position for such a time as this?"

Esther 4:14

You didn't land here by accident. God doesn't make mistakes. Just like Esther, you were created *for such a time as this*. Right now, right here, God has positioned you for a divine purpose. Esther was an ordinary young woman. She wasn't perfect or powerful—she was *willing*. She said yes, stepped out in faith, and walked into the role God prepared for her. That *same invitation is extended to you today.*

God delights in using ordinary people—like you and me—for His extraordinary plans.

When I began writing this devotional, I didn't feel qualified or worthy. But I said yes. That simple act of obedience led to healing, restoration, and a renewed purpose. Through this journey, chains were broken, courage rose, and my identity was realigned with God's truth. From that quiet yes came a finished book, a new chapter in Dallas, a nonprofit ministry, and a bold step into the calling God placed on my life.

And here's what I know for sure: the same God who worked in me wants to do something powerful through you.

So whatever God-sized dream is stirring in your heart—go for it. Start the fitness plan. Launch the business. Give love another try. Move to a new city. Begin the podcast. Try something new. Write the song. Lead the group. Tell the story!

God's not looking for perfection—just your *yes and obedience.* While this may be the end of our 365-day devotional journey, it doesn't have to be the end of our connection. If something this year sparked change in you, I'd love to hear from you. Share your testimony, send a prayer request, or just say hello.

Let's keep walking—one step at a time, one yes at a time.

Today's Verse:
"When the time is right, I, the LORD will make it happen."
—Isaiah 60:22

Afterword

FINAL THOUGHTS

"But seek first his kingdom and his righteousness, and all these things will be given to you as well."
Matthew 6:33

When we put God first, we experience an unshakeable peace—a peace that remains firm even when the world around us shifts and shakes. His presence anchors our hearts and souls in every storm. Wherever you are in your life or faith journey, I want you to remember this simple truth: **God loves you.** There is nothing you can do to earn His love or lose His love. He will never let go of your hand or your heart. God has a specific purpose and plan for your life. *You matter.* And you are deeply, unconditionally loved.

My dear brother or sister in Christ, I want you to know that I'm praying for you. Don't worry about being perfect or having everything figured out—our God is perfect, and He holds all the answers. He leaves the ninety-nine to go after the one, and **I know this personally—because I was once the one.**

If there's one truth I pray stays with you through every page of this devotional, it's this: **Jesus loves you more deeply than you can imagine**, and He delights in the steps you're taking toward Him. Keep Christ at the center of everything, and never stop pursuing His presence—whether in life's quiet moments or its biggest decisions.

Prioritize Scripture over screens and faith over fear—because with Jesus, we always win. In 2019, I quietly set a goal to publish my first book by 2025. And now, here we are. Only God—He gets all the glory! I'm so grateful you're holding this book and allowing my journey to be part of yours.

Don't cancel on yourself—keep showing up. Progress comes through consistency, not intensity. Pray boldly, believe big—God is still in the miracle business! Just like your body needs daily fuel, your soul needs daily time with Jesus.

Lift others up. As Proverbs 27:17 says, "*Iron sharpens iron.*" And before you scroll, pause—Scripture before screens. There's always time to seek the One who strengthens you.

With love always,
Wendi A. Irlbeck

Special Note: To my beautiful editor, Tamara Jolee—thank you. You were handpicked by God to help bring my dream devotional to life. This book would not have been possible without your incredible mind, heart, and courage to take on such a big project. I appreciate you more than words can express. May God continue to bless the amazing work you do.

About The Author

Wendi A. Irlbeck is a bold woman of faith, registered dietitian, certified sports nutritionist, and motivational speaker. She is the founder of two impactful platforms: *Devotions With Wendi*, a nonprofit women's bible study community, and *Nutrition With Wendi LLC*, a faith-driven private practice dedicated to health and performance nutrition.

Based in Dallas, Texas, Wendi is on a mission to equip others to walk in both spiritual and physical strength. Though many know her today as a passionate leader and expert, her journey began with brokenness. She didn't encounter the love of Jesus Christ until 2012, and she didn't fully surrender her life to Him until 2020, after a series of deeply painful and transformative events.

Through it all, she discovered that healing, hope, and wholeness are found in one place: the arms of Jesus Christ, our Lord and Savior. Her story is a testament to the redeeming power of Jesus, and her life's work is now devoted to helping others experience the same freedom and joy found in Him.

Wendi is the author of *Devotions With Wendi: 5-Minute Moments to Build Your Faith in 365 Days*. The book empowers readers to prioritize time with God, even in the busiest seasons of life. Whether she's speaking to teams, mentoring clients, or writing devotionals, Wendi uses her God-given gifts to uplift, teach, and point people to Christ.

Connect with Wendi:

Devotions With Wendi:
www.devotionswithwendi.com□
Nutrition With Wendi:
www.nutritionwithwendi.com□

X (Twitter): @Wendi_Irlbeck
Youtube & TikTok: Devotions_with_Wendi
Instagram (Nutrition): @nutrition_with_wendi
Instagram (Devotions): @devotions_with_wendi
Email: Wendi@nutritionwithwendi.com

www.ingramcontent.com/pod-product-compliance
Lightning Source LLC
Chambersburg PA
CBHW060807120726
47909CB00006B/1807